THE WORLD OF
DARKNESS

UNHOLY ALLIES

Masquerade of the Red Death Trilogy
Volume 2

A Vampire: The Masquerade™
novel by Robert Weinberg

D1608140

WHITE WOLF
PUBLISHING

The boundaries which divide Life and Death are at best shadowy and vague.

from "The Premature Burial"
by Edgar Allan Poe

iv

Dedication:

To Sax Rohmer and Dennis Wheatley, who
defined horror thrillers. And to Dean Koontz, who
took it one step further.

BOOK 2 - UNHOLY ALLIES

Author's Note:

While the locations and history of this trilogy may seem familiar, they are not our reality. The setting of *Vampire: The Masquerade of the Red Death* is a harsher, crueler version of our world. It is a stark, desolate landscape where nothing is what it seems. It is truly a World of Darkness.

Prologue

Tel Aviv, Israel — March 20, 1994:

Elisha sat in the parlor of his mentor's house and fidgeted. He had long since abandoned his studies, unable to concentrate on the words written on the pages of the grimoire. Though he knew the importance of patience, it was a virtue he had not yet conquered. He wanted to know what was being discussed in the back room. And he desperately wondered how it involved him.

The conference in the rear study had been going on for nearly three hours. Never before had such a meeting lasted more than sixty minutes. Whatever his teacher and his friends were debating had to be very important. And that worried Elisha, for he knew that his master only called such conferences when something terrible was about to happen.

The same four people always attended the meetings: three men, including his master, and one woman. They all appeared to be very ordinary citizens, middle-aged, the men with thick full beards, the woman with long flowing hair that fell halfway down her back. Their clothes were plain, nothing fancy. None of them drove. They always arrived at the doorstep on foot and departed in the same manner, as if they came from somewhere close by in the neighborhood, although it seemed, from their accents and the style of their clothing, that they actually lived somewhere very far away. Sometimes one of them was gone when the meetings ended, although the door to the back room was never opened.

If it were not for their eyes, he would have thought them to be government officials seeking his mentor's advice. Or members of the Mossad, the Israeli intelligence agency, for whom his teacher sometimes did work. But he knew instinctively that neither supposition was true. These three visitors were special. They possessed incredible powers just like his mentor. They were mages.

Even though Elisha had been studying with his teacher for over half of the twenty years of his life, he still could not meet his mentor's gaze for more than a few seconds without turning away. Those eyes glowed with a knowledge born of a thousand years of experience, burned with a will so strong it could overwhelm lesser minds with a glance. And as it was with his teacher, so it was with his three guests. Elisha was quite convinced that they numbered among the four most powerful magic-workers in the world.

Nervously, he glanced at the coffee table in front of the old sofa in the parlor. On it were scattered a half-dozen letters received during the past two weeks. Elisha suspected that the contents of those letters had been one reason for the conference. The letters, and the mysterious phone calls that came at all hours of the day and night during the same period.

UNHOLY ALLIES

The letters had come from all over the world. There was one from Australia, another from Switzerland, a third from Buenos Aires. There were several from Vienna and two from New York City. Elisha, who always brought the mail to his master in the morning, was fascinated by the names and the faraway places they represented. Born and raised in Israel, he had never traveled farther than nearby Jerusalem. Most of his two decades of life had been spent in study. He longed to see the world and experience some of its wonders.

"Elisha." His mentor's voice, firm yet mellow, resonated through the parlor. Though his teacher never spoke loudly, he had a way of projecting so that his words were always heard. "Please attend me in the study."

Trembling, Elisha rose to his feet. He had not anticipated a summons until after the meeting. He had never been summoned before then in the past. For some reason, his master and the three visitors wanted to see him. Heart in his throat, he stepped gingerly to the entrance. He opened the door and walked into the study.

It was an impressive room. As his master read constantly, the walls on all sides were filled with books. The thousands of volumes were all arranged by topic, and, within each section, by title. There were books on history, geography, medicine, philosophy. There was an entire wall devoted to magic, with many of the texts in Latin or Greek. And scattered throughout the room were hundreds of books written by his mentor, under his own name and many pseudonyms.

His teacher sat behind a large wood desk, a gift to him from the first Prime Minister of Israel, David Ben Gurion. Facing him, in high-back wooden chairs with red velvet cushions, were his three guests. They all turned and stared at Elisha as he walked into the room. Tall and thin, with thick, curly brown hair and wide brown eyes, Elisha felt like a canary under the gaze of four hungry cats.

The woman with the long hair smiled at him. The two male visitors nodded, as if in greeting. His mentor, his face an unreadable mask, beckoned him forward with a casual wave of one hand.

"My friends want to meet you, my son," he said. "Nothing to worry about. I have been bragging to them about your skill with the Art, and they expressed interest in seeing you in person. Come stand beside me."

His teacher rose to his feet as Elisha approached. Smiling broadly, he squeezed his star pupil affectionately on the shoulder with gnarled, callused fingers. As always, Elisha marveled that this plain-looking man, with his pleasant, mild features, browned skin, and thick black beard, was actually one of the most famous Jewish scholars and philosophers of all time. Though he had assumed many different identities over the past nine hundred years, his teacher had originally been born Moses ben Maimon. Or, named in the style of the times, Maimonides. Later, when he became famous, he was known by the title *Rambam*, an acronym derived from the words *Rabbi Moses ben Maimon*. For his immense contributions to Jewish thought and philosophy, he was known as the Second Moses.

"He looks fine to me, Rambam," declared one of the other men, winking at Elisha. "A little nervous, perhaps, but what young man wouldn't be nervous when confronted by such a group of ogres."

"Witches and warlocks, Simon," said the woman with the long hair. Her voice was so smooth and mellow that her words were more like song. "Keep your titles straight. The common folk stone ogres. Ones like us, they burn."

The woman stared at Elisha. Her deep brown eyes had the same look of incredible age and wisdom that his teacher's did. "Are you afraid of the dark, Elisha?" she asked.

"The dark, Mistress?" he replied, not sure what she meant. "No, I am not afraid."

"Not the darkness of the night," said the man addressed as Simon, "but the darkness of the soul."

Elisha shook his head. "I understood the question, sir. My teacher has lectured me many times about good and evil. Ours is a world of darkness that threatens to overwhelm the light. I realize that. But I am not frightened."

"He is very strong," said the third man, speaking for the first time. He was short and husky, with deep gray hair and matching beard; his voice rumbled like thunder. "He burns with the power. Though I don't like using one so inexperienced, I agree it is for the best. I approve the mission."

"As do I," said the man called Simon. "His youth and unassuming air serve as the best disguise. No one will suspect him. You have made a wise choice, Rambam."

"What say you, Judith?" asked Rambam.

"Like our friends, I dislike using one so young and naive," replied the woman, "but I do not see that we have a choice. We must make contact, and it must be done as soon as possible. This young man is our best hope. He is uninformed, but I assume you will take care of that, my friend."

"Assuredly," said Rambam. "He will learn everything he needs to understand from my own lips before he leaves this room today. And, though I must remain here to oversee the peace negotiations with Jordan, I will be with him in spirit. You have my guarantee that the message will be received."

"The word of Maimonides is promise enough for me," declared the man with the gray hair. "I must leave now. Other events of importance call. You will inform me when Lameth arrives?"

"Of course, Ezra," said Rambam. "I appreciate your attending today. You are my strong left arm. I will contact you the moment the Dark Messiah arrives. Though I suspect you will sense his presence immediately when he steps onto the soil of Eretz Yisrael."

The gray-bearded man chuckled as he opened the door to the study. "I expect I will. But in these turbulent times, who knows." He lifted one hand. "Shalom, my friends."

"I, too, must be going," said Simon, once Ezra had left. "The situation with the skinheads in Germany has deteriorated badly over the past few weeks. The old hatreds are rising again. I dare not spend too much time out of the country."

"I will summon you at the proper time," said Rambam. "Thank you as always for attending the meeting, Simon. You are my strong right arm."

"Shalom, Rambam," said Simon. He nodded to Elisha. "Good luck, young man. My prayers go with you. Shalom."

Then he was gone. With the blink of an eye, the space where he stood was empty. There was no noise, no flash, no explosion. It was as if Simon had never been there, as if a slate had been wiped clean. He was there, then he was not.

"The show-off," said Judith. "He could use the door."

"He has a far distance to travel," said Rambam, with a sly smile. "And Simon hates to waste a step. You sound jealous, my daughter."

The woman laughed. "Perhaps a little, teacher. He handles the most difficult spells with such ease. I could never bend space so effortlessly, no matter how long I practiced. Never."

"Your talents lie elsewhere, Judith," said Rambam. "Each of you is a master in your own right."

"If Simon is your strong right arm," she said, smiling, "and Ezra is your strong left arm, what does that make me?"

"You," said Rambam, his voice growing serious, "are the most important of all. You are my heart. You are my conscience."

Judith laughed and clapped her hands together

in delight. "As if anyone could give the Second Moses advice. Still, I accept the compliment as it was given, with good grace."

Judith stretched out her right hand to Elisha. Smiling, she nodded at him. Elisha reached out and took her fingers in his. The woman's hand seemed to radiate energy. A feeling of strength ran up his arm and spread through his entire body.

"Take some of my power, Elisha," she said, softly. "The task before you will be a journey into the very soul of everlasting night. I may not be a strong hand, but I have energy to spare. My strength is your strength. Use it well."

Then, the woman released her fingers from his and stepped back. The air in the room bent upon itself. Reality twisted, warped. And Judith was gone.

"She is right," remarked Rambam, more to himself than Elisha. "She is not as good at that trick as Simon. No matter. She handles it well enough."

The mage's gaze fixed on Elisha. "You have a powerful ally, my son. Judith may seem pleasant and gentle enough, but she is a terror in battle. She possesses the strength to shake the world."

"Yes, teacher," said Elisha meekly. He had never encountered magic that could be transmitted by a touch before. His body still burned with an inner glow. "Maybe someday she will teach me that teleportation spell. Or Master Simon will."

"It's a useful trick, but it only works if you are traveling to a well-defined, unchanging destination," said Rambam, with a shrug of dismissal. "Which, unfortunately, is rarely the case in these times of unrest."

Rambam dropped back in his chair. "Sit, sit, my boy," he said, directing Elisha to one of the red velvet armchairs. "Make yourself comfortable. We have a lot to talk about."

Leaning forward, elbows on the desk, the teacher stared at his pupil. "You have been chosen by this secret council to go on an important mission. We want you to find a certain person. While I dislike sending one so young and inexperienced, my friends believe that you are the best choice for the job, and I am forced to agree. Your age and innocence will cloak you in anonymity. Besides which, you are by far the most talented pupil I have ever instructed. Though you are still a very young man, your power to bend and shape reality to your wishes is incredible."

"Thank you, master," said Elisha, trying to sound modest and not succeeding. "Where am I going?"

"To America," said Rambam. "You are to locate a man named Dire McCann. You must find him as quickly as possible. I want you to personally deliver a message to him from me."

"A message?" repeated Elisha, puzzled. "Why not just use telepathy, master?"

"Telepathic communication is not as reliable as we like," said Rambam. "Besides which," and his teacher's face turned grim, "such messages can be intercepted by people other than those for whom they are intended. We dare not risk having McCann's enemies learn of our intervention in his battle."

"This man, McCann, his enemies," Elisha began,

trying to make sense out of what he was being told. "They are our enemies too?"

"They are the enemies of all humanity, my son," said Rambam. "An ancient and powerful bloodline of vampires, they call themselves the Children of Dreadful Night. Their leader is a monstrous being known as the Red Death. He has made a terrible bargain with creatures from the outermost darkness. If this unholy alliance is not destroyed, it will bring utter chaos to the Earth."

Elisha shivered. "Vampires. The Damned. You said to me once they are the immortal descendents of Caine, the Third Mortal. That some of them prefer the name Kindred, because they are all related by bonds of cursed blood. And that they have manipulated mankind for their own purposes for aeons."

"Correct, my son," said Rambam. "I spoke of them in passing last year when we were discussing the shifting nature of reality. How the past continues to change due to the beliefs of the present. Do you remember?"

"Of course, teacher," said Elisha, nodding. He knew Rambam was speaking rhetorically, for he never forgot anything his mentor told him. "You told me how God made Caine into a vampire because he brought murder into the world. That Caine, though he was ageless and possessed vast supernatural powers, grew bored and wanted companions. So, he created three new vampires, a Second Generation of the Damned. Then, those three created thirteen more, the Third Generation of vampires. And so it progressed down through the ages."

"Exactly right, Elisha," said Rambam. "I know, too, that we discussed how many thousands of years ago the Third Generation rose up against their sires, the Second Generation, and destroyed them. And Caine disappeared, never to be seen again."

"The Third Generation, the ones you called Antediluvians, founded the thirteen vampire clans that still exist today," said Elisha, "with the vampires of each clan inheriting certain traits from the vampire who created him. I remember that too. Then, after existing for millennia, these Antediluvians grew weary and sank into a deathlike sleep known as torpor, leaving the clans they founded to battle secretly among each other for control of the world."

"Though perhaps a little simplistic," said Rambam, "basically true. You said secretly. Do you remember why the Kindred keep their existence hidden from mankind?"

"Of course," replied Elisha. "Though they possess great supernatural powers, their numbers are small when compared to mankind. If humanity ever realizes that the Kindred exist, and that they have been preying on our species for thousands of years, it would mean a quick and total annihilation of the vampire race."

"Very good," said Rambam. "You not only remember the facts, my son, but you understand them as well. I assume you also recall how Caine's curse is passed from one generation of vampires to another?"

"The Kindred call it the Embrace, teacher," said Elisha. "Normally, a vampire just drinks the blood of its victim, killing him. However, if, at the moment the victim is dying, he is given a taste of the vampire's blood, that person becomes one of the undead. This new vampire is called a childe, while the creature who gave him the blood is called his sire."

"What about the childe's powers?" asked Rambam.

"They are diminished in comparison to their sires', teacher," answered Elisha. "The curse of vampirism is passed down through the ages by the blood of Caine. The less that is present in the veins of a vampire, the weaker his powers will be.

"Caine created the Second Generation with a mere taste of his vitae. They, in turn, invoked a Third Generation with a few drops of their blood, thus diluting Caine's vitae even further. With each following generation, the concentration of Caine's blood lessened. Thus, a sire's strength was always greater than that of its progeny."

"The lower the generation of a vampire," said Rambam, "the closer it stands in relationship to Caine the Damned. And the greater its power when compared to other vampires."

The teacher paused, staring directly into Elisha's eyes. "Pay close attention, for now it is time for you to learn secrets of the Kindred known only to a very few humans or vampires. Understand the motives of your enemy, Elisha, and you know his weaknesses."

"Yes, teacher," said Elisha. "You told me once that a wise soldier always strikes at his enemy's softest spot."

Rambam chuckled. "The strong survive, Elisha. The smart, conquer."

The mage's face grew serious. "With the Third Generation in torpor, the most dangerous vampires in the world are those of the Fourth Generation. Few in number, they are extremely powerful and incredibly ancient. Many of them are more than fifty centuries old. At least half have now retreated into torpor. Some are engaged in personal feuds with others of their generation, feuds that have continued uninterrupted for several thousand years. And, then, there are those who fight the Jyhad."

"The Jyhad, master?"

"It is the name given to the ongoing struggle among the mightiest of the Fourth Generation Kindred, known as the Methuselahs, for absolute mastery of the Children of Caine. The battle is conducted secretly, with these Methuselahs manipulating the Kindred of later generations and using them as their unsuspecting agents. Normally, we mages do not involve ourselves in the machinations of the Jyhad. Our concern is with mankind, not vampires. However, we suddenly find ourselves needing to act. That is why the council is sending you on this mission."

"To find this man, Dire McCann," said Elisha. "I am not sure I understand, teacher."

"The Red Death and his brood, the Children of Dreadful Night, seek to gain mastery over the

Camarilla and the Sabbat, the two warring cults to which most of the Kindred belong. It is quite possible that the Children may succeed. They control an awesome power, but at a price they do not truly comprehend. If the Red Death is not stopped, it could become the most powerful vampire in the world. And, in so doing, bring flaming doom to both mankind and the Kindred."

"You said that Dire McCann is the enemy of the Red Death," said Elisha. "How can one man stop an entire pack of vampires, especially if they are as deadly as you say?"

"Never underestimate the importance of a single individual, my son," said Rambam. "Dire McCann is no ordinary human. He conceals secrets that even I have not been able to unravel, though I have known him for many years. Somehow, someway, he is closely associated with perhaps the most enigmatic and dangerous Methuselah ever to exist, Lameth, the Dark Messiah."

Elisha blinked with unexpected excitement. "The Dark Messiah, teacher? What a fascinating title. I don't believe you ever mentioned such a being before. Tell me more about him. Please."

Rambam shook his head. "No, Elisha, that I will not do. Let Dire McCann provide you with that information when you find him. Assuming that you can get him to speak about Lameth at all. The detective prefers not to discuss the Dark Messiah, or his relationship with the Kindred in general. However, knowing both your curiosity and your persistence, I suspect you will learn everything you wish."

"I will accept your words as a challenge, teacher," said Elisha. "Is there anything else I should know?"

Rambam scratched his beard, shrugged, then shook his head. "Whatever other facts I might tell you, my son, would only confuse the issue. However, I have certain opinions that I think may prove helpful on this quest."

"The judgments of the Second Moses," said Elisha, "are as wise of those of Solomon."

"Perhaps not *that* wise," said Rambam, with a laugh, "but hopefully useful enough."

Lifting his right hand, Elisha's mentor stuck one finger into the air. Despite the importance of his advice, he could never abandon his teaching habits.

"First. Though you are still a young man, you are a powerful mage. Try to avoid using your powers if possible. Though we follow no specific Tradition, my allies and I have very powerful enemies, especially in America. The Technocracy thrives there, and its leaders hate me and my friends. They believe all magic must appear to be science. If threatened by their agents, the Men in Black, do not hesitate to bend reality to fit your needs. I prefer that my students not become dead heroes."

He raised another finger.

"Second. Beware the Kindred. Do not be deceived by their appearance. These vampires are no longer human, and their actions are based on needs and desires much different from yours. They are cursed with an insatiable lust for human blood. They call it the Beast Within, and they will commit any horror, any abomination, in order to quench that thirst."

Rambam held up a third finger.

"Last and most important. Believe nothing you are told by anyone. You are young and still naive. In this world of darkness, truth exists on many different levels. The Kindred are masters of deception; with them, nothing is ever what it seems on the surface. Their mortal allies are no better — in many ways, they are perhaps worse. They exist by treachery. Their promises are worthless. Beware bargains with both humans and vampires. Don't make deals with either. And, if you are unsure of the facts, trust your heart, not your eyes."

"I will not fail you, teacher," said Elisha, his voice thick with emotion. "Now, tell me the message I am to deliver to this man, Dire McCann."

Rambam told him. And, eyes wide with horror, Elisha realized that Maimonides had not exaggerated in the least. The fate of the world rested on his success.

PART

1

To conceive the horror of my sensations is, I presume, utterly impossible; yet a curiosity to penetrate the mysteries of these awful regions predominates even over my despair, and will reconcile me to the most hideous aspect of death. It is evident that we are hurrying onward to some exciting knowledge — some never-to-be-imparted secret, whose attainment is destruction.

from "Ms. Found in a Bottle"
by Edgar Allan Poe

Chapter 1

Washington, D.C. - March 23, 1994:

Sitting on the footsteps of the Lincoln Memorial at 4 a.m., Dire McCann contemplated his future. At the moment, it was not an inspiring picture. His clothes still damp from his unexpected swim in the Anacostia River, his eyes still aching from staring at the Thermit inferno that had engulfed the Washington Navy Yard, the detective felt like a laboratory rat who had just survived a maze from hell. Unfortunately, there was no cheese to reward him at the end.

Instead, he was exhausted, disgusted, and depressed. Besides which, he found himself faced with the problem of dealing with two distinctly different, and yet incredibly similar, female vampires. Both of whom were sworn to guard him against misfortune, whether he wanted their aid or not.

On his left, pacing back and forth, constantly flexing her fingers in a manner that resembled choking someone to death, was Sarah James, known among the Kindred as Flavia, the Dark Angel. Tall, blond, and beautiful, with lush curves and full red lips, she wore a white leather outfit that hugged her body like a second skin. A deadly Assamite assassin,

Flavia had come to Washington to serve as McCann's bodyguard. She had been assigned that duty by the vampire prince of St. Louis, who had sent the detective to discover the secrets of the Red Death. Flavia, however, had her own reasons for traveling to the capital. The Red Death had killed Fawn, her sister, and the Dark Angel had pledged a sacred oath to find and destroy the monster. Or perish trying.

On McCann's right, her arms folded across her breasts and seemingly in a state of rest, was Madeleine Giovanni. McCann noted with an inner grin that Madeleine never once let her gaze slip from Flavia. Though they had been thrown together as allies, neither woman trusted the other. It was only their shared concern for McCann's safety that kept the fragile peace between them.

As if in contrast to Flavia, statuesque in her white leather jumpsuit, Madeleine was short and slender, almost girlish in appearance. She had long, jet-black hair, thin bones and dark eyes. The only garment she wore was a black leotard, against which her pure white skin was a sharp contrast. Where Flavia looked trim and athletic, Madeleine seemed delicate and fragile. It was an illusion McCann suspected the woman strove to maintain. The one feature both she and Flavia shared were their blood-red lips.

Despite her gentle appearance, Madeleine was in reality one of the foremost saboteurs and espionage agents in the world. A member of the tightly knit and extremely secretive Clan Giovanni, she was not as famous as Flavia, but her reputation was equally grim. To friends and foes alike, she was known as the Dagger of the Giovanni.

"What now, little man?" asked Flavia, a sarcastic edge to her voice. "Dawn approaches and I must be leaving shortly. Will I be able to find you when I awaken? Or are you planning another wild venture of your own for the daylight hours? Remember, I can do nothing to protect you if you persist in taking actions independent of my counsel. Until tonight, I thought we were partners working together. Now, I am not so sure."

McCann grimaced. Earlier that evening, he had rendezvoused with the Red Death and had not taken Flavia with him. The detective had hoped to destroy the monster with powers he preferred not to reveal to the blond assassin. However, McCann had not been the only one planning treachery. The supposed truce had been a death trap. Only the intervention of Madeleine Giovanni had saved the investigator from a fiery end. Flavia was not pleased to be left behind, or to miss a chance to confront the Red Death.

"I made a mistake," said McCann, trying to sound sincere. "I admitted that already. The Red Death said he wanted to bargain. He swore an oath on his sire's honor. I was foolish enough to believe him. How was I to know that his hired killer had laced the entire parade grounds with Thermit bombs?"

"You're not supposed to know, McCann," said Flavia. "That's my job. I am trained to think of such things. Makish is a master assassin. No matter how devious you are, he is more so. Unless you utilize my skills, you are doomed."

"The past is dead history," said Madeleine. She spoke perfect English, with no trace of an accent. Having learned the language from tapes, she never used contractions. "What is done, is done. Berating Mr. McCann is a waste of time. I am sure that in the future, he will not act so unwisely."

"I'm not so convinced," said Flavia. "Anyway, why does it matter to you? You never did explain to me what your business is with McCann. All I heard was that your sire ordered you to find him. And that Prince Vargoss revealed that we were in Washington. What's the rest of the story?"

"I am under no obligation to reveal my secrets to you," replied Madeleine, her voice cold and emotionless. "My business with Mr. McCann does not concern you."

"Anything involving McCann concerns me," said Flavia, raising her voice slightly. "My prince commanded me to see he wasn't harmed. I'm to keep him safe from everyone, including the brood of Clan Giovanni. And I intend to do exactly that."

"I will make no comment upon the execution of your responsibilities," said Madeleine smugly, "other than to remind you that it was I who saved Mr. McCann earlier tonight."

The detective sighed. Flavia, angry because she had been left behind, was spoiling for a fight. Madeleine, who was not someone who would stand to be pushed around, was prepared to give it to her.

Neither of the women was a diplomat; their fighting skills lent them a certain arrogance, and they did not believe in compromise. Retreat was alien to their nature.

Both vampires settled into fighting stances. Flavia balanced on the balls of her feet, knees bent slightly, arms outstretched parallel to the ground. Her hands were raised shoulder high, her long fingers curled into fists. The Assamite assassin could punch through solid steel. Flesh and bone offered much less resistance.

Madeleine waited, hands on her hips, arms akimbo. She stood with her feet spread slightly apart, head tilted to one side, eyes shining unnaturally brightly. An expert at the shadow Disciplines, Madeleine possessed the power to merge instantly with the darkness. McCann felt sure that Flavia had the strength to rip her opponent's head right off her shoulders. But only if she was able to catch her. A duel between the two killers would prove to be an astonishing display of destruction. No matter who won, however, McCann knew he would be the loser.

"Hey," he declared sharply, raising his hands in protest, and making no effort to hide his annoyance. "I'm tired of this macho posturing. I'm amazed that you both actually think that eliminating the other is going to make me *safer*. Madeleine's sire gave her the same orders you have, Flavia. She's here to safeguard my well-being."

His tone became harsh and unyielding. "Each of you has been charged to protect me — not to prove that you're the toughest kid in the neighborhood. Or did you forget that assignment? I nearly died tonight; I was confronted by not one, but four Red Deaths! Maybe that number doesn't scare you two tough characters, but it sure as hell worries me. I have this uncanny feeling that now might be a very bad time for petty squabbling among ourselves."

Flavia glared at the detective. "Damn you, McCann," she snarled, lowering her hands and relaxing her stance. "I hate acting like a fool. And I *really* hate when someone rubs my face in it."

"Perhaps I may have overreacted as well," said Madeleine Giovanni softly. "Your point is well taken, Mr. McCann."

Madeleine bowed politely to Flavia. Somehow, McCann could not visualize the Giovanni saboteur curtsying. "Please accept my sincere apology. As I said earlier tonight, your skills are legendary among our kind. It will be a great pleasure to work with you."

McCann was equally sure that when Madeleine spoke of *their kind*, she was not speaking of the Kindred. She and Flavia belonged to a much smaller, more select group. The deadliest predators in a race of predators, they were members of the killer elite.

"Apology accepted and returned," said Flavia, pressing her palms and fingers together so that her hands formed a straight line in front of her face. She said nothing more. Apologies from Assamites were short and to the point. That Flavia even bothered was remarkable.

McCann knew Flavia was not in the habit of

forgetting a wrong, either real or imagined. He debated warning Madeleine Giovanni, then decided not to bother. The dark-haired beauty appeared to be quite capable of taking care of herself, in any type of situation.

"Great," he said, unable to keep the sarcasm from his voice. "Now that we're all friends, maybe someone has an idea about what to do next."

"I'm just your bodyguard, McCann," replied Flavia. "If I remember Prince Vargoss' instructions correctly, you're responsible for making the important decisions. I distinctly recall your having insisted upon being in charge."

"My sire commanded me to *protect* you, Mr. McCann," said Madeleine, the barest hint of amusement in her voice. "He did not order me to *think* for you."

She paused for an instant, then shook her head. "And, to be perfectly frank, at the moment my advice would be worthless. The Giovanni clan is strictly neutral in the ongoing conflict between the Camarilla and the Sabbat. We honor a pledge made many centuries ago. I know nothing about the Red Death other than what I learned in the brief conversations I have had over the past week."

McCann, who knew a great deal more about the Giovanni clan than anyone not born in the family should, wisely refrained from saying a word about their supposed neutrality. Like all of the thirteen clans, the Giovanni desired to have absolute control over the Kindred. A thousand-year-old covenant between the Giovanni and the rest of the Damned forbade them to interfere in the conflicts in which the other clans were involved. But, like most of the tenets that governed the political intrigues of the undead, this rule was meant to be broken.

Powerful necromancers as well as vampires, the Giovanni dreamed of controlling the realms of the living and the dead. Safely hidden in the Mausoleum, their huge headquarters in Vienna, the clan elders charted their devious, long-range schemes for global domination. Time meant nothing to the Damned, and the Giovanni were very, very patient. It was a trait they shared with Dire McCann.

"Well, it's nearly dawn," said the detective. "There's nothing more that can be done tonight. Better we all take a break and meet here once the sun sets tomorrow. I sure can use the rest."

"One question before you leave, McCann," said Flavia. "Did you learn anything from this insane venture tonight? Or was the risk entirely without gain?"

In the distance, the sky still glowed crimson from the fire at the Navy Yard. "Actually, I discovered more than I expected," said the detective. "I spoke with the Red Death for a few moments on the parade grounds. He needed time after he arrived to set his plan in motion. Because he was not expecting me to survive the encounter, the monster was not as guarded with his comments as he probably should have been."

McCann's features were like stone. "The Red Death set a double trap for me. When one plan failed, he switched immediately to the other. I was overconfident of my abilities and admittedly was caught off-guard. If it hadn't been for Madeleine, the monster would have triumphed.

"Instead of a solitary Red Death, as I expected," continued the detective, "there were four of the monsters at the rendezvous. Each being was powerful enough to burn me to a cinder with one touch of its fingers. Fortunately, my magic kept the quartet at bay. I was unable to attack them in return, but the best offense proved to be a good defense. Using their Body of Fire Discipline drained the Red Deaths of psychic energy. In a few more minutes, they would have collapsed from their effort. When the quartet realized what was happening, they abandoned their strike, turned into mist, and vanished. That's when Makish took charge, setting off the Thermit he had planted all through the Navy Yard."

"The rogue Assamite assassin," growled Flavia, her voice not sounding the least bit human. "He assists the Red Death for a fee, even when the maneuver is directed against his own clansmen. By Assamite tradition, Makish should have left the services of the monster when the Red Death destroyed my sister. The Red Death will pay in blood for Fawn's death. And so will Makish."

The detective nodded but said nothing. The Assamite clan had a secret code of honor called the *khabar*, and the clan's traditions were concealed from all — including Dire McCann.

"Debts of blood must be repaid in kind," said Madeleine. Her words held such conviction that

McCann suspected she had a feud of her own to settle. The detective knew that her sire had been slain in some sort of European feud.

"The Red Death dreams of leading the Kindred," said McCann. "He feels that the rising of several ancient monsters, grisly horrors known as the Nictuku, from their torpor signals that Armageddon is approaching. The Red Death is convinced that their awakening means that the Third Generation, the Antediluvians, are also stirring, and will soon follow. And when they do, the ancient ones will be extremely hungry for the blood of their descendants."

"What do you believe, McCann?" asked Flavia.

"I'm not sure," said the detective. "We know that as a vampire ages, it needs stronger blood to sustain itself. Many Kindred of the Fourth and Fifth Generation can no longer survive on mortal blood. They feast instead on the much more potent vitae of other vampires. Whispered legends hint that the Antediluvians drank only Kindred blood. And after thousands of years in torpor, they will need rivers of blood to survive when they awaken."

"Gehenna," murmured Madeleine. "The return of the Third Generation. How does the Red Death propose to stop the slaughter?"

"That detail he never explained," said McCann dryly. "The Red Death was looking for my blind obedience, not a partnership. When I refused, he admitted that he had expected no less. That's when he launched his attack."

"He sought your aid," said Madeleine. "How odd

for a Kindred elder to ask for the help of a mortal. Even if that request was merely a trick."

"McCann has his little secrets," said Flavia, with a laugh. "He is a very special mortal. Even vampires want his help."

"The blood war taking place here in Washington is the Red Death's doing," McCann said hurriedly. The last thing he wanted to come up in the conversation was Flavia's theory about his true identity. "He wants to heighten the conflict between the Camarilla and the Sabbat. For some unknown reason, he seems to desire total anarchy."

"What better scenario for a power grab than exactly such conditions?" said Madeleine. "Destroy the old to start anew."

"I'm not entirely convinced that the Red Death wanted to create a vacuum and start fresh," said McCann. "He stated that he'd been planning things for thousands of years. The unexpected rising of the Nictuku abruptly forced him to change his schedule. The Camarilla and the Sabbat have been in existence for mere centuries. I think he began this battle to manipulate the two organizations, not to destroy them."

"From what I've heard of the Jyhad," said Flavia, her gaze focused directly on McCann, "it sounds like this is typical of the Fourth Generation. They seek control, not destruction."

"My thoughts exactly," said McCann. "Tomorrow night, we search out the leaders of the Camarilla in Washington. And try to explain to them how they are being used."

"Easier said than done," declared Flavia. "The Sabbat's been hunting for the same elders for a week, with destruction on their minds. If the invaders can't eliminate the prince of the city and his advisors soon, this blood war is going to collapse in absolute disaster. So, they're desperate. What makes you think we stand a better chance of finding Prince Vitel than do hundreds of the Sabbat?"

"Because," said McCann, grinning, "I have much more competent help. With the Dark Angel of the Kindred and the Dagger of the Giovanni working together, how can we fail?"

The detective stretched his arms high over his head and yawned. "Enough discussion for one night. You two have to seek shelter before dawn. I'm falling asleep on my feet. Meet me here tomorrow, after sundown, and we'll map a strategy."

"One final question, Mr. McCann," said Madeleine Giovanni, as they prepared to depart. "I meant to ask this earlier, but I never had the chance. Who was the mortal woman standing at your side the instant before the explosion at the parade ground?"

McCann, caught by surprise, blurted out an answer without thinking. "She was an old friend. A very old friend and ally." His wits returned then and he quickly covered his tracks. "She was a mage, of course. Like myself. The Red Death considered her, for some unstated reasons, to be a threat to his plans."

"Then I regret that I was not able to save her as well," said Madeleine. "It took all of my speed to get you to the river before the Thermit ignited. I'm sorry she perished in the blast."

McCann, remembering a sudden distortion of time, shrugged. "I have discovered over the years that, no matter what the circumstances, it is not wise to assume that this particular acquaintance is dead without first seeing a body. Her talent for cheating fate is unmatched."

And then he added, because it had been a long, difficult night and he wanted to taunt Flavia, "Like me, my friend considers life to be one big *masquerade*. She is much older than she looks."

Chapter 2

Washington, D.C. - March 23, 1994:

Money, Alicia Varney decided, could not buy happiness. But it definitely could rent it for short periods.

For the hundredth time, she gazed at the gauges only a few inches from her eyes. The readings were still the same. Outside the coffin-sized black box in which she rested, an inferno of incredible intensity raged. It had been burning for hours and she expected it to continue burning for hours more. She was trapped inside the life-support system until it finally quieted.

A secret NASA invention, the escape capsule had been developed as an emergency backup system after several fatal accidents in the early days of the manned space program. The pods, built to withstand an atomic blast or direct reentry into the atmosphere, had never been used. Three of them had been sitting in storage in Florida until a huge bribe from one of Alicia's many businesses secured their release. The capsules had then been placed in strategic locations throughout the Washington Navy Yard as Alicia's last line of defense against the diabolical power of the Red Death. It had been an expensive gamble, but one well worth the investment.

Mentally, Alicia slammed her hands together in frustration. Certain matters demanded her immediate attention, but they would have to wait until she was free. She was lucky to be alive and she knew it. The proper combination of ancient vampire powers and modern scientific technology had saved her from the massive firestorm that had swept across the Washington Navy Yard just hours before. The Red Death had unleashed his most potent weapons against her. On two separate occasions, he had tried to burn her to ashes. And failed in each attempt.

Alicia did not intend to give him a third try. The Red Death had played her for a fool. She had allowed her arrogance and her greed for power to blind her to his schemes — but she was blind no longer. The Red Death had started a blood war, and Alicia intended to finish it. She was going to destroy the monster.

Closing her eyes, she let her mind drift. Mostly, Alicia wondered if Dire McCann had somehow survived the raging inferno outside. It seemed unlikely. There had been less than a split second between the moment she realized what the Red Death planned and the actual explosion. Her power to stop time for an instant had given her the chance to flee to the isolation capsule. McCann possessed no such skill.

Still, Alicia had a vague memory of a shadow darting across the Navy Yard, and she was not a believer in coincidence. She suspected that in some unknown fashion the detective had managed to avoid the blast. To kill the being who called himself Dire McCann, as she knew from her experience over the centuries, was almost an impossible task. He seemed to have an incredible talent for survival. The Red Death had sought to destroy them both with his trap, and they had vastly underestimated the monster's power; but he had equally underestimated theirs.

The fact that there were four Red Deaths haunted Alicia as she lay confined to her contemplations. She now had to deal with four enemies, and possibly even more, for if four such beings of unknown bloodline existed, there could be five, six, or a dozen of them. It was an extremely unpleasant thought. At least, only one of the monsters had been a Methuselah. The original Red Death, the vampire whose attack against the Sabbat archbishop of Manhattan had incited the Sabbat strike against Washington, was a member of the Fourth Generation. Alicia had no doubts about that fact. Among the most powerful of the Damned, *like* recognized *like*.

The other Red Deaths had been of the Fifth or Sixth Generation. She felt certain that they were the progeny of the Methuselah, his childer. They were dangerous, but none of them could match her in power. Alicia smiled. There were very few Kindred in the world who were her equals. Lameth, the Dark Messiah, was one; the Red Death obviously thought he was another. She, however, was determined to prove him wrong. Destroying him would be a pleasure.

Alicia yawned. The gauges had not changed. The inferno outside continued to burn. It would be many hours before the city fire departments could bring the blaze under control, and she was stuck inside this capsule until then. Even her time control powers could not aid her now. Exiting the capsule would place her in the midst of a blast furnace. Her spirit would survive, but not her physical form. And though earlier, she had been willing to sacrifice her body to destroy the Red Death, she was no longer feeling quite so generous.

The Red Death's plan had focused entirely on destroying Alicia Varney, controller of the huge Varney financial empire. If she was killed, Anis would be rendered powerless for decades, and this is exactly what the Red Death desired.

Alicia closed her eyes. It would be dawn soon, and she was weary and needed rest. Thousands of years of life had taught her patience, and tomorrow was soon enough to deal with the Red Death. Seconds later, she was asleep.

Alicia dreamed...

"The Lady in room 12 wants a bottle of fine wine," said Marcus Drum, a salacious leer crossing his ugly face. "She requested you, my sweet, to deliver it. Said to send you up early, she did."

"Me?" asked Alice, squinting at Drum as if to discern the truth from his twisted features. "Why me?"

The old man laughed nastily. "Why indeed?" he replied. "Maybe she's one who likes her pleasures from pretty young girls like you, my pet. A few fine ladies with such strange tastes do frequent my establishment. Who knows? As long as she's willin' to pay for your services, that's all that matters. Now, get moving before she gets tired of waiting. Take two glasses with ye. She said that too. And remember to bring me back every penny she pays you. No holdin' back or you'll get a whipping."

Alice stifled a curse. Drum was a greedy old bastard with a taste for the lash. She knew that no matter what money she gave him, he'd claim it wasn't the whole of it and then beat her senseless. Alice had allowed him his pleasure for three years. The fool never realized that his guess was correct and she had been hiding coins exactly as he suspected. Let him beat her. She didn't care as long as he didn't leave scars. Someday soon, she'd have enough to escape this rathole tavern and set up her own business. As for Master Drum, Alice had her plans for him. And for his leather whip.

At twenty-two, Alice Hale was one of the most stunning women in all London. A dark-haired vixen with flashing eyes and lush figure, she was as ambitious as she was beautiful. Born to the gutter, she had used her body, and sometimes her knife, to rise to the position of chief serving girl and tavern doxy of *The Bitter Brew*. To Alice, it was just one more step along the path of her quest for fame and happiness. Other women in eighteenth-century London had escaped the streets to become members of the aristocracy. All it took were certain sexual skills. And a lot of money.

She had the necessary skill. The money she was accumulating, but it was taking longer than she liked. Her good looks, she knew, would only last so long. She was not yet desperate. But she was growing anxious.

Tonight, she hoped that perhaps this Lady's unusual tastes might earn her more than her usual tip. Alice had made love to enough men not to be surprised by anything they demanded, but, although the other girls had sometimes talked about the strange desires of certain wealthy women, she had never before been asked to spend some time with a Lady.

Slightly nervous, Alice, balancing a tray with two goblets and a bottle of the inn's best wine, knocked on the proper door. The pair of glasses also had her wondering. Her male clients never shared their drink. They saw no reason to waste good ale or wine on a serving girl. That kind of thing just wasn't done. But Drum insisted that the Lady had asked her to bring two glasses. It was all quite strange.

The door opened. Except for a solitary candle, the room was completely dark. The noblewoman, her figure shadowy and indistinct, stood before her. Alice licked her lips. "I've brought your wine, milady."

"I know, Alice," said the woman. Her voice was rich and deep, cultured yet oddly exotic. She stepped back into the room. "Please come in."

Her suspicion flaring, Alice entered. She deposited the tray with the two glasses and the bottle on the small bedside table. The woman remained in the shadows.

"Should I pour you a glass, milady?" Alice asked, trying to keep a rein on her temper. She hated when Drum treated her like a piece of cheap jewelry, as he had this evening.

"Not for me," said the mystery woman. She was tall and very well dressed. From what little Alice could see of her features, she appeared to be very beautiful. Not the sort of woman who needed to pay for her sexual favors. Grimly, Alice wondered what sort of entertainment Drum had promised she would provide. And how much extra the old goat had received for the arrangement.

"No wine?" said Alice. "I don't understand."

"I don't care for wine," she said. "Please, have a glass for yourself. Take as much as you like."

Alice shook her head. "No thank you, milady. It's too good for the likes of me."

The woman laughed. She had the most sensual voice Alice had ever heard. "No reason to lie to me, Alice. Please, help yourself. A good vintage is meant to be enjoyed. Especially for the price asked by Mr. Drum."

Alice shrugged and poured herself a glass. It truly was fine wine. Marcus Drum kept an excellent cellar for his wealthy patrons. If nothing else, Alice reasoned, the wine would be a small payback for whatever would take place tonight.

"You are mistaken, Alice," said the Lady, emerging from the darkness so that her features were illuminated by the candlelight. She was the most ravishing woman Alice had ever seen, with long black hair, black eyes, blood-red lips, and an aristocratic air. She wore a simple black dress, against which her skin appeared white as snow, and she moved with a sinuous grace that Alice somehow found rather unsettling. "I made no arrangements with Mr. Drum. Your body does not concern me. At least, not in the manner you suspect."

"You knew my name," said Alice, never one to hold her tongue.

"I know your name, your place of birth, your history, and your innermost thoughts," said the Lady. Gently, she sat on the huge feather bed. "Your parents are Tom and Molly Hale. Of seven children, you are the last. Only four survive and you have not seen any of them for years.

"Your first sexual encounter was with Tom Smith, on Christmas Day, 1714, when you were thirteen. It was followed by many others over the past ten years."

The Lady smiled. "You want to take Mr. Drum's whip and strangle him with it. The image is quite vivid in your thoughts. Do I need continue? You have no secrets from me, young woman."

Alice shook her head in bewilderment. She should have been frightened, perhaps terrified, by the Lady's remarks. But she felt nothing, except the desire to have another glass of wine.

"Drink," said the woman, "then sit down here beside me on the bed. We need to talk."

"About what?" asked Alice, her suspicions immediately returning. "What does a fancy Lady like you want with the likes of me?"

"More than you can imagine," she said. The dim light of the candle glinted on her perfect white teeth. "My name is Anis, and I have been observing you from afar for months. Tonight's meeting was a long time coming. I dislike making the wrong decision, and now, seeing you in person, sensing your feelings, I know I did not. You are ambitious, unscrupulous, and strong. Exactly like me."

"I don't understand," said Alice. "What are you talking about?"

"A bargain, Alice," said Anis. "I am talking about a bargain."

"You are the devil," said Alice, remembering stories she had been taught as a child. Her eyes narrowed, as if she were trying to spot horns or a tail. "Or one of his servants."

"Would it matter if I was?" asked Anis. "Would it really matter, if I offered you all that your heart desired?"

"Not for a friggin' minute," said Alice, honestly. "I'm not afraid of spending an eternity in Hell if it means that I can live my days on Earth in splendor. It's the present that counts. That's the truth of it."

"Exactly my position," said Anis. "We think alike, you and I. Why worry about the afterlife? The material world is waiting to be conquered."

Anis leaned forward, her dark eyes burning with an unnatural light. "I am no devil, Alice, nor am I his imp. I am one of the Damned. I am a member of the undead, a vampyr."

"A vampyr? What's that?" asked Alice.

Anis laughed. "So much for my concern about frightening you. Ignorance, I suppose, is bliss. A vampyr, Alice, is a man or woman who has died and then returned to life to prey upon the living. Vampyrs subsist entirely on human blood. These undead creatures, or Cainites as many of them prefer to be called, are immortal and nearly invulnerable. They can be killed by sunlight, or fire, or by having their head cut off. A fall off a high cliff is often fatal. That's it. Some, like myself, have existed for over five thousand years."

Alice shook her head and giggled. The strong wine made her silly. "Beggin' milady's pardon, but you don't look no five thousand years old to me. Not a wrinkle on your face. You'd be more like twenty-five. Thirty at most."

With a gentle smile, Anis nodded. Unexpectedly, one of her hands shot out and caught Alice by the throat. Effortlessly, Anis rose to her feet, lifting Alice off the bed and into the air. With Anis's grip on her neck, she couldn't make a sound. Eyes bulging, she desperately tried to wiggle free. But she was unable to loosen the Lady's iron grip.

Anis opened her mouth, revealing two long fangs that belonged in no human mouth. "One bite and I could drain you dry," she declared. She shook Alice like a rag doll. "Now do you believe me? Or do you still doubt my word, Alice?"

Opening her hand, Anis let Alice drop to the floor. With a moan, Alice rubbed her neck where fingers like steel spikes had dug into her flesh. She looked up at the figure standing before her. "I believe you," Alice whispered. "I friggin' believe."

"Good," said Anis, sitting once more on the bed. "I hoped the demonstration would convince you. The alternative was... unpleasant."

Alice, thinking of the fangs, shuddered. "You'd have drunk my blood?" she asked. "Murdered me for no other reason than the fact that I know your secret?"

"Human life, my dear," said Anis with a shrug, "is cheap. After fifty centuries, mortals are little more than shadows to one such as me. I do not kill without a purpose. That is the way of the beast. But, when the need arises, I also do not hesitate. Remember what I say. It is a lesson you will need to learn. And must never forget."

"What do you want of me, if not my blood?" asked Alice, pouring herself a third glass of wine. She was cold sober again. "You spoke of a bargain."

"I want your body, not your soul," said Anis, calmly. "I desire to live again. Through you, I want to experience the joys of the flesh once more. I hunger to eat real food, drink red wine, make passionate love. As a vampyr, such pleasures are denied me. But, with your cooperation, I can indulge in such things once more."

"How?" asked Alice.

"After thousands of years of existence," said Anis, "my body has grown tired. Most of my time, except for brief interludes like tonight, I spend in a trancelike state known as torpor. My physical form remains in deep sleep, but my mind is free to wander anywhere I wish. Once a mental bond is forged between us, I can merge my thoughts with yours. It is a symbiotic relationship that causes you no harm. And it allows me to perceive reality through your human senses."

"You'll take over my body," said Alice, frightened. "Replace my soul with yours."

"Never," said Anis, shaking her head. "That would defeat my purpose. I don't want you to become me. I want to become part of you, to regain some of my humanity. There will be a change in your personality, without question, as my goals and ambitions become important to you. Plus, you will absorb much of my knowledge, my history, and my powers. But you will always be Alice, albeit a more powerful Alice. Alice and Anis bound together in a single entity. Call us...Alicia."

"You mentioned riches and power," said Alice. Much of what Anis was saying made little sense to her. She didn't care. What mattered was that she was tired of poverty, tired of having to fight to survive. She wanted everything that life had to offer. And she wanted it now, not later. The price didn't matter. "When?"

"As soon as you like," said Anis. "To complete our bargain, you merely need to drink some of my blood. Just a taste will suffice. The vitae will transform you into my ghoul. As such, your mental and physical powers will be greatly enhanced. My blood will also slow your aging process to a crawl. Your life will be extended for many hundreds of years.

"Once the pact is sealed, we shall take care of

some unfinished business in this tavern. Mr. Drum will reap the bitter harvest he has sown. Burning the hostel to the ground, with him tied to his bed, should serve our purposes admirably. You will have your revenge, dear Alice. And what little information Mr. Drum knows about me shall disappear with his unexpected demise.

"Afterward, we will return to my estate in the country. There I will instruct you in the many things you need to learn before you can function as my alter ego. The serving wench must be transformed into a lady. Even my powers cannot do that overnight." Anis' voice grew sober. "There is no rush. The one thing I do not lack is time."

"I'll live forever?" asked Alice. "Never die?"

"I can't promise you that," said Anis. "Mortal flesh ages. The process cannot be stopped, just slowed. However, you will survive vastly longer than any normal human. Perhaps a thousand years or more."

"Long enough for me," said Alice. Then, she came to a realization. "I'm not the first, am I? You said you were five thousand years old. This ain't the only time you've made this bargain with some young girl." She grinned, pleased with her discovery. "I'm right, ain't I."

"You're the third," Anis admitted. "My last host died a decade ago. I've been searching for another ever since. My tastes are quite selective. Few women have both the physical attributes and the mental traits I desire. I had almost despaired of finding another. Until tonight." Her voice grew soft, almost pleading. "I hunger for the pleasures of life. I am so terribly bored with undeath. I want to live again. In torpor, my mind is free to wander in daylight as well as night. I want to feel the sun on my flesh. I want to feel...warm. With your cooperation, using your senses, I can do so once more."

Alice licked her lips nervously. She wanted to believe Anis was telling her the truth. But she was afraid, terribly afraid of being tricked. And she suspected that once the deal was made, there would be no turning back.

"There are others like you?" asked Alice. "Other Cainites?"

"There are many vampyrs," said Anis, rising to her feet, her expression unreadable. "Thousands of them exist throughout the world. They are the secret masters of humanity, manipulating nations and races for their own ends. But that isn't what you want to know, is it, Alice? You wonder if perhaps there are other vampyrs, like me, who live on through human hosts. The answer to that question is no."

"Why not?" asked Alice, anxiously. "What secrets are you keeping from me? Are the rest pleased with their lot? Or are they frightened of the consequences?"

"You are no fool, Alice," said Anis. "Which is one of the many reasons I selected you to be my partner. The Damned are neither scared nor satisfied. Most vampyrs hate their existence. They must endure an eternal struggle with the lust for blood that rages inside them. It is called the Beast

Within. That is why such unions of Cainite and human spirits are doomed to fail. Any mortal who links with a vampyr soon goes mad, driven insane by their partner's overwhelming thirst for vitae. Only a member of the undead unaffected by that dark hunger can merge its personality with a mortal companion."

"What makes you so special?" asked Alice.

Anis smiled. "I chose the right lover."

"I—I don't understand," said Alice.

"There is a special state of being," said Anis, "known as Golconda, that a select few of the Cainites achieve. Normally, it is the result of hundreds and hundreds of years of rigorous mental discipline and intense spiritual meditation. A vampyr who attains Golconda gains complete mastery over the desire for blood. He is in harmony with the universe."

Anis chuckled. "Reaching Golconda, unfortunately, has proven nearly impossible for most of my kind. The inner circle of a mysterious sect known as the Inconnu are reputed to have attained it. Some say the brood of Saulot, the Salubri, also reached Golconda, but they are no more. Since no vampyr is willing to admit to belonging to either group, in my more than five millennia of unlife I have yet to meet one of these fabled beings."

"You achieved Golconda," said Alice. It was not a question.

Anis nodded. "As I said, the right lover made the difference. Almost six thousand years ago, in a fabled place known as the Second City, a brilliant vampyr alchemist and sorcerer, Lameth, created a potion of rare and esoteric ingredients that artificially induced Golconda. There was only enough of the elixir for two. He drank half. The other draught he gave to me."

"What happened to Lameth?" asked Alice.

"He still exists," said Anis, her voice wistful. "He too pretends to be a human, though whether he uses the same technique, I do not know. Over the centuries, we have drifted together and then apart many times, sometimes as lovers, others as bitter enemies. Both of us harbor ambitions that cannot be shared by another. Among the Cainites he is known as the Dark Messiah, for the formula for his elixir offers salvation to the Damned. Though, much like his mortal counterpart, he has yet to return."

"And you, Anis," said Alice, knowing the time for questions was over. "What are you called by other vampyrs?"

Anis held out her right arm, lifting her wrist to Alice's lips. "I am Anis, Queen of Night. Now, bite and drink. And let the masquerade begin."

Chapter 3

Rub al-Khali — March 24, 1994:

"This moment will live in our thoughts forever," declared Assad ben Wazir, his voice thick with emotion. Anxiously, he stood with his four companions and watched as Nassir Akhbar, the explosives expert of their party, set the proper charges. Nassir worked in a shallow gully a dozen yards away. In a few minutes, the massive stone door that blocked the entrance to the ancient temple they had uncovered would be gone. And they could claim the treasure inside.

Assad felt certain that he and his fellow archeological bandits were about to become rich beyond their wildest dreams. These ruins were ancient. Sealed nearly three thousand years ago, during the reign of Solomon the Wise, this structure had remained undisturbed ever since. It was the dream of every thief in the Middle East, a temple filled with relics from Biblical times. The objects that were within had to be worth millions, perhaps tens of millions.

"Are you sure you want me to use this much dynamite?" asked Nassir, as he completed his preparations. "The blast will completely destroy the barrier. The carving on the stone is remarkably preserved. The writing is gone, but Solomon's Seal remains intact. It would bring a handsome price from some museum."

"Smash it," said Isbn Farouk, the leader of their party. "It blocks the only entrance to the temple. The rock weighs tons. It would take days to move, if we could even move it at all. We have spent too many days here already. Our supplies are growing short."

"How would we carry it home, Nassir?" asked Assad, anxious to explore the temple itself. Dirt poor his entire life, he was thinking about the wealth that awaited. "On your back? It won't fit in either jeep."

Nassir shrugged. "It's not my business to worry about such details. Still, I hate demolishing anything that might be worth hard cash."

"Finish your work," said Isbn. "Assad is correct. The rock doesn't matter. This first trip, we need to take only the very finest items. Strike fast and steal as much as possible: that's the way to handle such finds. Once the Saudi government learns of this place, it'll close the site to hard-working businessmen like ourselves."

"And stash the loot for themselves in a Swiss bank account," said Assad. "The thieving dogs."

"Enough jabbering," said Ivan Burroughs, the only non-Arab in their party. A German geologist and engineer, it was Burroughs, who, while doing survey work for a major oil company, had stumbled upon the ruins three years before. It had taken him long months to find a band of thieves who were desperate enough to risk their lives to accompany his return trip. A big, burly thug of a man, with shaven head and beady, piglike eyes, Burroughs was always in a hurry. "I've waited a thousand days to see what's inside this damned hole. The night is half over already and we still haven't gotten in. Blow up the *verdammte* stone."

Isbn scowled. A strict Muslim, he disliked profanity; it was forbidden by the followers of his religion. In Burroughs' case, however, he made an exception, and did not complain — at least for the present.

The ruins were located in the southern corner of the Rub al-Khali, the "Empty Wastes" of the Arabian desert. One of the most inhospitable regions on the entire planet, the Rub al-Khali was a vast sandy wasteland, utterly devoid of life. Temperatures soared to over 130 degrees Fahrenheit during the day, and night offered little relief from the heat's intensity.

There was no water for hundreds of miles; in truth, only madmen or geologists dared challenge the silence of the "Empty Wastes," and much of the desert remained unexplored. Located in the most barren region of the wasteland, where not even scorpions could survive, the ruins had been buried beneath mounds of shifting sands, and essentially ignored or forgotten for the course of a millennium. Forgotten, that is, until Burroughs, driving across the desert in search of mineral deposits, noticed a small finger of stone projecting from the dunes, and soon realized he had found a lost outpost of the fabled King Solomon.

"It is ready," cried Nassir, scrambling out of the shallow gully as fast as he could. "Ten seconds. Get down."

The blast shook the earth. For an instant, darkness turned into bright daylight; and then the night, lit only by the moonlight and the glare of their electric torches, returned. They worked at night to escape the sun's scathing rays.

"Praise Allah," cried Assad. "The stone is gone."

The explosives had done the job. The huge rock blocking the way into the underground temple was destroyed, shattered into thousands of stone fragments. Where it stood gaped a black corridor leading at a sharp angle down into darkness.

"A good job," said Burroughs, grinning. "We go inside now, *ja?*"

"Yes," answered Isbn. "Immediately."

He pointed to the heavy cloth sacks they had brought from their camp. "Take the sacks. Fill them with everything you find. Even the smallest statue is worth thousands. Leave nothing behind for the government jackals."

Assad marched third into the tunnel, behind Isbn and Burroughs. Following him came Nassir, Fakosh, and Harum. Tough, wiry individuals, veterans of a hundred illegal enterprises, they were gifted with a complete lack of imagination. Or fear.

The air in the corridor was dry and stagnant with age. All five men wore wet cloths over their mouth and nostrils to help moisten the air they breathed. Ancient buildings were like leeches, sucking liquid from their bodies and absorbing it into the parched air like water to a dry sponge.

"There is something very strange about this place," declared Harum, the scholar of their group, after they had been walking for a few minutes. "It is not an ordinary temple. Such buildings never have long entrances. Even those located beneath the ground have only short foyers. And there are no pictures or sacred writings on these walls. There should be carvings everywhere. It is not right."

"*Ja*, I agree," said Burroughs. "I, too, find it very unusual here. This tunnel goes too far down into the earth. We are already fifty feet beneath the desert floor. I think this temple is no temple. It is a tomb."

"A tomb?" said Isbn, with a shake of his head. "Never. Why would King Solomon build a mausoleum in the middle of the desert? More likely, we are descending into an ancient storehouse. The above-ground ruins looked like a garrison. Perhaps those buildings served as headquarters for guards watching the goods collected here."

"Solomon's treasure house!" said Assad excitedly. "Don't legends say that the king hid many of his finest jewels in a secret location?"

"Fairy tales for children," declared Harum skeptically. "Most likely, there was an oasis here thousands of years ago. And this location served as an outpost along a trade route. That would make more sense."

"We will know who guessed the correct answer in a moment," said Isbn. "The tunnel widens into a room just ahead."

They emerged into a huge chamber, so vast that their flashlights barely touched its far walls. The room was circular, about forty feet in diameter. The solid rock ceiling was twenty feet high, and covered with strange writings, still bright after thirty centuries. Similar symbols decorated the walls and floor of the room as well.

Assad began to feel uncomfortable as he stared at the glyphs. They made his eyes hurt. Something about them was wrong. They were not meant to be read — or seen.

"These words are cursed," declared Nassir, shielding his eyes with one hand. "They make my head spin."

"They are in no language I recognize," said Harum.

"Who cares about the *verdammte* scribbling," Ivan Burroughs said angrily. He raised a beefy arm and pointed to the center of the room. "What is *that*?"

The focus of Burroughs' curiosity stood six feet high, fifteen feet long, and six feet wide: a gigantic box, capped with a massive stone lid. It was made from the same unyielding stone as the door they had destroyed to gain entrance into the hallway. It was the only object in the entire room.

"Perhaps the treasure is inside the box," said Assad, expressing hope he no longer felt. "It looks like a chest."

"Perhaps," said Isbn, his voice betraying his doubts. "We will need more dynamite to remove the

ROBERT WEINBERG

top. It must weigh a ton."

"I do not like this spot," said Harum. A practical, soft-spoken man with a degree in history, he was ordinarily cold and emotionless during their expeditions. "I think we should depart immediately. This place is cursed."

"Solomon's seal on the door," said Burroughs, muttering to himself. "He was the master of demons."

"But the treasure..." Assad began, sensing that a fortune was slipping from his grasp.

"Der treasure ist not, you dummkopf," bellowed Ivan Burroughs suddenly. The big German's face had turned beet red. "Don't you understand? That thing there isn't a treasure chest. It's a coffin. A gigantic stone coffin!"

"A-a coffin?" said Assad. "You are crazy. What creature is so large..."

He never finished his question. A grating noise filled the chamber as the gigantic stone lid on the box shifted a few inches. Something inside was sliding the top off the tomb.

"Mein Gott," said Burroughs, the color draining from his face. "What thing could live three thousand years trapped inside a sealed stone box?"

"I do not want to find out," declared Isbn, stepping backward toward the tunnel that had brought them to the chamber. "Nassir, do you have any dynamite?"

"I left it with our supplies," answered Nassir. "Outside, by the jeeps."

"When we get to the surface, use it to seal the

tunnel entrance," said Isbn. "Immediately."

Stone shrieked in protest as the lid shifted another few inches. An immense clawlike hand, the color of old bone, its five huge fingers capped with inches-long nails, emerged from the sarcophagus and grasped the edge of the cover. Fragments of rock exploded as the titanic digits curled into the stone.

"Allah protect us," said Isbn feverishly. "Flee for your lives!"

A cloud of dust rose from the tomb, filling the chamber. Isbn howled with fright and bolted for the exit, followed by Nassir, Fakosh and Harum. Assad, still bewildered by what was taking place, remained where he was. Next to him Ivan Burroughs stood frozen, as if hypnotized.

"We released a genie from the bottle," said the German. "When we destroyed King Solomon's seal, we broke the spell."

"Genie?" said Assad with a laugh. "Only children believe in such nonsense."

"*Gott in Himmel*," Burroughs whispered. A figure moved in the dust cloud that obscured the tomb from view. A gigantic creature, twice the height of its discoverers, stepped ponderously forward.

"Azazel," said the German. "It is Az..."

A monstrous hand whipped out of the darkness. Huge fingers wrapped around Burroughs' waist. The German shrieked as nails the size of spikes sank into his flesh. Effortlessly, the monster he named Azazel lifted him into the air.

Horrified, Assad stumbled backward. His feet tangled, and he sprawled to the ground. The fall jarred the flashlight from his grip, and it rolled across the floor; its beam, flipping over and over, produced a shifting kaleidoscope of flashes of light and dark.

For an instant, the monster from the sarcophagus was illuminated. It was immense and horrifying, shaped like a man but frightfully mutated. It had long, beastlike jaws and a mouth full of gigantic teeth. Its twin eyes burned red like coals. Crowning its hairless skull were two curved horns. And clasped in one hand was the limp body of Ivan Burroughs, blood dripping from the wounds in his side.

Assad screamed. The lamp landed face down on the floor and the chamber was enveloped in darkness. He curled himself into a ball, shuddering, as the monster roared words in a language he didn't recognize. The beast's voice echoed through the giant room like the beating of a huge gong. Assad felt certain the creature was trying to question Burroughs. But no response came from the German. He was either badly hurt or dead.

Again, the monster howled its queries and again Burroughs did not answer. Desperately, Assad searched the blackness for his flashlight. He couldn't find it, nor was he sure he wanted to see what was happening. The creature was no longer speaking. Instead, the room was filled with a terrible hissing, almost a sucking sound. And a gruesome crunching that made Assad bite his lower lip in terror.

Then, its feet thumping like triphammers, the monster stomped across the floor of the cavern to the tunnel that led to the surface. Assad swallowed, not sure what to do next. Astonishingly enough, he was still alive and unharmed; he had no idea, however, how long he would stay that way. He didn't want to know whether the creature was gone or if it planned to return. Following it to the surface did not seem like a good idea, but remaining in its lair was an equally unappealing alternative.

After five minutes of carefully running his hands across the ground, he recovered his flashlight. Miraculously, it still worked. With a sigh of relief, he swung the beam around the room. It came to rest on the a smashed pile of flesh and bones that had been Ivan Burroughs.

Cautiously, Assad approached the corpse. He gulped, fighting down the bile that churned in his stomach, when he saw the condition of the German's neck and chest. A huge chunk had been ripped right out of Burroughs' body. With a moan of terror, Assad realized that there was no blood visible in the wound. Or on the floor. The monster had sucked out every drop.

Gasping for breath, Assad rushed for the tunnel. Better to be caught in the passageway and die fighting then await the monster's return. Assad might be a thief, but he was not a coward.

Halfway up the tunnel, he felt the floor suddenly begin to shake. Dynamite. Assad remembered Isbn's instructions to Nassir. Cursing, he prayed that the blast hadn't sealed the entrance to the underground corridor, trapping him inside with the demon. Desperately, he quickened his pace. Until he heard the rattle of gunfire. And the screaming of men in agony.

Moonlight gleaming into the tunnel convinced him that the opening remained clear. But the horrible shrieks of his companions slowed Assad's ascent to a crawl. The silence that followed was equally unnerving. A dozen feet from the entrance, he dropped to his belly and wiggled the rest of the way forward.

Cautiously, he peered outside. Nothing moved in the moonlight. Though it felt like hours, he had been underground for less than sixty minutes. Anxiously, he scanned the area with his eyes; but as he was at the bottom of a gully, he could see nothing unusual.

Consigning his soul to Allah, Assad raised himself up to a standing position. He remained motionless, waiting for the demon to appear. After counting to a hundred, he decided the creature was no longer in the area. Nervously, he climbed out of the gully and went searching for his companions.

They weren't hard to find. Their bodies, in much the same condition as the German's, were scattered around their two jeeps. All of them were dead, expressions of incredible shock etched across their features. Gaping wounds bore mute testament to the fury of their attack. Yet not a drop of their blood stained the desert sands.

Bullets and dynamite had failed to stop the monster or even slow it down. Shaking his head in dismay, Assad wondered if any weapon could destroy it. He did not intend to learn the answer. After killing Isbn and the others, the thing had stalked off into the desert. Its footprints, impressed into the sands, pointed north. Assad turned the jeep south.

Upon reflection, he realized that his words of earlier that evening had been correct. The memory of this night would live in his thoughts forever.

Chapter 4

Washington, D.C. - March 23, 1994:

The small plane landed on a hidden airstrip at 4 a.m. According to records on file at the Virginia Department of Revenue, the field was owned by the Tobacco Research and Development Corporation of America. A lone, two-story red brick building sat on the corner of the grounds, facing a rarely traveled country road. Sitting in the parking lot beside the structure was a lone black limousine.

A sign on the structure proclaimed it the home of the Tobacco Research Institute of the United States. Papers filed with the Department of Revenue for the State of Virginia explained that the corporation, funded by grants from the major tobacco producers, sought to produce a safe, low-tar cigarette. The huge field in the back was home for thousands of genetically engineered tobacco plants.

No one bothered to mention in the declaration that the plants were anchored to huge movable boards that retreated with the flick of a switch, revealing a fully functional airplane runway beneath. Nor did any documents speak of the millions of dollars in bribes paid each year to law enforcement officials in the area, insuring that all flights to the Institute remained unnoticed and undisturbed. The employees of the Tobacco Institute of America were not scientists or researchers. They were Syndicate toughs. The field, located exactly twenty-seven miles from the White House, was a major drop-off point for drugs destined for the capital. Sometimes, it served as a stop-off for visitors to America who preferred not to pass through Customs. As was the case tonight.

Three men approached the Cessna as its powerful twin motors idled. As soon as the plane's sole passenger exited, it would take to the skies again. The boards would slide into place, and the landing strip would disappear, replaced once more by a tobacco field.

Leading the delegation was Tony "The Tuna" Blanchard, head of the East Coast branch of the Crime Syndicate. A big, beefy, red-faced man, Tony had been waiting nervously all evening for the small plane to arrive. His thousand-dollar Armani suit looked as if it had been slept in. Though there was a chill in the night air, he was sweating profusely as he stepped up to the door of the aircraft and wrenched it open.

Flanking Tony on his left and right were his bodyguards, Alvin and Theodore. Massive men, each nearly seven feet tall, with barrel chests and apelike arms, they were conservatively dressed in charcoal gray suits, white shirts, and solid gray ties. Though the landing field was dimly lit, the two giants wore dark sunglasses. Cold, ruthless mob enforcers, they exuded an air of menace. Alvin and

Theodore were afraid of nothing. Which was why Tony brought them with him tonight.

A dark figure stepped out of the airplane and onto the runway. He was wearing a heavy black overcoat, white scarf and gray fedora. His large hands were encased in black silk gloves. Short and stocky, the stranger was broad shouldered, with shortly clipped jet-black hair. His face was pale white, with a beak nose and narrow eyebrows that slanted upward, giving him a hawkish expression. He had thin, bloodless lips and eyes the color of old marble. He looked to be about forty, but Tony Blanchard knew he was much, much older.

"Don Lazzari," said Tony, trying to keep his voice steady. He held out his hand in greeting. "Your flight made good time."

"Very good time, Tony," replied Don Lazzari, shaking Blanchard's hand. The stranger had a grip like a steel vise. His fingers were ice cold. "I told the pilot if we did not arrive a half-hour early, I would rip off his genitals."

Don Lazzari laughed, a harsh, cruel sound. Tony laughed too, but more from fear than amusement. He knew Don Lazzari wasn't kidding. The Mafia Capo never made idle threats.

"Please, follow me," he said, gesturing toward the Institute headquarters. "We have to get off the field so the plane can depart. Besides, we will be much more comfortable inside."

"All of my belongings arrived here safely?" asked Don Lazzari as they walked to the building.

"Everything," said Tony. "Your coffin came this

afternoon. I had it placed in the basement of the Institute. Because of your late arrival, this seemed the best place to keep it safe.

"I've assigned Alvin and Theodore, my personal bodyguards, to the task of standing guard tomorrow. In the evening, when you awaken, we can have the box moved anywhere you like."

"The arrangement sounds acceptable," said Don Lazzari, "considering the lack of advanced warning. I think this location will serve as an adequate headquarters for my work. You have done quite well, Tony."

"Thank you, Don Lazzari," said Blanchard, sighing in relief. "I tried my best. If I had had a little more time..."

"Don Caravelli sent me here on account of some rather unexpected news," said Don Lazzari. "The Capo de Capo oftentimes forgets that major operations need a great deal of preparation. He expects miracles."

The Mafia Don smiled, revealing a mouthful of wolfish yellow teeth. "I, of course, never said such insulting words. Only a fool would ever criticize Don Caravelli. And I am not a fool."

"No, Don Lazzari," said Blanchard hurriedly. He was sweating again. "You are definitely not a fool."

"I am glad you understand me, Tony," said the Mafia chief as they entered the brick building. "You strike me as a man with a great future. I assume you can keep your mouth shut and your eyes and ears open."

"Yes, Don Lazzari," said Tony, his head bobbing

up and down like a buoy in choppy seas. "Your wish is my command. I swear it. I swear it."

"Good," said the Don. They were in a large meeting room, with a long table surrounded by six chairs. With a grunt of satisfaction, the Don settled into the black leather chair at the head of the table. "That is very good."

The Mafia chief gestured to the seat next to him. "Sit, Tony. Relax. We have business to discuss." Don Lazzari's eyes narrowed. His lips curled in the slightest of smiles. "My special request I sent you yesterday, for a young girl, a virgin. You found one for me?"

"Yes, Don Lazzari," answered Tony, his throat suddenly very dry. A hard-boiled career mobster, he had no problems dealing with adults. But he normally steered clear of children. "We found one. My men kidnapped the child from a convent school. She is tied up in the basement. As you requested, we used no sedatives or drugs. She is awake and alert."

Don Lazzari smiled. "Excellent, Tony. Send these two behemoths to fetch her. Meanwhile, you and I can chat about business."

"Whatever you wish, my Don," Tony said, and swung around to his henchmen. "Get the girl and bring her upstairs. The Don wants to see her. And make it quick."

Without a word, Alvin and Theodore left, heading for the basement. They rarely spoke. Neither of them had much to say. Besides, they weren't paid to talk, only to follow instructions.

"The blood of a virgin," said Don Lazzari, "tastes sweeter than any other. My fellow Kindred tell me that there is no difference, but they do not have my refined palate."

"Uh, sure, Don Lazzari," said Tony Blanchard, the sweat dribbling down the inside of his shirt. He was not comfortable talking about human blood. Especially when the proposed victim was an innocent teenage girl. "You wanted to discuss work?"

"The Giovanni bitch," said Don Lazzari. "Your men have discovered some trace of her?"

Blanchard grimaced. "Not yet. But they're still lookin'. We spread the word on the street. According to the information provided us by your man, Darrow, the dame is drivin' a big rig with the Giovanni crest on the side. Nice that she's advertising her presence. We hope to find the truck fairly soon."

"The sooner the better," said Don Lazzari. "I cannot risk her leaving the city. The stakes are too high. Raise the reward if necessary. The Mafia has plenty of money. I personally will pay twenty-five thousand to the man who first spots the truck."

"Twenty-five G's," said Blanchard, whistling. "That's quite a chunk of change for locatin' a dame. Don Caravelli must be anxious to off the babe."

"Madeleine Giovanni has been a thorn in his side for many years," said Don Lazzari. "The Capo de Capo is most anxious to be rid of her. He has offered a tremendous bounty for her elimination. I am here to personally supervise the operation."

"Didn't Don Caravelli say something about this

Madeleine not being no pushover?" asked Blanchard. With three other Syndicate crime bosses, he had just recently returned from a visit to the Mafia Overlord. It had not been a pleasant trip. "He told us how she wiped out six different hitmen sent after her."

"The bitch definitely has claws," said Don Lazzari. "But she is neither invincible nor invulnerable. Once I know for sure she is in the city, I will spread the special message I bring from Sicily. Don Caravelli has offered control of the entire American branch of our organization to the Cainite who destroys Madeleine Giovanni. The reward will have every vampire in the city out hunting her. Even she cannot cope with such numbers."

"That sounds promising," said Tony. "Nobody is that tough."

"If I found her," said Don Lazzari, his eyes blazing red, "I would nail her to the earth with a dozen daggers. Make sure that she couldn't move an inch. Then, I'd let her struggle until the sun came up and melted the flesh off her bones. And turned her body into powder."

The vampire paused, as if relishing the thought. "I'd videotape every second, so I could watch her perish a thousand times. And with each replay I would laugh and laugh."

Blanchard swallowed, feeling slightly queasy. The sound of footsteps reminded him that worse, much worse, was about to come.

Alvin and Theodore reentered the room. Held between them, a gag thrust in her mouth so she couldn't scream, was a fourteen-year-old girl. Standing around 5'4", the girl was thin as a beanpole. She had brown hair, done into braids. She wore a school uniform, white socks, and plain black shoes. Her cheeks were stained with tears, her eyes wide with shock. She had good reason to be afraid.

Don Lazzari stared at the child. His gaze met hers and for a second, the teenager stopped struggling, as if hypnotized by the vampire's glance. The Mafia boss chuckled. "Perfect," he declared. "Exactly as I desired. She has never known a man's touch."

"We aim to please, Don Lazzari," said Tony Blanchard, struggling to keep down his supper. The unholy desire in the Mafia Capo's voice nauseated him. "You want us to, uh, leave you here alone with the girl?"

The Mafia Don shook his head. "No. Much of the pleasure comes from the thrill of the chase. I want you to let the child go."

"Let her go?" questioned Blanchard. "Not to be doubting your good judgment, Don Lazzari, but if this kid makes it to the highway and gets help, this operation could be put in serious jeopardy."

"Do not fear," said Don Lazzari, chuckling. "I take full responsibility for whatever happens. Remove the gag. I need to talk to the child. It is important to me that she understands precisely what is about to happen."

Alvin yanked the cloth off the girl's face. "Who are you?" she asked, her voice quivering with horror. "What do you want with me?"

"I," said Don Lazzari, rising to his feet, "am Don

Nicko Lazzari. I am a vampire." He grinned, his lips stretching back to reveal two long fangs. "I hunger for warm human blood. You, child, are my prey."

"Why me?" asked the girl, tears trickling down her pink cheeks. "I didn't do anything to you. I never hurt anybody." The tears were flowing in a torrent now. "Why me?"

Don Lazzari shrugged his massive shoulders. "You were at the wrong place at the wrong time. Ours is a world of darkness. There is no justice. Life and death are accidents of an uncaring fate, with no meaning and no purpose."

The vampire paused, as if in contemplation. "However, I am not unreasonable in my pursuit of pleasure. I will offer you a chance to survive. You are young and strong, with a healthy body. You can run. If you can elude me long enough to get to the highway, I promise to let you go."

"Why should I believe you?" said the girl, through the sobs. "Tell me why I should believe you."

The vampire smiled nastily. "I don't care if you do or not. You have no choice. Run or die." He gestured to the two bodyguards. "Bring her outside. I am bored with talking."

Alvin and Theodore looked at Tony Blanchard. He was the man who paid their salary, not Don Lazzari. White-faced, knowing he was condemning the girl to death, he nodded. And entered the ranks of the damned.

"Which direction to the highway from here?" asked Don Lazzari, when they stood in front of the house. It was pitch black outside, in the dark hours before dawn. The only light came from the bright moon.

"A mile to the east," said Tony, pointing to the dirt road that wound past the Institute. "That's if you follow the road. It's even shorter going straight through the forest."

"A mile," said Don Lazzari to the teenager. "A six- or seven-minute run for a girl of your years. Are you prepared? I will give you a five-minute head start. Not a second more. But not a second less."

The vampire looked at Blanchard. "You are wearing a watch. As soon as she starts running, begin counting off the minutes. She is to have her full time. My word is my bond."

"Please," said the girl, looking first to Blanchard, then to Alvin, and finally to Theodore, "don't let him kill me. You can stop this terrible thing. Please."

None of them said a word. Sobbing, the girl turned to the road. "Oh dear God, please save me."

Don Lazzari laughed, a cruel, harsh noise sound without the slightest trace of pity. "Your God cannot help you now. I can wait no longer. Run, child, run."

The girl ran. Straight as an arrow, she sprinted for the dirt road leading to the highway. She was fast, faster than Tony Blanchard had expected. Nervously, he glanced down at his watch. Less than a minute had passed and already the teenager was out of sight.

"She moves well," said Don Lazzari, his eyes glowing with anticipation. "That pleases me. The naive fool actually thinks she can escape. Those I hunt in Europe are so resigned to their fate, they don't even pretend to try. Our peasants lack backbone. Their lack of enthusiasm takes the thrill out of the chase."

"Two minutes," said Tony. "That kid's damn fast, Don Lazzari. She might make it to the highway in five minutes. Like I said before, if the kid gets to the police, she could endanger our entire operation."

The vampire shrugged. "I gave the child my word, Tony, and I refuse to compromise that, under any circumstances. She has her chance. That's what makes the hunt exciting. Will she manage to escape my clutches? Will she survive the night? Not likely, despite her speed. Like many gifted members of my race, I am very, very fast."

"Four minutes," said Tony. "You want me to hold your coat or something? That kid is probably pretty damned close to the highway. This might take some extra effort."

Don Lazzari shook his head. Smoothly, he pivoted on one heel so that he faced the same direction the girl had taken. "No one escapes me, Tony," the vampire declared grimly. "I am not easily denied."

The mobster swallowed hard, understanding that the Mafia chief wasn't merely talking about the girl in the woods. The implied threat was clear. Crossing Don Lazzari was not a wise idea.

"Five..." began Tony, then paused, as the Mafia leader vanished, moving faster than the eye could follow, "minutes."

Less than ten seconds later, a child's scream of

incredible pain broke the silence of the night. Cut off after an instant, the horrible sound lingered in Tony's mind for the rest of the night. As did the terrible truth of what he had done. Don Lazzari was a depraved, evil monster, a creature of unnatural passions. And in cooperating with him, Tony was no better.

Chapter 5

Washington, D.C. - March 23, 1994:

"It's a spectacular fire, isn't it?" said the heavyset, gray-haired old woman. "Best I've seen in a while."

"A major conflagration," said the mahogany-skinned man who stood next to her. Short and slender, with oily black hair and white teeth, the man was staring at the blaze with a peculiar intensity. He was one of a crowd of nearly two dozen spectators who clustered by the gatehouse of the Navy Yard and watched the inferno rage. "It is definitely a masterpiece of destruction. The creation of a true artist."

"You like fires?" asked the old woman, wiping the sweat from her forehead. Though they were two blocks from the flames, the heat was still intense. She didn't bother to wait for the stranger to answer. "I love big blazes. The bigger the better."

"A well-done fire is a work of art," said the dark-skinned man. His voice was polite, his diction perfect. "A thing of beauty is a joy forever."

"I got a police band radio in my van," said the old woman, her voice low, as if whispering a secret. She glared at the other people in the crowd. No one was paying any attention to her. "Have 'nother one in my home. I keeps them tuned to the emergency frequency. That way I arrives at the fires while they're still blazing."

Her voice dropped even further. "Sometimes I gets there early enough to hear the people screamin'. Before the smoke and the flames shuts them off. You know who I mean. The suckers trapped inside. The ones that can't get out."

"Ah, I understand," said the little man. "You refer to the poor unfortunates caught in the blaze. A tragedy when they die before help arrives."

"Yeah," said the old woman, her eyes glistening. "Damn rotten shame. Makes me shivery all over. Thinkin' about their skin goin' all black and crackly, smelling their own flesh burnin'." She laughed. "Crispy critters, I calls 'em."

"An unpleasant comparison," said the little man. He grinned. "But I must admit, quite accurate. You are a perceptive critic."

"Summer's best season for fires," declared the old woman. "Bunches of 'em every night. More than the department can handle. Kids set most of them. They like burning things down. Can't says I blame the little buggers. Been tempted once or twice to light one myself. You knows, just to see what it would be like."

"But you never did, of course," said the dark-skinned man. "That would be a crime."

"I didn't say I dids," said the old woman, with a sly smile. "But I didn't say I didn'ts. If you gets my drift."

"You keep such interesting company, Mr. Makish," came a voice out of the darkness behind the pair. A tall, lean figure clad in a dark raincoat stood there, a slouch hat covering most of his features. He did not seem to be disturbed by the heat. "The lady sounds quite intriguing."

"She appreciates an expertly constructed fire," said Makish, calmly. He glanced over his shoulder as if confirming the identity of the newcomer. "It is a gift shared by only a few."

The dark-skinned man bowed from the waist. "A great pleasure speaking with you this evening, honored lady. I hope perhaps to continue the conversation at a future blaze."

"You knows where to find me," said the old woman, her laughter cackling like breaking glass. "If it's a good fire, I'll be there. Francine the Firebug, they calls me."

"Good night, Miss Francine," said Makish. "I feel certain that we shall meet again."

Makish turned to the Red Death. "I assume you came to discuss the results of our recent transaction. That is why I remained in the neighborhood. Shall we walk?"

"After you," said the Red Death. He gestured to the deserted streets leading away from the Navy Yard. The old dark houses were empty of life. "It appears that we will remain undisturbed by the residents."

"The inhabitants of the region fled shortly after the fire began," said Makish. "An unconfirmed but quite believable rumor stated that an old cache of explosives stored in the Navy Yard ignited, causing the blaze. The locals evidently felt that other eruptions were likely. They evacuated their homes like lemmings rushing to the sea."

The Red Death chuckled. It was a dry, emotionless sound. "The members of the fire department seem rather reluctant to battle the inferno. None are present at the site. I fear they lack the dedication of true public servants."

"A regrettable but astute observation," said Makish. "I believe they are letting the blaze burn itself out. It is a common procedure in these troubled times. The fire chief claims to lack the necessary equipment and manpower to deal with such a disaster. Good help is hard to find."

"So true," said the Red Death. Its voice suddenly turned harsh. "You, for example, did not fulfill your promise this evening. That fire was supposed to kill Dire McCann and Alicia Varney. It did not happen. They both survived the blast. You swore to me that there was no possible means to escape from your trap. I paid your fee and expected results. And I did not see any."

"I protest," said Makish, polite but firm. There was a hard, unyielding edge to his voice. Assamite assassins did not like to be accused of failure. "You withheld important information from me about my victims. I performed my duties to the best of my abilities."

The Indian glanced around, as if searching for other figures in the darkness. "You told me that McCann and Varney were mortal. I had no reason to suspect otherwise. During their fight with you and your disciples, the pair exhibited powers far beyond those possessed by any ordinary human. And, after your retreat, those same powers saved them from my magnificent fire."

"I may have underestimated their skills," said the Red Death. "They surprised me."

"An obvious understatement," said Makish, politely. "Where are the trio of doppelgangers who aided in your attack, if I may be so bold as to inquire?"

"Afraid they may be waiting in ambush?" asked the Red Death, his tone mocking. "You need not worry. I do not blame you for the disaster. Besides, using Body of Fire requires a tremendous amount of energy. After our encounter with McCann and Varney earlier, none of us are capable of using the Discipline again for many hours. My childer have returned to other responsibilities. They departed Washington hours ago. You and I are alone."

"I am much relieved that you are accepting this setback so well," said Makish. "It is a very mature attitude."

The Red Death laughed again. He was not amused. "One learns patience after a few thousand years. I made a major mistake. My ego overruled my good sense. It will not happen again."

"A wise man learns more from his disasters than from his triumphs," said Makish solemnly.

"I tried eliminating McCann and Varney by direct methods," said the Red Death. "That was an act of sheer folly on my part. In attempting to overwhelm them by force, I revealed more about myself and my ambitions than was prudent."

"Hindsight is always the clearest vision," said Makish. "Mistakes can often be rectified. Such decisions help keep assassins like myself busy." The Assamite hesitated, then continued. "I am still at a loss to understand how these two humans control such incredible forces. Would you perhaps care to explain?"

"Dire McCann claims to be a mage of the Euthanatos Tradition," said the Red Death. "Alicia Varney says she is the ghoul of a major Sabbat leader. Those are the rationalizations they use to explain their astonishing powers to others. Both of them are quite careful never to demonstrate the full extent of their impressive skills."

"A ghoul and a mage could not have stopped you tonight," said Makish. "Nor could they have escaped my trap."

"The two humans are possessed," said the Red Death. "They are puppets controlled by two legendary Cainites. The mortal shell merely conceals the Kindred intelligence pulling the strings. Their powers are but a small reflection of those of their controllers."

"I am almost afraid to learn the identity of this pair of masqueraders," said Makish. "However, it is always better to face the truth than suspect the worst."

"Dire McCann is the human agent for Lameth, the Dark Messiah," said the Red Death. "Alicia Varney is the puppet of Anis, Queen of Night."

Makish opened his mouth to reply, then closed it. He remained silent for several minutes. Finally, he spoke.

"I feared as much, but I hoped I was wrong. They are worthy opponents. I also suspect that they are unforgiving enemies. By now, the two of them surely know who set the trap in the Navy Yard. There is no turning back for me, that is for certain, sir. My services are at your disposal. You have, I hope, another course of action planned to counter this setback?"

"A minor modification in my program was necessary," said the Red Death. "I revised the details as soon as I discovered that our quarry escaped your trap. The scheme will proceed on schedule."

"I am quite positive they will be expecting trouble now," said Makish. "That is a real problem."

"I think not," said the Red Death. "Their attention is centered on me. Both of them want to find the Red Death. Therefore, I will disappear. I will do nothing. Instead, others will do my work for me."

"I am somewhat puzzled, sir," said Makish. "Would you care to explain?"

"As events unfold over the next few nights," said the Red Death, "you will understand better. A killing thrust is most effective. But a crippling blow serves equally well."

The Red Death paused. "In the meantime, I have another assignment for you. It should prove to be quite a challenge to you as both an assassin and an artist."

"What might that be, sir?" asked Makish. "I am anxious to prove my worth after the unfortunate events of this evening. I will even cut my fee by a small amount."

"How generous," said the Red Death, its voice dripping with sarcasm. "No need for you to suffer the agonies of reduced wages. I'll pay full price for this job. It's worth every dollar. I want you to kill a fellow Assamite."

Makish frowned. "I suspected you might say that. It is normally not permissible to accept such a contract. Since I abandoned my clan long ago, however, their rules of conduct are no longer valid in my eyes. I will, therefore, accept, though I do it with a certain amount of regret."

"I expected nothing less," said the Red Death. "My plans are progressing too swiftly for me to deal with every loose end. Prince Vargoss' pet killer, the Dark Angel, has sworn to destroy me in revenge for exterminating her sister. She is a dangerous enemy for several reasons. I want her eliminated, and the sooner the better."

"I will attend to her tomorrow," said Makish. "She is a deadly fighter, but I am better. Besides, this Dark Angel is blinded by her passions. An assassin must have no emotions. Her lust for revenge will be her downfall. Twenty-four hours from now, she will join her sister in hell."

Chapter 6

Washington, D.C. - March 23, 1994:

Madeleine insisted upon escorting McCann to his suite inside the Watergate Hotel. So did Flavia.

"Not in a million years," said the detective in protest. They stood, arguing, across the street from the entrance to the famous hotel. "Think of the attention it would attract. Neither of you is particularly inconspicuous. Or modestly dressed. The staff will think I'm bringing two hookers back to my room."

"Nonsense," said Madeleine. She was not willing to give an inch on her decision. Nor was she pleased by McCann's remarks. "I am not usually mistaken for a woman of loose virtue."

"Speak for yourself, dear," said Flavia. She stretched, pulling her form-fitting white leather outfit tight across her breasts. "Clothes like this number immediately lead to assumptions of the worst kind. Of course, I prefer to foster that impression. It often proves useful to be considered a cheap slut."

Madeleine's face crinkled with concern. She looked at Flavia, then down at her own black leotard. "I suppose we might be noticed," she declared, after a few moments of thought. "But I refuse to let you return to your hotel room without asserting that no enemy waits in ambush."

"I agree," said Flavia. "What better time for the Red Death to attack than immediately after a failed attempt? Your reputation isn't important to me, McCann. Your life is."

They compromised. McCann was to enter the hotel on his own, with Madeleine and Flavia following a minute later. The detective agreed to wait for them in the elevator. He promised to hold the *Door Open* button until they arrived. Then, they would proceed up to his suite together. The consensus was that at five in the morning there would be no one around to complain about the delay.

Unfortunately, they all forgot the house detective. He swooped down on Madeleine and Flavia before they were halfway across the lobby. A small, rat-faced man with a swarthy complexion, yellow teeth, and beady black eyes, he looked as seedy as his suit.

"You *ladies* going somewhere?" he asked, flashing his hotel identification card. His voice sounded more weary than sarcastic. "Only guests are permitted in the building this late at night. Our restaurant is closed. Sorry."

"Damn," said Flavia. "I was hoping to get a bite to eat."

"Sure you were," said the detective. "No offense, girls, but this hotel is a high-class establishment. The Hojo is across the street. We don't allow door-to-door solicitation. So, get lost."

"We are not prostitutes," said Madeleine, her temper flaring. "I resent your accusation."

"Well, ain't that too bad," said the detective, sneering. "Kinda young for this racket, aren't you, sister? Not much meat to your bones, either." He shrugged. "Guess some geeks like their women to look like boys."

Madeleine grimaced. She disliked the little man's attitude. And his assumptions were distasteful. Killing him in the lobby, however, would create a disturbance that would be hard to explain to McCann. It wasn't, she decided with regret, worth the trouble.

"Now, now," said Flavia, reaching out and patting the detective on the cheek. "You should know better. We have rooms here at the hotel. Don't we, Maddy?"

"Yes, of course we do," said Madeleine, unaccustomed to being called by any nickname, much less Maddy.

"Oh," said the little man, his eyes blinking rapidly several times. "That's right. My mistake. I must have been dreaming. My apologies for the inconvenience. Didn't mean to come across wrong."

The detective shook his head. He stepped away from them, his face flushed with embarrassment. "What a screwup. Please, don't say anything about this to the manager. Okay? Must'a had a few too many beers tonight."

"No problem," said Flavia. "We'll let it be our secret. Good night."

"Night," said the detective. "Sorry, again, for the

misunderstanding."

They hurried to the elevator. McCann was still waiting, an impatient expression on his face. "Stop for a candy bar?" he asked, pushing the button for the fifth floor.

"A minor disagreement with the local authority," said Flavia. "He had a weak mind. Altering his thoughts was not difficult."

"The fool was a disgrace to his profession," said Madeleine with more passion than she intended. "He deserved to be roasted over a slow fire."

"He thought Maddy was a teenage hooker," said Flavia, cheerfully. "I smoothed things over before she tore him to pieces."

"I was in complete control of my temper," declared Madeleine heatedly, realizing that neither McCann nor Flavia believed a word she was saying. In a more subdued tone, she continued, "I merely resented the lack of respect he displayed for women."

"A feminist statement," said McCann, smiling. "How intriguing."

The elevator stopped on the fifth floor. "Here we are," said McCann, as the door slid open. "Are you convinced now that I am safe? Or do you want to search my suite as well?"

"I sense no hostile presence in the area," said Madeleine. "However, just to be certain, I..."

"...want to check your rooms," finished Flavia. "Better safe than sorry, McCann."

Smiling in amusement, McCann watched them scourge the suite thoroughly. The rooms were empty and appeared to have remained untouched since McCann left them early that evening. The bolts on the bulletproof windows, standard in the capital, were closed. And the multitude of chains on the door were firmly anchored to the walls.

"I sense strong binding spells in the chambers," said Madeleine, when she and Flavia finished their tour. "Yours?"

"Mine," said the detective. "They're quite effective. I doubt that even the Red Death could pierce them without waking me." He grinned. "I'm a light sleeper. Nobody catches me napping."

McCann frowned, as his words revived an unexpected memory.

"Something wrong?" asked Madeleine.

"Just recalling a surprise visitor," said the detective, shaking his head as if to banish the thought. "Nothing to be concerned about. Now, both of you leave, so I can get some rest."

Despite his words, McCann was still frowning when he let them out of the suite. They waited until they heard him chain the door shut before they took the elevator to the main floor.

"What was that all about?" asked Madeleine, as they strolled across the lobby. The rat-faced detective was nowhere to be seen.

"I have no idea," answered Flavia. "McCann tells me what he wants. As I said at our first meeting, he is the most interesting human I have ever encountered."

"I remember," said Madeleine. The conversation had taken place shortly before midnight. It seemed like an eternity ago. "You also claimed he was the most dangerous."

They were outside, alone on the sidewalk. Flavia nodded. Without warning, her right hand, fingers outstretched like a chisel, shot forward. Her lethal blow sliced upward, aimed at the center of Madeleine's chest.

It never connected. Madeleine reacted instantly. Her hands clapped together, catching Flavia's fingers between her palms. Normally, she would have retaliated immediately with a sweeping kick or shoulder wrench. However, she did nothing, waiting for the Dark Angel to explain her action.

"A few days ago, I attacked Dire McCann in exactly the same manner," said Flavia. "He caught my hand in midflight and held it motionless."

"Impossible," said Madeleine, as they both relaxed. "No human can match the reflexes of the Kindred. Or counter our strength."

Flavia smirked. "Exactly. McCann begged to differ. I chose not to pursue the argument."

"I see why you find him so...fascinating," said Madeleine. The rumble of a large truck barreling down Virginia Avenue broke off further conversation.

The big rig came to a screeching halt, air brakes squealing, in front of the hotel. It was a sixteen-wheeler, painted black, silver and red; the letters MG were prominently displayed on its side. "My ride," said Madeleine, smiling. "Can I drop you off somewhere?"

"MG?" said Flavia, staring at the huge vehicle

in astonishment. "Rather ostentatious, don't you think? And who the hell is driving this thing? It looks like a bunch of kids in the cab."

"The MG stands for Mishkoff Granary," said Madeleine. "A small but popular brewery, they make deliveries throughout the country, so the truck actually blends in reasonably well wherever I travel. That is the main reason my family bought the business years ago. The inside of this unit is specially designed for Kindred use."

"Hey, Miss Madeleine." The voice was unmistakably that of a young boy. "You fuckin' ready to roll? Gonna be daylight soon. And you know what that means."

"Who is that?" asked Flavia. A baby-faced teenager, perhaps thirteen or fourteen years old, had lowered the window of the cab and stared out at them with limpid blue eyes. "Are you insane?"

"Hey, who's the broad in the white stretch pants?" asked the boy. He displayed no fear of, or shyness toward, Flavia. "Fuckin' A."

Madeleine shrugged. "I found the three of them in Louisville. They're children of the street, and they tried to hijack my truck. After foiling their plot, I made them an offer they could not refuse."

"Serving you or death?" said Flavia.

"Essentially that," said Madeleine, with a smile. "Though I threw in a cash reward to ensure their enthusiasm."

"Wow, some babe," called a second boy, peering out the window over the shoulder of the first child. "Nice outfit."

"Junior is the one with the big mouth and foul language," said Madeleine. "He and Sam, the other one, are fourteen. Pablo is sixteen. I let him drive." She waved a hand at the window. "Come down, all of you, and meet the lady."

The cab door popped open and three boys poured onto the sidewalk. They clustered around Flavia, making suggestive remarks. The Assamite shook her head in bewilderment.

"You like these kine?" she asked, sounding shocked. "They are your...pets."

"My allies," Madeleine corrected, with a wan smile.

She had to admit she could understand Flavia's confusion. Using young boys was not part of her standard operating procedure. She wasn't exactly sure why she had recruited the children to be her assistants. Her sire would have dismissed the action as foolishness. But she was not willing to abandon the children to cruel fate.

Their stories of adult neglect and abuse had struck a note that resonated to the core of her being. Though Madeleine was a vampire, part of her was still human.

"Miss Flavia and I are working together," said Madeleine. "I expect you will be seeing a lot of her."

"Another vampire babe," said Sam. "Cool."

"You a tough chick like Miss Madeleine?" asked Pablo, curiously. "Or you just kill the hombres with your good looks?"

Flavia chuckled. Soft and low and sensuous, the laughter had a weird, inhuman sound. Involuntarily, the boys surrounding her stepped backward, as if all at once comprehending the Assamite's true nature.

"Children should be seen," she purred, "not heard."

"My lips are sealed," said Sam.

"Ditto," said Pablo

"Fuckin' same for me," said Junior. He glanced at Madeleine. "Ain't that long till morning."

"I know," said Madeleine. She looked at Flavia. "Can we drop you somewhere?"

"No thanks," said Flavia. "My lair is not far from here. But I appreciate the offer."

The Assamite's dark eyes stared directly into Madeleine's. "I will see you tomorrow. In the meantime, I leave you with these two thoughts to ponder."

Flavia waved a hand at the three boys. "First. These children are a dangerous encumbrance. We are engaged in deadly enterprises. Beware of any emotional involvement with them. It will lead to disaster."

Madeleine nodded. Already, though she had known them for only a few days, she had grown attached to the boys. A loner for most of her existence, she longed for any companionship, even that of children.

"I will not fail my sire," she said. "I am a Giovanni."

"Good," said Flavia. "I hope you never forget that. Second point. You are Madeleine Giovanni, the Dagger of the Giovanni. Your clan has been dealing with mages for well over five hundred years.

More than most Kindred, you are familiar with the Traditions. The spells that McCann uses to bind his resting place are not those of a Euthanatos mage."

"I did not recognize them," Madeleine admitted. "Yet, the weavings were complex and very, very powerful. Those spells were old. They were older than my clan."

"Still," said Flavia, "Dire McCann set them in place with ease. And with the help of another mortal, he battled the Red Death and his brood — four powerful vampires — to a standstill."

"I serve the wishes of my clan," said Madeleine uneasily. "I am here on the direct order of my sire."

"That's my third point," said Flavia. "Dire McCann, mage or not, is kine. He is a mere mortal. Yet, you were sent all the way to America to protect him. Why? What makes Dire McCann so precious to the elders of the Clan Giovanni that they worry about his safety?"

It was not a question Madeleine could answer.

Chapter 7

Paris, France — March 24, 1994:

"Come into my parlor," said Marie, giggling. Careful not to exert too much of her strength, she tugged her young paramour into the front hall of her mansion. "Said the spider to the fly."

"You are much too beautiful to be a spider, my love," said Maurice. He leered at her perfect body with lustful eyes. Tall, dark and handsome, he was very much the gentleman rogue. And quite drunk.

"You underestimate me," said Marie, spinning on her heels. Like a fine dark mist, her near-transparent shawl whirled around her body. Beneath it, she wore an extremely short black velvet dress that clung to her curves like a glove. Her stockings were decorated with roses, which matched the painted red rose on her right cheek. Her hair was long and dark, and it curled across her shoulders like a gigantic snake. Her lips were bright crimson. "The black widow spider is both beautiful and deadly. She loves her victim to death."

"You are no black widow," said Maurice, grabbing her by the shoulders. Roughly, he pulled her toward him. His mouth covered hers in passionate embrace while his hands dropped to her ample breasts. Anxiously, he pushed off the velvet and reached for her exposed nipples. "Your lips are cold as ice. But I will warm them up quick enough."

"The night air makes them so," declared Marie, pulling away from her latest conquest. She made no effort to fix her dress. A little more provocation never hurt, she felt. Maurice was young and strong and full of life. First, she would let him make love to her. Afterward, when his energy and lust were fully spent, she would drain him of his rich, warm blood.

"Would you care for a drink?" she asked, pressing the bell to summon her maid. "A glass of wine, perhaps."

"Wine would be good," said Maurice. His face was flushed, his gaze fixed on her ruby-red nipples. "You are so young and beautiful. Your breasts are magnificent. I want to bury my face between their beauty."

"You will have plenty of time to examine them at length," said Marie, with a smile. "In fact, I will insist on it."

The young man laughed, a harsh, coarse sound in marked contrast to his flowery words. Involuntarily, Marie flinched. Despite his good looks and expensive clothes, Maurice was a typical country bumpkin come to the big city to make his fortune. Every year, hundreds of adventurers like him flocked to Paris in search of wealth and notoriety. Most of them ended up as waiters and bartenders in the city's many restaurants. A few, like Maurice, became high-class gigolos, catering to the exotic and depraved sexual excesses of the metropolis' idle rich. His disappearance would hardly be noticed.

Marie discovered him at a party of a friend of a friend of a friend. As one of Paris' privileged class, she went to many such affairs. He had come to the art gallery as escort for a wrinkled old hag with much too much money and little taste or culture. Getting rid of the old hag had not been difficult for Marie, who was an expert at disposing of anyone who stood in the path of her desire. Winning Maurice's attention had been even easier. A flash of bare thigh, a passionate whisper, and the sight of her Rolls-Royce limousine were all she needed to persuade him to accompany her back to her mansion in the Marais quarter of the city.

"Where is that girl?" Marie wondered aloud. She rang the service bell for a second time. "Yvette, attend me. Now."

No one answered. Marie frowned. The mansion was quiet — *too* quiet. Yvette should have come immediately. The girl, one of her ghouls, knew better than to keep her mistress waiting. There was no excuse for her absence.

"Something wrong, my little cabbage?" asked Maurice, swaying back and forth in place. He was very drunk. "Don't worry. I'll protect you."

"Nothing to worry about, I am sure," said Marie, striding over to the phone on a nearby end table. "However, I think I will summon Emile from his quarters. Just in case."

Emile was her driver. He had rooms over the garage. Like Yvette, he was a ghoul and had served

Marie for decades. A veteran of the Second World War, he could be an extremely deadly opponent in a fight. If there was trouble in the mansion, Emile could handle it.

The telephone line was dead.

Marie grimaced. The conclusion was obvious. A pack of thieves had broken into her home to steal some of her fabulous treasures. She suspected it was too late to worry about Yvette's fate. Though the burglars had probably departed several hours ago, Marie always thought it better to be safe than sorry.

"I think it would be wise for us to leave this place immediately," she said to Maurice, gripping his right arm. He blinked in drunken surprise at the power of her fingers. "We are in danger. Don't disagree or try to be a hero. And stay quiet."

Together, they turned to the front door. Marie gasped in shock. A man stood there. A very big man, whom she immediately sensed was a vampire like herself, dressed in a pair of faded jeans and a black T-shirt. Standing with his huge arms folded across his chest, he filled the doorway. He smiled cruelly. "Thinking of going somewhere, milady?"

"Get out of my way, you oaf," Marie commanded, summoning the force of her will. No man and few Kindred could disobey her direct orders. The vampire stared at her, then laughed. He did not move an inch.

"Wha-wha's going on?" asked Maurice, still in a drunken stupor. He seemed to be unaware of their peril. "Who is this clown blocking our exit? Send him away. I want to be alone with you."

"I am afraid that your wish is unimportant to us, *mon ami*," said a soft, smooth voice from behind them.

Marie whirled, suddenly very frightened. The speaker was a short, slender man with a pencil mustache and restless eyes. He was dressed much the same as his companion. And he also was a vampire.

"Who are you?" Marie demanded. "And what are you doing in my home?"

"My name is Le Clair," said the small man. "Not that it matters. I am the one who will ask the questions. And you will supply the answers."

"Another pain in the ass," declared Maurice, belligerently. He raised his hands, curled into fists. "You can't talk to a lady like that. I oughta knock some sense into your pointy little head."

"Be quiet, Maurice," said Marie. "The gentlemen are thieves. They merely want to know where I keep my jewels. Let me tell them so they can be on their way."

"I'm not afraid of them," said Maurice, swaying slightly. His lips curled in a sneer. "Two peasants. Their accents betray them. This one comes from Marseilles. Typical sea scum. Son of a cheap whore, I'd guess."

"My mother was an honest smuggler," said Le Clair coldly. "She cried bitter tears for her only son who died in the War."

"War," said Maurice. "What war?"

"The War to End All Wars," said Le Clair. He looked over Maurice's shoulder to the big man stationed at the door. "I grow tired of this kine's ramblings, Baptiste. Kill him."

"Whatever you say, Le Clair," the big man rumbled.

For someone his size, Baptiste moved with astonishing speed. He took two steps forward and with his left hand grabbed a surprised Maurice by the back of the neck. He lifted, raising the young man off the floor. Casually, effortlessly, Baptiste slammed Maurice face-forward into the nearest wall. Plaster cracked from the force of the blow.

Blood spurted as Maurice's bones broke into pieces. The gigolo screeched in pain. Ignoring the sounds, Baptiste pulled Maurice back a few inches, then slammed him a second time into the wall. Then a third time, and a fourth. By now, the young man was no longer screaming. And the wall was soaked with blood.

"Not much fun killin' humans," said Baptiste, dropping the battered gigolo to the floor. He lay there, unmoving. "Hardly seems worth the effort."

Grinning, the huge vampire slammed a foot into Maurice's head. The young man's skull exploded, sending bits of bone and brain and gore across the room. "I always liked doing that," declared Baptiste. "Nice and messy."

"I am a personal favorite of the Prince of Paris, Francois Villon," said Marie, trembling. "Harm me and he will make you pay."

"A frightening thought," said a third vampire, coming up behind Le Clair. A good-looking man with a casual, relaxed stance, he almost appeared human. Except for his red eyes, which burned with madness. In his fists he gripped the heads of Yvette and Emile. No blood dripped from either. They had been drained dry. "We promise not to be bad."

Le Clair laughed. "Truthfully, we three are gentle souls. We seek to harm no one. All we wish is some information."

"Information?" said Marie, conscious of the huge brute, Baptiste, close behind her. "What kind of information? And why come to me?"

"Because, madam," said the handsome vampire, carelessly tossing the heads of Marie's two ghouls at her feet, "you are reputedly the most notorious gossip among Paris' Kindred. If there are secrets to be learned, we have been informed during our short stay in Paris, you are the one who has the answers."

"Me, a gossip?" said Marie, indignant. "I am no gossip. I am an artist."

"All members of the Toreador clan claim to be artists," said Le Clair. "Big deal. Personally, I think art is crap. It's a waste of time."

Marie sneered. "You, sir, have the soul of a pig."

Le Clair sneered back. "And, you, madam, tread on dangerous ground. There are others in the city who possess the same information that you do. Insult me at your peril."

Marie realized the danger of her situation. Her powers meant nothing when she was confronted by three Kindred of equal strength. She was at the mercy of this hellish trio: she knew it, and so did they. "What do you want to know? Ask, and if I can answer, I will. On one condition."

"A condition?" said Le Clair. "I find it amusing

that you dare bargain with us, madam. You are in no position to make demands."

"I beg to differ," said Marie. "You want facts. I have them. No one knows more about this city than I. No one. Destroy me, and you may eliminate your only chance to learn what you wish to know. Am I not correct?"

"You're smarter than you look, that's for sure," said Le Clair. He glanced at his handsome companion. "What do you think, Jean Paul?"

"Make a bargain with the bitch," said the other vampire. "We're in a hurry."

"You're always in a hurry," said Le Clair. "It's a bad habit." He looked at Marie. "Name your fee."

"My life, of course," said Marie. She pointed to Maurice's body and then at the two heads on the floor. "I have grown accustomed to eternal life. Servants can be replaced. As can lovers. They are merely kine. Swear that I will not be harmed and I will tell you whatever you want to know."

Le Clair shrugged. "In return, we must have your oath that you will not reveal our mission in the city to anyone for a week. By then, we will be long gone. Either departed or destroyed, depending upon circumstances."

"I promise not to say a word," said Marie, trying to sound sincere. At the moment, she was willing to swear to anything to preserve her life. Promises meant nothing to her. As soon as the three departed, she intended to call the Prince of Paris and inform him of everything that had taken place tonight. "I swear it on the honor of my sire."

"The honor of your sire," declared Le Clair. "A powerful oath, to be sure. I, too, swear. By the honor of my sire, you shall not be harmed."

Marie pointed to the vampire named Jean Paul. "He should swear too. And the oaf behind me."

"I swear it," said Jean Paul. "By the sacred honor of my sire. I will do you no harm."

"Me too," said Baptiste. "What the others said."

"Ask, then," said Marie. "I will answer if I am able. Then, depart."

"We are searching for an ancient Nosferatu vampire known as Phantomas," said Le Clair. "We were told that he lives in catacombs far beneath the streets of Paris. Tell us how he can be found."

"Phantomas?" said Marie, laughing. "Surely you jest. He exists only in the pages of magazine stories. No such vampire lives in this city."

"Our quarry is no fiction," said Le Clair. "I am sure of that. Concentrate. Act as if your existence depends on your answer." The small man grinned. "It does."

"Catacombs beneath the streets?" repeated Marie, thinking furiously. She shook her head. "Paris is not Rome. There are no such tunnels."

Then, suddenly, the thought of Rome triggered a long-forgotten memory. "Perhaps, just perhaps, you mean the Roman tunnels in the Montparnasse section of the city. Vague tales claim that they are part of a greater network of passages that honeycomb the entire city."

"Exactly where are these Roman catacombs located?" asked Le Clair.

"The main entrance is at the place Denfert-Roucereau, near the Montparnasse cemetery," said Marie. "I remember them well. Many years ago, long before I was Embraced, I visited the place with my parents. It was a frightful sight. During the eighteenth century, the caves were stocked with the remains of millions of skeletons moved from the city's charnel houses. They covered the floor of the tunnels like a carpet of bones. My mama called the place the Gate of Hell."

Jean Paul nodded. "It sounds right to me."

"And to me," said Le Clair. He bowed to Marie. "Thank you, madam, for the information. You have been quite helpful. We appreciate your assistance."

He waved a hand at Baptiste. "Destroy her. You can drink her blood if you like."

Marie shrieked as the giant grabbed her by the throat. "You promised," she cried. "You swore an oath."

"We lied," said Le Clair.

Chapter 8

Paris, France — March 24, 1994:

Phantomas studied the computer screen intently. The news of the day, as reported by a dozen secret intelligence networks, was all bad. It had grown progressively more so every hour since the first appearance of the Red Death. Phantomas suspected it was going to get even worse before it got better. If it did get better.

A huge gray rat crawled across the top of the monitor. Phantomas ignored it. There were rats all throughout his lair. He liked rats. A solitary being, he enjoyed the small measure of company the rodents provided. Phantomas felt a little bit less lonely when he was surrounded by rats. They demanded nothing of him, and in return, he demanded nothing from them. It was a mutually satisfactory arrangement.

The rats, at least, were not frightened by his appearance. With a huge nose, bulging red eyes, and a mouthful of yellowed teeth, Phantomas defined absolute ugliness. All members of the Nosferatu clan of vampires were physically gruesome creatures, and Phantomas was more horrific than most. Yet, despite the grotesqueness of his outward features, he was actually a gentle soul who wanted only to be left alone with his rats and his computers while he pursued his great project. It was that endeavor, he was convinced, that had earned him the enmity of the monstrous vampire known as the Red Death. And, hopefully, it was that same project that would somehow enable him to defeat the monster's schemes.

Phantomas was a realist. He understood the desires and passions of the Damned better than most of his kind. For nearly a thousand years, he had been laboring to write a massive encyclopedia detailing the history of the Cainite race. The volume contained comprehensive biographies of all the major vampires who had ever existed. Or, at least, every one whose existence he had been able to verify through his endless studies. His genealogical chart linking vampires by clan and sire was the most complete family tree ever done of the Kindred. The work, though far from finished, contained more information about the Damned than any other single sourcebook in the world. And, thus, somehow, some way, its existence threatened the Red Death.

Wearily, Phantomas called up on his green monitor all the information he had been able to gather on the mysterious creature. It wasn't much. None of his usual sources had provided any useful information. The Camarilla and the Sabbat both believed that the monster worked for the rival sect. Phantomas suspected that he belonged to neither. The Red Death labored for no cause other than his own.

ROBERT WEINBERG

Unconfirmed stories described the monster attacking Kindred in a dozen different locations on several continents. A common link in the accounts was his use of an unnatural hellfire to burn his victims to ashes. The Red Death's power was not exaggerated. Phantomas had himself observed the charred remains of several vampires found in the Louvre a week before. Only his immediate reaction to his peril had saved him from a similar fate.

It had been in the same building, a few nights later, that Phantomas had discovered that the Red Death was a Methuselah, a fourth-generation vampire more than five thousand years old. In ancient Egypt, the monster had been known as Seker, one of the Lords of the Underworld. Unfortunately, no such being was listed in Phantomas' encyclopedia.

Phantomas muttered to himself in frustration. The thirteen vampire clans each possessed certain strengths and weaknesses unique to their specific bloodline. If he could discover Seker's sire, and thus his clan affiliation, then he would also know the monster's vulnerabilities. He was convinced that this was the reason why the creature desired to destroy him and his encyclopedia. The Red Death was extremely powerful, but he was not indestructible. No vampire was.

With a hiss of annoyance, Phantomas switched to another topic. His gnarled fingers flew with amazing speed over the keyboard. An obsessive seeker of knowledge, Phantomas was the ultimate hacker. No computer network in the world was safe from his intrusions. Sooner or later, he would learn the secret the Red Death was trying so desperately to conceal. All he needed was time.

Staring at the new information on his monitor, Phantomas wondered if perhaps time was more precious than he realized. Strange things were occurring across the globe. The evidence on the computer screen pointed to only one possible conclusion: the Nictuku were rising.

Unlike many younger Nosferatu, Phantomas realized that the Nictuku were not just the stuff of wild tales that had no basis in fact. The monsters existed, allegedly hidden in torpor, throughout the world. Now, according to cryptic news reports gathered from a dozen different sources, several of them were stirring.

How the Nictuku came about was a mystery to the vampire clans. However, working with hundreds of myths and legends gathered over the course of a thousand years, Phantomas had been able to piece together the probable story of their origin and purpose. He was not entirely sure of the tale's veracity — since much of it was based on legends handed down from sire to childe over five millennia — but he felt confident that the entry in his encyclopedia was the most accurate possible.

Once, in the earliest days of the Kindred, the Nosferatu were not ugly monsters. The founder of their clan, Absimiliard, was the most handsome of the thirteen Antediluvians — and the most vain. Somehow — the legends were not precise on what his exact sin was — he had managed to insult Caine, the Third Human, the father of the entire Cainite race. Swift in his anger and terrible in his power, Caine cursed Absimiliard and his entire bloodline. That night, every member of the clan in existence turned into a grotesque monster. Even worse, the curse extended to all of their descendants. Any human Embraced by a Nosferatu, no matter what the mortal's original appearance, immediately grew twisted and ugly in his vampire form. The entire clan became a collection of monstrous horrors, so ghastly that they chose to exist in hiding or dwell only in vast caverns beneath the earth.

The sight of his own hideous features drove Absimiliard insane. In his madness, he came to the conclusion that the only way to gain Caine's forgiveness was to destroy all of his childer, wipe out his entire bloodline. For centuries, he conducted a crusade across the world, seeking out and eliminating his descendants. But one fourth-generation vampire, a nameless woman, survived.

Despite her sire's wishes, she created numerous childer, and they in turn Embraced many others, until there were so many Nosferatu vampires that it became impossible for Absimiliard to destroy them all. It was then, in his fury, that he created the Nictuku.

The Antediluvian journeyed to the far corners of the globe searching for hideous monsters with just the barest trace of humanity. In ancient times, numerous freaks of creation still walked the Earth. Absimiliard found and Embraced as many of these creatures as he could. Already horrific monsters, these creatures were turned even uglier by the curse. Possessing incredible powers of destruction, the nightmarish hunters became known in the forgotten language of the Second City as "The Ravagers." They were the Nictuku.

Blood-binding his creations so that they obeyed his every wish, Absimiliard sent them out to locate and destroy every member of the Nosferatu clan. Satisfied that his curse would someday be lifted, and confident that his servants would finish the job he had started, the Antediluvian retreated into torpor. That had been over six thousand years ago. During the course of the millennia that followed, for reasons not entirely understood, the Nictuku also vanished into torpor. But now they were rising.

Not even Phantomas was sure how many of the monsters existed. Mostly, he was aware of names, titles that had been passed down through the Nosferatu clan over the centuries. There was Gorgo, She Who Scream in Darkness; Nuckalavee, the Skinless One; Abraxes, Lord of Mists; Azazel, the Abomination; and Echidna, the Mother of Foulness. Phantomas could only guess at their powers. He suspected, however, that their names were just a small hint of their true evil. It was not a pleasant thought.

In Australia, Nuckalavee had awakened. News reports from the past few weeks described how the unexpected migration of thousands of Aborigines from the deserts of the Northern Territories to the city of Darwin had resulted in race riots that had killed hundreds. No one was certain why the natives had fled their homes at the base of the MacDonnell Mountains, and why they refused to return there. However, one word was common to every explanation given by the Aborigines. That word was Nuckalavee.

Equally troublesome were the reports from Buenos Aires. Or, rather, the lack of reports. Buenos Aires had long served as a major Kindred stronghold in South America, and was home to dozens of vampires. But Phantomas feared that this was no longer the case. No word had come from the city in days. The Kindred there, both from the Sabbat and the Camarilla, had suddenly disappeared. No one was sure of the reason, although the enigmatic Red Death was the focus of a great deal of speculation. Phantomas was convinced that the blame rested with Gorgo, She Who Screams in Darkness. For nearly two thousand years, Gorgo had been sleeping inside a labyrinth of caves that honeycombed the Andes. Recently, the entrance to that vast network of passages had been opened. And, evidently, Gorgo had come out.

Perhaps the most frightening of all the incidents involving the Nictuku occurred in Russia. There, the seven-thousand-year-old Iron Hag, Baba Yaga, had returned to life. Eight feet tall, with iron teeth and claws, she had effortlessly overthrown the secret Kindred masters of the country. Using her incredible powers, the Hag had then sealed off the entire country from the Kindred. Rumors hinted that she was assembling a massive Army of Darkness and planned to march out of Russia and conquer Europe.

Phantomas groaned. He was a peaceful, quiet sort, not a fighter. He loved fine art and great literature. The thought of battling the Nictuku turned his mottled skin pink.

Still, he was not without courage. A strict moralist, whenever he craved blood he sought out those criminals and outlaws who had eluded justice through influence or bribes. The legal system of Paris was as corrupt as that of most modern cities, but there was one power that could not be swayed by wealth or position. The justice of Phantomas was swift, efficient, and always deadly.

"I don't like it," said Phantomas to his rodent companions, "but there are certain dangers that must be faced head on."

At the sound of his high-pitched, squeaky voice, a hundred rats started squealing. His pets were easily excitable. "Calm down," said Phantomas, waving his hands gently about, quieting the beasts. "I dislike the situation as much as you. However, there is no choice in the matter. As Caesar once said to me, 'Better to meet danger face-first than suffer a stab in the back'."

The rodents squealed in agreement. Or, at least, that's what Phantomas took their noisy replies to mean. A master of the vampire Discipline known as Animalism, he maintained a telepathic link with the rat hordes. Their minds were simple and primitive, but the rodents were not stupid. They paid close attention to everything Phantomas said. And, more importantly, they obeyed his commands.

"According to my computer analysis, the only

Methuselahs capable of defeating the Red Death are Anis, the Queen of Night, and Lameth, the Dark Messiah," Phantomas told the rats. "Most Kindred believe the pair to be myths, much like the Antediluvians."

He snorted in derision. "I know better. Both Anis and Lameth are still actively engaged in the Jyhad. If I could contact either one of them, they might aid me in my struggle against the Red Death."

Phantomas stared at the monitor, but his thoughts were not on the screen. The identity of the Red Death's sire was a mystery to him. As was the case with Anis and Lameth. None of the legends circulating about the pair contained any hint of their origin. Phantomas grimaced. There were no coincidences involving the Fourth Generation.

"No coincidences," he murmured. "That reminds me."

He typed a single word into his search menu. "Washington."

A blood war raged in the streets of the United States capital. The deadly conflict had caught the European councils of the Camarilla and Sabbat by surprise. Each side blamed the other for the outbreak of hostilities. Neither seemed exactly sure of what was happening. To Phantomas, the confusion indicated that other, secret adversaries were at work: the forces of the Fourth Generation engaged in the Jyhad.

There were one hundred and forty-seven pages of detailed reports on the day's events, gathered from seven different sources. Phantomas shook his head in disgust. He doubted that most of the material mattered. However, he couldn't chance missing an important fact buried amidst the details. A thousand years of research had taught him that often the most innocent statement covered a multitude of sins. If there was any hint of Fourth Generation interference in the blood war, it was contained in these pages of transcripts from agents of the Kindred clans to their masters in Europe. It was his job to find the relevant passages. He did not relish the task, but it had to be done.

Without the cooperation of Lameth or Anis, he stood no chance of defeating the Red Death. Locating them was more than a matter of satisfying his curiosity. For Phantomas, it had become a matter of survival.

Chapter 9

St. Louis — March 23, 1994:

As was his custom, Darrow knocked on the steel door of Prince Vargoss' inner sanctum an hour after the sun set. A meticulous dandy, the prince refused to set foot in his headquarters at The Club Diabolique before he was properly dressed. Darrow, who had been serving as Vargoss' personal bodyguard since the Dark Angel's departure for Washington, knew better than to criticize. The prince was notoriously touchy about his appearance.

Usually, Vargoss opened the steel door immediately. Tonight, he did not. Darrow knocked again. It was unthinkable that any vampire in St. Louis would dare challenge Vargoss, but lately the unthinkable had been occurring with astonishing regularity. Again, there was no answer.

Cautiously, Darrow pressed one hand against the door and pushed. A battle-scarred veteran of the nineteenth-century English Army, he was by nature a careful man. It was a characteristic that had kept him alive through a dozen famous battles, and had served him equally well in undeath. The door was not locked, and it swung inward without a sound. The room beyond, a small, mirror-lined dressing area, was empty.

"My Prince?" called Darrow, starting to worry. It was his responsibility to protect Vargoss. If some other vampire had managed to break into the prince's quarters and destroy him, Darrow would shoulder most of the blame. The Final Death would be the least of his punishments. "My Prince?" he repeated, this time a little louder.

A voice replied from the next chamber, where Vargoss kept his coffin and his extensive wardrobe. "Who are you?" came the question. The speaker sounded arrogant, unafraid. "And what do you want with me?"

Recognizing the prince's voice, Darrow felt a wave of relief, although he was puzzled by the questions. "It's me, Prince Vargoss. Darrow, your bodyguard. I've come to take you to the club."

The door to the inner chamber opened. Vargoss, tall and aristocratic-looking, stood framed in the portal. As usual, he was dressed in a black tuxedo, ruffled white shirt, red bow tie and matching cummerbund. He stared at Darrow suspiciously. "I did not call for an escort."

"No, my Prince," said Darrow, not sure how to respond. It was definitely Vargoss. There was no mistaking the prince's regal bearing. Or the raw power he exuded. "I come every night. Remember? I am merely following your instructions."

Vargoss scowled. "My apologies," he said, making it clear that he was not the least bit sorry. "I had forgotten. My mind was on other things."

Darrow nodded, feeling distinctly uncomfortable. He did not like the way the prince stared at him.

Nervously, he wondered if Vargoss had learned of his connections with the Mafia. If so, Darrow realized, his unlife was about to end very unpleasantly. Prince Vargoss demanded total loyalty from his subjects; there was no forgiveness for betrayal. The penalty was slow death by torture.

"Bad news?" asked Darrow, unable to remain silent. His gaze, shifting about nervously, fastened on a pile of ashes on the floor of the inner chamber. The cinders were still glowing. Evidently, the prince had just finished burning something when Darrow first knocked. That explained why he had not answered the door. It did not reveal the reason for his rotten temper.

"Very bad news," said Vargoss, stepping into the dressing room. He closed the door to the inner chamber. "I recently learned from an unimpeachable source that there are traitors to the Camarilla among my inner circle of advisors."

"Traitors?" said Darrow, his muscles tightening. A dozen tattoos, spread across his body, danced against the rippling flesh. "I find that hard to believe, my Prince."

"So did I," said Vargoss. He reached for his black cloak. "But the evidence was absolutely conclusive."

He beckoned for Darrow to take the lead. "Come. Take me to the club. This matter must be dealt with immediately."

They traveled in silence, Vargoss sitting in the back, brooding, while Darrow drove, wondering if he was doomed. The trip took twenty minutes, which seemed to the bodyguard to last for twenty lifetimes.

"Who at the club has been with me the longest?" asked Vargoss unexpectedly, as Darrow steered the limo into the prince's parking space at the rear of the nightspot. "Which of my confidants seem to be completely above suspicion, Darrow?"

Darrow's hands clenched the steering wheel so hard that the plastic cracked beneath his fingers. He was convinced that the prince was toying with him. But he couldn't be absolutely sure, and so he answered as truthfully as possible.

"There's Uglyface, for sure. That Nosferatu bloke's been around as long as anybody. Maybe longer. Nobody knows his friggin' age. He's been your advisor since I arrived in town, Prince. Devious bastard, that Uglyface. Typical Nosferatu sneak. Best kind of counselor there is, in my humble opinion."

"Who else?" asked Vargoss. He seemed amused by Darrow's discomfort.

"Flavia, the Dark Angel," said Darrow. "Though, she's in Washington, helping that pet human of yours, McCann. Dangerous lady. Like all Assamites, you pay for her loyalty. She's trustworthy as long as your credit's good. And your contract is in good standing."

"And?" said the prince.

"Brutus handles the crowds out front," said Darrow. If he had been human, he would have been sweating profusely. As it was, he felt ready to explode. "He's your ghoul. Can't buy loyalty better than that. He needs your blood to stay young."

"Aren't you forgetting someone?" said Vargoss, chuckling.

"You mean Melville?" said Darrow. "I never thought you cared much for 'im, Prince."

"No," said Vargoss, reaching for the handle of the door. "Not Melville. I meant *you*, Darrow. You are one of my most trusted advisors. That's why I have you escort me here. Because I trust you."

The prince laughed. It was not a reassuring sound. "Come, it's time for us to enter the club. Escort me to my regular table. Hopefully, Uglyface will be somewhere nearby. If not, find him. Once he is in attendance, go out front and summon Brutus. Answer no questions, not from anyone. I shall do all the talking. What I have to say concerns each of you."

Uglyface was in the club, waiting at the prince's usual table. Following Vargoss' orders, Darrow went for Brutus. He never once thought of trying to flee. The prince held St. Louis and the surrounding countryside in an iron grip. There was no escape. And, with the prince, there was no mercy.

The three of them stood silently waiting while Vargoss sipped a glass of blood. The rest of the Kindred in the club studiously ignored them. There were no friends when vampire honor was involved. Darrow had not said a thing to his companions about the prince's earlier comments, but there was no mistaking Vargoss' mood. His gaze, dark and brooding, slid back and forth between them.

"There is a traitor among us," said Vargoss, putting down his glass. "I have been betrayed. It is clear to me now that the Red Death's attack was part of a much larger plan by the Sabbat to gain control of our city."

Brutus growled. "A traitor? Tell me who it is; I'll rip his body into pieces."

Uglyface shook his head. His grotesque features twisted in fright. "I am loyal, my Prince. I have always been loyal."

Vargoss nodded. "What about you, Darrow? Will you protest your innocence as well? Have you nothing to say?"

"I let my actions speak for me, Prince," said Darrow. "No friggin' lies can change the truth."

Vargoss shook his head. "Three trusted servants. Three denials of guilt. One or more of you is lying. But, who?"

The prince tapped his fingers on the tabletop. His gaze fastened on his ghoul. "Brutus, how long have you served me? How many years?"

"Twenty-five, Prince," answered the ghoul. "You know that. Just the other night, you were remarking how we've been together for a quarter of a century."

Vargoss nodded. "Two and a half decades. Twenty-five long years. How disappointed I was to learn of your deceit."

"No," said Brutus, his jaw dropping with surprise. "Not me. I never..."

"Yes, Brutus," interrupted Vargoss. "You betrayed me." The prince looked to Darrow. "Kill him. Now."

Brutus stood a head taller than Darrow and weighed nearly twice as much. Before becoming Vargoss' servant, he had been a professional wrestler. As a ghoul, he was stronger and faster than any man. All of which postponed his execution by mere instants.

Darrow had learned to fight in the most brutal battles of the nineteenth century. He survived when others had perished because he was capable of any act to ensure his survival. Becoming a vampire only strengthened his inner resolve. Though he strongly doubted Brutus' guilt — feeling the ghoul was much too stupid to be involved in any conspiracy against the prince — it didn't stop him from following Vargoss' orders. Darrow never let his emotions override his good sense.

It was a quick, painless death. He felt he owed Brutus, who had been a close friend of his for more than two decades, at least that much. Brushing aside the ghoul's upraised arms, Darrow slammed him in the head with a fist like a steel hammer. The force of the blow crushed the big man's face to pulp, sending the cartilage of his nose directly into his brain. Brutus wobbled unsteadily on his feet, his eyes popped wide open in amazement. He was dead by the time he collapsed to the club floor.

"Hard to believe Brutus was a traitor," said Uglyface, staring at the lifeless body. "He never struck me as the type to turn against his prince. How did the Sabbat reach him?"

"Brutus was a fool," said Vargoss, waving to the bartender for another glass of blood. "As such, he was easily misled by promises. The real mastermind behind the Sabbat attempt was, of course, you, Uglyface. Destroy him as well, Darrow."

Uglyface shrieked in horror. He staggered back from the Prince's table, his grotesque, cartoonlike face contorted in shock. "Never," he screamed. "Never!"

Grimly, Darrow leapt forward and grabbed Uglyface by the neck. He meant to jerk the Nosferatu's head around and break his spine. However, though incredibly thin, Uglyface was no weakling. His hands shot up and caught Darrow's by the wrists. With a cackle of mad laughter, he wrenched the bodyguard to the side. Then, to everyone in the room's surprise, instead of fleeing, Uglyface launched himself at Prince Vargoss.

"Impostor," he cried, his long fingers clawing for the prince's features. "Your masquerade no longer fools me!"

Almost casually, the prince reached out and pressed one hand against Uglyface's chest. The Nosferatu howled in pain. He froze in place, his outstretched digits inches from Vargoss' skull.

The Nosferatu's body seemed to swell up like a balloon. In an instant, he was nearly double in size. Then, with a thousand cracks, Uglyface's form collapsed inward, as if the air had been released from the balloon's nozzle. He fell to the ground, a vampiric jellyfish. Only his flashing eyes indicated his mind was still functioning.

"Nice trick," said Darrow, staring at the pulsating mound of flesh and muscle. There wasn't a single solid bone left in Uglyface's body. If Darrow didn't know better, he would swear Vargoss had just used a Sabbat Discipline. Seeing what had happened to his colleague, however, Darrow did not plan to pursue the issue by inquiring. "Never knew you could do that, Prince."

"There are many things about me you don't know, Darrow," said Vargoss, finishing his drink. "Drive a stake through his heart. Or, as best you can determine, where his heart should be. Afterward, take the traitor outside and let him watch the sunrise. He should leave a nice oily blot in the parking lot."

"You're the boss," said Darrow. "Whatever makes you happy. I'll be back in a few minutes."

Two neonates, young vampires who served as waiters at the club, helped him drag Uglyface outside to a deserted lot behind the building. When he drove a wooden stake into the area he suspected approximated the Nosferatu's heart, the gelatinous mass gurgled in pain. It was a monstrous sound.

None of them said a word as they returned to the club. Darrow suspected the horror in his assistants' eyes reflected what was in his own.

The prince sat patiently at his table. "The job is done," said Darrow. "He'll fry like a poached egg when the sun comes out."

Vargoss smiled. In all of his years with the prince, Darrow had never seen him wear so savage, so diabolical a grin. "There is still another traitor to be dealt with, Darrow."

The bodyguard tensed. After nearly two hundred years of undeath, the Final Death was frightening enough. But perishing like Uglyface, reduced to a boneless puddle of flesh, was obscene. "What are you saying, Prince? If you don't mind me asking?"

"Dire McCann," said Vargoss, chuckling. His

knowing smirk made it perfectly clear that he realized that the detective's name was not the one Darrow expected to hear. "The mage has been conspiring against me since the first time we met. I will not be safe until he is destroyed."

"Taking care of him won't be so easy, Prince," said Darrow, trying to still his jangled nerves. "Mages never die easy. Besides, Flavia seems to be rather keen on the bloke. I'm a scrapper, but she's the real item. Friggin' Assamite would chew me up and spit me out without blinkin' an eye."

"The Dark Angel is scheduled for her own date with destiny," said Vargoss, cryptically. "I am terminating her contact. In the most permanent manner possible."

Darrow needed no explanation of what this meant. He felt distinctly uncomfortable. For reasons yet unknown, Vargoss had turned on his most loyal retainers. Never once had he spelled out their specific crimes. What accusations had convinced the prince of their guilt? Darrow wasn't convinced that any such evidence even existed. Remembering the pile of glowing ashes in the prince's inner sanctum, Darrow wondered what secrets had been destroyed in the flames. Where had they come from? And, more importantly, who had made them?

"I trust you will not forget tonight's lesson, Darrow?" said Vargoss, settling back in his chair. As he relaxed, the conversation throughout the rest of the room, stilled during the confrontation, started up again. "Only a fool tries to serve two masters. Remember that, always."

"I'm a quick learner, Prince," said Darrow, mustering in his voice as much sincerity as he could. Mentally, he promised himself never to turn his back on Vargoss again. "You can count on me. Nobody more loyal than Jack Darrow. I think I proved that tonight."

The prince folded his hands together and placed them on the table. It was not a gesture Darrow recalled Vargoss ever working before. His master was different somehow. The bodyguard wasn't sure what had taken place before his arrival at Vargoss' sanctum that evening, but whatever it was, he didn't like it.

"You performed as expected this time, Darrow," Vargoss declared, nodding his head in satisfaction. "Make sure you continue to do so in the future. There will be no second chances. None at all."

To Darrow, the prince's words sounded like a death sentence postponed, but not canceled. *His* death sentence.

Chapter 10

Washington, D.C. — March 24, 1994

Poker had taught Walter Holmes many important lessons, the majority of which had nothing to do with cards. Perhaps the most crucial of these was the importance of remaining calm and clear-headed, regardless of how unexpected or dangerous the situation. Walter took pride in his ability to deal rationally with the impossible, no matter what the circumstances. Behind his bland exterior lurked an incredibly cunning mind.

Walter's innocuous features had always served him well. Despite tight security, no one at the abandoned warehouse that served as headquarters for Justine Bern, the Sabbat archbishop of New York, during the cult's attack on Washington questioned his presence in the building. He was commonly viewed as a vampire of no importance. The Blood Guard, the elite order of Cainites who served as the archbishop's personal shock troops, tolerated Walter. Quiet, with an slightly confused expression, he was a good listener, a rare quality among the undead. While most anarchs constantly bragged about their kills, Walter rarely spoke of his triumphs. Instead, he preferred to quietly play cards.

Walter was an exceptional poker player. No one

in the warehouse realized exactly how good he really was. Practice made perfect, and Walter had been gambling for much longer than most vampires suspected. He was a lot older than he looked; in an odd, undefined way, Walter appeared ageless. Once he had labored as a Roman soldier. Now, he served as Inconnu Monitor of New York.

The Inconnu was the oldest and most mysterious sect of the Kindred. Its followers monitored the schemes and deceptions of the Damned for purposes they kept strictly to themselves. The sect's agents moved secretly among the Kindred, pretending to be ordinary Cainites, watching, waiting, never interfering. At least, not under ordinary circumstances.

Following the direct orders of his superiors, the group of ancient vampires known as "The Twelve," Walter had come to Washington to report on the Sabbat attack on the city. Tales of the mysterious vampire known as the Red Death worried the elders of the Inconnu. They wanted to know more about the monster's schemes — and his frightening control of fire. It was Walter's job to find out. In a rare deviation from sect policy, he had been instructed to use whatever means were necessary to discover the facts.

A few minutes past midnight on the evening after the tremendous explosion at the Navy Yard, Walter sat with four members of the Blood Guard playing five-card draw in the rear of the warehouse. They served as watchmen for the building. The rest of the elite troop roamed the streets of Washington, enforcing Justine Bern's edict against further violence within city limits. Meanwhile, in the rear office of the warehouse, the archbishop and two of her three closest advisors discussed possible ways to avert a major disaster.

An attack against her in Manhattan by the Red Death had supposedly prompted Justine's call for a blood war against Washington. The city, like most major metropolises in the United States, was secretly ruled by vampires. The archbishop claimed that the Red Death was working for the Camarilla elders who controlled the country's capital, and thus had to be destroyed.

In reality, Justine had long coveted the city of Washington. With New York City and the capital both under her thumb, she would effectively control the east coast of America for the Sabbat. Such power would set the stage for her rise to supreme authority over the sect. The current regent of the Sabbat, Melinda Galbraith, had disappeared months ago in an as-of-yet-unexplained disaster in Mexico City which had killed thousands. Justine was one of several archbishops who were vying to take her place. The Red Death had served as the perfect excuse for calling the blood war. If he had not arisen, sooner or later Justine would have been forced to manufacture a threat.

The only problem was that the attack had gone sour. Hundreds of anarch vampires, filled with an uncontrollable lust for blood, had descended on the capital, bringing death and destruction in their wake. Major riots had erupted throughout

Washington and its suburbs, as the local police were unable to cope with the huge surge in violent behavior. However, while anarchy gripped the city, the secret Camarilla masters of the metropolis were nowhere to be found. Somehow, they had learned of the attack in advance and had gone into hiding. Unless they were located and destroyed, the blood war would fail. And Justine Bern would be disgraced.

Time was short. Even the Sabbat dared not alert humanity to the reality of vampires in their midst. As usual, riots and looting had served as a disguise for the blood war. But, there was a limit to how much violence could be inflicted on a city before the death toll became suspiciously high. And as each hour passed, Justine grew more desperate.

Discussing the situation with her in the warehouse office were Hugh Portiglio, a renegade Tremere vampire wizard, and Molly Wade, a Malkavian of undetermined loyalties. Like most of her clan, Molly usually acted as if she belonged in a madhouse. Yet, she was a brilliant, unconventional tactician with a keen grasp of political intrigue. She served as an effective counterbalance to Portiglio, a no-nonsense strategist without a trace of imagination.

Missing from the group was Justine's ghoul and most trusted advisor, Alicia Varney. No one had seen Alicia for two days. Portiglio, who hated the ghoul for the influence she wielded over Justine, had already accused her of deserting the cause. Molly, in typical Malkavian fashion, had muttered something about Alicia being the only one who showed any common sense. Justine was angry about Alicia's disappearance but was anxious for her return. Walter believed he understood the real reason why.

Alicia Varney, he was convinced, was not really Justine's ghoul. Instead, she served another mistress — Anis, Queen of Night. Walter felt certain that Anis, through Alicia, dominated the archbishop's mind and was the prime mover in this attack on Washington. What role the Red Death played in the whole conspiracy he did not know, though he had a nagging suspicion that the spectral figure was involved in Alicia's mysterious absence.

A hundred different plots and counterplots swirled in Walter's head as he dealt out the cards. A master of sleight-of-hand, he made sure that his companions did most of the winning. Walter spread the good hands among the watchmen, breaking the string only rarely with a score of his own. Money meant nothing to Walter. Information was what mattered.

The mental web of perception he kept draped over the entire warehouse provided Walter with a second's warning of approaching disaster. Instantly, he let the psychic aura collapse and withdrew his mind into an inner shell, letting the fanatical card player section of his personality surge to the surface. A telepathic scan of his thoughts would confirm that Walter Holmes was exactly what he appeared to be — a vampire of no consequence, obsessed with poker. From a tiny peephole in his mind's eye, the Inconnu Monitor of New York watched and waited for the worst.

The front doors of the warehouse exploded off their hinges. Howling like a banshee, a fierce wind roared through the building. Light bulbs melted as the electricity flickered, surged, then disappeared altogether. The air crackled with unseen forces.

The four members of the Blood Guard were on their feet, their knives and guns drawn. Walter, staying in character, slipped back to the warehouse wall, his gaze fixed on the open door of the building. A lone woman stood there, her figure starkly etched in the moonlight. Walter recognized her immediately. She was the missing regent of the Sabbat, Melinda Galbraith.

A petite, extremely beautiful woman with dark brown hair and light brown eyes, Melinda burned with inner power. Dressed in a black satin dress and high heels and wearing long black gloves, she looked more like a fashion model than a Sabbat leader. But appearances were deceiving. Melinda was one of the deadliest vampires in the world. She was an ancient member of the Lasombra clan, a group known for its ruthlessness and depravity. Since the founding of the Sabbat, Lasombra elders had been the only vampires to serve as regents.

"Where is Justine Bern?" asked Melinda, her voice a cold whisper that split the wind that roared about her. "I want to see that stupid bitch right now."

"Who the fuck are you?" demanded a member of the Blood Guard, a tall, thin killer named Lopez with too much arrogance and not enough sense.

"The archbishop don't see nobody without an appointment. And you, babe, ain't got one."

Melinda smiled. She almost seemed pleased with Lopez's response. "I am Melinda Galbraith," she declared. Slowly, she raised her left hand to eye level. Her fingers curled into a fist. Then tightened. Lopez shrieked in pain. "And I demand respect from scum like you."

Lopez screamed again. His head jerked to and fro, as if a massive invisible hand held him by the throat. Desperately, he tore at his neck, trying to break the grip that was squeezing his neck to pulp. His mouth opened again, soundlessly, in an unheard cry of despair. Clearly visible now were five deep gouges in his pale white flesh. Eyes bulging, the Blood Guard dropped to his knees. The finger marks in his neck grew deeper and deeper, and Lopez's struggles became more frenzied.

Melinda laughed and twisted her hand. With a crack that echoed through the warehouse, Lopez's spine snapped. Like a lead weight, the vampire's head dropped forward, his chin slamming into his chest. The Cainite's body wobbled like a marionette whose strings had been cut loose.

With a satisfied smirk, Melinda opened her fist and sharply clapped her two hands together.

Lopez's skull burst as if caught in the center of a hydraulic press. A narrow stream of gore, gristle and brain rocketed to the ceiling. Nothing remained of his head from the neck up. His decapitated body toppled to the floor, crumbling into rotted flesh as it fell. In seconds, except for some scattered bits of metal and cloth, there was nothing left to show that the vampire had ever existed.

"Does anyone else want to play games?" asked Melinda sweetly. "If not, tell Archbishop Bern I am waiting to see her."

"No need for an announcement," said Justine. She had appeared in front of the door to the warehouse office. Standing next to her were Hugh Portiglio and Molly Wade. The archbishop's expression was a mixture of rage and apprehension. "I heard you arrive."

Melinda's smile widened. "Dramatic, wasn't it." She waved a hand and the howling wind died down. "I thought it might catch your attention."

"Rumors reported that you died in Mexico City," said Justine. "There was talk of a demon rising. Reports claimed that thousands of kine and dozens of vampires perished in the quake."

"Talk means nothing," replied Melinda, walking forward. "I think you can see that I survived."

She glanced around as she moved, her eyes missing nothing. Her gaze touched Walter, crouching against the far wall; she examined him briefly, then continued on. He was an unimportant vampire of no worth, his mind filled with thoughts of cards.

"What happened?" asked Portiglio. "We thought..."

"As if I care what you thought, Tremere slime," said Melinda sharply. She sneered at the quivering wizard. "What took place in Mexico City is over. Forget it. It doesn't matter."

In the small section of his brain where his intellect still functioned, Walter noted that Melinda seemed reluctant to offer any explanation for her long absence. Nor was she accompanied by her usual entourage of bodyguards, sycophants, and advisors. From what he knew of the regent's personality, her appearance here at the warehouse tonight, unannounced and unexpected, seemed quite out of character. He wondered exactly what had occurred in Mexico.

"Why are you here, Melinda?" asked Justine. Dressed in a shapeless dark blue dress, with gaunt, drawn features, piercing black eyes and dark hair pulled back in a bun, the archbishop resembled Hollywood's version of a spinster schoolteacher. Justine cared nothing about her appearance. She only cared about power. And obtaining more of it.

"You summoned me, Justine," Melinda said softly, standing a few feet in front of the archbishop. "Or, should I say," her voice rising in anger from a whisper to a scream of fury, "your incredibly stupid, mishandled, ill-conceived, ineptly planned and executed attack on this city! You misshapen rotting carcass, who authorized this misbegotten blood war? How could you be so damned fucking incompetent!"

Eyes blazing, teeth clenched in restrained anger, Justine looked ready to tear Melinda to shreds. "What are you raving about?" she managed to ask.

"The prince of this city, you stupid bitch," said the regent. "Why do you think I gave strict orders that Vitel be left alone. Why? Why! WHY!"

Frightened by the sheer malevolence Melinda

projected, Justine took a step back. "Orders? What orders? I don't remember receiving any such instructions."

"Fool!" shrieked Melinda and slapped Justine hard across the face. "You don't remember! Months and months of negotiations ruined because you forgot."

Cautiously, Walter crept to the entrance of the warehouse. The rest of the proceedings he watched from the outside corner of the doorway, ready to flee instantly if Melinda glanced in his direction. He had a bad feeling about this confrontation. And over the course of many long centuries, Walter had learned to trust his instincts.

"I — I — I didn't recall any messages," sputtered Justine, completely cowed by Melinda's towering rage. "I had no idea that a bargain was in the works."

"Of course you didn't," said Melinda, her tone calmer, though her voice dripped with sarcasm. "How could you? If you did, the negotiations wouldn't have been secret."

The regent shook her head in disgust. "Come. We have to find a way to cut our losses and retreat. The sooner that's done, the better."

Thoroughly browbeaten, Justine shrugged her shoulders and turned to the office door.

As if from nowhere, a machete materialized in Melinda Galbraith's hands. A powerful misdirection spell had kept it hidden until the precise moment it was needed. Gracefully, Melinda swung the blade high above her head, then brought it down in a sweeping blow aimed at Justine Bern's exposed neck.

Like most powerful vampire elders, Justine employed the protective measure known as Skin of Steel to deflect such attacks. It hardened a Cainite's flesh into a near-impenetrable barrier. The machete should not have cut into Justine's neck. The blade should have shattered on contact. Neither happened. Instead, the shiny blade sliced into the archbishop's throat with incredible force, cutting right to the bone.

Justine, caught completely by surprise, gurgled inarticulate sounds. Tiny streams of black blood dribbled down the archbishop's dress.

Reaching forward, Melinda grabbed Justine by the clump of hair bundled behind her ears. Viciously, the regent yanked the archbishop's head backward, exposing the gaping wound made by the machete. Laughing wildly, Melinda raised the machete a second time and drove it into Justine's exposed flesh.

Like a flash of silver, the burnished blade chopped clean through the archbishop's flesh and bone, severing her head from her body. Sizzling like bacon on a grill, Justine's body fell to the floor. Howling with pleasure, Melinda tossed the archbishop's head high into the air.

"Try to take over my job, you bitch," screamed Melinda, not sounding entirely sane. "Look where that ambition got you."

Machete still in hand, she whirled to stare at Hugh Portiglio. There was a dazed, horrified expression on the wizard's face. "She was an archbishop," he croaked, his fear making it difficult for him to speak. "You can't just execute an archbishop like that."

"I'm Melinda Galbraith, regent of the Sabbat," said Melinda, her face glowing with unholy blood lust. "I can do anything I want."

She swiveled her head and looked at the three remaining members of the Blood Guard. "Those not with me are against me. Where do you stand?"

"With you, mistress," declared the quickest of the three. "We are loyal."

Anxiously, the other two guards nodded in agreement. Melinda smirked.

"Take this scum," she said, pointing to Hugh Portiglio, "and drive a wooden stake through his heart. That should quiet him down. When things settle here, I'll do some carving on him. He'll be sorry he was ever Embraced."

"No-o-o," bellowed Portiglio, waving his arms frantically in the air, without results.

"Don't worry," said Melinda. "I've neutralized his magic. The traitorous bastard is completely harmless."

The regent spun around, looking for Molly Wade. The Malkavian was gone. She disappeared the instant the machete cut into Justine's neck. Molly might be crazy, but she was not stupid.

"The Malkavian showed a lot more sense than you," Melinda said, chuckling, as Hugh Portiglio struggled futilely in the grip of two of the Blood Guards, while the last searched for a piece of wood to use as a stake. "She can run, but there's no escape from Melinda. I'll get her in the end."

"No, no, no," begged Hugh, as he spotted the guardsman returning with a sharpened broom handle. "Please, please, please. Not me, not me."

"You've outlived your usefulness, Tremere," said Melinda. "With Justine destroyed, I no longer need you. However, I promise you an interesting end. Your Final Death will provide me with hours of entertainment."

Melinda laughed. "Still, it's nothing compared to what I have planned for Miss Alicia Varney when she finally reappears. Knowing your affection for her, it's almost too bad you won't be around to witness the execution. But, then, nobody said undeath is fair."

It was then that Walter Holmes' suspicions solidified and he realized the truth about Melinda Galbraith.

Chapter 11

Washington, D.C. - March 23, 1994:

The attractive young couple sat in the rear of Colabouno's Seafood House, nibbling on shrimp and drinking Coca-Cola. Though located in one of the safer neighborhoods of the city, the restaurant wasn't very crowded. The riots had put a damper on people's desire to eat out. There were only a dozen tables filled, although the restaurant seated several hundred. No one on the staff remembered when the pair had arrived or who had taken their order. But, as the guests seemed to be pleased with the service and their meal, no one worried about them.

The man was tall and slender, with wavy blond hair and sky-blue eyes. His bronze skin radiated good health. He wore an open-necked, short-sleeved white shirt and white slacks. His shoes and socks were also white. Though it was March and barely spring, he wore no coat or hat.

The woman sitting across the table bore enough of a resemblance to the blond man to mark her as his sister. She wore a red sequined top, a matching skirt, and red heels. Her hair was also red, and her eyes the same bright blue as her brother's. She had the kind of figure that attracted attention. Her companion was simply handsome — she was beautiful.

The couple spoke in moderate tones that somehow did not carry beyond their table. Not that anyone ever eavesdropped on their conversations. They required privacy. And when they concentrated in tandem, whatever they desired came to pass.

"Well," said the young man who used the name Reuben on occasion, "they survived the flames."

"Alicia used Temporis," said the woman, who took the name Rachel from a certain children's song. "Drawing on Anis' power enabled her to stop time just long enough to make it to the survival capsule. McCann surprised me. He pulled a rabbit out of the hat with Madeleine Giovanni."

"Father once told me that Lameth has strong precognitive powers," said Reuben. He popped a shrimp into his mouth. "I'm not sure he understands in advance why he does certain things, but intuitively those acts pay off with unexpected dividends."

"What hold does he have on the Giovanni clan?" asked Rachel, sipping on her Coke. "I never heard of them doing favors for an outsider."

Reuben shook his head. "Don't ask me. Lameth's a Methuselah. He's between six and seven thousand years old and as devious as they come." He paused, then grinned at his sister. "He has secrets about secrets. Have you figured out his relationship with Dire McCann? I'm still trying to piece that puzzle together."

Rachel sighed. "He could be a masquerader, like

Anis and Alicia. That's what I originally suspected. But now, I don't think so. McCann doesn't act like he's possessed. He's too... independent."

"I know what you mean," said Reuben. "Lameth communicates with the detective in his dreams. That much we've determined from reading McCann's surface thoughts. But the vampire's exact connection with the human remains a mystery."

"We'll learn the truth sooner or later," said Rachel, confidently. "We always do. Patience is a virtue."

Reuben laughed. "The Red Death could use a little of it."

Rachel dipped a shrimp daintily in cocktail sauce and ate it before answering. "He's impatient, that's for sure. His entire bloodline is in a hurry. They're convinced that the apocalypse is rapidly approaching and they are the only ones capable of stopping it."

"They might be right," said Reuben. "The Nictuku are rising across the globe. Their appearance may be a sign of further disasters to follow. That's a belief common to many of the Kindred. It doesn't matter. What counts is that Seker and his brood are using the Sheddim to further their ambitions. The unsuspecting fools truly believe they are manipulating the fire elementals. Of course, that's exactly what the Sheddim want them to think. Those creatures have been scheming since the beginning of history to gain a foothold in our reality. Now, the Red Death and his brood are enabling them to finally achieve their ambition. If they succeed in breaking through to our world, every inhabitant on earth will pay dearly for Seker's folly. That's why McCann and Alicia must stop the Children of Dreadful Night."

"The Red Death and the Sheddim," said Rachel, shuddering. "They are truly unholy allies."

"Lameth can destroy the union between the two," said Reuben. "Or Anis. They control powers equal to the horror."

"I couldn't help but notice that your friend in Israel felt the same," said Rachel, chewing on another shrimp. "Funny how he came to the same conclusion."

Reuben shook his head in mock dismay. "I can't keep anything hidden from you, can I?"

"Nope," said Rachel. "That's the peril of being a twin."

"Well," said Reuben, "I worried that McCann might not realize the gravity of this situation without a little prompting. Remember, we spoke the other night about how arrogant the Methuselahs can be. They think they know everything. But I doubt that even Lameth understands the peril the Sheddim represent. They are pretty obscure.

"So, the last time I played chess with Rambam, I dropped a few hints about Seker and his plans. Nothing definite, of course. We both know *that's* forbidden."

"Definitely forbidden," interrupted Rachel, her eyes twinkling. "It's against the rules we've already bent and distorted until they are unrecognizable."

"Maimonides is nobody's fool," said Reuben. "He

knows the *Kabbalah* from cover to cover. The merest whisper about the Sheddim extending their tendrils into our reality started him investigating. He's an extremely powerful mage, and so are his friends. They uncovered the truth in short order. He recognized immediately that no human could deal with the menace; it requires a being with ties to both mankind and the Kindred. That's why he sent his messenger to look for Dire McCann. The detective is the logical choice to deal with the Children. He has to succeed."

"What I don't understand," said Rachel, pushing the plate of shrimp away, "is how Seker ever managed to contact the Sheddim. They dwell in the darkness outside our reality. Where did he find the spell that enabled him to communicate with the creatures?"

"Ever hear of a book called *The Necronomicon?*" asked Reuben.

"Oh please," said Rachel, raising her eyebrows. "Get serious. The forbidden text written by Abdul Alhazred. It's purely an imaginary work. H.P. Lovecraft invented the book as a background for his stories. The Red Death didn't find any instructions in there about the Sheddim."

"Just testing," said her brother, grinning. "I wanted to make sure you were paying attention."

He looked at the last few remnants of fish on the platter and shook his head.

"I've had enough shrimp," he decided. He gulped down a final swallow of Coke. With a wave of a hand, he summoned a busboy over to clear the table.

"How about dessert?" he asked his sister. "Nothing's happening yet. It's too early in the evening. The chocolate mousse cake here is supposed to be fantastic."

"Sounds fine to me," said Rachel. A brief look of concentration flickered across her face. "It's part of our order. The waiter should bring it in a minute, along with coffee. Now, enough silly stuff. Answer my question. No more stalling."

"The Sheddim and the shattered worlds were described in a lost section of *The Book of Enoch*," said Reuben, naming the fabled volume of Kindred lore of which only fragments remained. "A Tremere scholar found the forgotten passage carved on the wall of an ancient tomb in the Middle East. Seker killed him before he could report the discovery to the clan elders. The formula inscribed on the stones enabled him to contact the Sheddim. And the Red Death was born."

"The Tremere still don't realize how Seker has been manipulating them for centuries," said Rachel, shaking her head. "Those fools. He's stolen so many of their greatest discoveries. And used the House of Mystery for his own ends."

She brightened as a waiter approached. "Ah, here's dessert. And coffee."

Looking slightly befuddled, the server set out two slices of chocolate mousse cake and poured them each coffee. "Can I get you anything else?" he asked, and then hesitated. "You are my table, right?"

"Definitely," said Reuben. "And we've had excellent service. You've done a fine job. I think we're set for the moment. Bring the check whenever."

Shaking his head in bewilderment, the waiter departed. "Good choice on the cake," declared Rachel, already on her second forkful. "It *is* excellent."

"I sent Etrius a dream," said Reuben. "It got his attention. Unfortunately, the rest of the Inner Council refused to believe what he told them. Nothing more I could do. It would be stretching coincidence beyond belief if I transmitted similar dreams to other members of the Seven. In any case, Etrius acted on his own. He dispatched an underling of his own to hunt for St. Germain. At least, that's a start."

"Better than nothing," said Rachel. She stared at her brother. "What do we do now?"

"Sit back and wait, I guess," he replied. "Things should start bubbling shortly.

"The Red Death tried to kill Anis and Lameth — and failed. He'll try again. Fanatics like him never give up. I'd be willing to bet he started a new plan the instant his original scheme collapsed. But, his targets know a lot more about him after that attack. And they won't be tricked so easily again.

"Lameth is an extremely dangerous foe. He's slow to anger, but when he's enraged he has the power to shake the world. And Anis isn't a pushover either. Drawn out of torpor, either of them could destroy the Red Death and his entire brood. Assuming that they unravel Seker's plot before it is put into action."

"They need to contact Phantomas," said Rachel. "His encyclopedia holds the solution to the conspiracy."

"I agree," said Reuben, his face serious. "Phantomas is the key. The Nosferatu is the sole Kindred who can unravel the Masquerade of the Red Death."

Chapter 12

Washington, D.C. - March 24, 1994:

"There will be thunderstorms tonight," said the voice inside McCann's mind. *"Violent storms, filled with lightning."*

McCann, as always, remained silent. He never spoke in his dreams. He just listened and remembered.

Lameth offered no explanation for the oncoming storms. McCann accepted the information as fact. The Methuselah who spoke in his brain controlled great forces. If he claimed there would be *thunderstorms* that evening, then it was merely a matter of when, not if.

Violent storms, filled with lightning. The words echoed in McCann's mind as he emerged from sleep. Groggily, he stretched his arms high above his head. Glancing over at the clock on the nightstand, he saw that it was nearly 9 p.m. It was a hell of a time to wake up.

Mentally, the detective checked the psychic defenses layered throughout the suite. They remained intact. No one had tried to break into his hideaway while he rested. Nor were there any messages on the hotel voice mail. He had nearly two hours to grab a bite to eat before his rendezvous with

Madeleine and Flavia at the Lincoln Memorial.

Sliding off the bed, McCann padded on bare feet over to the thick curtains that cloaked the suite from the outside world. He pulled them back and stared at the city lights. The sky was clear, with a lustrous moon high in the heavens. The stars twinkled brightly. There was not a single cloud. The detective shrugged. Neither the newspaper nor the television weather forecasters predicted rain. But Lameth had said there would be a thunderstorm tonight, and the vampire did not make idle promises.

Forty-five minutes later, as McCann made final preparations to depart for his meeting, dark clouds had gathered overhead. The detective wasn't sure how Lameth had created the weather pattern. It didn't matter. For some as yet unexplained reason, the vampire wanted a storm in Washington that evening. The distant rumble of thunder was a sign that whatever Lameth wished, happened.

Carefully, McCann checked his equipment. Secure in his shoulder holster was his Ingram Mac-10 submachine gun. The powerful automatic fired thirty .45 caliber bullets in a continuous burst. The impact from those rounds could daze and confuse most vampires. The razor-sharp steel garroting wire hidden in the detective's belt provided the necessary finishing touch.

Sewn to the inside of his long, black trench coat was a nearly invisible eight-inch flexible leather tube. Nestled within the container were three slender slivers of wood, each a half-foot in length.

Though they looked like children's toys, they were actually effective killing devices. Reinforced by an inner steel pin, the stakes were sharpened to a needle point. McCann used the sticks like darts, throwing the projectiles at his enemies as if they were tiny spears. Despite their size, a sliver through the heart would kill a man or paralyze a vampire.

Satisfied that he was ready for anything, the detective shut off the lights to his suite and stepped into the hotel's hallway. He glanced at his watch. It was ten o'clock. He was due at the memorial at eleven, and the statue was only a short cab ride from his hotel. He was running well ahead of schedule.

Walking the length of the hallway, McCann pressed the call button for the elevator. As he waited for the car to arrive, he smiled, thinking of Madeleine Giovanni's expression the night before. The vampire assassin was a curious combination of deadly killer and naive country bumpkin. She was definitely not typical of her clan.

The arrival of the elevator cut off any further thoughts McCann had about his protector. Stepping into the car, he pressed the button for the main floor. With a hum of machinery, the doors closed and the elevator started to descend.

Then, without warning, the car lurched to a sudden stop between the third and fourth floors. The overhead light blinked and went out. Alone in the darkness, McCann scowled. He was in no mood for machinery failure. Anxiously, he waited for the car to continue, but after a minute he came to the conclusion that it was not going to move. Cursing, he felt along the front panel until he discovered the emergency phone. He lifted the receiver to his ear, only to discover that the phone was dead.

Temper rising, McCann pounded his fists against the elevator door. "Anyone there?" he called. "What's going on?"

No answer. McCann sighed in despair. The riots had brought disaster after disaster upon the city. It seemed quite possible that Sabbat anarchs had blown up the D.C. power plant. He was stuck in this car until a rescue party arrived. And that might not be for hours.

"Like hell," the detective muttered to himself. Closing his eyes for a moment, he tried to recall the elevator car interior. McCann nodded. If he remembered correctly, there was an emergency trap door directly above him.

Locking his hands together in a double fist over his head, McCann leapt for the ceiling. His fingers smashed into the roof with the force of a jackhammer. Steel screeched against steel as the metal exit plate went flying. McCann dropped back to the floor of the car, a dim light filtering in from the opening above. There were battery-operated emergency lights in the shaft.

Jumping a second time, the detective grabbed hold of the edge of the trap and pulled himself onto the roof of the car. Standing up, he was able to reach the sliding doors that led to the fourth floor. Taking hold of the edge of a door with each hand, McCann exerted pressure. With a sigh of compressed air, the portal opened.

McCann frowned. The lights were on in the hallway. The power outage had just hit the elevators. That the electricity had failed precisely when he was inside the detective knew was no coincidence. Hastily, he pulled himself onto the floor of the corridor. Company was coming, and with malicious intentions.

"Mr. McCann?" asked a voice softly, catching the detective totally off guard. He jerked his head around, the Ingram Mac-10 flashing into his right hand. A young man, tall and thin, with curly brown hair and huge brown eyes, stood by the elevator call button. The stranger was dressed in plain brown slacks and wore a pale gray sweatshirt with the words "Notre Dame" embroidered on the chest. On his head was a black yarmulke, the skullcap worn by religious Jews.

"Who the hell are you?" asked McCann, shouldering the machine gun. Alone and unarmed, the young man radiated good will. He was not at all a threat. "And how do you know my name?"

"I'm Elisha Horwitz," said the newcomer. He looked down the hall. "No time to talk at the moment. The group that cut the power to the elevator is nearly here. A bunch of vampires, armed with flamethrowers, hunting for you. We better leave."

McCann nodded. He was beyond surprises after the past night's encounter. "You've come to rescue me?"

"Not really," said the young man, grinning. "I

suspect you can handle danger pretty well on your own. Sensing you would exit on this floor, I thought it best to meet you here. I'm just a messenger boy."

The fire door leading to the emergency stairs located at the other end of the hall slammed open. Four figures, dressed in black leather, with shaven heads and menacing expressions, crowded into the corridor. Each of them carried a flamethrower. Spotting McCann, they hooted in triumph.

"Shit," said the detective, pulling out the Ingram again. "Fighting vampires in the hallway of an expensive hotel. I feel like a character in a John Woo movie. Follow me, kid. Try to keep back, so you don't get hurt. I want to hear that message you're here to deliver."

Squeezing the trigger of the Ingram, McCann sent a burst of bullets down the passage. The ammunition slammed into the frontmost vampire, lifting it off the floor and hurtling it into its companions. They sprawled onto the carpet, arms and legs flailing.

McCann moved with inhuman speed. He waded into the quartet before any of them could rise. Reaching down, the detective seized the bullet-riddled body of the ringleader and slammed the listless vampire into the wall. It collapsed in a motionless hulk. Though steel couldn't destroy a Kindred, it would take the monster weeks to regenerate. It was no longer a problem.

The second and third monsters the detective transfixed with his long wooden "toothpicks." Their hearts pierced, the Cainites were frozen in place. A single vampire remained. It was nowhere in sight.

Puzzled, McCann looked around for the creature. It had disappeared. Finally, the detective noticed a thin line of ashes forming the outline of a body etched into the plush hall carpeting. In the midst of the soot was a flamethrower. The detective's eyes widened in astonishment. Evidently, when the vampire was knocked to the floor, the nozzle of its flamethrower had wedged into its chest and had accidentally switched on. The resulting brief instant of flame, concealed entirely by the Cainite's body, had destroyed it. It was an improbable answer but it fit the facts.

The detective turned his head and stared at Elisha. "You have anything to do with this?" he asked, pointing to the ashes.

The young man looked at McCann with wide, innocent eyes. "Me? How? It looks like he fell on his own weapon and destroyed himself. I never touched him."

"Sure," said McCann, sarcastically. He glanced at the two transfixed vampires. "Let's get out of here. I've noticed that these punks hunt in packs. The hotel is probably crawling with them."

Elisha nodded. "I sense at least a dozen more stalkers in the building. They seem anxious to locate you."

"The Red Death probably offered them a big reward for my head," said McCann. "Delivered separate from my body. Come on. You perceive any more vampires sneaking up on us, yell."

The emergency stairs were deserted. It was cold

and damp and poorly lit in the hall, but it was empty. Hurriedly, McCann and the young man clattered down the steps to the first floor.

"You realize," said the detective as they descended, "that what you told me is the standard excuse used by mages for centuries when unusual incidents occur in their vicinity. *I never touched him.* Better find a new variation. That message you're delivering. Who's it from?"

"My teacher," said Elisha. "Rabbi Moses Ben Maimon."

McCann's usually impassive features lit up with unexpected pleasure. "Rambam. It's been a long time since I heard from him. He still plays chess, I assume?"

"Of course," answered Elisha. "Though he constantly complains about the lack of competition. The only person who really presents a challenge is a man named Reuben who visits..."

Elisha broke off in midsentence as two vampire anarchs hurtled down the steps. Their shrieks echoed off the stairwell walls. The creatures had managed to muffle their thoughts until they were very close. McCann cursed. He had allowed himself to be distracted by conversation when he should have been keeping alert. Power channeled into his fists. He would destroy the pair with his bare hands.

He needn't have worried. A half-dozen stairs away, the first vampire, armed with a bowie knife, tripped as the heel of its black leather motorcycle boot caught the edge of the step. With a bellow of outrage, the Cainite shot into the air. It sailed over

McCann's head like a runaway rocket. The vampire's fall was broken suddenly when its head impacted against the heavy-duty steel pipe railing that lined the staircase. McCann blinked in amazement as the bowie knife flipped high up into the air, spun around once, then dropped earthward and plunged into the rear of the creature's neck. The anarch jerked spasmodically for a few seconds, then lay still. It wasn't destroyed, but it would not be going anywhere for a long time.

Its companion fared equally badly. Whirling a heavy steel chain in a deadly circle over its head, the vampire approached them cautiously. It took one step at a time, not rushing. Yet, for all its preparations, the anarch was still caught by surprise when the floor beneath its feet suddenly gave way. With a scream of rage, the creature disappeared through the gaping hole. It was a long drop to the basement. The vampire's cry of anger ended abruptly with a sickening crunch of bones against cement.

"Definitely find another excuse," said McCann, with an incredulous expression, as they eased past the anarch with the bowie knife through its neck. "You manipulate coincidences far too easily for people to believe they're chance."

"I'm new to this stuff," admitted Elisha as they exited the stairway and emerged into the hotel lobby. The young man's eyes glowed with excitement. There were no anarchs in evidence on the main floor. They were all searching for McCann upstairs. "Producing believable accidents takes practice."

"It appears to me that you just need to concentrate on style," said McCann, "not results. You handled those vampires without pausing for breath."

"Rambam drilled me thoroughly in coping with the unexpected," said Elisha. "I reacted without thinking."

"Speaking of your teacher," said McCann as they marched out of the hotel's front door and into the street, "what was that mention you made about Maimonides playing chess with a man named Reuben? Reuben who?"

"I don't know his last name," said Elisha. "He has blond hair, bright blue eyes, and always dresses in white. Once a month, he comes to our house in the evening to play chess. He looks young, but I suspect he's older than he seems." The teenager smiled. "Everyone who visits my master is older than they seem. I don't know a thing about his background. However, he does play excellent chess. He's beaten my master as often as he has lost."

"Very interesting," said McCann. It was another piece in a puzzle that seemed unsolvable.

Together, they started walking down Virginia Avenue toward the Potomac. A street running parallel to the river went directly to the Lincoln Memorial.

It had started to rain. Flashes of lightning lit up the sky in the distance. The detective didn't care. After this most recent encounter with the anarchs, he preferred to avoid automobiles. He was going to be late for his meeting, but that could not be helped.

ROBERT WEINBERG

"Okay. We're alone," said the detective. "What's this important message you came all the way from Israel to deliver in person?"

"My master wants to see you immediately," said Elisha. His face was flushed. "You're supposed to return with me as soon as possible. He needs to tell you the truth about the Red Death."

McCann shook his head in disbelief. "I'm not sure I grasp the importance of this communication. Since when does a mage of Maimonides' power involve himself in the affairs of the Kindred?"

"Don't you see," said Elisha anxiously. "That's exactly the point. Rambam isn't concerned with the Kindred. The plans of the Red Death don't just affect the Damned. If he's not defeated, the monster could destroy the entire world!"

Chapter 13

Washington, D.C. - March 24, 1994:

They parked the truck at a public rest stop twenty miles outside Washington. The lot was deserted. The riots and civil unrest in the capital had convinced independent truck drivers to stay clear of the city. Madeleine reasoned that the rig would remain safe and unnoticed in this out-of-the-way location until she returned in the morning. It was not a popular decision with her three young assistants, who longed for the excitement of the big city.

"You're fuckin' paranoid," declared Junior. Though he delighted in using the language of the street, Junior was a lot smarter than he sounded. "Nobody gives a damn 'bout this truck or its contents. We parked in Washington last night without a bit of trouble."

"Yeah," said Pablo. "We should be in the city, havin' fun."

"Right," said Sam. "They have video arcades that stay open all night. They advertise on the radio. I wanted to go there."

"Pizza," said Junior. "Those Big Macs for dinner were okay, but I wanna fuckin' pizza. I'm starving."

"We bought plenty of food at the 7-11," declared

Madeleine, looking up from her desk. "You can gorge yourselves on potato chips and pretzels. But leaving the rest stop is out of the question. I will not change my mind."

They were in the cargo container of the huge truck. The inside of the rig had been arranged like an office. There was a desk, several chairs, and a row of filing cabinets. Everything was bolted to the floor so as not to shift when the truck was in motion. There was even a cellular phone and fax system which linked Madeleine directly with the Mausoleum, the Giovanni headquarters, in Venice.

Beyond the office equipment was a large closet filled with Madeleine's clothes. Past that was her coffin. Alongside it were two sleeping bags. One was for Junior, the other for Sam. Pablo hated sleeping on the floor. He spent his nights resting in the cab of the truck.

"Remember," said Madeleine, "this endeavor is no game. There are many Kindred who would like nothing better than to destroy me. I fought such a gang of rogues in your home city, Lexington, the night I first met you. There are surely others, perhaps in this area, searching for me. My identity has been compromised. For me, staying hidden is a matter of survival."

"Yeah," said Junior. The boys sat on folding chairs arranged in a semicircle around the desk. "We understand, Miss Madeleine. Honest. Ain't no problem with anything you say. We were jus' givin' you a hard time. It's so fuckin' easy to yank your chain."

Madeleine finished typing her entry into her

computer journal. She pressed the key to print out the pages. Before she left, she wanted to fax her description of last night's activities to her sire. It was part of her daily routine. Not mentioned in the report, or in any of the others she had sent to Venice, were her trio of assistants.

Madeleine knew her grandfather would not approve of her recruiting the three waifs. However, she was also certain he would not command her to abandon them. As the Dagger of the Giovanni, she was allowed to act in the manner she thought best. She worked independently of any outside control. Her choice of helpers was strictly her own.

The problem was that Madeleine didn't fully understand her own motives in drafting the children as her accomplices. Despite what she had told them, she could have managed well enough on her trip alone. They were useful but not necessary.

As a girl born in the House of Giovanni, Madeleine had been raised with no friends — just responsibilities. The execution of her father by Don Caravelli of the Mafia when she was eleven years old destroyed any chance she may have had to lead a normal life. An intense, grim child, Madeleine found her purpose in death.

Instead of learning the family business or marrying some important business leader the Giovanni elders wanted to bring into the clan, Madeleine devoted herself to revenge. She trained with the greatest masters of sabotage, subversion and deception in Europe. She became an expert in armed and unarmed combat. And, she learned strategy and tactics from crooked politicians.

Twelve years she spent learning everything necessary to becoming a perfect terrorist. Then, when she had achieved her goal, Madeleine asked her grandfather to Embrace her. Under the Rite of Blood and Revenge, it was a request he could not deny. The solitary, quiet child became the solitary, quiet vampire.

She spent another decade melding her skills with her Kindred powers. Madeleine was extremely patient. She never grew bored. Twenty-two years after she swore she would not rest until the Mafia chieftain who destroyed her father was likewise executed, the secret weapon of the Giovanni elders entered the shadowy underworld of European espionage and intrigue.

Though the Giovanni refused to acknowledge any participation in the murder of Archduke Franz Ferdinand, his death was indirectly laid at Madeleine's feet. As were, over the decades that followed, the murders of dozens of other politicians who dared challenge clan schemes or ambitions. The Dagger of the Giovanni struck with swift, silent precision. She never failed.

Eighty years passed. Madeleine never ceased training. Nor did she stop waiting for the night when she would finally confront Don Caravelli. And settle her debt of honor.

"It is inconceivable to me that there could be spies in the Mausoleum, my clan headquarters," said Madeleine as she fed the printed pages into the fax machine. The message was in code, one that had been used by the Giovanni for centuries. Based on the hierarchy of the clan, among both the living and the undead, it was unbreakable by anyone who had not been raised in the family. "Among my bloodline, loyalty is not bought and paid for by the highest bidder. It is a matter of honor."

She looked at her three charges; the hero worship they felt for her was clear in their faces. The boys didn't care that she was one of the Damned. All that mattered to them was that she cared. It was a responsibility that caught Madeleine by surprise. But one that she took very seriously.

Vengeance had occupied Madeleine's life and her undeath. For more than a century, she had known nothing else. Yet, enough humanity remained in her that she instinctively realized that there was more to existence than destruction. Her unexpected attachment to the three runaways, she vaguely understood, was at least in part as much a reaction to her lost childhood as it was to theirs.

"So who turned you in?" asked Sam. "Who squealed?"

"I do not know," said Madeleine. "I am certain I was not recognized in passing by some unknown Kindred. My features are not well known." She smiled briefly. "Usually, those who realize my true identity meet the Final Death shortly afterward."

Madeleine shrugged. "It is possible that the Prince of St. Louis mistook my mission for more than it was and set assassins on my trail. Though, personally I doubt Alexander Vargoss would have employed such inept killers. Someday, I will learn

158

the truth. And pay back my betrayer in kind."

"If you're so worried about our safety," said Junior unexpectedly, "you could make us into fuckin' vampires. Then, you wouldn't have to worry 'bout nothing. We'd be strong like you. And fuckin' invincible."

Madeleine glared at the boy. Angrily, she walked over to where he was sitting, eating potato chips, and snatched the open bag out of his hands. She mashed the contents between her fingers until only crumbs remained. Dropping the bag to the floor, she ground it beneath her feet.

"I cannot eat these intriguingly named potato chips," she declared, her voice icy cold. "Nor can I indulge in the foamy mug flavor of root beer. I have never tasted a hot dog or sampled apple pie, both American standards. My entire diet consists of blood." She bared her fangs, nodding with satisfaction as the boys shrank into their seats, horrified. "Warm, human blood."

Her eyes fixed on Junior, with a gaze he could not meet. "If you were Embraced now, you would remain children forever. You would never mature, never become real men. Your existence would be a nightmare of unfulfilled dreams, unrealized ambitions. My race is called the Damned because we are exactly that. Damned."

Junior swallowed. Hard. "I was kidding," he said. "Really."

"I understand the lure of living forever," said Madeleine. "When you reach manhood, you three will become my ghouls. A taste of my blood, from

UNHOLY ALLIES

time to time, will extend your years tenfold. And you will still be able to experience the joys of life denied the undead."

"Ghouls?" said Sam. "That sounds cool. Sam the Ghoul. It kinda fits my personality."

"Yeah," said Pablo, who rarely had much to say. "It sounds like a good deal to me. I could live with that."

Madeleine nodded, permitting herself a small smile. In the course of her years of training, she had learned how to feign anguish perfectly. It was a lesson that continued to repay its costs. "Exactly what I want for you, my brood. Serve me in life, not in death."

"We won't fail you, Miss Madeleine," said Junior solemnly. "Never ever. You know that. We're fuckin' solid. No joke."

"I know, Junior," said Madeleine. "I could not ask for more dependable allies. Now, I must leave. My sire sent me to America to protect a man, not to sit discussing potato chips with three Giovanni recruits."

The boys swelled with pride at her words, as she knew they would. Though she had never dealt with children, Madeleine instinctively understood their needs. They were much the same as her own.

"Wait with the truck," continued Madeleine. "Keep watch. If you notice anyone suspicious, leave the area immediately. Drive to where we parked last night. Be very careful. I would rather you err on the side of caution than bravery."

"Nothin' to worry about, Miss Madeleine," said

Pablo. "We'll guard this big fuckin' rig with our lives. Nothing gonna happen to it. We're tougher than we look."

"You look tough enough," said Madeleine, with a grin. "I am off. Stay safe. I shall return before morning."

She left. But death, her constant companion, remained.

PART

2

In the deepest slumber — no! In delirium — no! In a swoon — no! In death — no! even in the grave, all is not lost!

from "The Pit and the Pendulum"
by Edgar Allan Poe

UNHOLY ALLIES

Chapter 1

Washington, D.C. - March 25, 1994:

The time for dreaming was over. Alicia opened her eyes and let her senses roam free. The fire still burned but no longer raged. Escape from the parade grounds was possible now, provided she watched her every step carefully.

The clock on the lid of the containment unit read nearly 2 a.m. She had been stuck inside the protection pod for more than twenty-four hours. Alicia wasn't sure what had happened during that period — but she intended to find out as soon as possible.

The Red Death, she felt certain, had not remained idle. The monster's scheme to seize control of the Camarilla and the Sabbat was convoluted and labyrinthine. The blood war that had engulfed Washington was just one phase of the phantom's master plan; the attacks upon and elimination of members of both sects had been another. The Red Death had made it quite clear that he sought nothing less than total control of the entire Kindred race. Alicia understood the monster's motivation perfectly. It was a dream shared by every Methuselah engaged in the Jyhad.

The lid of the coffin-shaped box swung open

ROBERT WEINBERG

with a touch of her hand. Alicia sat up and looked around. The escape pod had originally been placed inside a storage depot at the edge of the marching grounds. The building no longer existed. The explosion and the fire it created had wiped the structure off the face of the earth. All that remained were the charred stumps of several walls.

A steady, constant rain was falling. The drops sizzled in the flames that still burned in a dozen places around the base. The storage depot appeared to be relatively free of danger. Anxiously, Alicia scrambled over the side of the pod and lowered her feet to the ground. She could feel the heat of the earth through the soles of her shoes. Although of nearly volcanic intensity, it was bearable. She did not plan to remain on the premises very long.

She was still dressed in dark slacks and a midweight winter jacket. Her hat had disappeared in her desperate scramble for the escape pod. Beneath her clothing she wore a thin suit of fiberglass body armor. The communications headset she had been using was now a crushed strip of metal: the first seconds of the blast had shaken the earth like a major earthquake. Alicia had been lucky to survive with merely a smashed headphone and assorted minor bruises.

Another gentle push closed the lid of the escape pod. Obtaining the use of the three devices scattered throughout the Navy Yard had cost her millions in bribes. It was, she realized now, a wise investment. The pods had saved Alicia's body from destruction, which had been one of the primary goals of the Red

Death's trap.

The Red Death had realized that destroying Anis would be nearly impossible. Like most elder vampires, she used an agent to do her work while her actual body remained hidden in torpor. However, destroying that host body would have been almost as effective as eliminating Anis. Killing Alicia Varney would have forced the Methuselah to establish a new puppet identity — an effort that took months, sometimes years. Maintaining her grip on the huge financial empire Anis had assembled over the centuries would be difficult. More importantly, regaining her influence among the Kindred would take even longer. Alicia had to remain alive in order for the Red Death to be defeated.

Her senses alert for possible faults in the earth, Alicia wove a path out of the desolation. The naval yard looked as if it had been hit by an atomic blast. Not a building remained standing. Blackened, crumbling remnants of metal and concrete were the only evidence that something had once existed in the area. Makish, the renegade Assamite assassin with a taste for Thermit, had outdone himself. The whole area was as grim and gaunt as the dark side of the moon. And about as hospitable.

The rain pelted Alicia's body with increasing ferocity. Overhead, lightning flashed. Thunder roared. Hair pasted to her head, clothing clinging to her body like a second skin, Alicia threaded her way out of the smoldering inferno and back onto the streets of the capital.

There were no signs of any police or fire fighters, other than a row of horses that blocked off the entrance to the disaster scene. Both of these departments were critically understaffed. Whenever possible, the fire chiefs avoided trying to put out major blazes, but waited instead for them to burn out on their own. This saved manpower, time and money. In an era of tight budgets and indifference toward the lower class, a limited number of casualties, especially in the poorer neighborhoods of the city, were deemed acceptable by the city fathers. It was a harsh, but necessary, judgment.

Alicia looked and felt like a drowned rat. The rain was hard and steady. The sky flared every few minutes with another bolt of lightning. A hot bath and a steaming cup of coffee, preferably laced with brandy, called to her. But Alicia knew there were more important things to be done first. Rest could wait.

It took her a few minutes to locate the exact spot where she had entered the park the previous night. The van, which had served as her headquarters and held all of her sophisticated electronic gadgetry, was no longer there. The parking place just outside the blast perimeter where she had left it was empty. Alicia breathed a sigh of relief. The scorch marks ended a few feet before the parking spot, and there was no sign of any wreckage. As best as she could tell, her assistant, Sanford Jackson, had survived the explosion.

Alicia frowned. She wondered why Jackson wasn't still in the area. Her second-in-command had been instrumental in obtaining the NASA emergency pods, so he was well aware of their ability to withstand disaster. He also knew, from personal observation, that Alicia wasn't easy to kill. It seemed odd that he had not waited for her to emerge from the fire before leaving. The thought worried Alicia. Jackson was loyal to a fault. If he was gone, there had to be a very good reason.

The streets were deserted. The houses close to the fire zone were pitch black. Obviously, the inhabitants of the rickety old shacks and ramshackle apartment buildings had fled the inferno and were not in a hurry to return home. Alicia didn't blame them. She had lived both in poverty and in wealth, and she knew that poverty sucked. Wealth was infinitely better.

It felt good to walk again. After more than a day confined in the escape capsule, Alicia relished her freedom. The rain didn't bother her at all; her monthly taste of Anis' blood kept her in perfect health. The splashing water beneath her feet was a minor nuisance, nothing more. Meanwhile, the deluge kept traffic off the streets, enabling her to make good speed.

She was anxious to return to Justine Bern's headquarters. Trapped inside the survival pod, Alicia had been unable to establish any sort of mental link with the archbishop. She was anxious to learn whether the Blood Guard had found any traces of the Prince of Washington or his brood. Unless Prince Vitel was located and destroyed soon, this blood war would be judged a failure by the

Sabbat hierarchy. And the penalty for failure in the sect was severe.

Justine had long coveted the position of ruling Prince of Washington. The Red Death had provided her with the necessary excuse to invade the city. The archbishop had never realized that she was acting in accord with the crimson spectre's master plan. The attack had lured Alicia to the capital, and the hundreds of vampires involved served as perfect mental cover for the presence of four distinct Red Deaths. That section of the scheme had nearly resulted in Alicia's destruction. What concerned Alicia was the rest of the Red Death's plan: She had no idea what the monster intended to do next. But she felt sure that whatever it was, it would not be to her liking.

Thunder bellowed seconds after lightning flashed in the sky. The last few bolts had struck in the center of the city. Alicia shivered, pulling her coat tighter around her neck. It was unusually cold for a thunderstorm. Normally, temperature changes never bothered her. Tonight, however, she felt vaguely uneasy. There was a strangeness in the air, and the weather seemed to be a reflection of it. The rain continued to fall, a steady sheet of water that, combined with the darkness, served to cut visibility down to less than a hundred-foot radius.

There was a haunting air of familiarity to the storm that stirred long-forgotten memories. Pausing for a moment, Alicia let her mind range back over the thousands of years of her lifetime. The answer came to her in seconds: Lameth. The Dark Messiah was a master of violent weather. Having made that connection, she recalled several instances during their relationship when her lover had summoned similar abnormal thunderstorms to aid their machinations.

Alicia smiled. As she suspected, Dire McCann had also managed to escape the Red Death's trap. He was the force behind this ongoing torrent. Alicia had no idea why Lameth wanted the rain. But she suspected from the intensity of the storm that the reasons were not pleasant.

With a dismissive shrug, Alicia continued her journey. She had not had anything to eat or drink in nearly 36 hours. Even a ghoul needed physical nourishment. Her uneasy feelings were probably attributable to lack of food and water. A steak and a bottle of wine would shake the doom and gloom from her. Unfortunately, she suspected it would be hours before she would be able to indulge in those pleasures. There were more important things to be done first.

She was just a few blocks away from the warehouse. At least she should be able to obtain some dry clothing there, although she knew she would not find anything fit for human consumption. What the Sabbat didn't need, it didn't keep around. Hopefully, Justine and her advisors would be present. A quick probe of the archbishop's mind would provide all the information Alicia required. Afterward she could gently point Justine in the proper direction. The archbishop was devious, but she was nowhere near as devious as a seven-thousand-year-old Methuselah named Anis.

As she approached the warehouse, Alicia could see light streaming from the front door, although there was no sign of any activity in front of the building. The place appeared to be deserted. She wondered why the portal was open. It didn't make sense. The worry lines on her face deepened as the uncomfortable feeling she had been experiencing grew even more ominous. Something was very wrong.

"Alicia," a voice whispered from the darkness. "Don't go any nearer. I'll be clearer. It's a trap. The jaws are waiting to snap."

Alicia gazed sharply to her right. "Molly? Is that you? What the hell are you talking about?"

"It's me, it's me, happy as can be," rhymed Molly Wade, invisible in the pitch darkness. "Happy to see you ain't dead. But you will be if you march on ahead."

Alicia glanced back at the open doorway. She thought she saw movement inside but with the rain and the distance, she couldn't be sure. She continued to move her legs as if walking, but instead of going forward, stepped in place. It would fool anyone watching her for a few seconds.

"Explain yourself, you maniac," she hissed. Molly was a Malkavian, the vampire clan noted for its lunatics. Understanding her in the best of circumstances was difficult. "Who's waiting inside? Hugh? Justine?"

"No time for chatter," said Molly, appearing as if from nowhere at Alicia's side. "It don't matter.

We gotta run, if you wanna see the sun."

The Malkavian grabbed Alicia by an arm and yanked her into the blackness between two deserted buildings. Someone inside the warehouse bellowed in surprise.

"Hold my hand," whispered Molly. In the dark, she sounded perfectly sane. "Don't let go. I know my way through the alleys. You don't. If we're separated, the Blood Guard will find you for sure. That's something you definitely don't want to happen. Not with the witch back in town."

"The witch?" repeated Alicia, as, clinging tightly to Molly's fingers, she ran with the Malkavian through dark streets. She had a terrible feeling she knew the answer to her next question, but she had to ask it nonetheless. "Who are you talking about?"

"Melinda Galbraith," said Molly. "The regent's returned from the ranks of the missing. And she's out for blood."

Chapter 2

Washington, D.C. - March 25, 1994:

They ran for thirty minutes, following a convoluted path that seemed to cross itself a dozen times, before Alicia signaled that she needed to rest. Crouching at the edge of the curb, she rested her arms on her knees and tried to catch her breath. The rain had settled into a muted drizzle. An all-pervasive mist filled the air, dropping visibility to near zero. They could have been standing at the base of the Washington Monument and Alicia would not have known. Or cared. She was tired, hungry, thirsty, and annoyed. Mostly annoyed, at herself and at the world in general.

"What happened to Justine?" she asked, gulping in deep lungfuls of air. "And, for that matter, my buddy, Hugh Portiglio?"

"They're gone," said Molly. The Malkavian looked like a teenager. She wore her hair in pigtails and was surrounded by a perpetual air of innocence. "Exterminated. First thing Melinda did when she surprised us was dispatch the two of them to the Final Death. Would have been three if I wasn't fast on my feet. When she stabbed Justine, I guessed right away unlife had taken a turn for the worse. So, I faded from the picture."

Molly grinned. "It's a special talent of mine. I can earth-meld into walls. During the instant no one was watching me, I slipped into the side of the warehouse office. It saved me from getting my head handed to me on a platter. Honest."

"I believe you," said Alicia, stretching her arms over her head. "Subtlety has never been one of Melinda Galbraith's major faults. She believes in blunt, decisive action. Everything you said sounds like her style. She uses a slash-and-burn method of terrorism. No compromises, no concessions. Melinda makes a very dangerous adversary. She's nobody's friend."

"Well, put her at the top of your list of enemies," said Molly. "She wants you killed and chopped into little pieces. Before I maneuvered my way out of the building, I heard her instruct the Blood Guard to exterminate you the minute you arrived at headquarters. That's why I was waiting for you outside. I'm on the same list, too, for what it matters. Anyone associated with Justine is condemned."

Alicia grimaced. Events had careened out of control while she had been trapped by the inferno. A dozen years of planning were lost in the matter of a few minutes. It was bitter medicine to swallow, made worse by the fact that it was so unexpected. Melinda had been missing for months. Everyone believed she was dead, killed in the Mexico City catastrophe. Everyone including Alicia.

Shaitan, another Methuselah, had been the force behind that disaster. Alicia wasn't sure of the

details, but evidently Shaitan had tried, with
Melinda's help, to rise from hundreds of years of
torpor. Other vampires, from the Camarilla, had
interfered, and the effort ended in a major
earthquake and explosion that had devastated the
Mexico City region. Shaitan disappeared, having
either been destroyed or returned to unending sleep.
Melinda had vanished. Until now.

"What a fucking mess," Alicia said aloud,
forgetting Molly's presence. She shook her head in
disgust. "What a mess."

"Destroying Justine eliminated your source of
Kindred blood, huh?" said Molly, misunderstanding
Alicia's concerns. "Without the archbishop, you'll
age and die like a normal kine."

"I never even thought of that," said Alicia, her
annoyance growing. Though she had never touched
a drop of Justine's blood, all the members of the
Sabbat in New York were convinced that she was
Justine's ghoul. Explaining her survival for any
length of time after the archbishop's murder was
going to be difficult. It was another hassle Alicia
was not prepared to deal with. "Son of a bitch."

"We better start moving," said Molly. "The Blood
Guard are expert trailers. If Melinda's set them after
us, we can't stay in any one place for too long."

"Whatever you say," declared Alicia. She was
still trying to coordinate the sudden reappearance
of the Sabbat's regent with the schemes of the Red
Death. There were no coincidences in the affairs of
the Kindred. Alicia was certain that Melinda's
return was directly associated with the crimson

spectre's master plan. She just didn't know how. Not yet.

They set off at a brisk clip. Molly seemed to know exactly where she was going, though as best as Alicia could determine, they were running in a jigsaw pattern that crossed itself more often than a Russian revolutionary. The Malkavian didn't say a word while they ran, which perfectly suited Alicia's mood. She needed time to think.

The streets were deserted. It was as if the rain had washed all life from the city. There were no cars; driving in the incredibly thick fog would be suicidal. They were alone on the pavement. They and their hunters.

"There's five of them on our trail," announced Molly unexpectedly. "The good news is that they're a noisy bunch. Three blocks away and I can hear them jabbering. The bad news is they're moving a lot faster than us. We can't outrun them."

Alicia gritted her teeth. "Can anything else go wrong tonight?" she declared, her voice ringing with frustration. Her temper flared. She decided it was time to strike back.

She stopped running. Standing in the middle of the thoroughfare, Alicia closed her eyes and concentrated. "Five, you say? Three blocks back?"

"Less than that, now," said Molly. She looked at Alicia with a mixture of curiosity and admiration. "You planning to fight them? A single ghoul against five Cainites? Remember, they're Blood Guard. Vampires don't come any tougher than that."

"Wrong," said Alicia, viciously. Her lips twisted,

mouthing words in a long-dead language. The air trembled with the force of the spell. Something stirred. The pavement beneath their feet shifted.

Alicia opened her eyes and stared directly at Molly. Her voice purred with satisfaction. "There are things in this world of darkness that are much more deadly than those poor fools. As they have just learned. We can hopefully proceed to our destination without further interruption. You do have a final destination in mind, I assume? We haven't been dashing through the streets for the past hour just on some insane Malkavian whim?"

Molly licked her lips nervously. "He's right, isn't he? You are possessed by the spirit of Anis. Legends say she has the power to raise demons with a word."

"Myths tend to exaggerate, Molly," said a voice from out of the fog. A very ordinary-looking man emerged from the mist. Even the tone of his voice was plain. "I believe it took Ms. Varney an entire sentence to summon the forces of Hell."

"The card player," said Alicia, recognizing the speaker instantly. "Walter Holmes. You started telling my fortune at Perdition a week ago. I never saw anyone handle playing cards with such skill."

"I have always been a gambler," said Holmes cryptically. "Meeting you in the streets is perhaps my greatest risk."

"I criss-crossed the city like you asked, Walter," said Molly. "Figured you would show up sooner or later. I didn't count on those wolves finding us too."

Alicia turned and stared at Molly. "You, an

advisor to the archbishop of New York, obey the requests of a poker player? How interesting."

"Advisor no longer," chanted Molly, resorting to her lunatic Malkavian pose when faced with a question she obviously preferred not to answer directly. "Besides, Walter is stronger."

"I felt there was something odd about you that night at Perdition," said Alicia. "Now I know I was right. You masked your thoughts extremely well."

"I still do," said Walter with the faintest of smiles. "It is part of my charm. Meanwhile, may I suggest we depart this area immediately? There are other Blood Guard prowling the streets in search of you. Destroying them all might strain even the Queen of Night's powers."

"Perhaps," said Alicia. She never admitted limitations to her abilities. As a human, she was able to channel only a fraction of Anis' power through her body. She could use Disciplines like Temporis only for mere seconds. A major summoning spell, like *Edge of Hell's Abyss*, drained her strength for hours. She had no intention, however, of revealing that fact to anyone. Better to let them worry than allow them to realize her weakness.

"I could use something to eat and drink," she declared. "And, my body needs a rest. I'm exhausted."

"My car is parked a few blocks away," said Holmes. "Driving in this fog, while difficult, is not impossible using the Auspex Discipline. I suggest we leave the city entirely. With Melinda in charge, the Sabbat's blood war has come to an abrupt end.

Besides, I assume you want to return to New York City as soon as possible."

"Manhattan?" said Alicia, instantly alert. "What are you talking about?"

"Sorry," said Holmes. "I thought you knew. Immediately after Melinda seized control of the Sabbat, she sent a group of ghouls north with instructions to attack the Varney Building in New York. Your headquarters is very likely under siege as we speak."

Chapter 3

Paris, France — March 25, 1994:

The floor of the catacombs was covered with bones. There were millions upon millions of bones, extending seemingly forever into the dark tunnels. Le Clair, who often claimed he had the soul of a philosopher, though he did not believe in the supernatural, found the sight inspiring.

"Look on my works, ye Mighty," he declared solemnly, as they descended into the blackness. They had long since left the tourist section of the catacombs and were in a region without well-defined paths or electric lights. Neither mattered. All three of them possessed the power to see in the dark. And Baptiste delighted in crushing the brittle, dry bones beneath his feet. "And despair."

"Nicely put," said Jean Paul. "But, I think the line has been used somewhere before."

"Great minds think alike," said Le Clair.

"I thought you told the Toreador bitch that art was a waste of time," said Jean Paul, as he watched Baptiste plow ahead, smashing a path through mounds of skeletons. "Remember, *mon ami?*"

"Painting is crap," said Le Clair defensively. "Dance is crap. Music is crap. But poetry, that is different. Poetry is philosophy. Like science, it is truth."

"Ah," said Jean Paul. "My apologies. The difference escaped my uneducated mind. I understand now."

After learning of the entrance to the catacombs from Marie Rouchard, they had decided to wait until the next evening to enter the tunnels. They spent the daylight hours resting comfortably in the Countess' mansion. Now it was shortly after sunset. They had all night to find and destroy Phantomas.

Le Clair spat blood in annoyance. "Don't mock me, Jean Paul. I hate... "

"I found it," roared Baptiste, drowning out Le Clair's protest. "I found it. Here it is."

It was a narrow passage leading off to the right of the main tunnel. The corridor sloped downward at a sharp angle, beneath the very heart of Paris. The ceiling was so low that Baptiste could not walk without bending his head. A thick layer of dust covered the floor, indicating that the passage had not seen use in many years. But, there were no skeletons.

"You think this tunnel leads to the Nosferatu's lair?" asked Jean Paul.

"I expect so," said Le Clair. They were spread out in a line, with him in the lead, Baptiste second, and Jean Paul bringing up the rear. Le Clair was the quickest thinker. Baptiste was the group's strong anchor, while Jean Paul provided the necessary dose of caution. "Those ugly Nosferatu bastards always design their hideaways with five or six exits. They're terrified of being trapped underground by their enemies. With a bit of luck, we'll surprise this

Phantomas as he emerges from one of his own escape routes."

"That's if we're lucky," said Jean Paul. He was a pessimist by nature. "What if we're not?"

"Then, he'll sense our approach and flee before we arrive," answered Le Clair. "It won't make a big difference. Wherever he goes, we'll follow. And squash him like a bug when he's caught."

"Ain't this tunnel ever gonna end?" asked Baptiste. "Seems like we've been heading down forever. And the damned passage twists and turns too much."

"I wouldn't complain," said Le Clair. "Most Nosferatu fill these antechamber corridors with giant poison fungi. They don't like visitors."

"Don't matter none to me," said Baptiste. "I'm after his blood. And I'm... "

The sound of metal screeching interrupted the giant's words in midsentence. A steel slab five feet long and five feet wide, covered with six-inch-long spikes, swung out in a vicious arc from the right wall. Le Clair shrieked in surprise.

Almost casually, Baptiste stepped forward and shoved his companion out of the way. Two massive hands slammed into the space between the spikes. The giant was incredibly strong. Groaning in protest, the deadly gate came to an abrupt stop. With a shove, Baptiste pushed the slab backward until it touched the wall. A lock clicked, the spikes folded over and all was as it had been seconds earlier.

"A typical Nosferatu trap," declared Jean Paul,

gingerly examining the mechanism as they stepped carefully past the gate. "Triggered by pressure from a floor plate, I would guess. Crude but effective. Might I suggest that we let Baptiste take the lead?"

"Good idea," said Le Clair, motioning the giant forward. "Stay alert. There will be more such ambushes before we find our quarry's lair."

"Like I was sayin'," declared Baptiste, "I'm after his blood. Ain't no dumb traps gonna stop me."

The ceiling collapsed a hundred feet further, burying them in tons of rock and debris. Veterans of the First World War, they had endured similar disasters in the trenches. It took the trio twenty minutes of feverish digging to reemerge from the cave-in.

"*Mon dieu*, that brought back old memories," said Le Clair. "It is fortunate we no longer require air."

"Holding our breath for that long might have been difficult," said Jean Paul laconically. "This Nosferatu scum seems determined to protect his privacy."

"These traps are aimed at mortals, not vampires," said Le Clair. "I suspect Phantomas relies on anonymity to protect him from those like us. All the better. It means he will be unprepared for our attack."

"Maybe," said Jean Paul, always the skeptic. "Though I suspect any Kindred who has survived for two thousand years is no cretin."

"Enough yakking," declared Baptiste. "Night ain't gonna last forever. Let's start moving."

They forged onward. An exploding container of

poison gas added further evidence to Le Clair's assertion that Phantomas' traps were aimed at humans. As did the automatic machine guns spread along a section of corridor and set to start firing when the victim was halfway through. Jean Paul easily disabled their circuits with his mind.

"Feels like we're walking to Berlin," said Baptiste. "I wish this damned tunnel would come to an end."

It did. Fifty feet farther, the corridor stopped abruptly at a blank wall.

"Merde! It can't end like this," said Le Clair, his brow wrinkled in bewilderment. "Why bother setting traps in a passage that leads nowhere? It makes no sense."

"Since when did the thoughts of the Nosferatu make sense?" Jean Paul remarked. "But, I agree with you. The tunnel cannot stop. Thus, it does not. It merely seems to."

Grinning, Jean Paul stepped forward, into the stone. He disappeared without a sound, then reappeared, an instant later, still smiling.

"As I thought," he declared. "It is nothing but an illusion. It is good enough to fool the kine. But not hunters like ourselves. Ignore it. The corridor continues as before on the other side."

A hundred feet further, the passage took a sharp turn to the left. A dim light, the first they had seen since they entered the corridor, came from around the corner. Le Clair laid a cautioning hand on Baptiste's arm.

"Beware. I sense life ahead. But nothing natural

lives this deep beneath the earth."

"I'm not afraid," said Baptiste. "Nothing scares me, Le Clair. You should know that by now."

His expression arrogant, the giant vampire rounded the bend. Much more cautiously, his two companions followed. They didn't need to hurry. Baptiste stood frozen in place, his eyes wide with astonishment, a step beyond the turn.

"*Mon dieu*," whispered Le Clair. "A spawning pool."

They stood in a circular cavern forty feet across and ten feet high. Six other passages opened into the chamber. It was the center room of a gigantic underground labyrinth. Oddly out of place, a lone electric light hung from the ceiling, illuminating the area with a sickly yellow glow.

In the exact center of the cave was a small pool of liquid perhaps eight feet in diameter. The water was tinted dark pink. More than a dozen creatures surrounded the basin; several of these were drinking from its contents. It was the sight of them that had stopped Baptiste. The inhabitants of the cavern were monstrous beyond belief.

There were rats the size of ponies lapping up the water with incredibly long tongues. A black beetle as big as a dog, its mandibles clicking, circled the edge of the chamber. A pair of gigantic centipedes, the size of pythons, were intertwined on the walls. A foot-long lizard scurried across the ground, its huge eyes the size of tennis balls.

"By the mercy of my mother," whispered Le Clair, "it is exactly as the stories say. The beasts feed off the pool water, transformed by drops of the Nosferatu's blood. The mixture makes them huge. And it twists their form just as the vampire is twisted."

"Stop gawking, you cretins," Jean Paul snapped. "These horrors are ghouls of a sort. Their minds are most likely linked telepathically with Phantomas. We must leave this cursed place at once, or they will undoubtedly make trouble."

Baptiste shook his head. "I'm not going in that place. I can't. It ain't natural."

"*We're* not natural," Jean Paul shot back. He strode forward and gave the big man a stinging slap across the face. "Turning back is out of the question. The tunnel collapsed, remember? It's kill or be killed now. Either Phantomas dies or we do. Now, follow me. And hurry along. You, too, Le Clair."

Jean Paul took the lead. Baptiste, his face a mask of barely repressed horror, followed. Le Clair, mesmerized by the size and grisly appearance of the creatures, came last.

They walked slowly but steadily, with Jean Paul watching their every step. The rats stared at them but made no move to delay their passage. The huge bugs ignored them. The lizard scuttled out of their path.

"There is no reason to be afraid," said Jean Paul as they approached a massive log covered with moss that stretched from the edge of a corridor right to the pool. He swiveled his head and grinned at Le Clair. "These ugly brutes take after their master. They hide beneath the earth, afraid of the surface world. We have nothing to fear from them."

As if in response to Jean Paul's remark, the mottled green and brown log, a dozen steps ahead, rose up from the ground. Le Clair's jaw dropped. What they had assumed was a gigantic piece of wood, a remnant of some long-abandoned building project, was a gigantic crocodile. Blood-red eyes, huge as saucers, stared at them hungrily.

Opening its immense jaws to reveal yellow teeth the size of carving knives, the monster lunged forward. It moved incredibly fast for something so huge. Jean Paul never had a chance. The crocodile's mouth closed on his head like a child fastening on a piece of hard candy. With a click that rang through the cavern, the monster snapped its teeth together, decapitating Jean Paul before he could even scream.

"*Merde*," croaked Le Clair, numb with shock as he watched the body of his friend dissolve into dust. "Jean Paul."

With a croaking roar that shook the cavern, the crocodile opened its jaws again. Le Clair felt like he was staring into the mouth of hell. He stood immobilized with fear as the monster took a giant step forward. Behind him, the huge rats, squealing in panic, plunged into the open tunnels.

"Come on, Le Clair," said Baptiste, grabbing him by the arm. The giant half-dragged, half-carried Le Clair toward the passage directly behind the crocodile. "You wanna be next? We gotta move."

Stumbling clumsily through the darkness, they soon left the horrors of the spawning pool behind.

Nothing followed them. The crocodile was too big to squeeze into the passageway. Le Clair had no way of knowing how many years the monster had lived beside the tainted pool. But, from the size of the creature, he suspected it had been feasting on the water mixed with Nosferatu blood for centuries.

"We must be getting close to Phantomas' hideaway," he declared after fifteen minutes of silence. "I can sense the presence of a powerful vampire in the vicinity. He cannot be far from here."

"Good," grunted Baptiste. He did not seem to be affected by Jean Paul's unexpected demise. "I want his vitae. Think of the power it contains."

"You will get all you deserve, my friend," promised Le Clair, his mind whirling. With Jean Paul gone, he alone was responsible for Baptiste. The giant was incredibly powerful but also incredibly stupid. Keeping him in line was a full-time job. It was not something Le Clair enjoyed. If Baptiste also perished on this quest, Le Clair would be free to feast on Phantomas' blood — and gain mastery over the Nosferatu's domain.

It was a tempting prospect. And Le Clair had never been able to resist temptation.

Chapter 4

Vienna, Austria — March 25, 1994:

Etrius scowled at the neonate. "What do you want?" he demanded, his voice cold as the night wind. "I left word that I was not to be disturbed."

"I—I know, master," stuttered the apprentice, sounding confused. "But the lady insisted. She said to give you this note."

Etrius' frown deepened. As a member of the Inner Council of Clan Tremere, he was not accustomed to being disobeyed. Normally, he would have had the neonate severely disciplined for interrupting his studies. It was clear to him, however, that the force of his unknown visitor's personality had overwhelmed the novice's conditioning. The lady had to be a vampire of incredible mental powers, and he was not expecting any such visitor. His curiosity aroused, he opened the folded slip of paper.

Written on it, in elaborate calligraphy, was the single letter E. Etrius looked at the neonate sharply. "Who saw this stranger other than you?"

"No one, master," said the novice. "She arrived a few minutes ago. I—I brought her here immediately. It seemed the right thing to do."

Etrius nodded. He had expected nothing less. His

visitor traveled in secret. Which left him with the annoying decision of what to do with the neonate who had ushered her to his chamber.

Destroying the novice, he decided quickly, would raise questions. Solving a mystery by creating another never worked. It was easier to erase memories than apprentices.

"When you leave this chamber," he said, his gaze fixed on the neonate, "tell the lady to enter. Then, return to your post. When you arrive, forget what occurred in the past thirty minutes. No one came to the door. You never escorted anyone to my chambers. Nothing happened. Understand? Nothing at all."

The apprentice nodded, mesmerized by the sound of Etrius' voice. "Yes, Councilor. Nothing happened. I understand."

"Good," said Etrius. "Now, depart."

Etrius rose to his feet as his visitor entered the room. The woman wore a long hooded cloak that shrouded her features in shadows. In her left hand she gripped an elaborately carved wooden staff. The presence of the mystic talisman merely confirmed the stranger's identity.

"My dear Elaine," said Etrius, with a slight bow. "I am honored by your presence."

The stranger threw back her hood, revealing the attractive face of a young woman. She had high cheekbones, milky-white skin, and ruby-red lips. Her thick golden hair fell in two long braids nearly to her waist. Her dark blue eyes blazed with an intense inner fire. She was Elaine de Calinot.

ROBERT WEINBERG

Originally a noblewoman of the fifteenth-century French court, she was a member of the Inner Circle of Clan Tremere.

"Always the gentleman, Etrius," she replied, with a slight curtsy. Raised among nobility, Elaine retained her sense of style no matter what her outfit.

"Sit," said Etrius, pointing to a high-backed wooden chair directly facing him across his desk. "Your visit, though unexpected, is welcome. We have hardly been in contact since that unfortunate episode at the Brocken."

Elaine was puzzled by his remark. "The Brocken?"

"Last year," said Etrius. "The failed attempt to return our lost mortality. You were not present in person, but you followed the events telepathically."

"I remember now," said Elaine. She smiled faintly. "The attempt failed."

"A miserable night," said Etrius, "filled with chaos and deception." He fingered the key dangling around his neck. "It was a dangerous gamble. Luckily, none of the Inner Circle were destroyed."

"I didn't come here tonight to discuss the past," said Elaine. "We need to speak of the present. And the future."

"You come in secret," said Etrius, his eyes narrowing to slits. "Are there new troubles in Africa?"

The Inner Circle had divided the world into seven regions. Elaine was the Councilor for Africa. It was a difficult area to control.

"There are always troubles in Africa," replied

Elaine. "I suspect ancient Kindred sleep beneath the sands, trying to manipulate my actions."

"Your predecessors as Councilors for the region disappeared under unexplained circumstances," said Etrius.

"I know," said Elaine. She sounded weary. She needed an assistant, but like most Tremere elders, she trusted no one. "The fact that certain members of our clan, Embraced hundreds of years ago, dislike being led by a woman does not make my job any easier. Keeping them in line is not a favorite task of mine."

"They are fools," said Etrius. "You are among the most competent of the Inner Circle."

"I do my best," said Elaine, leaning forward in her chair so that her elbows rested on Etrius' desk. "At the moment, my pontifices can handle the minor problems. And compared to the horror we face, all other difficulties *are* minor."

Etrius nodded, as a strange feeling overwhelmed his senses. For an instant, he felt as if he was sharing his body with another. Everything he saw through his eyes, heard through his ears, was absorbed by him and a ghostly, invisible companion. It was an eerie sensation. And as quickly as the sensation had begun, it came to an end.

"Did you experience that?" Etrius anxiously asked his guest.

"Experience what?" replied Elaine. "I experienced nothing unusual."

"Forget it," said Etrius, with a shake of his head. "My imagination. Tell me why you came."

It had been Tremere, Etrius decided silently. The clan founder had Blood Bound the Inner Circle and could mentally eavesdrop on their conversations whenever two or more of them gathered. Though he rested in torpor, Tremere still maintained a tight grip on the Order he had started.

"I read with great interest the account of your recent dream about the mysterious Count St. Germain and his alliance with Tremere. Perhaps, since I was Embraced long after the events took place, I found the story a great deal more believable than did the other Councilors. They dismissed your tale because it conflicted with their memories of the event. Since I had none, I found your suspicions frightening."

"You believe, then, as I do, that St. Germain existed as a vampire before the creation of our clan," said Etrius. "And that he persuaded Tremere to drink the formula that converted us from a society of mages into an order of vampires?"

"I believe," said Elaine.

"You did not answer my letter thus," said Etrius. "Nor did you support my claim with the others."

"Just because I agreed with you does not mean I will act like a fool," said Elaine. "I thought it best to contact you in secret, then reveal my suspicions to the others. I do not trust them."

Etrius folded his arms across his chest. He did not like the direction in which this conversation was turning. "What do you mean?"

Elaine did not answer immediately. Instead, she rose from her chair, staff in hand, and walked around the chamber. Her voice, soft and sweet, chanted in an ancient tongue as she marched. Every few steps, she raised and then lowered her staff, weaving a complex series of designs in the air. Etrius, one of the most powerful sorcerers in the world, immediately recognized the spell as a powerful privacy bond.

"You actually think someone would dare listen to our deliberations?" he asked Elaine when she returned to her chair. He smiled. "We are two of the most powerful Kindred in the world."

"I make no assumptions," said Elaine, her features grim. "I deal in facts. We both know that I am the third Councilor to Africa. The first two disappeared under mysterious circumstances. In the past few months, I have been subjected to an increasing number of psychic attacks. My enemy remains unseen. Defending myself has become more and more difficult. Whoever works against me has powers equal to my own."

"You suspect a member of the Inner Circle?" asked Etrius.

"No," said Elaine. "I would recognize the magic. My enemy is a stranger."

"And you think the same enemy was responsible for the elimination of your predecessors?" asked Etrius. "The implications are not pleasant."

"My thought exactly," said Elaine. "That's why your letter worried me so much. Is it possible that my hidden adversary might be the mysterious Count St. Germain? Is he still manipulating Clan Tremere for his own purposes?"

Etrius scowled. "I do not know. My search of the chantry journal has turned up nothing about St. Germain. He is a name, nothing more. Whatever legends exist about his execution in the nineteenth century, I believe he started to conceal his true nature. It is quite possible he yet exists."

"And that he orchestrates our moves like pieces on a gigantic chessboard," said Elaine.

"The possibility that St. Germain controls my destiny disturbs me greatly," declared Etrius. "I am not a pawn."

"Nor am I," said Elaine. "But, how many of the mortals we used to further our plans, our ambitions, said the same things, never realizing that we were pulling their strings? How can we be sure that we are free, Etrius? How can we be *absolutely* sure?"

"You are leading up to something, Elaine," said Etrius. "Stop playing word games with me. What exactly do you want?"

"We cannot trap St. Germain on our own," said Elaine. "Not if he has been dominating us for centuries. Finding and destroying him is impossible for Clan Tremere. What we must do instead is persuade the elders of the other clans that compose the Camarilla to do the job for us."

"How?" Etrius demanded. His lips curled into a sneer. "Appeal to their spirit of cooperation? I don't think that will work. Most of the Kindred hate us. They consider our clan to be dangerous upstarts, trying to become the rulers of the undead. Which, of course, is absolutely true. Why would they agree to help us find St. Germain?"

"They will do it if they feel it is in *their* best interests," said Elaine. "Greed and fear motivate the Damned. We merely need to persuade them that the Count threatens their rule."

"I assume you have such a scheme?" said Etrius. He appeared amused. "I must admit I am amazed. You never struck me before as being so devious. It is an entirely new side of your personality."

"With my existence threatened," said Elaine, "I rise to the occasion."

"What is your plan?"

"We need to address an emergency Conclave of Kindred elders," said Elaine. "The sooner it is held the better."

"Such meetings can only be called by a Justicar," said Etrius.

Elaine nodded. "As the enforcers of the Traditions of the Camarilla, it is their right. Moreover, as they serve as both judge and executioner for the sect, they take their responsibilities very seriously." She chuckled. "Such serious-minded Kindred are the easiest to manipulate."

"There are seven Justicars, representing each clan in the Camarilla," said Etrius. "Not all of them are fools."

"We need only to convince one," said Elaine, laughing. "It will be easy. Especially when we explain the threat that needs to be addressed. Clan leaders from all over Europe will attend the conference."

"I don't understand," said Etrius. "What threat?"

"Conclaves are often held to declare a Blood Hunt against an enemy of the Camarilla," said Elaine. "Oftentimes, it is an unruly prince whose actions threaten the Masquerade. At this meeting, however, we will present evidence that the Count St. Germain menaces the very actuality of the sect. The Conclave, having been presented with the facts, will be forced to demand that St. Germain be destroyed. What we cannot accomplish on our own, the Justicars of the Camarilla will do for us."

"An excellent notion," said Etrius, "except for one small detail. How do you intend to convince the elders of the Camarilla that the Count St. Germain is a threat to anyone other than Clan Tremere?"

"It is all quite simple, my dear Etrius," said Elaine. "We shall tell them that the Count St. Germain is the Red Death."

"What!" roared Etrius, half-rising from his desk in shock. "How do you know? What proof do you have?"

Elaine smiled. "Calm yourself. I have no proof. To the best of my knowledge, none exists. We will have to manufacture some. It can be done."

"St. Germain and the Red Death," said Etrius, thoughtfully. "You think the clan elders will believe us?"

"I am convinced they will," said Elaine. "The leaders of the Camarilla are terribly worried about the Red Death. His attacks frighten them. They are fearful of that which they cannot understand."

Etrius sat silent for a few minutes, mentally

reviewing the notion in his mind. Finally, he nodded his agreement. "The best lies are the most outrageous ones. They might swallow it."

"Good," said Elaine, rising from her chair. "It grows late. I must leave. Tomorrow, we can decide what proof the Conclave will demand from us. Manufacturing a few clues shouldn't require much effort."

"You will not stay at the chantry house?" asked Etrius.

"The less we are seen together, the better," said Elaine. "Too many eyes watch us already."

"Good night, then," he said, escorting her to the door of his chamber. "Be careful. If St. Germain is the enemy behind the attacks against you, he will not take kindly to this new offensive."

Elaine nodded. "That is why I prefer to lodge elsewhere. His power is greatest inside these walls. You are the one who should be careful, not I."

Left alone, Etrius stroked his chin thoughtfully. He had not said a word to Elaine about Peter Spizzo, the vampire he had set on St. Germain's trail several days earlier. Nor did he intend to do so when they spoke again. Some secrets were best kept concealed.

He did not entirely trust Elaine. Her sudden personality change bothered him. Plus, she seemed totally unaware of the old ties that bound them closer than most Kindred. Some bonds were never forgotten. Etrius planned to cooperate with her scheme, but he vowed to be prepared for any treachery she might be planning.

Very prepared.

Chapter 5

Washington, D.C. - March 25, 1994:

Tony Blanchard hung up the phone. Grinning broadly, he turned around to face Don Lazzari. The vampire sat in a black leather armchair at the head of the long table in the meeting room, reading an Anne Rice paperback novel. An amused expression on his face, the Mafia chief raised his gaze from the printed page to stare at Tony.

"Good news?" he asked.

"Very good news," said Tony. "That was Joey Campbell, a cheap hood working out in the 'burbs. He spotted the truck. I told him to come by and pick up his loot. He should arrive in thirty minutes."

"Excellent," said Don Lazzari. "Excellent."

The vampire rose from his seat with a fluid, snakelike motion. Tony shivered. The Cainite gave him the creeps. Despite the fact that he looked human, Don Lazzari was not. He was a monster with a heart of ice, a true member of the Damned.

"Joey won't talk unless he's paid in advance," said Tony. "No offense, but, like I said, he's a small operator. He's not big on trust."

"I understand perfectly," said Don Lazzari, with a nod. "The Mafia has deep pockets, Tony. We can afford to be generous."

The vampire walked to the phone and dialed a number. A few seconds later, he murmured a few lines into the receiver. Nodding with satisfaction, he hung up.

"Give me a pen and paper," he said to Tony.

The Don scribbled a Washington address on the sheet and handed it to Tony. "Send one of your bodyguards to this location. Ask him to tell the doorkeeper that Don Lazzari sent him. The money will be waiting in small bills."

"Fine," said Tony. He looked at the paper. With a start, he realized that the address was that of a prominent political figure. "Alvin can go. He drives fast."

"Tony," said Don Lazzari, as Blanchard headed for the door, "it would be wise for you to forget that address. Wipe it from your memory."

"Uh, yeah, sure, Don Lazzari," said Tony, beads of sweat tricking down his back. The vampire's tone of voice made it quite clear that this request was not a suggestion.

"Likewise," continued the Cainite, "any hint that my conversations on this phone line might be tapped would cause me equal displeasure."

"Record your messages?" said Tony, chuckling nervously. "Never happen, Don Lazzari. After all, the Syndicate is cooperating fully with the Mafia. I'm your point man in America. Your ghoul. We trust each other."

"Good," said Don Lazzari, returning to the head of the table. Settling down in his chair, he opened his book. "Trust between a leader and his loyal troops is a wonderful thing, Tony. I'm glad we agree on its importance. Now, leave me to Lestat and his foolish enterprises. Go."

"Yes, sir, Don Lazzari," said Tony, hurrying to the exit. "I'll tell you the minute Joey Campbell shows up."

Tony forced himself to walk down the stairs slowly; he did not want to appear to be hurrying. His heart was pounding so hard that his chest felt as if it would burst. He had to send Alvin after the money. And he needed to dial Preston and tell him to stop monitoring the outgoing phone calls — immediately.

Joey Campbell arrived in twenty minutes. He was early. Short and thin, with coal-black hair and eyes that blinked constantly, he reminded Tony of a ferret on speed. Joey always looked ready to bolt for the exit at the first sign of trouble.

He lit his new cigarette with the butt of the old one. "Okay," he said, his head bobbing back and forth like a puppet on a string, "where's this big, bad Mafia dude? I wanna see the color of his fuckin' money before I spill my story."

Tony glared at Joey. "Watch your mouth, shithead," he said angrily. "You talk like that to Don Lazzari and you're fucked. And not the way you like it, either."

"I'm not scared of some dickless wonder from I-tal-y," said Joey, pronouncing each syllable distinctly. "Nobody spooks Joey Campbell."

"Ain't that nice," said Tony, looking over at Theodore, his other bodyguard. He smiled. "Joey's a tough guy. At least, he talks a good fight. I think it's time for him to meet Don Lazzari. They have business to discuss."

Joey's eyes nearly popped from their sockets when he saw Don Lazzari. The vampire exuded menace. When he smiled, Campbell would have bolted from the room if Tony and Theodore hadn't been holding him by each arm.

"Please sit down, Mr. Campbell," said Don Lazzari, politely. He pointed to a chair. "Do not be afraid. I mean you no harm. In fact, I am prepared to make you a rich man for the information you possess."

Joey slid into his seat. His gaze never left Don Lazzari. When he spoke, his voice was barely more than a whisper.

"I found the truck you want. Spotted the rig this evening. Didn't see any dame inside the cab, but it's the right one. I checked the description real close."

"No one saw you?" said Don Lazzari.

Joey shook his head. "Naah. I'm no dope. I never went too near to the truck. Scoped it out long-distance with a pair of binoculars. Figured it was best to be real careful."

"You told no one else of your discovery?" asked the Mafia chief.

"Are you crazy?" said Joey. "I ain't splitting this cash with no partners."

"A good policy," said Don Lazzari. "A wise man keeps his own counsel. Now, Mr. Campbell, please tell us where to find the vehicle."

Joey licked his lips nervously. "There was, uh, a

reward for finding this here rig. Not to be pushy or nothing, but I got my expenses."

The Mafia chief nodded. "I understand perfectly what you are saying. After all, we are both businessmen, Mr. Campbell. As an independent contractor, you expect to be paid on delivery of the merchandise. Or, in this case, the information."

Don Lazzari looked at Tony. "The money? Where is it?"

"That sounds like Alvin right now," said Tony, breathing a quick sigh of relief as a car rumbled to a stop in front of the house. Don Lazzari was playing the gracious host to Joey Campbell. Tony wasn't exactly sure why. But he definitely did not want to be the one who burst the bubble.

A minute later, Alvin handed the Mafia chief a black leather attaché case. It wasn't locked. Don Lazzari popped open the top, revealing stacks and stacks of tens and twenties, banded together by elastics.

"Twenty-five thousand dollars in small unmarked bills," he said, passing the briefcase over to Joey Campbell. "Feel free to count it if you like, Mr. Campbell."

Joey shook his head. He was smart enough not to push his luck. "Ain't no need. I trust you."

"Thank you. The location, please?"

"The rig's parked in a rest stop twenty miles outside D.C.," said Joey. He proceeded to give Tony exact directions to the lot. "You won't have any trouble finding it."

"You agree, Tony?" asked Don Lazzari.

UNHOLY ALLIES

"Yeah, no problems," answered Tony. "I know the spot. It's nice and deserted. Coordinating an attack there will be easy. If that's what you still want to do."

Don Lazzari closed his eyes, as if contemplating his plans. "I think that would be best," he said. "Why should I allow another Kindred the honor of the kill? Who better to execute the bitch than me?"

The Mafia chief opened his eyes and stared directly at Joey. "Thank you for your information, Mr. Campbell. Your help has been greatly appreciated. You are free to go." Don Lazzari hesitated for a moment. "Please give me back the briefcase, though, before you leave."

"Huh?" said Joey, as he was rising out of his chair. "Whatcha say?"

"I want the cash returned," said Don Lazzari coldly. "Money is worthless to a dead man."

The Don signaled Theodore. The huge bodyguard grabbed Joey from behind, wrapping powerful arms around the crook's neck. Caught completely off-guard, Campbell never had a chance. With a quick twist, Theodore wrenched Joey's head around and back. His spine broke with a crack like a gunshot. His face blue, his eyes wide with shock, Joey dropped to the floor. A boot to his chin finished the job.

"Efficiently done," said Don Lazzari. He held the briefcase in both hands. "The fool actually thought I was going to let him leave with the money. How refreshingly naive."

"Yeah," said Tony, licking his lips nervously.

"The guy was awfully stupid."

"Summon your men," said the vampire. "Let them surround the truck. But tell them not to act until we arrive."

The Cainite walked around the table, the attaché case dangling from one hand. "A wise man trusts no one," he said, stepping over Joey's corpse. "Especially those in power."

He gave the briefcase to Alvin. "Put this in the safe. It might prove useful later."

Tony swallowed hard, noticing that Alvin now obeyed Don Lazzari's orders without hesitation. He could feel control of his men, and his organization, slipping through his fingers. The vampire's words about trust, in complete contradiction to his earlier statement, made it absolutely clear that nothing he said could be believed. Tony's future began to look increasingly dark.

As if reading his thoughts, Don Lazzari smiled at Tony. "Better to live as a loyal servant," he said, "than die a martyred leader."

Numbly, Tony nodded. There was absolutely nothing he could say.

Chapter 6

The East Coast — March 25, 1994:

Walter Holmes drove in the same way that he existed: inconspicuously. Alicia, who believed that speed limits were meant to be broken, was not pleased.

"Can't you go any faster?" she asked, for the twentieth time, as they raced through another small town in Maryland at twenty-five mph. "It will be sunrise in another hour."

"Speeding through a tiny community at 5 a.m. is sure to attract attention," replied Walter, calmly. He gestured with his head at the cigarette billboard on their left. "There's a police car waiting behind that sign, tracking us with a radar gun. Getting stopped by them would be a disaster."

"I can buy and sell towns this size," said Alicia, impatiently. "Tickets don't worry me."

"They should," said Walter. "You're not carrying any money on you. If Melinda is as smart and ruthless as her reputation claims, she's guessed by now that you are heading for New York. Her agents are probably not far behind us. We can't risk even a minute's delay."

Once outside city limits, Walter stepped on the gas. "Besides, as a member of the Sabbat, you know that many police forces in this area are on the take from drug dealers. It's quite possible that your picture is being circulated among them as we speak. With orders to shoot to kill."

Alicia grimaced. She hated to be wrong. Especially so obviously wrong. "That's why you've avoided the major highways?"

"Exactly," said Walter. "We can't trust anyone. Melinda wields the power now, not Justine. The hunter has become the hunted."

"Melinda knows what I look like," said Alicia. She glanced at Molly, sitting silently in the back seat, playing games with her fingers. "Same for Molly. Not you, though. Why bother with the two of us? Nobody's aware of your involvement in our escape. If you left us now, you'd be in the clear."

"Under normal circumstances," admitted Holmes, "that's exactly what I would do. However, these are unusual times. I find I can no longer merely monitor events. The situation calls for direct action on my part."

Alicia stared silently at Walter for a few minutes. She seemed lost in thought.

"Inconnu?" she asked unexpectedly.

"Anis, Queen of Night?" Holmes replied, immediately.

Alicia burst out laughing. "Two mysterious characters in search of identity," she declared. "Keep your secrets, card shark, and I will do the same. I apologize for asking."

"Apology accepted," said Holmes, smiling.

"No more joking," said Molly from the back seat

suddenly. "The Red Death's smoking."

Holmes' expression turned serious. "We are united in a common belief," he said. "The Red Death threatens the very existence of the Kindred. He must be stopped."

"He's definitely no favorite of mine," said Alicia. "But, I am surprised to hear you make such a statement. It is a commonly held belief that certain elements of the undead merely observe the struggles of their race, but never interfere."

Holmes nodded, his expression bland and unchanging. "I have heard such rumors myself. There is probably some truth to them. However, I also suspect that any such group is wise enough to realize when an exception must be made to the rules." He paused. "Or at least certain members possess such insight."

"Walter's cool," said Molly. "He's no fool."

"How did you ever recruit Molly?" asked Alicia, glancing at the Cainite in the back. Molly, her hands folded together in a fist, was thumb wrestling. "She's demented."

"We shared a common love of gambling," said Walter. "Some years ago, I proposed she take an even bigger risk by spying on Justine for me. I thought the idea would appeal to her Malkavian sense of the absurd. Obviously, I was correct. She accepted and has worked for me ever since."

"I can see how she would be a marvelous poker player," said Alicia. "It is impossible to read her expression."

"Molly is quite cunning," said Walter. "When I

concentrate on the game, I am an expert card player. I rarely lose. Except when I play against Molly."

Walter shook his head. "She's typical of her clan," he declared. "I often wonder if the Malkavians are anywhere near as demented as they act. Perhaps they are the truly sane ones, and the rest of us belong in the madhouse."

"I'll leave such ponderous thoughts to the philosophers," said Alicia. "Meanwhile, why don't we discuss the Red Death?"

"An excellent suggestion," said Walter. "I believe an exchange of information would be to our mutual benefit. Perhaps in combining our knowledge, we will discover a method behind this madness."

"Fair enough," said Alicia. "Between the Red Death and Melinda Galbraith, I feel as if the entire world is conspiring against me." She smiled nastily. "I'd like to return the favor."

"Anis is mad," chanted Molly, "which makes her bad."

"The Red Death is a fourth-generation vampire, a Methuselah, who schemes to rule both the Camarilla and the Sabbat," said Alicia, ignoring Molly's latest remark. "He claims that after many centuries spent in torpor, the Third Generation, the Antediluvians, are stirring. Like many elder Kindred, the Red Death fears that when they awaken, the Antediluvians will be consumed by a terrible hunger for blood — Kindred blood. They will become cannibals, devouring their descendants by the thousands. The Red Death feels he is the only Cainite who can prevent the ensuing slaughter from taking place."

"A familiar tale," said Walter Holmes. "I've heard variations of it many times. What proof did this monster offer to bolster his claim about the Antediluvians?"

"The Nictuku are rising," said Alicia. "Baba Yaga has awakened in Russia. Nuckalevee prowls the deserts of Australia. And Gorgo, She Who Screams in Darkness, haunts the Amazon rain forest."

"Depressing news," said Walter Holmes. "The return of those abominations is thought by many Kindred to be a sign of Armageddon approaching. Did the Red Death state how he was going to stop the Antediluvians?"

"Of course not," said Alicia. "He was long on generalities but very short on specifics. Nor did he ever explain why he in particular was the right choice to lead the Kindred, though he implied there was a reason."

"Maybe he thinks his control of fire is justification enough," said Holmes. "It is an awesome Discipline."

Alicia nodded. "The Red Death is quite powerful. He belongs to an unknown bloodline. And," she paused dramatically, to emphasize her point, "he has at least three childer with the same command of fire."

Walter Holmes turned his head and stared at Alicia for a moment. His eyes glinted with surprise, but his voice remained relaxed. "Four Red Deaths? Are they similar in appearance?"

"Exact duplicates of the original," said Alicia.

"They even spoke with the same voice. They differed only in the degree of their psychic power."

Holmes nodded. "Interesting. That explains a great deal about the attacks. I've seen reports claiming the monster struck in several locations throughout America and Europe at approximately the same hour. A multiplicity of Red Deaths would make such claims possible."

"The creature claimed that the attack on Washington was part of a gigantic master plan that would enable it to gain control of the two major sects," said Alicia. She hesitated, debating about whether she should mention her own enterprises to the same end. Such information, she quickly decided, was not relevant to the current conversation. "The same scheme, on another level, was aimed at destroying me and another mortal the Red Death feared."

"Dire McCann," said Holmes. "I've encountered his name before. The rogue mage with powers possessed by no other mortal. I will restrain myself from making the obvious connection between two mortals and two legendary Kindred."

"Restraint is a splendid discipline," said Alicia. "I think I've told you everything I can about our common enemy. What do you offer in exchange?"

"I know nothing more about the Red Death than what you already stated," said Walter Holmes. "However, I believe I know how the monster plans to gain control of the Sabbat. Actually, I should say I know how the Red Death has already gained control of the Sabbat."

"What?" said Alicia and Molly in unison.

"I have been a monitor for hundreds of years," said Walter Holmes. "Along with keeping track of important events, it is my duty to track influential Kindred. During the past century, I have kept a close watch on Melinda Galbraith, scrutinizing her steady rise through the ranks of the Sabbat. She waged a particularly effective campaign of extortion and murder to become regent of the sect. The Melinda Galbraith I observed over the past hundred years *was not* the same Melinda Galbraith I saw earlier tonight."

"Explain yourself," said Alicia curtly.

"The body was the same," said Holmes, "but the personality was all wrong. There were too many inconsistencies in her story, she acted too strange. Her behavior was totally out of character. The more I watched, the more convinced I became. Another Kindred controlled the mind of Melinda Galbraith."

Holmes' voice lost it usual neutral tone. He sounded frightened. "Your story provided the final clue. Melinda's return tonight was no coincidence. It was carefully timed to eliminate Justine Bern and reestablish Melinda's absolute control of the Sabbat.

"Her emergence from hiding is part of a vast conspiracy. The regent of the Sabbat is a puppet controlled by a master schemer. *She is a pawn of the Red Death.*"

Chapter 7

The East Coast — March 25, 1994:

Alicia left the car thirty minutes later. Dawn was approaching and Walter Holmes and Molly needed to find shelter from the sunlight. An isolated motel with a flashing "Vacancy" sign provided them with a place to stay. Anxious to return to Manhattan, Alicia elected to continue on by herself.

"Be careful," Walter Holmes warned as they parted. "While you control vast forces, one ghoul cannot defeat the entire Sabbat. Don't attempt the impossible."

"I realize my limitations," said Alicia. "Still, it will take days for Melinda to marshal the sect's full strength against my headquarters. By then, I plan to be gone. The Red Death may be in charge for the moment. But, I assure you, it is only for the moment. He will learn soon enough that Anis is called the Queen of Night for good reason."

Heeding Walter Holmes' advice, Alicia continued her journey with a minimum of fuss. A farmer bringing goods to early market, with no intention of stopping for hitchhikers, gave her a lift to town. A truck driver heading up the turnpike provided her a ride into Delaware. A traveling salesman, with appointments scheduled throughout the day in Newark, New Jersey, told her dirty jokes the entire drive along the Garden State Parkway. None of the men questioned her presence, and when she left, they instantly forgot she had ever been there. Simple minds called for simple solutions.

Needing cash, she spent twenty minutes in the Greyhound Terminal casually talking to the hookers who were waiting for business. Six different women provided her with ten dollars each. Only once did anyone notice. An irate pimp approached her, obviously intending some sort of violence. Allowing her restraint to slip for a second, Alicia quietly told the man exactly where to go and what to do when he got there. His grotesque suicide made the front page of the next day's newspaper.

Alicia took the Hudson Tubes from downtown Newark to Jersey City to Manhattan. She arrived in New York's business district shortly after 11 a.m. Twenty minutes later, a gypsy cab deposited her a block away from the Varney Building.

The huge superstructure dominated the surrounding scenery. Alicia felt a twinge of satisfaction as she stared at the skyscraper. The building had served as her headquarters for years. She had been instrumental in its design, and many of its special features were known only to her. Everyone else involved in the edifice's construction was long dead. One of the benefits of immortality was outliving all those who knew your secrets.

Alicia sighed. She regretted having to abandon the skyscraper but she had no illusions about the necessity of leaving. Within a few nights, Melinda would have hundreds of vampires swarming through the corridors. Dealing with them would take time and energy. Both were too precious to waste on lesser Kindred. Alicia wanted a second chance at the Red Death. On her terms.

Unlike Walter Holmes, she was not convinced Melinda Galbraith was under the control of the spectral menace. Decades earlier, when Melinda had first assumed command of the Sabbat, Alicia had tried to dominate the regent's mind. Her attempt proved to be too late. Another fourth-generation vampire, a demonic figure out of Mexico's past, had already insinuated itself into Melinda's consciousness. However, even that extremely powerful Cainite was not able to control Melinda completely. It could influence her thoughts, just as Alicia did with Justine, but manipulating the regent's every motion was impossible. If that abomination had been unable to control Melinda after years of trying, Alicia felt certain the same was true for the Red Death. The regent might be acting out of character, but it wasn't because her thoughts were not her own.

There was a small restaurant, called Alice's, located directly across from the Varney Building, featuring a picture of Arlo Guthrie in the window. The place thrived on breakfast and lunch business from employees of the skyscraper across the avenue. Still, people often wondered how the eatery managed to survive offering food at such reasonable prices in a city where rent everywhere was sky high. The answer was simple. The restaurant operated at a loss. It was subsidized by a grant from the Varney Corporation.

The standard excuse the company offered for its actions was that employees needed somewhere to go other than the company cafeteria. It didn't really matter. Nobody cared. Most city taxes were routinely pocketed by the men in charge of collecting the bills. With numerous crack houses and numbers parlors in the neighborhood, worrying about a legitimate restaurant seemed foolish.

Alicia owned every building within a three-block radius of the skyscraper. Most of them she rented to whoever had the money to pay. A few, like Alice's, she maintained absolute control over. In emergencies, those locations proved useful.

Entering the restaurant, Alicia said hello to the manager on duty. "How's business?" she asked.

"Slow," said the man, with a shrug of his shoulders. "Considering the unemployment rate, I guess we should be happy anybody still goes out for lunch."

Alicia nodded, her eyes scanning the occupants of the dining room. A tall, thin, middle-aged man, bald, with bushy eyebrows, caught her attention. He sat at a table near the entrance to the kitchen, eating a bowl of soup and reading the newspaper. He was a ghoul. Which, as far as she was concerned, meant that he was an enemy. "Ever see him before?" asked Alicia.

"Nope," said the manager. "First-time customer."

"Last time, too," said Alicia. "He's going to need medical attention in a few minutes. No need to rush.

They won't be able to help. I'll be in the office in the rear. Don't disturb me."

"You're the boss," said the manager. "I hope no one will think the soup is bad. It's actually quite good today."

Chuckling, Alicia walked over to the bald man's table.

"Enjoying your food?" she asked.

Slowly, the bald man raised his gaze from the newspaper. His eyes widened in recognition. He opened his mouth to say something but whatever it was never emerged. His body froze, his eyes popping open and his hands clutching the paper in a death grip. According to the medical report filed later that afternoon, he died of a massive heart attack. It was definitely not the soup.

"Arrogant bastard," muttered Alicia, sweeping past the unmoving corpse and through the swinging double doors that led to the kitchen. "Watching for me in one of my own restaurants. He was lucky to die so easily."

The three cooks in the kitchen nodded to Alicia but otherwise kept working. They were paid to prepare food, not ask questions. She nodded in return and marched past them to the door marked EMPLOYEES ONLY. Opening it, she stepped inside. The room was empty.

There was a small desk, several chairs, a bulky black iron safe, and a metal file cabinet in the office. Normally, it was used for minor business dealings, paying graft and bribes to city officials, and counting the day's receipts. Only Alicia knew the room's other purpose.

Carefully, she reached out to the rear wall of the chamber, locating a latch only she could see. It turned smoothly. Without a sound, the entire section of the wall disappeared, revealing a tiny cubicle behind the office. Alicia stepped inside, then pressed another invisible button. The paneling slid back into place.

Instantly, a low hum filled the tiny chamber: it was a hidden elevator. It descended to a secret tunnel far beneath the street that connected the restaurant to the subbasement of the Varney building. There were three such elevators within a block of the skyscraper, and three such tunnels. They dated back to the period when the skyscraper was built. Alicia had long believed in being prepared.

A brisk walk down the corridor ended at a wide black door, on which were painted the words DO NOT ENTER. There was no lock or keyhole of any sort. Alicia pushed against the barrier. It yielded without a bit of resistance. She entered the next room, and the door immediately closed behind her. It was recessed in the wall, and there was no handle on its interior. The portal could not be opened from the inside: upon entering the chamber, there was no going back.

Smiling nastily, Alicia crossed the floor of the square room and pressed her palm against a metal plate on the far wall. Just as before, a section of the wall slid back, revealing the interior of another elevator. Alicia stepped inside, the door closing behind her. The strip was coded to her fingerprint only. Anyone else entering the room would be trapped — though not for long. Five minutes after the black door was pulled open, the chamber floor dropped away, sending the hapless intruder plummeting a hundred feet into a pool filled with flesh-eating acid. It was a cruel but effective deterrent to spies trying to break into the skyscraper.

The second elevator deposited her on the thirteenth floor of the skyscraper. Officially, the structure had no such floor. No elevator stopped there. Nor did the emergency stairs. On the outside of the building, a huge mural stretching from the twelfth to fifteenth floor covered the walls. None of those floors had windows. The picture's height off the ground and immense size made it impossible for anyone to guess that it covered four floors, not three.

The hidden floor was unmarked by any dividers or walls. There was no carpet or furniture. Several wooden cabinets, containing clothes and weapons, were set against the walls. The space was clearly designed for function, rather than comfort.

A special high-speed elevator, which Alicia alone could access, provided the only means of entrance or exit to the level. Three of them led to secret passageways like the one she had used to return to her headquarters. A fourth, at the south end of the floor, led upward, to her penthouse apartment. It also connected to a room located far beneath the foundation of the building, a hidden chamber that did not appear in any plans or designs for the skyscraper. A small cell which she alone could enter, the crypt held one object: a silver sarcophagus — Anis's coffin.

Alicia was anxious to return to the suite on the top of the building. She suspected that this was where she would find Sanford Jackson, her second-in-command. She did not know whether he was alive or dead. But in either case, she felt certain that he was not going to be alone.

Alicia considered taking a gun with her on the trip upstairs. There was a small but well-equipped armory on the floor. Though she rarely used firearms, she was a crack marksman. Unlike vampires, ghouls were vulnerable to high-velocity bullets; unfortunately, so was Jackson. After a short internal debate, she vetoed the idea of carrying a weapon. If her aide was not dead, she didn't want to kill him by accident. She would attack using her psychic energy. And her wits.

Alicia stepped into the elevator to the penthouse. Her enemies would pay any price to discover the location of that secret room beneath the foundation of the skyscraper. The blood of a fourth-generation vampire was a prize to die for. She grinned. Tonight, she just might let some of Melinda's minions do exactly that. With this cheering thought, she pressed the button that would send the tiny lift shooting up to the roof.

With the barest whisper of sound, the elevator stopped on the top floor of the skyscraper. The door slid open into Alicia's clothes closet. Careful not to disturb the folding doors that opened to her bedroom, Alicia stepped out of the lift.

Quickly, she did a mental scan of the apartment. No one was in the bedroom. They were all clustered in the large front parlor, close to where the main elevator banks leading to the lower floors were located. Six powerful ghouls, all men, waited there, along with Sanford Jackson. She breathed a small sigh of relief. Though her assistant's thoughts were incoherent and garbled, at least he was still alive.

Alicia was not thrilled by the odds. The past twelve hours had been a hectic scramble and she was starting to feel the strain. The spell she had used against the Blood Guard the night before only worked in darkness, and she needed to be at full strength to use it. Catching a solitary ghoul by surprise in a restaurant and squeezing his heart was easy. Confronting and eliminating six of them was going to be a lot more difficult.

As a ghoul, she was stronger and faster than most humans. As Anis' ghoul, she was also stronger and faster than most other ghouls. However, she was neither invulnerable nor immortal. She was quite mortal. As were her enemies.

That last thought decided her course of action. Her opponents were humans, not vampires. They still possessed some bare traces of emotion. They could be surprised. It was possible to divert their attention for a few moments, though not, perhaps, by ordinary means. Sabbat ghouls were mentally twisted lunatics. Although the men in the other room were not physically twisted, as was the case with many servants of the sect, their minds were bent in strange shapes. It would take a lot to stun them into inaction.

A determined expression on her face, Alicia quickly stripped down to her undergarments. She needed to be as unencumbered as possible for what she wanted to do.

Alicia was an exceptional-looking woman and was in top condition. Though she was several hundred years old, her body had only aged a few years since she had become Anis' ghoul. Physically, she just approached twenty-five. Her body was taut and lean, well muscled and the color of burnished bronze. She worked out regularly and had the reflexes and skills of a trained athlete. She was an expert gymnast.

Taking a deep breath, she flung open the door leading to the front room. "Looking for me?" she asked the startled ghouls. "Here I am."

They were trained killers, twisted madmen dedicated to the service of the Sabbat. Human life meant nothing to them. But they could still be startled. The sight of their intended victim, standing in the doorway behind them, caught them off-guard, and before they could raise their weapons, Alicia hurtled across the room in a lightning-fast series of cartwheels and backflips. The bewildered ghouls watched in astonishment, their weapons momentarily forgotten. It was all the time Alicia needed.

Sanford Jackson, his clothes sliced and shredded in dozens of places, was tied to an inverted wooden crucifix facing the elevators. He hung upside down, a silver plate beneath his head, on which rested a massive butcher knife. His face and chest were caked with blood. Only the slight rise and fall of his chest indicated that he was still alive. Alicia's face flushed with rage as her own anger combined with the fury of Anis. Blackness filled her mind.

The fastest ghoul was just reaching for his gun when she lashed out with her thoughts. The man shrieked in pain, his weapon forgotten. His face turned bright red as blood rushed to his head. Eyes bulging, he dropped to his knees, his screams rising in volume and intensity. With the sound of a rotten pumpkin being hit by a hammer, the man's head exploded, showering his companions with blood and brains.

Another ghoul collapsed to the floor, his body twitching spasmodically as his heart stopped beating. A third and fourth killer managed to draw their guns, only to find themselves aiming at each other's heads. Neither was able to stop his finger from pulling the trigger. Or duck out of the way of the armor-piercing slugs that slammed into their skulls.

That left two assassins. Surrounded by death and destruction, the ghouls somehow managed to step back and raise their weapons. They never had a chance to fire.

Behind them, the massive wooden cross holding Sanford Jackson crashed to the floor. Involuntarily, the pair of killers spun around. Alicia, settled in a crouching position twenty feet away, took full advantage of the opportunity.

Both men's eyes glazed. Dropping their weapons, they stepped around the fallen crucifix and marched to the nearest elevator door. Each taking a sliding panel, they wrenched the portal open, revealing the open elevator shaft. The car was forty stories below. Without a sound, the two ghouls stepped forward. They dropped like stones.

Shaking her head in disbelief, Alicia walked across the room to her assistant. He looked up at her with weary eyes.

"Nice performance," he mumbled through bruised and blackened lips. "I didn't know you were an acrobat. About time you arrived. I was starting to get dizzy hanging upside down."

"How the hell did you get this thing to tumble over?" she asked, kneeling next to the cross. Letting strength flow into her fingers, she tore at the ropes binding Jackson to the wooden cross.

"When they tied me to it, I pretended to be barely conscious," said Jackson. "My muscles were relaxed. That gave me a bit of slack. Then, when I heard your voice and the gunfire, I figured a distraction was in order. So, I tightened up the muscles in my legs. Doing that jerked my body upward and caused a shift in weight. I learned the trick in Vietnam."

He grinned, starting a dozen cuts on his face and chest bleeding. "It's not the first time I've been crucified."

"I'm surprised to find you alive," said Alicia, helping Jackson sit up. "I thought you'd be dead."

"They were saving me for when you came up on

the elevator," said Jackson. "I think they planned to cut my throat just before the doors opened. The sight of my blood pumping out onto a plate was supposed to stop you cold, giving them enough of an edge to cut you to ribbons in a crossfire."

"They should have waited for me doing jumping jacks," said Alicia, grinning. "It would have been more of a shock. I killed six of the creeps here. Do you know if any more of them are in the building?"

"Nine of the bastards came north with me," said Jackson. "I recall one of them saying something about posting lookouts on the street."

"Seven down, two to go," said Alicia. "I'll handle that minor detail shortly. They won't escape. First thing, though, is to get you cleaned up and back on your feet again."

"No problem," said Jackson, trying to stand. He crumpled to the floor with a groan after rising only a few inches. "On second thought, maybe I need a little assistance."

Alicia half-walked, half-carried Jackson to a nearby sofa. He had been badly beaten by the gang of ghouls, but nothing was broken. Using a roll of surgical tape and bottled antiseptic, Alicia patched him up as best she could for the short term.

"It's not pretty," she declared, staring at his cuts and bruises, "but you'll survive."

"I'm fine," said Jackson, "other than feeling like I was just run over by a tank."

Both of his eyes were black and blue, his cheeks battered and swollen, his lips split and cracked.

"So, Miss Alicia," said Jackson, "tell me."

"What?" she asked.

"How was *your* day?"

Chapter 8

New York City — March 25, 1994:

Two hours later, Alicia felt that she was once again in control. The two remaining ghouls had been located and dealt with. Feeling that three unusual deaths in the neighborhood during the span of an afternoon might raise a few eyebrows, she planted an overwhelming compulsion in the Sabbat agents' mind to investigate the bottom of the Hudson River. Her directions specifically suggested that they attempt the chore without diving equipment. New York City's suicide rate was so high already that two more victims would not even merit mention in the newspapers.

While she was handling the ghouls, a team of clean-up specialists paid the penthouse a visit and cleaned the place of blood and bodies. Afterward, the resident skyscraper physician examined Jackson's injuries. The ex-soldier was given strict orders to stay off his feet for a week and get plenty of rest. The doctor knew from previous experience with his patient that the orders would be disobeyed. But he never stopped trying.

Fifteen minutes after the medic left, Jackson was on the phone, issuing orders to building personnel about transferring control of various Varney enterprises to branch offices throughout the world. Several thousand workers discovered they were suddenly on vacation until further notice. The skyscraper was closing down that night, with no date set for it to reopen.

By the time Alicia returned from her headhunting expedition, the mass exodus had begun. Having dealt with major disasters in the past, she had structured her vast business empire in such a way that authority could be routed to regional corporate officers with a minimum of fuss. The Varney Corporation would continue to run smoothly. It just would not be directed from a central office in New York.

"You called our public relations firm?" asked Alicia. She wore a pair of black stretch pants, a black tank top, and black high heels. A sterling silver icon hung from her neck. "They know to put a positive spin on the situation?"

"As best as they can," said Jackson. His sole nod to the physician's advice, he was sitting instead of standing. And, between phone calls, he was devouring a steak, baked potato, and chocolate shake. "It's going to take a lot of imagination to come up with a logical explanation for closing down this building."

"I pay them a fortune to put a positive spin on my business dealings," said Alicia. "They'll invent something."

"When are you planning for us to leave?" asked Jackson. "I assume you have a schedule for our departure."

"We should leave before sundown," said Alicia. "That's when the Kindred will arrive."

"Should?" repeated Jackson. "Meaning otherwise?"

"The death of a few ghouls won't disturb Melinda," said Alicia. "She considers humans expendable. They're cannon fodder.

"The regent sent them because they're able to function during the daylight hours. Unless she's lost her mind, she knows they won't be able to harm me. Melinda's just using them as a message. She wants me to know that wherever I go, whatever I do, trouble will follow. I'm sure this evening, after sundown, the real shock troops will arrive."

Alicia grinned savagely. "I need to send her a message back. An RSVP, so to speak, to both the regent and her loyal followers. Something unpleasant, that will make it clear that Alicia Varney doesn't intimidate easily."

"Whatever you say," declared Jackson. "Though it sounds like risky business."

"We'll merely bait the trap, then leave," said Alicia. She watched him wolf down the baked potato off his plate. "Not to change the subject, but would you care to tell me how you were captured and how they brought you here?"

Jackson shrugged. "It's not much of a story, I'm afraid," he said between big chunks of steak. "The explosion and resulting fire shook the van but otherwise left me and my equipment intact. As you know, we videotaped the entire encounter from a distance, using high-powered telephoto lenses.

Worried about whether you survived the holocaust, I replayed the last few minutes of the tape before the blow-up at frame-by-frame speed. The footage made for pretty fascinating viewing."

"What happened?" said Alicia. "What did you see?"

"Four seconds before the explosion, you vanished from the picture. It was like a switch clicking off a lamp. One moment you were on the tape; a hundredth of a second later, you were gone. I guessed that your disappearance meant you had escaped to the life-support pods."

"What happened to the man standing beside me?" asked Alicia, curious to learn how McCann managed to avoid the blast.

"Damned if I know," replied Jackson. "He dropped out of the video right before you did. The picture shows a dark blur intersecting his image, even at stop motion, for a few frames, then both it and the guy were gone. Spooky stuff."

Alicia grimaced. She hated mysteries. And she knew from experience that anything involving Lameth also involved a mystery.

"Continue," she said. "What happened next?"

"The fire department arrived, with the chief not far behind. He took a quick gander at the blaze, then declared the Navy Yard off limits," said Jackson. "There was no way he was going to have his men tackle a blaze that ferocious. Especially with sporadic riots occurring throughout the city. It was easier to erect a few barriers and tell everyone they were going to let it burn itself out. Exactly how I thought he would play the situation. The chief believes in simple solutions."

"Amazing how cost-effective politicians can be," said Alicia, "when the problem involves a poor neighborhood. No matter. When did the ghouls arrive?"

"Not until the next afternoon," said Jackson. "I had dismissed our crews and was waiting in the van for the fire to burn out. I assumed you would want me around when you emerged from the pod, so I kept myself busy." He shook his head. "It's going to cost a hell of a lot in bribes and cover-up money to explain the loss of that NASA equipment. Our pet congressmen were not pleased to learn that billions of dollars' worth of space technology burned to a crisp in the blaze."

"We can worry about that later," said Alicia. "You said those ghouls arrived in the afternoon?"

"Around 4 p.m.," said Jackson. "They broke into the van while I was taking a brief nap. Damned geeks ripped the door right off its hinges. I tried to fight, but they outnumbered and outmuscled me. It wasn't much of a contest."

"Nothing to be ashamed about," said Alicia. "You did your best."

"They bundled me up like a Christmas turkey and threw me into the back seat of a tour limo. One creep who was more talkative than the rest informed me that they needed me alive for a day or two, otherwise I would have been tossed into the fire." Jackson touched a huge welt over his right eye. "Alive didn't mean untouched. The gang took turns beating the stuffing out of me over the entire trip north. It amused them. Nice bunch of guys."

"The Sabbat doesn't believe in using lots of ghouls like the Camarilla," said Alicia. "The sect elders consider humans to be food animals, nothing more. The mortals they utilize are like attack dogs. Savage, brutal, extremely loyal, but lacking in intelligence."

"They weren't sure when you would arrive in the city," said Jackson. "My face helped them bluff their way up to the penthouse. Incredibly enough, they carried the wood for the cross from D.C. in the second limo. Those jokers were determined to make an impression."

Alicia walked over to the huge picture window that provided a spectacular view of Manhattan's west side. Her expression thoughtful, she stared out across the rooftops of the city. The sun, burnt orange in the pollution haze, was approaching the New Jersey Palisades. In a few hours, it would be dark. And with the darkness would come the Kindred attack.

"Melinda didn't eliminate Justine until last night," said Alicia. "Yet, those ghouls captured you during the daylight hours *before* the regent regained control of the Sabbat. Taken separately, the facts don't seem very important. However, when examined together, they yield an unpleasant conclusion."

"It's pretty clear that Melinda wasn't just acting on impulse when she confronted the archbishop," said Jackson. "You were targeted long before the regent destroyed Justine. She had already set this operation in motion."

"Which also directly implies that Melinda realized I was not going to be present when she attacked the warehouse last night," said Alicia. "The only way she could be sure of that would be to know where I actually was and that, since I was trapped, I wouldn't be able to come to Justine's aid."

"Makes sense to me," said Jackson. "It appears the entire scheme was set up in advance."

"I'm sure there were some small adjustments," said Alicia. "I wasn't expected to survive the inferno at the Navy Yard. The basic plan didn't require any major changes, though. It is clear to me now that the Sabbat attack on Washington and Justine's execution were designed and executed with the intent to return Melinda Galbraith to power, stronger than ever before. And that the mastermind controlling both events was the Red Death."

Jackson laughed, not sounding amused. "You surprised?"

"Not really," said Alicia. "I'm impressed but not overwhelmed. The Red Death is pretty clever. He's won a few skirmishes. The big battle, however, is yet to come. That's the one that counts. And I don't intend to lose."

"What's next?" asked Jackson.

"There's a prophecy I want to study," said Alicia. "I'm hoping a certain card player can help me find someone."

"Find someone?" repeated Jackson. "Who?"

"A vampire called the ratman," said Alicia. "He knows the answer. If I can figure out the right question."

Chapter 9

Washington, D.C. - March 25, 1994:

The sound of raindrops hitting the side of the truck woke Junior. Groggily, he looked at the glowing numbers on the clock near his sleeping bag. It was a few minutes past midnight. Madeleine had been gone for hours. Pablo was keeping watch — assuming he hadn't fallen asleep too — in the truck's cab. A night owl, he liked to listen to CB chatter and stay awake through the long, dark hours.

"Hey, Junior," whispered Sam. "Is that you?"

"Who else, dickhead?" asked Junior. "You expecting Freddie?"

"No," said Sam. "Hope not. It's raining outside."

"Sure is," said Junior. "It happens. Makes the flowers and stuff like that grow. Enough talking. Let's get back to sleep."

"I can't," said Sam. "Not yet. I gotta go to the bathroom."

Junior groaned softly. As a vampire, Madeleine did not have the needs of normal human beings. She neither ate nor drank, and also did not use a bathroom. There was nothing available on the truck. They had used restrooms at gas stations the past few days. But now they were parked in the middle of nowhere.

"There's a john in that abandoned service center," said Junior, vaguely remembering the layout of the park. "You can use that."

"But that's real far away," said Sam. "I don't wanna walk there in the dark. Besides, it's raining. I'd get soaked. We don't got no towels."

"Yeah, yeah," said Junior. He was tired and in no mood for an argument. Sam was the baby of their group. He wasn't tough like Junior. "Why not just hop underneath the truck?" said Junior. "You can do your business there, without getting too wet. It won't be real comfortable scrunching down there behind the tires and everything, but you'll stay dry. That sound good?"

"Not great," said Sam. "But it's better than nothin'. All I wanna do is go pee."

"Well, then go do it," said Junior, "and shut up. I need some sleep. Okay?"

"Sure," said Sam, rising to his feet. His voice grew nervous. "You'll stay awake until I get back, right Junior?"

"Yeah, Sam," said Junior, "I'll stay awake. Nothing's going to hurt you. Remember, we're working for Miss Madeleine. Nobody dares mess with dudes like us."

"That's right," said Sam. "We're tough. I remember you saying that. We're tough, we're tough."

Sam repeated the line softly to himself as he pushed open the rear door of the container and jumped to the ground. Junior imagined he heard Sam whispering the words to himself while doing his business beneath the truck. The thought made him chuckle.

His laughter came to an abrupt end when he heard the cab door of the truck slam unexpectedly. There were voices, loud voices, shouting words that were indistinguishable in the rain. Someone yelled. Guns roared.

"Shit," whispered Junior and scrambled out of his sleeping bag. Something bad was going on outside. Something real bad. He was halfway to the door of the cargo unit when the metal slab swung open and a half-dozen flashlights caught him in a brilliant glare.

"Son-of-a-bitch," a man cursed, sounding disgusted. "It's another kid."

Junior peered at the lights. It was difficult to make out the figures in the glare. It didn't make much difference. He was trapped inside the truck by a bunch of guys with guns. Running wasn't going to get him out of this mess. He needed to stay calm and use his brains.

"Who are you guys?" he asked, in his best kid's voice. "Whatcha want with me? I didn't do nothin' wrong."

"Sure, kid, sure," said a big, beefy middle-aged man, stepping forward a few paces. His face was as red as a tomato. Dressed in a badly rumpled suit, he didn't look happy. In one hand, he held a large-caliber pistol. It was pointed right at Junior. "You're sweet and innocent. Where's the babe?"

"Babe?" asked Junior, trying to sound innocent and confused. "What babe?"

"The babe that owns this rig," said the red-faced man. "Drop the innocent shit, punk. Tell us where the Giovanni babe went or you'll end up like your friend."

The man signaled with a finger. Someone grunted and Pablo came tumbling out of the darkness. He hit the floor of the truck with a thud and didn't move. A thin trickle of blood crept out from beneath his body and pooled by his head.

"He tried to run when he should've stayed put," said the man with the red face. "Don't make the same mistake, kid."

Junior's throat turned dry and his eyes blinked rapidly in shock. Pablo was dead. Murdered. A few hours ago, he had been laughing and joking and eating chips. Now he was lifeless clay, killed by these creeps. Tears welled up in Junior's eyes, but he didn't cry.

"I—I don't know what you're talking about," said Junior, his voice cracking with emotion. That he didn't have to fake. "We—we just found this truck, open-like. So we decided to spend the night. Didn't mean to cause no trouble. Really."

"Sounds legit to me, boss," came another voice from behind the circle of lights. "No dame this dangerous is gonna leave a couple of kids in charge of her rig."

"Fuck," said the red-faced man. "Then why did this shit," and he kicked Pablo viciously, "head for the woods when we pulled him out of the cab?"

"M—m—maybe he thought his father hired you to find him," said Junior, his mind speeding into overdrive. "Pablo's dad, he's a crazy man. Beats Pablo with a belt all the time. He was running away from home. Like me."

"Two runaways discover a truck by the side of the road and decide to stay for the night," said the red-faced man, with a sneer. "They just walk in, find the door open, even find the keys in the ignition. How convenient."

"No tellin' what the Giovanni dame thinks, boss," said the unseen speaker. "Maybe she thought it was safe leaving the rig unguarded. Ain't that so, Mr. Lazzari?"

Another person spoke. Junior swallowed hard. This new voice was icy cold, like the hissing of a huge snake. Remembering what Miss Madeleine had said just before leaving, Junior had no doubt that the guy was one of the Kindred. And that, as such, human life meant nothing to him.

"In my country," said the monster named Lazzari, "no kine dares touch anything marked with the seal of the Giovanni. It is conceivable that Madeleine left the truck exactly as the boy claims. The arrogance of her clan knows no bounds. Where the bitch is concerned, anything is possible."

"Damn," said the man with the red face. He looked worried. With a wave of his hand, he beckoned one of the goons to his side. A giant of a man, he wore sunglasses inside the dark truck. He held a semiautomatic machine gun in one hand and carried a flashlight in the other. "Alvin, search this fuckin' rig. Let's see if this little bastard's story holds together."

Junior squeezed his eyes shut as the big man, gun waving back and forth as he moved, strode past him into the rear of the truck. Silently, Junior prayed that Sam had enough brains to stay hidden beneath. If he did, he might actually survive the night.

He had no illusions about his own life, however. These goons were killers. They had murdered Pablo and were going to kill him as well. Guys in the mob never left any loose ends. Shooting people was their business. There was no escape.

It didn't matter much to Junior. His life, except for the past few days, had been one long losing streak. Miss Madeleine, although she was a vampire, was the only person ever to treat him right. He was determined to pay her back. No matter what happened, he was not going to betray her trust.

The big thug whom red-face had called Alvin returned in just a few minutes. In his left hand, he held an empty potato-chip bag. "It's the dame's hideout, for sure. Her coffin's in the front. There's two sleeping bags there. And a bunch of garbage."

"The bitch is gone for the night," said the guy who sounded like a snake. Mr. Lazzari, Junior assumed. The man stepped into the circle of light created by the flashlights. Squat and powerful, he had pale white skin and jet black hair. His eyes were tinged crimson, and on his hands, he wore black silk gloves. "We arrived too late. Bad timing on your part, Tony."

Tony, the man with the red face, shivered but didn't say a word. He was frightened of his companion. Junior understood why. Miss Madeleine was a vampire. This Mr. Lazzari dude was a monster.

"It seems that I will have to post the reward for her head as originally planned," said Lazzari. "So be it. The Don's wishes are law. Executing her would have been a pleasure, but I will find my joys in other ways."

The vampire looked at Junior. "Tell me, child," he said softly, his eyes glowing red, "have you ever known the true taste of a woman's flesh? Are you a man or still a boy?"

"Wh-whatcha talking about?" asked Junior, avoiding Mr. Lazzari's gaze. Madeleine could tell if he was lying just by looking into his eyes. Junior didn't want to risk learning this vampire could do worse. "I don't like girls. They're dumb."

"You ever get screwed, kid?" asked Tony, his face redder than ever. The man's voice was shrill, frightened. Junior wasn't sure about what. Not knowing how to answer, he told the truth.

"No."

"How fortuitous," said Mr. Lazzari. He turned his back and stepped out of the light. "Then this outing is not a total waste. Take the boy with us, Tony. He's seen too much to leave behind. At least he can provide me a few moments of entertainment later in the evening."

"Whatever you say, Don Lazzari," said Tony, his voice barely audible. The red was draining out of his features, leaving him a pasty white. "You're the boss."

Two thugs grabbed Junior by his arms. He was absolutely helpless in their grip. Lifting him off his feet, the men carried him outside. The rain had settled into a thick, all-pervasive mist. Parked a dozen feet from the Giovanni vehicle were three huge black touring limos. Their engines roared in defiance of the surrounding darkness.

"Destroy the truck," said Don Lazzari, climbing into the passenger seat of the lead car. Junior's escorts shoved him to an open door in the third vehicle. "Use plenty of explosives. I want the bitch to understand that we are on her trail. And that for her, there is no place she can hide."

Silently, Junior prayed that Sam had enough brains to crawl into the forest before the explosives went off. If his friend survived the blast, it was still possible that he could find Miss Madeleine and tell her about Junior's kidnapping. It wasn't much of a chance. But, it was the only hope Junior had left.

Chapter 10

Paris, France — March 25, 1994:

After walking for another twenty minutes, Le Clair began to grow suspicious. Though they had been in the tunnels for several hours, they had yet to come across any signs of Phantomas. The passages went on and on, leading nowhere.

"I still sense the Nosferatu's presence," he said to Baptiste, giving voice to his frustration. "The ancient one is present somewhere in the heart of this maze. Earlier I detected him ahead of us. But now, he is off to our right."

The giant shook his head. "I don't understand. What does it mean, Le Clair?"

"We are circling him," said Le Clair grimly. "Instead of leading to his lair, this tunnel goes around but never through it. Which makes no sense. Why build corridors that don't connect with the central hub?"

"Maybe," said Baptiste, his brow wrinkled in concentration, "Phantomas closed the doors when he heard us coming."

"There are no doors, *conchon*," Le Clair snapped. He wondered why he bothered telling Baptiste anything. The giant was an idiot. "We are in a maze, not a boarding house. There are no secret passageways with sliding..."

Le Clair paused, considering exactly what he was saying. "Sliding panels," he declared. "*Merde*."

Baptiste grinned, as if realizing he had said something significant. He didn't know what, but the expression on Le Clair's face made it clear to him that it could be important.

"The Nosferatu are an insane cult of paranoid gophers," said Le Clair. "They build huge warrens beneath the earth, filled with traps, to keep them safe from some sort of bogeymen. That's our problem. Phantomas designed these tunnels. And he's afraid of his own shadow."

"What about the sliding doors, Le Clair?" asked Baptiste, anxious to learn more about his great discovery. "What did you mean about the sliding doors?"

"That's the secret of the maze, my friend," said Le Clair. "We've followed corridors that wind through the earth like the meanderings of a drunken poet, leading nowhere. However, I suspect that many of these passages actually connect with the heart of the maze. What Phantomas has done is block off those tunnels with movable walls. We're traveling in a gigantic circle around the Nosferatu's sanctum. If we continued long enough, we would end up where we started."

"Then there's no way to get to the center?" asked Baptiste, frowning. "How does Phantomas enter and leave his headquarters?"

"The walls move, *conchon*," said Le Clair, shrilly. He missed Jean Paul. "That's what I have been saying. They slide back and forth, changing the shape of the maze. When Phantomas wants to depart, he presses a switch and a clear, straight passage leading to the surface appears. When others are in the tunnels, he pushes another switch, and voilà, the tunnels reform into a gigantic labyrinth that goes nowhere. Now, do you understand?"

"I think so," said Baptiste, slowly. "We are like bugs in a wood maze. We want to get to the middle, but the man in charge won't let us. He's put plugs in all the entrances. It's a game that we can't win, because Phantomas has made up the rules. What are we going to do, Le Clair?"

Le Clair laughed, a harsh, cruel sound that echoed through the passage. "We stop playing by Phantomas' rules, my friend. Instead, we invent new rules. Ones that make us the winners."

"New rules?" said Baptiste, looking puzzled. "I didn't know you could make new rules."

"That is what makes us special," said Le Clair. "We refuse to be governed by the decisions of others. We are our own masters."

"When do we start, Le Clair?" said Baptiste. "I'm bored walking these tunnels. Let's change the rules right now."

"My thoughts exactly," replied Le Clair. "Now, remain silent. I must concentrate."

Closing his eyes, Le Clair reached out with his mind. He could sense Phantomas' presence in the maze. What he needed to do was pinpoint the Nosferatu's exact location, then find a path to reach him.

"Follow me," he said after a moment. Eyes still closed, he placed his left hand on the inner wall and began to pace slowly back the way they had come. Anxious for action, Baptiste lumbered along behind him.

They walked nearly a hundred feet before Le Clair stopped. He paused, then spun on his heels and faced Baptiste. Right hand touching the wall, eyes pressed tightly shut, he took five steps back. Finally, he came to a halt. Turning, he faced the wall. "He is closest to this spot," he declared, opening his eyes. "I can sense the ancient one's presence most clearly from here."

He looked at Baptiste. "You said you were tired of walking. Good. Our quarry is beyond this wall. There must be a passage leading to him beyond the stones. Find it."

Baptiste stared at the solid wall, then looked back at Le Clair. The giant shrugged. He never argued with Le Clair's orders. It was the crux of their relationship, and had been so since before they had been Embraced. Le Clair did the thinking. Baptiste provided the muscle.

"Stand back," said Baptiste, curling his huge fingers into balls. "This will not be easy."

Le Clair shifted down the tunnel a few feet. "Go ahead," he commanded. "There is another corridor on the other side of the wall. I am sure of it."

"I hope so," declared Baptiste and slammed a massive fist into the stone. He had hands like steel. Fragments of rock went flying. Baptiste smashed his other fist into the same spot. Chunks of debris splattered across the corridor. Feet planted in place, the giant pounded the wall like an inhuman jackhammer.

A dozen blows proved to be enough. Baptiste lurched forward as his right fist crashed into the barrier, then through it. It took the giant a second to regain his footing. Grinning, he pulled his hand back, ripping stones out with his fingers. "That was easy," he declared. "It's open on the other side."

"Of course," said Le Clair, keeping his temper in check. His companion's strength was a constant source of amazement. Insulting Baptiste, especially now that Jean Paul was gone, could be dangerous. "I told you there had to be a passage there. Widen the hole so we can crawl through."

"No reason for us to crawl," said Baptiste. Stepping back, he threw himself into the wall. The passage shook with the impact. The wall shifted an inch. Pebbles rained to the floor. Hastily, Le Clair checked the roof of the tunnel. It appeared stable. Baptiste, never one to worry about the effects of his acts, hurtled himself forward a second time.

With a crash of stone, the wall collapsed, revealing a passage at right angles to the one in which Le Clair waited. Baptiste, covered with dust but otherwise unharmed, grinned. He stood in the space between the two tunnels. "See," he said proudly. "No reason for us to crawl when we can walk."

"An impressive display," said Le Clair, stepping into the new corridor. "This passage leads in the right direction. The Nosferatu is directly ahead. He cannot be far away."

"I want his blood," said Baptiste, as they hurried along through the tunnel. "I've earned it."

"That you have, my friend," said Le Clair. "First, though, we must catch him. Somehow, I suspect there is still an obstacle or two in our path."

"Look!" yelled Baptiste, his voice ringing through the passageway. "There he is, up ahead!"

Le Clair's eyes bulged in astonishment. The giant was right. Fifty feet ahead, watching them calmly, stood the ugliest individual Le Clair had ever seen. It had to be Phantomas. Short and stocky, with mottled skin the color of moldy cheese, his eyes glowed crimson in the darkness. He was smiling.

"Take care, Baptiste," shouted Le Clair, as Baptiste rushed ahead. "There is something strange about the passage ahead."

The warning came just in time. Baptiste jerked to a sudden stop twenty feet ahead. Le Clair hurried to meet him — and beheld the pit.

The tunnel ended abruptly at the edge of a gigantic hole in the earth. Thirty feet in diameter, it neatly separated one end of the corridor from the other. The sheer walls of the pit dropped three hundred feet down. Peering into the darkness, Le Clair could vaguely make out huge five-foot-high metal spikes sticking up from the chasm floor. Even vampires could be badly hurt by such a drop. And Le Clair was certain the huge spikes were not the only danger.

Phantomas stood less than ten yards away, but it could have been miles. There was no bridge across the gulf.

"We have come for your blood, Monsieur Phantomas," cried Baptiste boldly. "You cannot escape us."

"Tell that to the pit," Phantomas called back. His voice was surprisingly mellow for one so ugly. "It awaits you."

Behind them, rock scraped against rock. Le Clair whirled, then cursed. The corridor down which they had come was sealed shut. A massive stone door filled the tunnel, cutting off their retreat. They stood on a slice of tunnel ten feet long by five feet wide. Unseen machinery whirred. Slowly but steadily, the back end of the platform started to rise, tilting them toward the pit. Le Clair howled in shock. Within seconds, the stone ledge would be standing straight up, and they would slide into the chasm. And there was nothing they could do to stop it.

"Goodbye, fools," called Phantomas. Turning, he walked back into his sanctum, leaving them alone to face their doom.

"Quickly, Baptiste," said Le Clair, as the platform continued to tilt. "There is still a chance. Remember the mansion in Transylvania? You tossed me across the collapsed floor. You can do it again. Throw me over the pit. Just be sure to aim carefully!"

Obediently, Baptiste hoisted Le Clair over his head. "What about me?" he asked suddenly. "I can't throw myself."

"The same as the other time," said Le Clair.

"Your legs are strong. Jump. If you need help, I will catch you."

"It is a good plan," declared Baptiste.

Without another word, he hurtled Le Clair across the abyss. For an instant, Le Clair glimpsed the walls rushing up to meet him. His mind filled with grisly thoughts of smashing flat against the stone. Then, before he could even close his eyes, he found himself lying on the floor of the far corridor. Baptiste's aim had been true.

"I'm coming," yelled the giant, as Le Clair scrambled to his feet and hurried back to the edge of the pit. The giant balanced precariously on the edge of the abyss, the stone platform pressing into his back. "Right now."

Even Baptiste was not strong enough to leap thirty feet from a standing position. He came close, but his body crashed into the opposite wall fifteen feet below the tunnel entrance.

Amazingly, he did not fall. The giant's fingers, like steel pitons, had dug into the surface of the stone, anchoring him to the rock. He dangled there, his entire weight supported by his hands.

Le Clair shook his head in amazement. He had thought himself finally rid of Baptiste. The giant, however, was proving hard to kill. But Le Clair was quite determined to put an end to his friend's career.

"Baptiste," he called, leaning over the edge of the pit. "Can you climb? Hold yourself by one hand and use the other to make new handholds."

"I think so, Le Clair," answered Baptiste. He stared up with worried eyes. His nose was smashed flat against his face, and his features were covered with blood. "I have to be careful. My grip isn't too steady."

"Don't wait too long," said Le Clair. "Phantomas is gone but he may return at any moment. And the longer you hang there, the more tired you will become. See if you can start now."

"I—I will try," said Baptiste.

Cautiously, Baptiste pulled the fingers of his left hand out of the stone. Nothing happened. He remained unmoving, his body held to the rock by his other five digits. Slowly, he snaked his free arm up over his head until it was stretched as high as it could go. Then, curving his fingers and spreading them wide apart, he dug them into the stone.

Awed, Le Clair watched as Baptiste tightened the muscles in his extended arm. Like a pulley lifting a weight, the giant raised his body up the side of the abyss. The fingers of his right hand pulled free and dangled at his side as he steadied his new position. Then, without hesitation, Baptiste repeated the entire operation, reaching over his head with his right hand.

Left, right, left, right, the giant hauled himself up the cliff face toward Le Clair. The little man snarled in frustration. In another moment, Baptiste would reach the safety of the tunnel. Le Clair knew he would not have such an opportunity again.

Desperately, he scanned the corridor. The passage was free of debris. There wasn't a thing to throw at the giant. Le Clair considered his boots. He shook his head. By the time he unlaced them, it would be too late. There was no choice. Much as he disliked the idea of physically confronting Baptiste, it was the only solution.

"Come on, Baptiste," he urged, as he lay down flat on the tunnel floor. He positioned himself in a direct line with the giant's head. Propping himself up on an elbow, he waited for the big man's face to appear over the rim.

Like four immense worms, the fingers of Baptiste's right hand snaked over the rim of the pit. They wriggled forward, the rest of his hand and thumb following. Le Clair grimaced as the giant dug his digits into the stone only a few inches away. He tensed, aware that timing was everything.

For a few seconds, his left hand free of its grip, Baptiste balanced entirely on the grip he held on the floor. Inch by inch, the big man's head rose from the abyss. First came his hair, then his broad forehead, then his eyes. The giant's pupils widened in surprise as he caught sight of Le Clair's face inches from his own. That was when the small man struck.

With all the strength in his body, Le Clair slammed his hand into Baptiste's face. His index and pointer finger, extended like spikes, dug deep into the giant's eyeballs. The big man screeched in shock as his pupils burst. Involuntarily, he jerked his head back, trying to escape the pain.

Rock crumbled into powder as Baptiste's fingers clenched into a fist. Savagely, Le Clair twisted his fingers, shoving the palm of his hand into the big man's nose. Bare flesh dragged across stone as the giant's extended right arm slithered along the tunnel floor. Then gravity took over. Screaming incoherently, Baptiste tumbled backward into the abyss.

Smiling in triumph, Le Clair watched his friend fall. The giant waved his huge arms desperately all the way down, as if trying to fly. He landed with a sickening splat on the immense steel spikes. A dozen of them snatched the giant up in their horrid embrace.

Seconds later, fire roared across the floor of the pit. Evidently, anything touching the metal spears set off flame-throwers embedded in the walls. Even if Baptiste had survived the fall, the blaze meant his end. The big man was no more. The Unholy Three had been reduced to one.

Le Clair rose to his feet. Jean Paul was gone. Baptiste was gone. Only he remained.

He shrugged. According to certain philosophers, the strong survived. It wasn't true. Strong was good. Smart was better. Ruthless was best.

Chapter 11

Vienna, Austria — March 26, 1994:

Etrius opened the door to his study and stepped inside. The lights in the chamber, sensitive to his presence, flickered on, casting shadows across his annoyed features. He was running late, as usual. Despite being one of the most powerful Kindred in the world, a member of the Inner Circle of the Tremere, he still had to approve bills and invoices for the Vienna Chantry House. Though he refused to admit it, Etrius had an obsessive-compulsive personality: he found it nearly impossible to delegate authority. It was not a trait that made him popular with other members of the Order.

He checked the clock on the mantle over the fireplace as he dropped into the plush chair behind his desk. It was half past eleven. Elaine was not due for another thirty minutes. That was barely enough time for him to jot down some thoughts he had about her proposed course of action. He reached for a pen and pad on the desktop, then froze. Something moved in the shadows on the far side of the chamber.

"Who's there?" he demanded, summoning the force of his immense will. "Show yourself."

"Hold, Sire," came the reply. A short, powerfully

built man, with broad shoulders, jet black hair, and swarthy features, moved forward with quick, jerky steps into the light. It was Peter Spizzo, Etrius' childe and special agent.

"I didn't mean to startle you," said Spizzo, approaching his sire's desk. "The entrance was open so I slipped inside. As per your instructions, I thought it best to remain unseen."

Etrius nodded, his body sinking into the deep comfort of his chair. He was quite sure that he had locked the door to the office the previous night. And that he had used powerful binding spells to ensure that the room remained undisturbed.

"You caught me by surprise," Etrius admitted, keeping his thoughts to himself. "I did not realize you were here."

"I have a talent," said Spizzo, a faint smile crossing his grim features, "for going unnoticed."

"A necessary ability for a spy," said Etrius, dryly. He leaned forward on his desk. "Why have you returned so soon? What have you learned?"

"I've been doing a lot of traveling," said Spizzo. "Using the House of Secrets for shortcuts. I visited a number of Chantries both here in Europe and in America. Everywhere I went, I asked a few questions, said hello to some old friends."

The House of Secrets was a bizarre structure that existed just outside normal space and time. It had been discovered by a Tremere elder centuries ago and had quickly become one of the clan's most closely guarded secrets. No one knew who had built it or when. It merely existed.

A huge palace with thousands of rooms, many of them unexplored, the House of Secrets touched the real world in a hundred different locations across the globe. A Tremere wizard could enter the building through one door, walk past three rooms, then exit out another door a thousand miles away. Using the dimensional gates helped the clan maintain strong ties with its scattered membership. Chantry Houses across the earth were built on entrances to the House of Secrets. As was the clan headquarters in Vienna.

"Did you discover anything about the Count St. Germain?" asked Etrius, drumming his fingertips on the edge of the desk. Elaine was due shortly, and he did not want Spizzo in his office when she arrived. Still, the spy had returned for a reason. Etrius wanted to know what it was.

Etrius frowned as a weird sensation clouded his vision. Just like the night before, he suddenly felt as if another mind was sharing his body, staring out at the world through his eyes, listening to what was being said through his ears. He felt certain that the mental eavesdropper was Tremere, in torpor, using his telepathic powers. It was a strange feeling — one not to his liking. And, once again, as quickly as the perception came upon him, it was gone.

"I spoke to several elders who had sharp recollections of having met with him several times in the past," said Spizzo. "However, none of them could provide me with his description. I found that rather odd. The Count made a strong impression on all those he encountered, but no one could remember his features."

"That, too, is a talent valued by spies," said Etrius, his composure returning. "Why resort to a disguise when your features fade from memory as soon as you depart."

"Exactly the case," said Spizzo. "Nor could any of those I questioned tell me when they actually spoke to our mysterious Count. They could recall several instances in which they discussed certain subjects with him. But none of them were sure when the exchanges took place."

Etrius shrugged. "Obviously, he is a master of deception. But I already suspected that. He fooled the Inner Council of the Tremere for a thousand years. That he managed to do the same with our underlings means little. Tell me something I don't know." Etrius' eyes narrow to slits. "You mentioned *certain subjects*. What information did he review with these clan elders?"

Spizzo chuckled. "I thought those words might pique your interest. As best as I could determine, St. Germain sought out the leading scholars and historians of our clan. Each of them was known for their research into the ancient legends of the Kindred. He discussed two topics, *the same two topics*, with them all. On numerous occasions."

Etrius glanced at the clock on the mantle. Elaine was due in a few minutes. He definitely did not want her to encounter Peter Spizzo. Nor did he want Spizzo running into Elaine. It was best, he felt, if neither knew about the other.

"What two subjects?" he asked. "Enough

dramatics, Spizzo. I am tired of waiting."

"The Count wanted to learn everything there was to know about the Nosferatu legends of the Nictuku," said the spy. "He was interested in their names, their descriptions, their origins, their vast powers, the legends surrounding their disappearance, and the prophecies regarding their reemergence."

Etrius suddenly felt very cold. He remembered the unusual circumstances concerning the Final Death of Tyrus Benedict, his envoy to the prince of St. Louis. Reports had tied the murder to a mysterious group of photos supposedly of Baba Yaga, one of the fabled Nictuku. And to the first appearance of a spectral horror known as the Red Death.

Elaine de Calinot schemed to convince the Camarilla that the Count St. Germain was the Red Death. Etrius wondered if perhaps by sheer accident she had stumbled on the truth. "What was the other subject about which he inquired?"

"*The Book of Nod*," answered Spizzo, naming the notorious collection of primitive folk tales that supposedly detailed the true history of the Damned. Etrius, who was as much a student as a practitioner of the occult, was quite familiar with the volume. He had spent years studying the infamous text. His research had convinced him that the collection had been written by several different people over the span of a thousand years. He was not convinced that all of the stories were true. But, he wasn't sure that they were not.

"What did St. Germain want to know about *The Book of Nod?*" he asked. "Or was that another fact that these scholars could not remember?"

"They remembered," said Spizzo. "The Count wasn't interested in anything they could tell him about the book. Instead, he inquired about the unknown. He desired to learn what was missing from the tome. St. Germain hunted for the lost pages of *The Book of Nod.*"

"*The Apocrypha of the Damned,*" whispered Etrius, almost as if afraid of the words. He didn't like what he was hearing. "The unrevealed truths of Caine, the Third Mortal, as told by Seth, his ghoul. The final secrets of the Kindred."

"A prize equal in value to the legendary Lameth's Cup," said Spizzo. "Or the Sword of Troile."

"And probably equally imaginary," said Etrius, feeling his anger rise. "Over the centuries, there have been hundreds of rumors about *The Apocrypha* resurfacing. It never has."

"Are you sure?" asked Spizzo. "My Sire, are you quite sure?"

"What do you mean?" asked Etrius, a dread anticipation creeping through the core of his being.

"I asked the scholars why St. Germain stopped returning to them to ask for more information," said Spizzo. "None of them were positive of the answer. But most seemed to think that there was an obvious explanation."

"Which is?" asked Etrius. He could guess the reason but he wanted to hear it confirmed by Spizzo.

"The Count no longer needs to inquire about the

secrets of *The Lost Apocrypha*," said Peter Spizzo, "because he holds them in his hands. Somehow, the mysterious Count St. Germain has acquired the missing chapters of *The Book of Nod*."

ROBERT WEINBERG

Chapter 12

New York City — March 26, 1994:

A full moon cast its bright glow through the huge picture window in the parlor of Alicia Varney's penthouse suite. The room was otherwise dark. The lights were off. Nothing moved. The only sound was the ticking of a small clock on the table where Alicia normally ate breakfast. It was nearly one o'clock. The chamber was deserted.

A shadow drifted across the moon's face, casting the parlor into semidarkness. Something large and sinister drifted out of the night sky, heading for the window. It had immense, leathery wings, tiny clawed feet, and a face out of a gothic nightmare.

With a soft plop, the horror touched down on the ledge. Its black body pressed tight against the window like a gigantic suction cup. Huge wings folded to its sides. It stood there for a moment, waiting for a reaction from inside. None came.

Slowly, the form quivered in the moon's light. It turned indistinct, mistlike. Soundlessly, the vapor sank into the panes of the picture window. In an instant, it was gone, merged with the glass. Five, ten, fifteen seconds passed. Then, inside the chamber, a dark film formed on the window. The black blot quickly grew larger and more distinct, until a figure took shape. In place of the bat stood a massively built vampire with a bullet-shaped head and clipped silver hair.

Blood-red eyes surveyed the room. Nothing had changed in the few moments it had taken the creature to gain access to the chamber. Other than the ticking clock, the suite remained silent. The man nodded as if answering his own question. He had to be very careful. Transforming from one form to another took a great deal of power. For the next few hours, he was bound to remain in human form. Rising to his feet, he turned to the picture window, twisted the lock and flung open the glass doors. He was expecting three others, and while they could all fly, he was the only member of their hunting party who possessed the power to pass through man-made materials.

The bat-vampire stood six feet seven inches tall and weighed three hundred and fifty pounds. His shoulders were unnaturally broad and his arms were as long as those of a gorilla. Four hundred years ago, as a mortal, he had been known as Otto the Butcher, the Terror of the Black Forest. An infamous bandit and mass murderer, he had disappeared mysteriously at the height of his bloody career, never to be seen again. Otto was assumed by historians to have been killed by his own men, who were sickened at last by his gruesome excesses.

In reality, he had been Embraced by a Brujah *antitribu* and recruited as a member of the Sabbat Blood Guard. Otto continued his reign of terror, but with Kindred, not kine, as his victims. For the past fifty years, he had labored for Justine Bern. When she was destroyed, he immediately switched allegiance to her executioner, Melinda Galbraith. Loyalty meant nothing to Otto the Butcher. All he cared about was killing.

Dark wings in the moonlight signaled the arrival of the rest of Otto's pack. Three huge bats sailed into the parlor. Two landed on the carpet, a third on the nearby easy chair. Moments later, they had transformed into a man and two women. Otto had no prejudices regarding the sexes. His only concern was that his companions were consumed by an insatiable lust for destruction.

Hanns Heinz was a notorious SS *Hauptmann* wanted on three continents for crimes against humanity. He had escaped execution by becoming a member of the Damned. A sadistic maniac, Hanns was always grinning as if he enjoyed some private joke. Even Otto refused to turn his back on Hanns.

Debbie Sue Mauser had robbed twenty-two banks in Texas during a three-month spree in the late 1950s. Seven security guards died before Debbie Sue met her end in an FBI ambush in Waco. However, not everyone believed that she had been killed. The same people who claimed John Dillinger didn't perish in front of the Biograph Theater in Chicago declared Debbie Sue Mauser's death a cover-up. They were correct. It was a conspiracy by the Sabbat. An innocent woman died while Debbie Sue Mauser joined the ranks of the Blood Guard.

The fourth member of Otto's pack was Sha'una Teague. A slender black woman with finely chiseled features and soft brown eyes, Sha'una was proof that appearances could be deceiving. In life she served as minister of interrogation for Ugandan dictator Idi Amin. Her taste for torture with branding irons and small, sharp objects made her one of the most feared women in Africa. When Amin had been forced to flee the country, Sha'una had turned freelance. She was recruited by the Sabbat for her skills in making people suffer. As a member of the Blood Guard, she had far exceeded sect expectations.

"Remember," said Otto the Butcher, his gaze sweeping the apartment, "none should escape. They must die in much pain."

Otto spoke English with a thick, Germanic accent. He was not particularly adept at languages. It didn't matter. He was very good at what counted: killing.

"This fancy fuckin' pigsty is damn deserted," said Debbie Sue Mauser. She spoke with a grating nasal twang. "We're fuckin' wasting our damn time here."

"We are following the directives of Commandant Galbraith," said Hanns Heinz stiffly. "A true soldier never questions his superiors."

"Well, maybe I don't see Melinda as my fuckin' superior," said Debbie Sue, glaring at Heinz. "Who the hell put her in charge, sudden-like? And, who the fuck are you, butt-kisser, to tell me what to do?"

"Shut up," said Otto harshly. "Both of you. There not is time for arguments. We must split up and search the apartment. Nobody is here, I feel it too. But, we must look anyway. Melinda will want a whole report."

"Fuckin' waste of time," muttered Debbie. She snapped her mouth shut when Otto glared at her. The Texan had no respect for authority when she was alive, and she respected it even less in unlife. Even the Final Death didn't frighten Debbie Sue. But Otto the Butcher did.

"We split up," said Otto. "Me with Hanns we explore this room und the hall. Debbie, you go with Sha'una and search the bedroom. Somewhere, dis Alicia, she leave a clue. We dare not return to the regent with nothing."

"I'd like to find this Alicia bitch and rip off her fuckin' head," declared Debbie, heading for the door to the bedroom. Sha'una, who let her actions speak for her, remained silent. "Maybe the broad has some nice clothes in her closet. She sure as hell can afford them."

"That imbecile should be left out in the sun to bake," snarled Heinz when Debbie had left the room.

"She ist a pain," said Otto. "But she fights well. Enough of the talking. Search for leads."

The two vampires spent the next fifteen minutes ripping the parlor to pieces. They tore the furniture to shreds hunting for a clue to Alicia Varney's destination. They found nothing. Searching the area by the elevators proved equally fruitless. Otto was not pleased.

"Sending 'dose ghouls here first was a big mistake," he declared, surveying the wreckage. "They were no match for this Alicia woman. She kilt them and left this building hours ago. Debbie was right. We are wasting our time."

"It's been awfully silent in the other room," said Hanns. He stared at the entrance to the bedroom. "That's unusual for Debbie. Usually, she's screaming obscenities."

Otto frowned. "Funny. I don't sense Debbie or Sha'una in there. Dey are gone."

Hanns snarled, revealing his fangs. "Gone? How is that possible? What could have happened to the two of them? They can't have disappeared into thin air."

"We will find out how," said Otto, striding purposefully to the door. Heinz trailed behind him, fingers extended in front of his face like claws. The Butcher feared nothing living or dead.

Ready for a fight, Otto grabbed the door and ripped it off the hinges. Tossing it to the side, he clumped arrogantly into the bedroom. His bullet head turned from side to side as he searched for an enemy to smash and destroy. The chamber was deserted.

There wasn't much furniture in the bedroom. In the center of the chamber was a king-size bed, flanked on each side by a wood nightstand. The bed was covered by red satin sheets and a thick black comforter. The wall to the right was taken up by a huge picture window, a duplicate of the one in the parlor. A small writing table and chair faced the outside world. The opposite wall consisted entirely of closet space. A door by the bed evidently led to a bathroom.

"They're gone," said Hanns Heinz. Anxiously, he

hurried across the thick white carpet and checked the huge picture window. It was locked, from the inside.

"Look," said Otto, pointing in the opposite direction. "In der closet. They found a secret door."

"A lift?" said Heinz. "Maybe the bitch took a trip and forgot to tell you."

"I don't know what she did," said Otto, his features twisting with annoyance. The Butcher stepped over to the open elevator. "But I intend to find out. Come on. We will take a ride and see where it goes."

Heinz started across the room. He stopped in front of the huge bed.

"That's funny," he said, staring at the floor, "the carpet's wet here. It's stained black."

Kneeling, Heinz felt the plush floor-covering with his fingers. His voice grew shrill. "It's blood."

Without a sound, the black comforter rose up on the satin sheets. What had appeared to be merely a dark blanket suddenly became a huge black panther. Its blood-red eyes glared with near-human intelligence at the unsuspecting vampire only a few feet away.

Hanns Heinz never saw his doom's approach. With a casual grace, the immense jungle cat lashed out with a gigantic paw at the German's unprotected head. Razor-sharp yellow claws the size of knife blades caught Heinz full in the throat. The cat's talons ripped through the vampire's neck, shearing muscle and bone like paper. The SS officer's decapitated body dropped like a sack of cement to the floor. His head, dripping black blood, sailed across the chamber and came to rest at the foot of the picture window.

Snarling deep in its throat, the black panther turned to face Otto the Butcher. Opening its jaws, the beast roared its defiance at the remaining Cainite.

Frantically, Otto crowded into the elevator. There were three buttons on the control panel. He pushed the lowest one. With anxious eyes, he watched the door slide closed. After witnessing the ease with which the black panther had disposed of Hanns Heinz, the Butcher no longer wondered at the fate of the other members of his pack. Their bodies had either dissolved into dust or were hidden beneath the bed in the chamber. It didn't concern him. All that mattered was that he was on his own.

The elevator dropped steadily for several minutes. Otto felt his spirits rise the farther down it went. He was obviously descending to a hidden chamber far beneath the foundation of the Varney Building. Melinda had said there had to be such a hideaway. Through luck alone, he had found it.

Smoothly, the car glided to a stop. With a soft whisper of displaced air, the elevator door opened. Nervous but excited, Otto stepped forward. As soon as he did so, the door closed behind him.

The Butcher found himself in a rectangular room twenty feet long by ten feet wide. The roof was low enough that he could touch it by reaching over his head. The chamber was made of cement, without a seam showing. A row of electric lights in the ceiling provided illumination, and a vent in the far wall kept the air circulating.

The compartment was empty. Whatever had been kept here was gone. He cursed in annoyance. There was nothing left for him to do but reenter the elevator and try the second button. Turning, he looked for a switch to open the doors, but found nothing on the smooth wall's surface. Furious, he slammed a massive fist into the metal panel. It didn't budge. He was trapped here until he regained enough strength to transform into a bat.

Otto shook his head. First the black panther, now the abandoned storeroom. He wondered what else could go wrong.

With a whoosh, a strong-smelling liquid began to pour into the room from the air vent above. Otto shrugged. As a vampire, he no longer breathed and thus could not drown. If the flood continued, when the room filled to the ceiling the pressure would force the elevator door open.

It wasn't until a few minutes later that Otto the Butcher realized the liquid filling the chamber was gasoline. He was just considering what that implied when the power surged, shattering the light bulbs and showering the room with sparks.

Chapter 13

Paris, France — March 25, 1994:

Ever since first entering the maze that led to Phantomas' lair, Le Clair worried that the Nosferatu might flee, abandoning his lair for safety. Now, finally entering the ancient vampire's sanctum, Le Clair realized that his fears were meaningless. Everywhere he looked there were computers. The entire cavern was filled with machinery. The green glow of dozens of computer monitors cast weird shadows on the walls. It was inconceivable that Phantomas would have abandoned this equipment to invaders. He was a prisoner of his own possessions.

Rats, dozens of rats, scurried out of Le Clair's path as he walked forward. His gaze flicked from location to location, hunting his elusive quarry. He could sense Phantomas' presence in the chamber, but from this distance, it was impossible to pin down his quarry's exact location. He need not have worried.

"Welcome to my home, Monsieur Le Clair," came a pleasant, relaxed voice from the far end of the cavern. A grotesque figure clad in a formless gray robe rose from a chair that faced a vast array of circuit boards. Phantomas stood five feet tall, with broad, twisted shoulders, mottled green skin, and a face out of a Picasso painting. A small rat sat on his left shoulder, while another five clustered about his feet.

"My congratulations on your persistence," said the Nosferatu. "Over the centuries, others have tried to find this place, but you are the first to succeed."

"I am determined by nature," said Le Clair. He stopped moving, content to exchange information for a moment. Phantomas was trapped in a corridor of machinery. "You know my name?"

"But of course," said the other. He waved a hand negligently at the rows and rows of computers. "You are one of many thousands of undead who find a place in my great project. I am working on an encyclopedia of the Kindred. It was not difficult to discover your identity after listening to your conversation in my tunnels. The passages are, of course, under constant audio and video surveillance."

"Of course," said Le Clair. "I expected no less from such a master of construction."

"Thank you," said Phantomas. "I take that as a high compliment, coming as it does from an expert of deceit. Considering the loss of your two companions, I feel my traps performed quite well."

"I appreciated the assistance," said Le Clair. From his back pocket, he pulled out a large switchblade. He pressed the snap, revealing a six-inch steel blade. "After decades, their presence had become tiresome. I disliked the notion of having to share the spoils."

"I fully understand your position," said Phantomas. The rat on his shoulder leapt to the floor, but the Nosferatu seemed not to notice. "We vampires value our independence. It is part of our solitary nature."

He paused. "Yet, despite such feelings, I suspect you are working for another. I am correct in my assumption, am I not?"

Le Clair took a step closer to his victim. Then another. He was in no rush, but he did not have all night. "You mean the Red Death? He is an instrumental part of my mission, but I am not his servant. Or his partner. I am the sole master of my destiny."

"So think all of the Kindred," said Phantomas, chuckling. A dozen rats swarmed across the floor in front of him, their squeals echoing his laughter. "We refuse to admit that many of our actions are the direct result of more powerful vampires manipulating us for their own ends."

"The Jyhad?" said Le Clair, with a sneer. He inched forward, his attention focused on Phantomas. Members of the Nosferatu clan were famed masters of illusion. Le Clair had no intention of letting his quarry escape by turning invisible. "Surely you don't believe in that fable? It's a myth fostered by the Camarilla to keep the herds in line. I am not so easily fooled."

Phantomas shook his head slowly, as if disappointed. Kneeling, he reached out and gently picked up a large rat, cradling it in his arms like a kitten as he returned to an upright position. "You

272

are a fool, Monsieur Le Clair," he said quietly, "blind to the truth that glares at you out of the darkness. The Red Death is no myth. He is a Methuselah, one of the incredibly ancient Kindred engaged in the Jyhad. And you are his puppet. You let him pull your strings."

Le Clair raised his knife. The steel glowed green from the lights of the monitors. "Enough of this senseless babble," he declared. "I have won. The taste of your blood will make me strong."

"I think not," said Phantomas. "You made a terrible mistake, Le Clair, when you let your friends die. You stand before me alone. While I am surrounded by allies."

Le Clair laughed, a harsh, cruel sound. "Allies? What allies?"

Holding the rat close to his chest with one arm, Phantomas pointed to the ground with the other. "I have loyal friends, Monsieur. Thousands upon thousands of them. Like me, they are ugly. But they are true."

All at once the cavern floor came alive. Rats covered the earth like a blanket. Le Clair felt the first stirrings of uneasiness, as thousands upon thousands of pairs of eyes looked straight at him. The knife he held suddenly seemed useless.

Phantomas let the rat in his arms slip to the ground. "They cannot kill you, Le Clair. But they can keep you very busy until I finish the job by slicing off your head."

From the desk which held his keyboard, Phantomas picked up a long metal object. It was a

Roman soldier's gladius.

"Just because I hide in the darkness, Le Clair," said the Nosferatu, "does not mean I cannot defend myself."

Phantomas raised his arm and pointed at Le Clair. "Get him," he commanded.

Le Clair managed to scream once before he was engulfed by a swarm of rats.

PART

5

UNHOLY ALLIES

The impetuous fury of the entering gust nearly lifted us from our feet. It was, indeed, a tempestuous yet sternly beautiful night, and one wildly singular in its terror and its beauty.
from "The Fall of the House of Usher"
by Edgar Allan Poe

ROBERT WEINBERG

Chapter 1

Washington, D.C. - March 24, 1994:

Though he murdered for money, Makish did not think of himself as an assassin. Instead, he believed that he was a performance artist, creating three-dimensional tapestries of destruction. Death was merely the final scene in his elaborate tableaus. The act of committing murder was as important to him as the result. Makish was truly dedicated to his craft. No matter what the pressure, he refused to compromise his beliefs. To him, style meant everything.

Tonight, as he had promised the Red Death, Makish planned to kill the female Assamite assassin known as Flavia, the Dark Angel. In doing so, he was violating one of the seven basic tenets of Assamite code called the *khabar*. According to the tradition known as *Ikhwan*, assassins were members of a shared brotherhood that took precedence over any contract or obligation. They were strictly forbidden to fight one another. The penalty for violating the *khabar* was the Final Death. Makish didn't care. He had been condemned by the clan inner council, the Du'at, centuries ago. He could only die once.

Shortly after sunset, Makish completed his

preparations for the upcoming battle. He pulled on a pair of baggy, olive-green silk pants and a matching silk topshirt. The garments provided him with freedom of motion and were difficult for his enemies to grasp. The inner lining of the shirt, at the waist and sleeves, hid a number of small, secret pockets. In each of them he placed a handful of tiny Thermit charges, along with a detonator. Makish planned to immobilize Flavia, then circle her neck with a chain of explosives. Their detonation, which would burn her to cinders, would be a supreme moment of artistic expression.

Completing his clothing ensemble, he pulled on a pair of black cloth sandals. Finally, he looped over his right shoulder a large, light-blue cloth bag. It contained his wallet and identification papers. Makish was a superior forger and never traveled anywhere without the correct, though entirely fictitious, documentation. Like all professional assassins, he was an expert at appearing innocuous.

Resting at the bottom of the cloth sack were two black plastic blocks approximately four inches wide by four inches long and an inch and a half thick. He had retrieved them from his suitcases last night. Each of the blocks had four holes on one end the size of a small man's fingers. The size of Makish's fingers.

The plastic slabs looked harmless, and they were, until Makish slipped his hands into them. Then, the blocks were transformed by the force of his will into a unique pair of weapons known as *Bakh Nagh*, tiger claws.

Each claw was a molded piece of shatter-resistant plastic that hugged Makish's knuckles like a second skin. Embedded in them, pointing straight out, were curved, three-inch-long adamant steel spikes. The nails were honed to a razor's edge, able to cut through muscle and bone like scissors through paper. By clenching his hands into fists, Makish effectively changed his fingers into gigantic metal claws.

Normally, he did not use weapons in the performance of his duties. Makish disliked separating himself from the actual kill by artificial means. Though he needed human blood to sustain himself, he was careful never to kill any of the mortals he fed upon. Murder was reserved solely for his art. Makish drank vitae to survive; he killed to give his existence meaning.

In dealing with the Dark Angel, however, he felt justified in using the tiger claws. All of the reports he had found on Flavia's skills credited her as a spectacular fighter with double-swords. Armed with two sixteen-inch blades, using vampire Disciplines that canceled out against his, the Dark Angel would be a dangerous opponent. Makish was confident about his dueling skills, with or without the claws, but he also did not believe in gambling. Though he was committed to destroying the Dark Angel, he was equally intent upon surviving the encounter.

Satisfied with his preparations, he checked the appearance of his headquarters carefully, making sure that the place did not look occupied. The best hideaways were those which no one suspected to be in use.

The deserted cellar of a burned-out apartment building on the capital's southeast side served as Makish's base of operations. He had discovered the room on the first night he had been summoned by the Red Death to Washington. It was in the center of the worst slums of downtown D.C., not far from the Navy Yard that he had destroyed in spectacular fashion. To the west were both Houses of Congress, and to the north were the presidential memorials. The location served as a base, where he could store his garments, remain hidden during the daytime while he slept, perform his exercises upon rising each night, and launch his attacks upon the Red Death's command.

It was just starting to rain when he departed. The skies were dark, with thick clouds blotting out the moon and stars. Thunder rolled and lightning flashed in the distance. Makish set a steady pace, somewhere between a walk and a jog. His destination was the large office building across the street from the Watergate Hotel. It was there, he was certain, that he would find the Dark Angel.

Makish's confidence stemmed from the fact that he had been raised and trained as an Assamite assassin himself. He understood as only an insider could the practices and philosophies of the clan. As such, he could predict how Flavia would act in specific situations based on his own reactions to similar circumstances.

She had been given the assignment of protecting Dire McCann from enemies among the Kindred. The detective, however, refused to allow her unlimited access to his room. Besides which, conforming to hotel rules and regulations often caused vampires serious problems. Makish therefore surmised that the Dark Angel must be staying close to McCann's quarters while remaining out of sight. The challenge then shifted to locating the detective. For an assassin of Makish's stature, that was no more than an annoying riddle.

Like many powerful Kindred, Makish had no childer or ghouls. He preferred to work entirely on his own. He did not want any followers or assistants cluttering up his existence. However, whenever foot soldiers were necessary, he made use of clanless vampires known as Caitiff mercenary fighters. Willing to work for payment in cash or innocents' blood, the Caitiff performed the necessary chores that Makish could not cover on his own.

A dozen such Caitiff had scoured hotel journals in the Washington area until they matched McCann's description with that of a guest at the Watergate hotel. The same band of renegades had been promised a huge reward for eliminating the detective that evening. Makish had no illusions about the group's chances of success. He was sending them to certain death. But their attack on McCann would provide the necessary time for Makish to contact Flavia. And issue a challenge she could not refuse.

An impressive business complex faced the west side of the Watergate Hotel. Makish scanned the directory for new companies. He stopped when he found Vargoss Imports. It didn't take a great leap of the imagination to connect the Dark Angel with a branch office of her prince's business concern. Many vampires who traveled from city to city relied on short-term rentals to provide safe havens. Offices could easily be sealed shut each night, with instructions for the cleaning crews to come in the morning. They offered a viable alternative for Kindred who preferred that their resting places not be known to the Cainites of a city. Or a vampire who had more enemies than friends.

Riding the elevator to the seventh floor of the building, Makish considered breaking down the correct door and attacking Flavia without warning. With a little luck, he would catch the female totally off guard and slice her to ribbons before she could mount a counterattack.

The assassin shook his head. He never relied on luck or chance. Gambling was for fools. He had not survived for hundreds of years by taking unnecessary risks.

Flavia might have a strong paranoid streak, a common trait among professional killers, and have the door rigged for a surprise attack. Or, he could break into the room just as she was preparing her weapons. Either circumstance would mean disaster. Makish, instead, preferred the cautious approach. He planned to trap the Dark Angel by her own code. The hallway leading to Office 714 was deserted. Moving without a sound, Makish glided down the corridor and knocked three times on Flavia's door.

"Who's there?" a woman's voice asked without

hesitation. Flavia sounded neither worried nor surprised. Revealing doubts was not part of Assamite tradition. "Identify yourself."

"I am a tiger among leopards," said Makish. Among the Kindred, the Assamites were often referred to as "leopards among the jackals." Makish, who numbered himself among the greatest assassins of the bloodline, felt he deserved a title befitting his status. "May I enter?"

The door to the office opened. Standing inside the chamber, her back to the far wall, was Flavia, the Dark Angel. She was dressed entirely in white leather, and was taller and heavier than Makish. She waited for him to enter, a ghostly smile on her lips. "You've come to surrender to face clan justice?" she asked, as he walked into the office and closed the door. "Or did I guess wrong?"

Makish chuckled. He appreciated the Dark Angel's sarcasm. Most Assamites were much too serious. Inwardly, he rejoiced. The wheels had begun to turn and there was nothing that could be done to stop their motion. Flavia was doomed.

Folding his hands just beneath his chest, he bobbed his head up and down swiftly several times. "I am so sorry, Miss," he announced in a high-pitched, singsong voice. "You are very mistaken in your belief. I have not come to surrender my humble self to your care. My sincere apologies."

"Then why are you here?" asked Flavia. Makish noted that while the Dark Angel sounded amused, she still held a short sword in each hand. He expected no less. She had been properly trained. A good assassin never confronted a stranger unarmed.

"I have come to issue a challenge," said Makish, abandoning his mock-Indian accent. "Your continued presence in this city threatens my client, whom I am sworn to protect. I fully understand that you cannot leave until you have destroyed him. You are bound by your word, as I am by mine. The only honorable solution is a battle to the death between the two of us."

"You speak of *Muruwa* — honor," said Flavia, her voice devoid of humor, "but you are a renegade and a traitor to your clan. Why should I believe anything you say?"

Makish shrugged. "Believe whatever you wish. It is true that I disobeyed the commands of the Du'at. But realize, please, that clan politics forced me to that decision."

"Explain," said Flavia. "I'm listening."

"Jamal, leader of our clan, always considered me his greatest rival as Master of the Assassins," said Makish. "He knew someday I would challenge him for his position and he feared my skills. Thus, he resorted to trickery and deceit to brand me an outlaw.

"When my sire was killed by a mortal, I demanded, as was my right and my duty, vengeance against his slayers. Jamal and his puppets denied my request. They said my actions could jeopardize the Masquerade. As if the Assamites care for such foolishness! I suspected they were in league with the killers, but had no proof. Blood called out for blood. My sacred honor permitted me no other path than to disobey the commands of the Du'at When I did so, I was declared an outcast and an outlaw."

Makish's voice turned cold. "But I did avenge the death of my sire. His wraith is at rest in the land of the dead. Some debts must be paid. I think you understand. The spirit of your sister, destroyed by the Red Death, calls to you, demanding that you honor her name. I am the deputy of the Red Death; he has contracted me to protect him from harm, and, once given, my word is law. Your path to revenge lies through me. The choice is clear: accept my challenge and face me in single combat, or forfeit your claim and abandon your honor."

"The choice you offer is no choice," said Flavia. There was a note of desperation in her voice. She had been cornered by her own code. "I will fight. As you knew I would. I accept your challenge. Where? And when?"

"Tonight, of course," said Makish. As if echoing his words, lightning flashed in the window. A crack of thunder shook the building. "As soon as you are ready. The time is right. As I have picked the hour, you have the right to choose the location."

Flavia's eyes narrowed. Behind her, lightning flashed again. Slowly, she nodded, as if answering an inner question. "On the grass mall linking the Lincoln Memorial and the Washington Monument," she said, an odd look of satisfaction on her face. "Between the weather and the riots, the area should be deserted. We should be completely alone."

Makish had no choice but to accept, although the Dark Angel's pleased expression made him wonder whether he had made a dangerous mistake.

UNHOLY ALLIES

Chapter 2

Washington, D.C. - March 25, 1994:

Elisha pulled the collar of his sweatshirt tighter around his neck. The rain was coming down with increasing force, and he was thoroughly soaked. His entire body felt like a gigantic sea sponge.

Overhead, lightning flashed, answered almost instantaneously by thunder. The storm, in all its fury, was upon them. In the glare of the electricity, Elisha glanced at his companion. Dire McCann's face was etched with worry. The big detective appeared to be lost in thought.

According to McCann, the walk from the Watergate Hotel to the Lincoln Memorial was not a major outing. With the rain, however, going from one place to the other was like swimming upstream in a waterfall. Elisha would have suggested taking a cab except they hadn't seen a single moving vehicle for the past twenty minutes. The streets were empty of life. Even his magic couldn't make a taxi appear from thin air.

"Is something wrong, Mr. McCann?" Elisha asked, not sure why the detective appeared so disturbed. "You look worried."

"It just occurred to me," answered McCann, "that maybe that attack wasn't actually expected to catch me by surprise. The Red Death knows by now that I'm not vulnerable to scum like those vampires who attacked us in the halls. They're a minor inconvenience, nothing more."

"Then why were they sent?" asked Elisha.

"I'm not sure," said McCann, "but I suspect we'll learn the answer in..."

"Someone's approaching," Elisha interrupted, his mental defenses tingling. "I can sense a presence drawing closer."

Anxiously, he scanned the area, looking for trouble. It wasn't hard to find. Grabbing McCann by the arm, Elisha pointed to a black blot on the street fifty yards away. "There. That shape on the ground. It's moving toward us."

The detective smiled. "Nothing to worry about. She's on our side."

"She?" repeated Elisha.

"Watch," said McCann. "Some powers can't be explained. They have to be seen to be believed."

The shadowy blotch rushed forward. As it approached, it gradually took on form and shape, seeming to solidify out of the surrounding darkness. Elisha rubbed the rain out of his eyes. Though he had been surrounded by magic most of his life, he had never witnessed three dimensions emerging from two in quite so spectacular a transition. What had been shadow was now substance. The phantom blot was gone. Replacing it, standing just a few away, was an intriguing young lady dressed entirely in black.

The newcomer wore a very short black dress,

black stockings, and black shoes. Even her hair and eyes were black. Around her neck was an elaborate silver necklace. Her features were pale, broken only by the crimson of her lips. Elisha thought her stunning. It took a few seconds for him to realize that she radiated no warmth, no life. She was a vampire.

"Madeleine Giovanni," said McCann, sounding amused. Elisha wondered if his disappointment was so obvious. "I'd like to introduce you to Elisha Horwitz. He came to see me at the request of an old friend."

The detective paused. "Actually, the two of you have that in common. Madeleine comes from Venice. She's the childe of another close acquaintance."

Reacting by instinct, Elisha stepped forward, holding out his hand. "Pleased to meet you," he said.

"The pleasure is mine," said Madeleine, her expression enigmatic. She touched his hand for a moment. Her fingers were ice cold. "You are a mage?"

"Just an apprentice," said Elisha. He was somewhat bewildered. "How did you know?"

"There are certain unique traits that set mages apart from normal humans," said Madeleine. "I have come to recognize the signs. It helps me avoid possible painful business confrontations."

Elisha had absolutely no idea what Madeleine meant, but he had no intention of saying so. "I always felt I was pretty ordinary looking," he declared instead. "Nobody has ever seemed to think otherwise."

"Most mortals are fools," she declared, her dark eyes shining brightly. "They merely observe the physical, but cannot see what lies beneath the surface. Personally, I find you quite attractive."

Dire McCann laughed. "Enough flattery, Madeleine. Poor Elisha is blushing."

Elisha opened his mouth to say that he was not. But no words came out.

"I only spoke the truth," said Madeleine, a puzzled note to her voice. "Please do not be embarrassed by my remarks."

Elisha gulped. The rain had quickly soaked Madeleine's black dress so that it clung to her slender figure like a second skin. She was not wearing much beneath. Though she was not mortal, Elisha still thought she was the most beautiful woman he had ever seen. "I'm fine," he croaked, feeling anything but. "Really."

"Let's move," said Dire McCann. He looked up apprehensively. "Standing on a path right by the Potomac River with lightning flaring overhead makes me nervous. Besides, we're late for our meeting. Flavia is probably cursing already, wondering where I am tonight."

"Flavia?" asked Elisha, as they started walking again. With McCann taking the lead, it seemed only natural for him to walk with Madeleine. "Who's that?"

"An Assamite assassin," replied the young lady in black. "She is acting as McCann's bodyguard."

Elisha shook his head, remembering the fight in

the hallway. "Mr. McCann doesn't need a bodyguard."

Madeleine smiled. "Everyone needs a bodyguard sometime. Even a mage like Elisha Horwitz. Even Dire McCann."

She paused, then changed the subject. "Which of the Nine Traditions do you follow?"

"My teacher does not adhere to any one particular system of magic," said Elisha, cautiously. He remembered Rambam's three warnings. Madeleine seemed pleasant, and McCann evidently trusted her. But she was a member of the Kindred. "He honors them all equally."

"A diplomatic answer," said Madeleine laughing. "Your mentor sounds like a wise man. Who is he?"

"He's the smartest man in the world," said Elisha, proudly. He spoke without thinking. "He goes by the name Rambam. It's his nickname."

Madeleine's eyes widened. "You study with the Second Moses? Maimonides is numbered among the most powerful mages in the world. He instructs only a chosen few. No wonder your aura burns so brightly."

Elisha felt his cheeks turning red again. It didn't occur to him that, despite his earlier misgivings, he was revealing more about his background than he should. His teacher's cautionary words were forgotten. It would only be much later that he would realize his mistake.

"What's your relationship with Mr. McCann?" he asked, trying to regain his composure.

"Probably the same as yours," said Madeleine.

Again, she switched subjects without providing a definite answer. "He is quite mysterious. You know, of course, that he claims to be a mage? Of the Euthanatos Tradition."

"So I've been told," answered Elisha. "Though I find that hard to believe. Mr. McCann acts too...unusual."

"I understand," said Madeleine, flashing him another smile. "Everything Dire McCann says about himself seems to be highly questionable. I am not sure anyone knows the truth about him. Actually, I suspect he prefers it that way."

They reached the Lincoln Memorial ten minutes later. The path from the river led directly to the rear entrance of the huge structure. There was no sign of anyone else. The monument appeared to be deserted.

"Dry off," said McCann to Elisha. "I'm going to check the guard station. I'll be back in a minute. Madeleine, you keep watch. Maybe Flavia's scouting the grounds, hunting for us."

Left to his own devices for a minute, Elisha peeled off his sweatshirt and squeezed out the water as best he could. That job complete, he decided to play tourist until McCann returned. Thus far, his tour of America consisted of an airport, a hotel and some city streets.

It only took him a few minutes to do a quick walkaround of the magnificent sculpture of Abraham Lincoln. Sadly, he shook his head. He found the monument both inspiring and depressing. The statue was impressive, as were the great orator's words, carved on the marble walls. However, the impact was considerably lessened by the presence of gang symbols and graffiti spray painted everywhere. Even the massive sculpture had not escaped defacement. In a grotesque statement of modern values, an unknown hoodlum had decorated Lincoln's forehead with a bull's-eye.

"She's not here," declared McCann, breaking into Elisha's melancholy thoughts. The detective stood at the base of the statue. He was frowning. "I checked everywhere. That's odd. After her lecture last night, the one thing I did not expect was for us to arrive before Flavia."

"I agree," said Madeleine, appearing as if by magic at Elisha's side. She smiled when he jumped. "The Dark Angel did not strike me as the type to ever be late for a meeting."

The Giovanni vampire closed her eyes. "Let me try to pinpoint her location," she said. "I have the power to determine the whereabouts of powerful Kindred by their mental patterns. Last night, I found Makish and the Red Death to determine where you were. I located Flavia in the same manner. Spotting her again shouldn't be difficult."

Elisha stared at Madeleine in amazement. He wondered what other incredible powers she controlled.

Her eyes stayed closed for just an instant. When they blinked open, she looked startled. "Out in front," she declared. "Flavia is right outside, on the grassy mall separating this building from the Washington Monument. But she is not alone. I sense a second powerful Assamite presence there as well."

"Makish," said McCann, hurrying around to the front of the memorial. Madeleine was a step behind. "The rogue killer. It has to be him."

Not sure what was happening but knowing he did not want to be left on his own, Elisha followed the others. Near-constant streaks of lightning lit up the sky so that it was easy to see where the detective was going. McCann flew down the front steps of the Lincoln Memorial and across the closed street beyond. He came to an abrupt stop at the edge of the grass. An instant later, Madeleine froze at the detective's side. It took Elisha a few seconds to catch up. A dozen questions died unspoken as he stared in amazement at the drama unfolding less than a hundred feet beyond.

Two figures moved about on the grass in what appeared to be a complex ritual dance. One was a small, slender male, dressed entirely in green silk. The other was a woman wearing white leather. They were both Kindred. The rain obscured their features, but Elisha knew they had to be Flavia and Makish. Watching them intently, the young man realized that the vampires were not dancing. They were dueling with swords and claws.

"What's happening?" Elisha whispered to Madeleine. He dared not raise his voice, for fear of distracting one of the fighters.

"Makish is a rogue Assamite assassin employed by the Red Death," Madeleine replied softly, her lips close to his ear. "He is the one who nearly killed

McCann the other night. Flavia has sworn a sacred oath to destroy the Red Death. Obviously, Makish somehow found Flavia and challenged her to a death duel. Bound by her code of honor, she could not refuse the traitor, even though her chances of winning this fight are minimal."

"He's better than she is?" asked Elisha. Watching the two Assamites moving in the rain, it seemed their skills were equally matched.

"She is very good," said Madeleine. "There are few among the Kindred who can match both her speed and her skill. But Makish is in a class by himself. He is one of the very best. It will take a miracle for Flavia to defeat him."

"We could help her," said Elisha. "That would even the odds."

"Never," replied Madeleine. "She would suffer the Final Death before she would accept aid. We can only watch. None of us may interfere. Flavia is bound by her honor and the honor of her clan to battle Makish without assistance."

"If he destroys her, then what?" asked Elisha.

"She will be avenged," said Madeleine, her voice grim. There was no doubt in her words. "I cannot intervene while they fight. However, once the battle is over, I am free to act as I wish. And I promise you that there will be a reckoning. A reckoning in blood."

Chapter 3

Washington, D.C. - March 25, 1994:

Five minutes after the duel began, Makish knew how it would end. He fought using his tiger claws. Flavia used twin short swords. Their weapons were evenly matched. Neither of them dared use magic because it placed such a tremendous drain on the caster's strength. They depended entirely upon their physical skills. She weighed more than he, and was stronger, but he was slightly faster. The differences evened out. The grass was slippery, as were the garments they wore. Only their years of experience separated them. The Dark Angel had been an Assamite for slightly over a hundred years; Makish had been an assassin for twice as long. She had spent most of her time working as part of a team with her sister. He had always worked alone. The disparities between them were minor, but they were enough. Makish felt certain of victory. It was only a matter of time until Flavia made a fatal mistake.

The rules of the duel were simple. The fight was to the death, and would continue until one of them was destroyed. There were no other rules. Anything was permitted, as long as the fighters remained in the agreed-upon arena and no aid was provided by outsiders.

For every move she used, he employed the proper counter. Flavia had been taught double short-sword fighting from Salaq Quadim, the greatest weapons master in the world. So had Makish. They knew the same tricks. And the same counters.

"You fight well for an old man," she said, after they had been dueling for five minutes. "It will be a shame to send you to the Final Death."

Makish smiled, his attention never wavering from Flavia's swords. He was not easily distracted.

"I appreciate the compliment," he declared. "But, as before, you have made a terrible mistake. I am not going to perish. You are."

As if to prove his point, Makish aimed a quick series of punches at Flavia's head. His hands, moving faster than the eye could follow, directed the metal spikes right at the Dark Angel's eyes. She didn't blink. Nor did she retreat.

Her swords came up, slamming hard against the dark plastic of the claws. With a quick twist of her wrists, the Dark Angel deflected the feints over her shoulders. Then, with Makish's arms spread wide apart, she pushed herself toward him, trying to ram the assassin with her body. Flavia knew that with her superior body weight, if she could knock Makish to the ground and land on top of him, the fight would be over. But, being no fool, he realized the truth as well.

Like a springboard diver launching himself against a hardwood board, Makish kicked his feet hard against the wet ground. Incredibly powerful leg muscles sent him flying straight up into the air. His arms flattened against his body. Flavia charged on, but Makish was no longer there. Curving his torso, he flipped head over heels and dropped to the ground ten feet beyond the leather-clad assassin. Landing on his feet, he immediately raised his tiger claws in a defensive stance.

"I plan to spend many more years on this earth conducting my business, thank you," he declared smoothly, as Flavia spun around to face him again. "I do not think it is time for me to retire yet."

"The choice isn't yours to make," said Flavia. "Why don't..." she began, then leapt forward, the sentence unfinished.

The Dark Angel moved quick as the lightning above them, swinging a short sword in an upward pass at Makish's stomach. Reacting with equal speed, he parried, catching her blade on the steel claws of his left hand and deflecting it to his side. At the same moment, he slashed downward with his other arm, aiming his claw at her unprotected shoulder. Her second sword clashed against the steel hooks, stopping them inches from her flesh. Together, they spun around, hand to hand, twirling in a tango of engaged steel.

"...you listen to what I am saying," continued Flavia, picking up where she left off, while each struggled to break the other's counter. "You cannot defeat me."

"Why not?" Makish asked, gathering his strength. Twisting both hands around, he thrust upward, trying to rip Flavia's blades out of her grip. With a whisper of metal, she pulled away, sliding out of his latest trap. In doing so, however, she shuffled her feet instead of lifting them. The slick, wet grass, battered to the ground by hours of rain, betrayed her. The Dark Angel's feet skidded a step. For a bare second, Flavia stumbled off-balance and off-guard.

Makish, his hands still raised above his head, reacted instead with his legs. He lashed out with toes harder than stone. The blow caught the Dark Angel in her right knee. Bone shattered.

Cursing in despair, Flavia slashed wildly with both swords at Makish's exposed chest. The rogue assassin danced out of their path, laughing merrily. Like most vampires, the Dark Angel possessed tremendous recuperative powers. But using those powers required concentration and blood. And Flavia had neither.

Cautiously, Makish circled his victim. Crippled, the Dark Angel maneuvered as best she could on one good leg. The other dangled helplessly at her side as she tried to turn, to keep facing Makish.

"One small mistake," he declared sanctimoniously, "is the difference between survival and destruction. You are undone."

"I'm not dead yet," said Flavia. Her gaze flickered over his shoulder as she focused on something in the darkness. "I am the Dark Angel. It is not my destiny to be destroyed tonight. It is yours, traitor to the *khabar*."

"You think your companions watching our duel will save you?" said Makish, moving a little faster. He was in no rush. Making his opponent suffer physically and mentally was part of his art. Without pain and cruelty, death was merely an act. It needed passion and hate to make it beautiful. "Their presence is noted. They will not intrude in your duel. Eluding them in the rain and the darkness once you are destroyed will not be difficult."

"I don't need saving," replied Flavia. "The end is near. Not for me. For you."

Savagely, Makish swung a ferocious blow at Flavia's side. He found her constant taunting irritating. Especially now that he had won the fight. Reacting instinctively, the Dark Angel blocked his claw with a sword. Steel strained against steel. Makish expected no less. Instantly, he jerked his arm up and around in a tremendous loop. The action sent Flavia reeling. With only a single leg for support, the Dark Angel crashed, flat on her back, to the ground. Brutally, Makish stomped on her good knee, crushing cartilage and bone to pulp.

Flavia was helpless, with both of her legs mangled. There was no possible way for her to regain her feet. With a knowing smile, Makish walked around her limp body. He was careful not to get too close. The Dark Angel still held two swords, though in a minute more it wouldn't matter. She was finished. His triumph was complete.

"You think you've finally beaten me," she said, her eyes blazing, as he removed the tiger claws from his hands. Makish no longer needed the weapons. He preferred to have his hands free. He planned to break Flavia's elbows, rendering her completely helpless. Then he would destroy her using his

Thermit charges. "You haven't."

"Considering your position," said Makish, "I find your remarks quite amusing. Would you care to explain them to me in the few moments of unlife you have left?"

"Better yet," said Flavia, the rain forming a puddle beneath her head, "I'll demonstrate."

Her right hand flashed forward, sending her short sword flying like a dagger at Makish's face. He reacted without thinking. Letting his reflexes take over, he reached out and grabbed the blade from midair, inches from his left eye. The second sword, a moment later, he caught with his other hand.

"Somehow," he said pensively, holding the two swords at arms' length, "I expected a different answer."

"You arrogant, ignorant bastard," said Flavia, mockingly. "I'm an angel. Dark or light, I can call down the lightning."

The sky turned molten white. The tremendous electrical discharge drawn by the steel swords might not have destroyed Makish. But there was no escaping the exploding Thermit bombs that filled his pockets.

Chapter 4

Washington, D.C. - March 25, 1994:

Gingerly, Dire McCann raised himself off the muddy ground. None of his bones felt broken. He had been caught completely off-guard by the massive lightning stroke and accompanying explosions. The blasts had slammed him to the earth. His eyes hurt, and he was sure that he was partially deaf. Still, he was alive and functional, which he suspected was no longer the case with Makish. Thermit was extremely effective.

Shaking off the effects of the blast, McCann climbed to his feet. A few yards away, Elisha Horwitz sat on the wet grass, his head buried in his hands. The rain, which earlier seemed to be easing off, had returned full force. The detective splashed his way through a series of small puddles to the young man. There was no sign of Madeleine Giovanni.

"You okay?" the detective asked.

Elisha raised his head and squinted at McCann. "Sure," the young man said with a laugh, "other than the fact that I'm barely able to see, my hearing is shot, and I have a headache wide enough to march the Israeli army through. I'm fine."

"Good," said McCann, chuckling in return. "I worried it might be something serious." The detective paused. "I take it you didn't have anything to do with this lightning strike."

"Me?" said Elisha. "Not on your life. My teacher has warned me about fooling around with the weather. Coincidence can be stretched only so far before it breaks. Raising a storm is beyond that limit. It takes a lot more skill than I possess to toss around lightning bolts. Remember, I'm just an apprentice."

"I haven't forgotten," said McCann. "Though I suspect you underestimate your talents. Meanwhile, do you have any idea where our female friend might be?"

"Madeleine?" asked Elisha. "She was here a minute ago. She helped me sit up and checked to make sure I wasn't hurt. Then, she muttered something about going to take a look for Flavia. Though I'm not sure why she bothered. Nobody could survive an explosion that powerful."

"You haven't associated with the Kindred long enough," said McCann. "These vampires, especially Assamites, are astonishingly difficult to destroy. Give me your hand. It's time for you to get out of that puddle. The walk will do you good. Let's go see what she's discovered."

They found Madeleine sitting cross-legged in the middle of a scorched, ten-foot-wide patch of grass. Stretched out next to her was the battered and burnt body of the Dark Angel. Her white jumpsuit hung in tatters on her figure. Much of her skin had been baked to a crisp, like meat left too long over a fire. In several places, muscle and bone lay exposed to the rain. Both of her knees were broken, and her arms and legs hung limp at her sides. But the Assamite's eyes were wide open and glowed with intelligence.

There was nothing left of Makish. He was gone, as if he had never been. The only remnant of his passing were two fused pieces of dark plastic.

"McCann," Flavia croaked as he stepped into her line of vision. "My apologies. I'm the one who is late tonight."

"You're excused," said the detective. He knelt beside the assassin. "I didn't realize you could call down lightning."

"Neither did that arrogant son-of-a-bitch, Makish," said Flavia. "My sister and I both claim that power. That's where the Dark Angels nickname originated. We looked like we were angels from above. And we controlled Heaven's fire."

"He underestimated you," said McCann. "A fatal mistake."

"The rogue was overconfident," said Flavia. Wearily, she closed her eyes. "He considered himself above the honor of his clan. He forgot that a wise assassin must always bury his pride. He paid the price for his vanity."

"She needs blood," said Madeleine. "The longer she waits, the more she'll require. Burn wounds take vast amounts of vitae and much time to heal. Assamites possess incredible regenerative powers. But she can't regenerate without blood."

"Not mine," said McCann, instantly. He rose to his feet and took a step back. The notion of Flavia drinking his blood frightened him. "Sorry. But that's impossible. She can't have a drop of my blood."

Flavia reopened her eyes. Looking at the detective, she smiled, her black lips cracking like dried bacon. "Somehow, I thought you might feel that way, McCann."

The Dark Angel turned her head and stared at Madeleine. "I can't drink your blood," she said. "As you well know, Assamites are cursed. We cannot touch the vitae of other Kindred. We can only feed on the blood of mortals. Like that of your young friend standing behind you."

Elisha, who had been following the conversation with interest, turned bleach white. "She wants to drink my blood?"

"Just a small amount," said Madeleine. "That's all she needs to enable her to move. Please, Elisha. It won't be painful. Just the opposite, in fact. I swear it."

"How do I know she'll just drink a little?" said Elisha, his eyes wide with panic. There was a wild sound to his voice. "You said she needs a lot to heal. Once she starts, what's to make her stop?"

"McCann and I will be watching," said Madeleine. "There is no danger."

"I—I—I'm not sure," said Elisha. He licked his lips, his gaze flicking back and forth between Dire McCann and Madeleine Giovanni. "I just met both of you tonight. Why should I believe what you are saying? You could be lying to save your friend."

"Boy," said Flavia, harshly. Somehow, she had raised herself up on her arms to a half-sitting position. "I am an Assamite. My clan is not like the rest of the Kindred. *Our word when given, to humans or vampires, is never broken.* On my sacred honor, I swear that I will take just enough of your blood to enable me to regenerate my broken body so I can return to my hideaway. Tomorrow, I will obtain the necessary vitae from others to complete my healing. You will not be harmed. And, I will be forever in your debt."

Elisha's hands tightened into fists. He took several deep breaths. The frightened look disappeared from his eyes. Gradually, the color returned to his cheeks.

"I'm probably making the biggest mistake of my life," he declared, his voice shaking with emotion. "But I'll do it."

Trembling, the young man dropped to his knees on the wet ground beside Flavia. Snaking an arm under the Assamite, Madeleine carefully raised the Dark Angel to a sitting position. The rain had lessened into a soft steady drizzle. Elisha tugged at his wet sweatshirt. "I assume you want me to take this off," he said, with a wan smile.

"Not necessary," said Flavia. "Biting necks is out of style. Give me your left arm. Pull back your sleeve. That's all. Close your eyes and forget where you are."

Biting his lower lip, Elisha did as he was told. Anxiously, Flavia raised the young man's wrist to her mouth.

"Don't be frightened," said Dire McCann, resting a hand on Elisha's shoulder. The detective willed some of his inner calm to the terrified young mage.

"It's not what you think."

Flavia bit and drank. Elisha's jaw dropped in surprise. McCann knew why. The kiss of a vampire caused not pain but pleasure. The sensations for both kine and Kindred were intense beyond belief. It was the supreme moment of fulfilled passion.

It lasted mere seconds. "Enough," said Flavia, her voice thick with emotion. She pulled her mouth off Elisha's wrist and pushed the young man away. "I need no more."

McCann marveled at the Assamite's self-control. Few vampires had the willpower to break contact so quickly. Blood not only gave the Kindred life, it *was* their life. They called their dark hunger the Beast Within, for it was exactly that.

"Well?" asked McCann, as Elisha opened his eyes. Already, the two incisions on the young man's wrist had closed. A few seconds more and they would be gone. The Kindred never left any trace of their presence. "How do you feel?"

Elisha shook his head, appearing bewildered. Slightly wobbly, he stood up with an assist from McCann. "I'm fine. Slightly dazed and confused, but otherwise all right. It felt... strange. Very strange." He grinned. "My headache's gone, though."

The detective kept a hand on Elisha's arm to make sure the apprentice didn't take a sudden tumble. "You'll be dizzy for a few minutes," he said. "Take it easy. Meanwhile, you might be interested in seeing how Flavia uses your blood to renew her body. It's a transformation rarely witnessed by mortals."

ROBERT WEINBERG

McCann wasn't exaggerating. The Dark Angel was undergoing a startling metamorphosis. Her skin was flattening out, turning smooth and white, and regenerating where it had been burned to cinders. In seconds, the black and crumbling remains had disappeared, replaced by healthy, supple flesh. At the same time, the bones in her knees reformed, knitting together exactly as they had been before the fight. Her legs straightened, as did her arms. All that remained unchanged was Flavia's leather jumpsuit, which still hung in ripped fragments across her rejuvenated body.

"Incredible," said Madeleine Giovanni. She licked her lips. "His blood is incredibly powerful."

Flavia, appearing equally astonished, slowly ran her fingers down her body, touching every spot that had been damaged. She looked up with a bemused expression. "I was broken, now I am whole."

"You've seen the power of a mage's blood," said McCann quietly to Elisha, "and you've also endured in small measure a vampire's kiss. Few mortals have experienced either. Remember them both, for in these dangerous times, such knowledge is the ultimate power."

"You also are owed a debt by an Assamite assassin," said Flavia, rising like a white ghost in the mist. There was not a mark on her. Her lush figure played havoc with the remaining bits of her outfit, but she made no effort to cover herself. A sardonic smile crossed her blood-red lips. "We do not regard such obligations lightly. It shall be repaid."

"Good enough," said Dire McCann. "But let's

continue this conversation under shelter. I'm tired of being soaked."

"I agree," said Elisha, shivering. "I'm not partial to this type of weather."

"I like the rain," declared Madeleine Giovanni as they walked toward the Lincoln Memorial. "It adds character to the night."

"It saved my skin," said Flavia, with a laugh. "Without it, I would never have defeated Makish."

"I thought you were finished when he knocked you to the ground," said Elisha. "Then the lightning came."

"I taunted him throughout our fight," said Flavia, "telling him that I couldn't lose. The words annoyed Makish but he never gave them any credence. Thus, when the moment came for him to finish me, he paused for an instant to gloat. Those few seconds were all I needed to summon the lightning. Makish never realized that his peril came from his own attitudes, not from me. The renegade had a basic character flaw which proved to be his doom."

"Overconfidence," said Dire McCann. "He was so positive of victory that he forgot to be cautious."

Flavia smiled. "A sin suffered by both mortals and immortals," she declared, staring directly at the detective. "A typical male attitude. Makish was so convinced that he was my superior..."

"NO-O-O!" screamed Madeleine Giovanni, cutting off Flavia's remark in midsentence. Clutching her hands to her forehead, she screamed again. "No, No, NO!"

The Giovanni vampire collapsed to the ground,

an expression of unbelievable despair on her face. Elisha looked stricken. McCann had no idea what was wrong. Only Flavia understood.

"The children," whispered the Dark Angel. "Something has happened to those three children."

Chapter 5

Washington, D.C. - March 25, 1994:

When he was thirteen years old, Tony Blanchard had been told by his mother in no uncertain terms that he was on a road straight to hell. With a wisdom born of fast money and boundless ambition, he had laughed in her face. A stern, unyielding woman, Lucia Blanchard had thrown her son out of her home. He never looked back. Fifteen years later, a short letter from his sister informed him that his mother had died of cancer, still cursing his name. Tony didn't bother to send a card. Now, for the first time ever, Tony wished he had paid more attention to what his mother had said.

There were six people in the room. Of them, Tony was the only one breathing. The other five were vampires. Tony was not heading toward hell. He was already there.

The foursome had been waiting for Don Lazzari to return from Madeleine Giovanni's truck. Tall, gaunt figures, dressed in long black overcoats, with dead white skin and crimson lips, their eyes blazed red in the steady drizzle. The Mafia Capo acknowledged their presence with a wave of a hand and a nod of greeting.

"Put the child in the room downstairs, Tony,"

Don Lazzari ordered. "Let Alvin and Theodore stay with him, to make sure he doesn't try to escape through suicide. Send the rest of your men home for the night. We don't need them anymore. Once that is done, attend me upstairs. I want to introduce you to some of my new business associates."

"Whatever you wish, Don Lazzari," Tony answered, as his stomach did flip-flops. "I'll be there as soon as possible."

"Be quick, Tony," said Don Lazzari. "Our visitors do not like to be kept waiting by a mere ghoul. When I return to Sicily, it is likely that you will be working closely with these gentlemen. First impressions are very important."

"Understood, my Don," said Tony, a lump in his throat the size of an anvil. "Immediately. I swear."

The introductions put Tony on edge. The quartet of vampires said not a word during Don Lazzari's presentation. Their expressions, a mixture of amusement and hunger, were enough.

Blanchard had dealt with vampires for more than three decades. As a part of the Syndicate, he couldn't avoid them. The Kindred were involved in every illegal racket in the world. Creatures of the darkness, they believed in no laws other than their own. Murder was part of their birthright. And addiction the tale of their heritage.

In Europe, the Mafia controlled organized crime. While there were thousands of independent operators — thieves, blackmailers, rapists and murderers — any major criminal undertaking required the sanction and approval of the Capos of the Secret Brotherhood. Don Caravelli, boss of bosses, wielded as much power as many clan elders. On the Continent, his word was law.

In America, however, the Mafia had never taken root. Instead, crime was a regional affair, controlled by a number of powerful gangs loosely confederated into an organization known as the Syndicate. Vampires were involved with the mob, but they didn't belong to the innermost gang hierarchy. The sale of vice in America was strictly a human affair.

Tony Blanchard had been part of the Syndicate for most of his life. He had risen over the years from street tough to crime boss through a combination of guts and greed. During that time, he earned the nickname "The Tuna" for his cold-fish demeanor in the most desperate situation.

As leader of the East Coast branch of the criminal empire, he had been the one to suggest they form an alliance with the Mafia to combat the growing influence of the Far Eastern Triads in the United States. It was Tony who made a deal with Don Caravelli, only to learn that he had signed a contract with a devil in human form. And, it was Tony who, in a desperate effort to preserve his own power base in the face of ever-increasing competition, was now pandering to every wish of Don Caravelli's top lieutenant, Don Lazzari.

Normally, Tony dealt with vampires from a position of strength. He worked hand-in-glove with a number of princes of major cities on the coast. They treated him with respect, knowing he controlled resources they needed to maintain their grip on the community. Blanchard, in turn, understood that he depended on the Kindred to ensure the safety of his gangsters after dark. It was a mutually beneficial partnership.

The creatures meeting with Don Lazzari were of an entirely different breed. They had neither the class nor the style of the princes or their councilors. They were outcasts from the fringes of Kindred society. Dangerous, solitary vampires, these four followed no prince, obeyed no archbishop. They were neither Camarilla nor Sabbat. They were lackeys of the Mafia.

Much like Alvin and Theodore, they were brutal, vicious thugs, hoping to make the big score. The quartet were killers who had found their place working for the criminal overlords of the Mafia. They were loose cannons, used as shock troops in the crime organization's attempt to establish a foothold in the United States. Don Lazzari had summoned them to the farm to reveal Don Caravelli's offer concerning Madeleine Giovanni. Tony had the uneasy feeling that the moment Don Lazzari left America, the four would come looking for him. And not to pay tribute.

Obviously, the Mafia Capo sensed the quartet's desires. In short, clipped sentences, he made it clear to all concerned that he was the boss. And let it be known what he expected from his subordinates.

"When I depart," he declared, his tone entirely devoid of humanity, "Tony Blanchard speaks for me. He is my voice in America. *Any move against him is a move against me.* And, I speak for Don Caravelli,

Capo de Capo of the Mafia. Is that understood?"

There was no humor in the faces of the four any longer. Don Lazzari was a dangerous foe, and his reputation for being both bitter and relentless earned him the respect of the Kindred outlaws. However, Don Caravelli was terror personified. None dared face his wrath.

"We understand," growled Tito Gagliani, the leader of the quartet. "We hear and obey, Don Lazzari."

"Good," said Don Lazzari. He gestured to chairs around the table. "Sit down. I have a message I want you to spread throughout the city. The words come from Don Caravelli himself. Needless to say, the communication is quite important. I think you will find it to be of great interest."

Twenty minutes later, the Mafia Capo finished describing Don Caravelli's blood bounty on Madeleine Giovanni. It was an offer that would tempt even the most powerful Kindred. Whoever destroyed the Don's most hated foe would be elevated to the post of Capo de Capo of America. And given the opportunity to increase his power by drinking the blood of a Cainite elder.

"Destroying the bitch is not enough," said Don Lazzari. "The act must be verified before payment is made. Don Caravelli requires proof. The silver necklace she wears around her neck will suffice."

"I'll spread the word as you require," said Tito Gagliani, rising to his feet. His three companions did the same. "But that doesn't mean I don't plan to claim that reward for myself."

"Only if you find her first," snarled one of the other outlaws.

"Excellent," said Don Lazzari, standing. "That is the proper attitude. Madeleine Giovanni is somewhere in the city. Her base has been destroyed. There are still hours till dawn. Let the blood hunt begin."

He gestured to the door. "Now, leave me. I have other matters of importance to attend to."

Tony shuddered as the four vampires filed out past him and into the night. He knew exactly what other matters Don Lazzari meant. The vampire hungered again for the blood of a child.

"Have the boy brought to the front yard, Tony," said Don Lazzari, confirming the gang leader's worst suspicions. "I am in the mood for a little diversion. The child appears spirited. Tracking him should be good sport."

Tony nodded, unable to speak. His insides felt as if they had been turned to ice. Don Lazzari considered this monstrous pursuit merely "sport." To the vampire, human children were no more than game animals, to be chased, caught, and devoured. The Mafia chief had as much pity for his victims as an ordinary mortal did for cattle or hogs. It was a frightening notion. Especially since Tony realized that the only thing separating him from Don Lazzari's victims was fifty years.

His throat dry, his eyes burning, Tony walked slowly down the thirteen steps to the basement. Alvin, Theodore and the boy sat around a wooden table in the center of the room. They were playing poker.

"Aces over sixes," said the kid, laying down his cards as Tony approached. "I win again."

"Son-of-a-bitch," Alvin swore, tossing his hand onto the table in disgust. "My hand was crap."

"Same as mine," said Theodore, dropping his cards as well. "You're up sixteen bucks, kid."

The hoodlum looked up at Tony. "This damned kid plays a hell of a game of cards, boss. We should hire him as a shill. I never saw such a run of luck."

"Well, it looks like his luck's taken a tumble," said Tony. "Take him outside. Don Lazzari's looking for a bedtime snack."

The boy turned pasty white. He obviously understood what Tony meant. Which indicated, at least to Tony, that he knew more about Madeleine Giovanni than he had let on earlier. Tony didn't care. The kid was about to die. Whatever secrets he held would die with him.

"Do we gotta do it, boss?" asked Alvin. "The kid's kinda fun. He don't deserve gettin' killed."

"You want to tell Don Lazzari that?" asked Tony. "Feel free, Alvin. Just keep me out of it."

Alvin shook his head. "I'm no brain," he declared, "but I ain't that fuckin' stupid. Come on, kid. We got an appointment with the big boss out front."

The boy climbed to his feet. Short and scrawny, he was not a very impressive figure. The blood had drained from his face and his eyes shifted wildly about the basement, as if searching for some escape. Yet, his voice, when he spoke, was absolutely calm.

"You're all fuckin' ghosts," he said. "You just

don't know it yet. But it's fuckin' true. You're dead meat walkin' around. I might be going to hell. But I'll have plenty of company pretty fuckin' soon."

Tony squinted at the boy. "You got a dirty mouth, kid. And now ain't the time for you to be making threats to nobody."

The kid laughed. Tony felt cold chills ripple down his back. The boy was about to die. He shouldn't be laughing.

"Miss Madeleine will get you," said the kid. "She's the toughest, meanest babe in the world. I know. I've seen her. She'll come for you — count on it. And that snake upstairs, too."

"Enough of this shit," Tony said angrily to Alvin and Theodore. "Take the kid upstairs. Right now. The Don's waiting. He's probably wondering what's taking so long."

The mobster shook his head, as if clearing his thoughts. There was no room for doubts, for second guesses. He had made his choice and there was no turning back. "Damn kid has us all spooked. It ain't natural."

Don Lazzari met them in the front yard. His lips twisted into a thin smile when he saw the boy. The look in the Mafia Capo's face was enough to convince Tony that any mention of the conversation that had just taken place would be a major mistake. He kept his mouth shut and prayed the kid would do the same.

The mist was so thick that it was difficult to see anything beyond the front yard. Tony suspected that the mist wasn't a problem for Don Lazzari. At least, the vampire didn't seem to be concerned.

"I," he said to the boy, "am a vampire. In a few minutes, I intend to drink your blood."

"Big fuckin' deal," said the kid, before Don Lazzari could continue.

The Mafia boss frowned. He was not prepared for mockery. Eyes glowing dangerously, he continued. "However, I like taking risks. So, I am willing to give you a chance to escape."

Don Lazzari paused, as if daring the boy to make another remark. After a few seconds, the vampire resumed his speech. "The state road is not far from this hideaway. You will be given a five-minute head start. After that, I will come hunting for you. Escape to the highway and I will not pursue. You will be free. If I catch you," and the Capo smiled, revealing his fangs, "your blood is mine."

"I get it," said the kid. "I run like a fuckin' idiot trying to get to the highway. I bust my balls for five minutes, then you swoop down on me and drain me dry. Lots of fun, right?"

Tony expected Don Lazzari to explode. But instead, the Capo nodded.

"Essentially correct. You are smarter than you look. Obviously, I made a mistake in believing your story back at the truck. It is of no consequence. Your blood will still taste as sweet. Are you ready, child?"

The boy stared at Don Lazzari, as if memorizing the vampire's features. Then, he turned the same look on Tony. "I'm ready anytime you are," he said.

"Tony, check you watch, please," said Don Lazzari. "What time is it?"

"Three o'clock," Tony replied. His hand was shaking but Don Lazzari didn't seem to notice. "On the dot."

"You are the timekeeper," said the vampire. He smiled. "Your last five minutes of life have begun... right now."

Chapter 6

Washington, D.C. - March 25, 1994:

"One of the boys is dead," said Madeleine, her voice filled with anguish. Tears of blood trickled down her cheeks. "I felt his life flicker and vanish like the flame of a candle. The others are still alive. At least, I think they are. I'm not sure."

She looked at Dire McCann, her eyes wide with confusion. "I can sense the presence of powerful Kindred in a city. Usually, I can even determine their clan. But, my talent never extended to mortals. Not until now."

McCann's expression was filled with sadness. "That's because you never had such close emotional ties to humans before. It's the price you pay."

"I never cried before," said Madeleine. "Not even when my father was slain. I was Giovanni, and the Giovanni never cry."

She wiped the black blood from her face. Then, in one fluid motion, Madeleine was on her feet. "I must request a favor," she said to McCann.

"Ask," said the detective.

"I am here in America to protect you," said Madeleine. "My sire gave me very explicit instructions. I cannot disobey them. But, if you were to request that I defend your honor by avenging the murder of a friend, or the death of a child..."

McCann nodded. "Debts of blood must be repaid in kind," he said, repeating the sacred oath of revenge spoken by Madeleine the night before.

The detective's voice seemed to deepen, to vibrate with power. It was as if another, more potent being spoke through his lips. "The enemies of my friends are my enemies as well. Go, find those who would kill children to further their schemes. Be they Kindred or kine, show them no mercy."

"They will drown in their own blood," promised Madeleine, solemnly.

She nodded to Flavia, then to Elisha. The young man looked as if he were about to say something but she gave him no time. All of her years, Madeleine had been a loner. She had no desire for assistance now. The sacrifice was hers alone to make. With that, she disappeared into the ground.

It took her thirty minutes to reach the rest stop where she had left the truck. Though consumed with the need to know who had died and how, Madeleine wasn't foolish enough to approach the rig without scouting the area first. She had to make sure the murder hadn't been calculated specifically to lure her back to the location. Twenty yards into the surrounding forest, she returned to human form. Moving without a sound, she crept forward to the edge of the woods. And found herself staring at a gigantic slag heap of fused metal that had once been a truck.

The rest area appeared to be deserted. Madeleine couldn't sense any Kindred in the area, and a quick visual scan of the lot revealed no humans. Her foes had discovered the truck, killed one of the boys, destroyed the vehicle, and then left. She felt a rush of anger. The scum were evidently so confident of their eventual triumph that they hadn't even considered setting a trap. It was a mistake she intended to pay back in black blood.

Twenty feet away, the bushes rattled. Instantly, Madeleine was there, moving as so fast that her figure was a blur in the heavy mist.

"Sam," she exclaimed in relief, as she caught the boy in her arms. A deadly stranglehold turned into a hug of affection. The youngest of the trio was disheveled, wet, and very scared. But at least he was uninjured.

"Miss Madeleine, Miss Madeleine," Sam gasped, starting to sob. "They got Junior. They took Junior and drove away."

"Who, Sam?" asked Madeleine, knowing now that it had been Pablo who died. Pablo, the oldest of the trio, the tall quiet boy who had little to say. His murder would be avenged, she swore silently, before the night was over. "Who took Junior? And where?"

"I don't know," he answered, looking young and frightened. He was working hard to hold back a river of tears. Madeleine hated to ask him about the attack, but she had to know the answers immediately if she was going to rescue Junior. "It was hard to hear underneath the truck."

"What were you doing beneath the truck?" asked Madeleine. Coaxing the story from him might take precious minutes, but hopefully the information would provide a clue. Any clue.

"I went to take a leak," said Sam. "Junior said to go beneath the truck. I did. That's when the cars came."

"Cars?" asked Madeleine. "How many, Sam?"

"Three," said the boy. "I counted them when they drove away. Big black limos, like the kind the president rides in. Some of the bozos from the last car put bombs inside the truck and by the wheels. But I ducked out in the darkness. They never realized I was there. Never, ever."

"Very good, Sam," said Madeleine. "Three cars drove up. Then what happened?"

The boy shook his head. "I'm not too sure, Miss Madeleine. I was gonna come out. It was scary and dark under the truck. Still, there were a bunch of guys outside. I could see their feet, nothing else. But I remembered what you said about being hunted and all that, so I hid close to the tires, where nobody could see me."

The teenager shivered. "Some of them went up to the front of the truck. There was a lot of shouting. I couldn't hear about what. Then...then...they started shooting."

Sam's eyes suddenly filled with tears. "They killed Pablo, Miss Madeleine. They shot Pablo and killed him. Pablo's dead!"

"I know, Sam," said Madeleine, holding the boy close. Gently, she stroked his back as he cried on her shoulder. Sam's body felt cold, terribly cold. But Madeleine had no warmth to give him.

"After that," said Sam, struggling to continue, "they went into the truck and talked to Junior. They weren't real loud, so it was hard for me to hear what they were saying. I tried. I tried real hard. But I didn't want them to see me. I—I was afraid they might shoot me too."

"You did fine, Sam," said Madeleine. "There's nothing to be upset about. You did the best you could. I'm proud of you."

She paused, giving the boy a moment to compose himself. "Did you hear them say anything?" she finally asked, when he seemed ready to continue. "A name? A place where they were going? Anything at all? Think. Think hard. It could be important."

Sam frowned in concentration. "I heard one of the men talking. He said someone's name. At least, I thought it was a name. He called the other guy, Don."

"Don?" said Madeleine, making an effort to keep her tone neutral. "Don what, Sam?"

"Don...Don...Lasers," answer Sam. "When I heard it, I thought it sounded like a video game."

"Don Lazzari?" asked Madeleine. "Was that the name, Sam? Don Lazzari?"

The youth nodded. "That was it, Miss Madeleine. Don Lazzari. Do you know him?"

Madeleine nodded. "I know him, Sam," she said, a terrible cold rage filling her mind. Her voice remained calm. "Though we have never met, I know him very well by his reputation. He is the henchman of an extremely evil creature named Don Caravelli, who murdered my father. Don Lazzari is just slightly less a monster."

Sam stared directly into Madeleine's eyes. His features twisted in fear. "He's a vampire, isn't he, Miss Madeleine? Don Lazzari is a vampire and he's got Junior." The boy's voice grew shrill. "That's why he took Junior with him when he left. He's gonna drink Junior's blood. Isn't he? Isn't he!"

"Don Lazzari is notorious for his perverted desires," said Madeleine. "He drinks only the blood of innocent children. Junior is in dire peril. But he is still alive. I would sense it if he was dead."

Madeleine closed her eyes. It took mere seconds to locate Don Lazzari. She could reach him quickly.

"I have to leave you, Sam," she declared. "I do not like doing so, but I must, if Junior is to be rescued. Stay here. Stay hidden. I will return as soon as possible. Or a man named McCann will come instead. You can trust him."

Sam glanced nervously at the forest. "Can't you take me with you?" he asked.

Madeleine shook her head. "I cannot. It is time for me to depart." She stepped back, releasing her grip on the boy. "Be brave, Sam. Be strong."

Fixing Don Lazzari's location in her mind, Madeleine let her body meld with the earth. Though she wore no watch, she always knew the exact time. It was 3 a.m. It would take her a little more than five minutes to reach the Mafia chief's headquarters. She could only hope she would not be too late.

Chapter 7

Washington, D.C. - March 25, 1994:

Junior knew that running for the highway was a waste of breath. If Don Lazzari moved even half as fast as Miss Madeleine, a five-minute head start meant nothing. And Junior felt certain that for all his talk of being fair, the Mafia chief would never actually let him escape.

Instead, as soon as the vampire said go, Junior set off in the other direction. Much of his short life had been spent as a runaway. In his years on the road, Junior had learned a lot about evading capture. The most important factor was to take advantage of his size. Don Lazzari might be fast and strong, but he was almost a foot taller than Junior and a lot bulkier. And the Cainite couldn't stand exposure to the sun.

Junior realized that this wasn't a race to the highway. It was a race against the clock. He had to keep out of the Don's hands until sunrise. That was his only chance for survival.

The farmhouse was surrounded by forests. The woods were dark and it was hard to see. The ground was covered with vines, bushes and broken branches. Junior trampled a path through the underbrush, not worried about leaving a trail. He was sure Don Lazzari could find him with or without a path. Junior needed to find a thick patch of thornbushes before his five minutes ran out. Without them, he was doomed.

Luck was with him. Three minutes into the forest, he came upon a huge tangle of shrubs, twenty feet long and ten feet wide, curled around and between a half-dozen maple trees. The branches of the bushes were devoid of leaves, but they were long and pointed, with immense thorns sticking out in a hundred different directions. Woven together in a gigantic net, the bushes made an impenetrable barrier. With a whoop, Junior dropped to his stomach and began to crawl.

There was just enough room for him to slide beneath the lowest thorns. The ground was soft and muddy, slowing his progress. But, by the time his five minutes had passed, Junior was nearly at the center of the bramble patch. He had just rolled over onto his back when he knew his grace period was over.

"A neat trick, boy," said Don Lazzari. The vampire sounded more amused than annoyed. "You have brains as well as courage. I commend you. Unfortunately, I do not give in so easily. These obstacles are an annoyance, nothing more."

The ground shook as if it were being pounded by a gigantic hammer. Junior's eyes widened in dismay as he realized that Don Lazzari was reaching down to the base of each thorn bush and ripping it out of the soil. The vampire was inhumanly strong. With a sob of frustration, Junior began crawling for the other end of the thicket. There was nothing left for him to do but run.

A minute later, scratched and torn by the thorns, Junior staggered to his feet. Not ten feet away, in the center of the thistles, stood Don Lazzari, casually holding an uprooted bush in one hand. The vampire's eyes glowed red when he spotted his frightened prey.

Heart thumping, Junior dashed between the trees. He wound a broken path through the undergrowth, hoping somehow that the monster pursuing him would not be able to follow his trail. Except for his gasping breath, the woods were silent. Don Lazzari didn't make a sound.

The ground dipped into a small gully. A tiny freshwater spring ran through the center. Huffing and puffing, Junior stamped into the cold stream. According to a movie he recalled seeing at the orphanage, vampires couldn't cross running water. He prayed that Don Lazzari had seen the same movie. And believed it was true.

Twenty feet downstream, Junior plunged back into the forest. The stream curved toward the farmhouse. That was definitely the last place he wanted to go. Feeling lightheaded and slightly dizzy, he stumbled through the darkness, listening anxiously for the sounds of pursuit.

Unexpectedly, the woods came to an abrupt end. The trees fell away, yielding to an open field a hundred yards across. A few broken-down picnic tables proclaimed that this had been a picnic area years before. At the far end of the clearing was an empty parking lot and single-lane access road.

Beyond that, Junior realized, had to be the highway. It was a forlorn hope, but it was better than nothing. Junior refused to surrender. He had never been a quitter.

Every breath an effort, he staggered across the deserted field. His lungs were burning, his feet felt as if they were worn to the bone. There was no sign of Don Lazzari. Anxiously, Junior glanced over his shoulder, expecting the vampire to burst out of the wood any second. Nothing stirred. The rain had stopped and the mist was lifting. A hint of moonlight touched the earth. The pavement was fifty yards away, then thirty, then ten, then just a few feet distant.

The tall grass surrounding Junior rustled as if touched by an unexpected breeze. There was a flicker of motion, and Don Lazzari, a knowing leer on his lips, stood between Junior and the parking lot. The vampire chuckled, shaking his head in mock bewilderment. "I could have caught you at any time," he declared. "But I thought it best to let you think there was a chance. It makes the game so much more entertaining if the prey keeps struggling until the end."

Junior collapsed to the ground. Flat on his back, he stared up defiantly at Don Lazzari. "It ain't over till it's over, you fuckin' monster," he groaned.

"It is over," said Don Lazzari, his eyes glowing. Bending over, he reached for Junior's shoulder. Then froze, as another voice rang through the clearing.

"*It is over*, devourer of children. Not for the boy, but for you."

Don Lazzari whirled about to confront the speaker. The barest trace of fear echoed in his voice as he confirmed the identity of the newcomer. "Madeleine Giovanni."

"Miss Madeleine," cried Junior, raising himself on one elbow. "I knew you'd find me."

Madeleine Giovanni stood a few feet beyond Don Lazzari. She had risen out of the shadows without a sound. The Dagger of the Giovanni made a contrasting picture of dark and light, with her black dress and ivory-white skin. Her hands rested at her sides. She seemed perfectly at ease. Her face was serene, deadly calm, an icy smile frozen on her lips. Her eyes burned with a fire as intense as an inferno.

"I believe you have been looking for me?" said Madeleine. "I have arrived, Don Lazzari. Where is your courage now that you are faced with an enemy who is not a child?"

The Mafia Capo growled, an inhuman sound rising from deep in his chest. "Bitch," he snarled. "I'm not afraid of you."

"Liar," said Madeleine, taking a step forward. Don Lazzari stepped back. "Or, if you mean what you say, *fool*. I am your doom. A century ago, you helped your master kill my father. Tonight, you murdered a child I befriended. You dared hunt another. The penalty for each crime is the Final Death. I have waited too long for this moment. There is no mercy, no forgiveness. My only regret is that I cannot bring you back with me to the Mausoleum. There you would suffer a thousand years of torment before you would be allowed to perish."

"I merely did as I was told," said Don Lazzari, his voice wavering. "I was only following orders."

"Tell that to your victims," said Madeleine, "when they confront you in hell."

"Never!" Don Lazzari shrieked. The Mafia Capo flung himself at Madeleine, his hands grasping for her neck. Only a few feet separated them, and he moved faster than the wind. Yet, when his fingers clenched together, Madeleine's flesh was not between them.

"You are a witless buffoon," she declared, a dark shadow standing at his side. A tendril of blackness reached out and touched Don Lazzari's neck. Bones snapped like dried twigs. The Mafia Capo screamed as his body crashed forward into the dirt. He lay there, his body twitching like a fish out of water, his head pressed so tightly into the mud that he couldn't make a sound.

"The blow snapped his spine," said Madeleine, sounding quite satisfied with her work. She stepped over the Capo's body to Junior and helped the boy to his feet. "He won't be able to use his arms or legs until it heals. Unfortunately for him, he needs blood to regenerate a wound that serious. He can hear, he can see, he can speak, he can certainly feel, but he cannot move."

"You did that with one fuckin' slap, Miss Madeleine," said Junior. "It was fuckin' amazing."

"No, Junior," said Madeleine Giovanni, with a smile of sheer malice. "*It was a pleasure.*"

Madeleine stared at her helpless prisoner. Her

face was a grim death-mask. "I am not finished with Don Lazzari. There is not much time till dawn, so I need to act quickly. The scum must suffer for his crimes. It is probably best if you do not watch what I do next."

"No fuckin' way," said Junior. "This son-of-a-bitch had Pablo killed. And he was gonna fuckin' drink my blood. I wanna see every fuckin' thing you do to him."

"If you wish," said Madeleine. She didn't attempt to argue. Her expression was unreadable. "Just stand clear as I work."

Lifting the helpless Don Lazzari like a baby, Madeleine carried the Mafia chief to the concrete parking lot. She dropped him face-up on the pavement. Unable to move other than to twist his head, he watched in silent horror as she searched the area for some loose blocks of cement.

"Mother of mercy," he cried when she ripped a two-foot slab out of the road. "What are you going to do to me?"

"You crushed my dreams," said Madeleine, raising the concrete block over his legs. "Before you die, I intend to pay you back in kind."

"Let me go," pleaded Don Lazzari, his gaze fastened on the cement slab. "I beg you. Please, let me die fighting. Not smashed like an insect."

"An apt comparison," said Madeleine, without a hint of remorse. A faint smile crossed her lips. "I grant you the same mercy you gave to my father."

Still smiling, she slammed the stone down on Don Lazzari's legs. The vampire shrieked as his limbs were ground to a pulp. The sound seemed to last forever. Madeleine laughed and raised the rock off the ground. Junior, no longer so interested in revenge, heaved up what little of his dinner still remained in his stomach.

"I'll wait by the picnic tables, Miss Madeleine," he gasped, when he could speak again.

"This interlude will take me a few minutes, Junior," said Madeleine, without turning her head. Don Lazzari, his eyes glazed with horror, was babbling incoherently. "I want to make sure Don Lazzari remains here until the sun rises. First I need to finish destroying his legs. Then I will crush his arms. And finally, I think, some of his torso. By the time I complete my task, he will welcome the dawn's fiery embrace."

Don Lazzari screamed and screamed. But the Dagger of the Giovanni was relentless. And she was entirely without mercy.

Chapter 8

Washington, D.C. - March 25, 1994:

Nervously, Tony Blanchard glanced at his watch again. Ten minutes had passed since they had let the boy loose. Don Lazzari had departed five minutes ago. However, there had been no screams from the forest. Tony couldn't help but wonder if something unexpected had occurred.

"I don't like this crap," he muttered. "It ain't right."

"That kid was no pushover, boss," said Alvin. He and Theodore appeared ill at ease. "He played cards awfully good for a little punk."

"Cheating at poker is a lot different than getting past a vampire," said Tony. "Don Lazzari's probably just taking his time, playing cat-and-mouse with the kid."

"Yeah," said Theodore, peering out into the darkness. The mist was finally lifting, and the soft glow of the moon was filtering out from behind the clouds. "That Mafia dude is a mean SOB. And those friends of his were no bargain either."

Tony shuddered, remembering the hungry look in the renegades' eyes. "They won't cause any trouble," he declared. "We don't got nothing to worry about as long as we play it straight with

Don Lazzari."

"Sure, Tony," said Theodore. "I bet Joey Campbell was thinking the same thing right before he got his."

"You killed him, not me," said Tony, checking his watch again. The Mafia Capo had been gone for ten minutes. And, so far, there had not been a sound from the forest.

"I did what I was told," said Theodore. "I sure the hell wasn't gonna say no. Looking at Don Lazzari, I saw it was Joey or me. And I ain't that noble."

"You and me both," said Alvin. "Sorry, boss, but Don Lazzari's the guy in charge now. You're second in line. Not much any of us can do about it."

"Well, I still got some..." Tony abruptly stopped speaking. "You hear something?"

"Shit," said Theodore. "That sounded like somebody screaming down by the old picnic grounds."

"Yeah," said Alvin, his face turning the color of ashes. "And that wasn't no damned kid."

"No way that boy could hurt a vampire," said Tony. "Not in a million years."

The second scream came a minute later. It lasted a long, long time. There was no mistaking Don Lazzari's voice.

"I got a sneakin' suspicion that Don Lazzari ran into that dame he was hunting," said Alvin. "For all his big talk, I sorta suspected he wasn't in any rush to meet her on his own."

"Yeah," said Theodore. "He didn't seem real

anxious to hang around her truck, waiting for her to come home."

"But...but..." said Tony. Each shriek drove another nail into his coffin. He had gambled everything on the vampire's favor. Without Don Lazzari's protection, Tony was nothing more than a Syndicate boss with dreams of grandeur. "It can't end like this. It can't."

"Sorry, Tony," said Alvin, "but I don't plan on staying around to find out different. Once those four geeks learn Don Lazzari is history, they'll be back. I ain't sticking around to say hello."

"I'm leaving too," said Theodore. He looked at Tony. "You can come with us if you like, boss."

"I'm not running out," declared Tony angrily. "This can't be real. It's some kind of mistake. Don Lazzari's just testing us. That's all it is, a test. He wants to see who's loyal and who's not. Drive off now and he'll hunt you down one by one."

"I'll risk it," said Alvin. He drew his gun. "Stay cool, boss. Maybe the kid was right. See you in hell."

Alvin and Theodore climbed into the black limo and drove off into the darkness. Tony stood alone, his face a mask of anguish. "It can't be over," he cried at the departing car. "It can't be over."

Shaking his head, Tony turned and headed for the door. He had just entered the farmhouse when the first shots rang out.

Flashes of gunfire were visible from the entranceway. There were five, six shots, from two different guns. Then a man bellowed in pain. Tony recognized Alvin's voice. All the blood drained from

Blanchard's face. He slammed the door shut and bolted it closed. Muttering prayers he had not uttered since childhood, he hurried up the stairs leading to the second-floor meeting room.

"It's that crazy dame who's after Don Caravelli," he told the chairs as he rushed past the black leather seat near the front of the chamber. "She killed six guys the Capo de Capo sent after her. I remember him telling us that. Damn bitch is hell on wheels. I shoulda never got involved with this Mafia crap. Big mistake on my part, big mistake."

There was a compact submachine gun hidden in the window box against the front wall. Tony pulled it out and checked the magazine. The weapon was loaded and ready for use. "Nobody catches Tony Blanchard unprepared," he declared. "I ain't no fucking pushover."

The door downstairs shattered. Eyes glazed with fear, Tony raised the submachine gun. He aimed it at the stairwell.

The lights went out.

Tony fired. He squeezed the trigger and kept on squeezing. Bullets splashed across the meeting room, slamming chairs to the floor. The walls exploded as shells pounded into plaster. Tony screamed wildly, as he swung the gun back and forth, blanketing the chamber with lead.

Tony kept his finger on the trigger until the magazine was empty. Nothing stirred. He laughed. Nothing could have survived that blast. Even vampires were made of flesh and bone.

Behind him, a hand reached out and plucked the

submachine gun from his fingers. Choking in surprise, Tony whirled. A slender young woman, wearing a black shift dress, her skin white as chalk, stood before him. She held the automatic rifle in her hands. Wordlessly, she took the hot muzzle and bent it in half. "You aimed too high," she said, sounding amused. "And you were a second too slow."

"Who-who are you?" asked Tony, knowing the answer.

"I am Madeleine Giovanni, of Clan Giovanni," answered the young woman. "Junior said your name is Tony."

"Junior?" asked Tony. "The kid?"

"The child you gave to Don Lazzari to use in his hunt," said Madeleine. "He heard your name mentioned in my truck. He has a good memory. He doesn't forget his enemies. Ever."

Tony felt lightheaded. "You gonna kill me?"

Madeleine Giovanni shook her head. "Not unless you force me to do so. You treated Junior badly, but you were not intentionally cruel. The two men in the car tried to run me over when they saw me. I was forced to defend myself. They paid the price for their stupidity. Otherwise, I would have let them depart in peace. Junior seemed to like them. 'Easy Marks,' I believe he called the pair."

"If you're not going to kill me," said Tony, feeling a small measure of his courage returning, "then why are you here? What do you want?"

"I need a messenger," said Madeleine. "There is an important communication I want delivered to someone to whom I do not have immediate access. But you do."

Tony swallowed as the meaning of Madeleine's words became clear. "A message," he repeated, beads of sweat forming on his forehead. "You want me to deliver a letter for you?"

"Not a letter," said Madeleine. Her dark eyes seemed incredibly large. Tony found that he couldn't stare at anything else; he seemed to sink into the depths of her gaze. Her voice came from far away, and her words rang with truth.

"I want you to fly to Sicily tomorrow," she declared. "Use Don Lazzari's name whenever necessary. It will open the necessary channels. You know where to go: the stronghold of the Mafia."

"Their headquarters," said Tony, nodding. He listened carefully, knowing that he had to follow the vampire's instructions exactly as stated. It was the proper thing, the right thing to do.

"Once you have arrived there," continued Madeleine, "I want you to convey a message from me to Don Caravelli. Make sure that you relay my words to him in person. Don't let anyone else do it for you. It is your mission, your responsibility. Do you understand?"

Tony nodded. "I understand. It's my mission." He would do anything Madeleine wanted. It was his duty.

"Very good," said Madeleine. "I want you to say the following to him. 'Madeleine Giovanni sends her regards to the coward on the rock. Your puppet, Don Lazzari, has seen the glory of the sunrise. Soon, you will do the same.'"

Tony repeated the words. "That's all I have to say?" he asked. "Do you want me to wait for a return message?"

"That will not be necessary," said Madeleine. "I do not expect a reply. Don Caravelli has a vicious temper. I suspect he makes the mistake of equating the messenger with the message. Maybe he will forgive you for your part in this drama. Though I sincerely doubt it."

"I'll make the arrangements right now," said Tony. He reached for the phone, half-buried in the demolished plaster. Astonishingly, it still functioned. "Glad to be of service."

Tony was speaking to empty air. Madeleine Giovanni had disappeared. The only sound in the room was the telephone dial tone. With a shrug, the mobster dialed the phone number of his headquarters. A vague feeling of uneasiness stirred in the deep recesses of his mind. He dismissed it with a mental shrug. He was doing the right thing. His mother would definitely approve.

Chapter 9

Washington, D.C. - March 26, 1994:

"I think the time has come to leave Washington," said Dire McCann. After a day of undisturbed rest, the detective felt human once again. He had called this late-night conference to decide his small band's next move in their ongoing struggle against the Red Death.

"No argument from me," said Flavia. She lounged on the couch in the parlor of McCann's suite. Her leather jumpsuit having been destroyed, the Dark Angel was now conservatively dressed in a navy blue pants suit. The color went well with her pale white skin and red lips. "I was never much of a tourist anyway. I've done enough sightseeing for a hundred years."

"The blood war has come to an abrupt conclusion," added Madeleine Giovanni. She was dressed, as always, in a basic black slip dress cut to midthigh. Though the truck carrying her belongings had been destroyed by Don Lazzari's thugs, it had not taken the Giovanni saboteur very long to assemble a new wardrobe. Or buy another vehicle to serve as her hideaway. As the favorite childe of Pietro Giovanni, she had a credit line in the multi-millions. What Madeleine wanted, she got without delays. "The anarchs are deserting the city in droves. When the regent commands, her subjects obey. Melinda's reputation as a ruthless maniac serves her well. By tomorrow, control of the capital will be firmly back in the hands of the Camarilla."

"Discussing the situation with Prince Vitel doesn't seem very important anymore," said McCann. "I doubt if he knows anything we don't. Whatever the Red Death wants to accomplish in the city no longer seems important. I think we're faced with a dead end here."

"The sudden reappearance of Melinda Galbraith seems to have caught a lot of Kindred off-guard," said Flavia. "She's stirred up a real buzz in the clubs surrounding the city. Everyone's trying to guess her next move. From what I gather, she's regained total control of the Sabbat by the sheer force of her will. The consensus is that she will set up her new base of operations in New York City."

"Justine Bern was one of Melinda's most serious rivals," said McCann. "The regent destroyed her quick enough. Ditto that rogue Tremere wizard who was serving the archbishop as councilor. Any more word of the archbishop's other two advisors?"

Flavia smiled. "Not a mention. They vanished, swallowed up by the night." She paused. "One of them was your friend, Alicia Varney."

"Alicia can take care of herself," said McCann. "I'm not worried. It's the Red Death who concerns me."

"You think that monster is involved with Melinda's seize of power?" Madeleine inquired.

"Do you believe in coincidences?" asked McCann, sarcasm dripping from his voice.

"Of course not," said Madeleine. She paused. "I see. Please disregard my earlier question."

"The Red Death has proved to be a master schemer," said McCann. "Despite our limited successes against him, I strongly suspect that his plans are progressing on schedule. He told me that he intends to gain control of both the Camarilla and the Sabbat. I think that definitely links him with Melinda Galbraith's unexpected return."

"The regent is titular head of the Sabbat," said Madeleine. "But she rules with the cooperation and approval of the Black Hand."

"The Black Hand?" asked Elisha, who had been sitting in a chair in the corner of the room, listening intently to the conversation. "Who or what are they?"

"The true strength of the Sabbat," said Flavia. "They are the killer elite of the organization. Not much is known about them. They are a secret sect within the sect. Their numbers are few but their influence is widespread. Their four leaders are known as the Seraphim. Rumors are already running about that they are planning to visit Manhattan shortly to confer with Melinda."

"For the moment, I don't see that there is much we can do about the Sabbat," said McCann. "Or, for that matter, with the Camarilla. Until the Red Death strikes against them, we're helpless to act."

"We just sit on our hands and wait?" Flavia said.

"Not exactly," McCann replied. "I thought I

would take a trip."

"A trip? Where?" asked Madeleine.

"Yes," repeated Flavia. "Where, McCann?"

"To Israel. Elisha came to America to give me an invitation to visit his teacher. I think now is the time to go. I'm curious to discover what Maimonides feels is so important that it needs my personal attention."

"Pietro Giovanni commanded me to protect you," said Madeleine. "He did not say where. If you go, I go." She smiled. "Besides, I've always wanted to meet Rambam."

McCann shrugged. He looked at Elisha. "Do you have any objections to Madeleine coming along?"

The young man grinned. "Are you kid..." he began, then realized what he was saying. His cheeks turned bright red. "Of course not. My mentor would be pleased to welcome her. But what about the two boys you rescued last night?"

"They are safe and in good company," said Madeleine. "I made arrangements for them to live with ghouls loyal to my family. They will be treated like royalty and are well protected. I understand now that as long as I must deal with the Mafia, forming entanglements of any kind," and her gaze fastened on Elisha for an instant, "would be a dangerous mistake."

"Well," said Flavia. "Prince Vargoss instructed me to keep an eye on you, McCann. He didn't say anything about returning home if you decided to take a side trip. He wants the Red Death destroyed. And so do I. I doubt that the prince would object if

I went along for the ride."

"Why not," said Elisha. "Do any of you play chess?"

"I guess that's settled, then," said McCann. "All that remains is to find a means of transportation. Crossing the ocean in company with several vampires presents a minor logistical problem."

"Some difficulties are more easily solved than others," said Madeleine, smiling. "My clan controls several large shipping lines. If you and Elisha do not mind keeping vampire hours, I can secure us accommodations on a liner catering specifically to Kindred and ghouls traveling across the ocean. It is not as quick as an airplane. But it is much safer."

"I've been working at night so long that I don't remember what the sun looks like," said McCann. "Just book me a private cabin. I like my privacy."

"No company, McCann?" said Flavia, licking her lips sensually. "Think of the fun we could have rooming together."

McCann shook his head. "Dead or alive, you're too much woman for me, Flavia. Alone is best."

The Dark Angel nodded. "Just testing," she declared, with a chuckle. "Remember the offer I made in St. Louis, McCann. It still stands."

Madeleine had an odd expression on her face. "Offer?"

"Flavia is convinced she knows a deep, dark secret about me," said the detective. He sounded amused. "It frustrates her that I refuse to confirm or deny her suspicions."

McCann laughed. "Life is a masquerade on many

different levels. Flavia wants to know what truth lurks behind my mask." The detective's voice sounded strange, almost threatening. "But there are some mysteries best not revealed. To anyone."

Chapter 10

St. Louis - March 29, 1994:

Jack Darrow read the fax from Sicily three times. Then he carefully fed the paper into an open flame and watched it burn until it was utterly consumed. Scooping up the gray ashes, he crumpled them into a fine powder, opened the window of his apartment, and tossed the dust into the night winds. Magic could do amazing things, but even sorcery had its limits. Darrow had not survived as a Mafia agent serving a Camarilla prince without being very careful.

The contents of the letter had been short and to the point. Don Lazzari, the trusted first lieutenant of Don Caravelli, leader of the Mafia, was no more. He had been destroyed by Madeleine Giovanni, the nemesis of the organization. The Capo de Capo was not pleased. Especially since Madeleine had been working entirely on her own in America, while Don Lazzari had had the full cooperation of the East Coast Crime Syndicate.

Though nothing definite was stated in the fax, Darrow was no fool. He could read between the lines as well as anyone. Don Caravelli was worried. For nearly a century, Madeleine Giovanni had been pursuing him. She was like one of the Furies — persistent, relentless and unforgiving. There was no swaying the huntress from her course of revenge. Backed by the incredible resources of Clan Giovanni, she haunted the Capo de Capo's existence. Don Caravelli was growing desperate. Sooner or later, he knew Madeleine would catch him. And, despite his deadly reputation, the Boss of Bosses knew that the Dagger of the Giovanni was his death.

The fax described an offer brought to America by Don Lazzari. Whoever killed Madeleine Giovanni became the Mafia overlord of the United States. And was given the opportunity to lower his generation through diablerie. It was a heady gift, an offer that indicated just how desperate Don Caravelli had been when he dispatched his lieutenant to oversee the operation. But it had not saved Don Lazzari from the Final Death. And, despite its generosity, there had been no takers. Even the most foolish Caitiff knew the difference between ambition and suicide.

Confronted with the death of his agent and bound by an inflexible code of honor, Don Caravelli had raised the stakes. A single sentence spelled out the incredible details. Though the paper had disappeared in flames, the words remained etched in Darrow's mind.

Whoever eliminates Madeleine Giovanni will become Master of the Hunt of the Mafia.

By Mafia tradition, the Master of the Hunt was the vampire in charge of night-to-night operations of the organization. The position was, next to Capo de Capo, the most powerful office of the Mafia. The Kindred holding it was considered the logical successor to the Boss upon his death or destruction. At present, the office was unoccupied. The previous Huntsman had made the mistake of assuming that he was his leader's equal. Don Caravelli had taught him the error of his ways. Permanently. There had been no Master of the Hunt for nearly twenty years. That Don Caravelli was willing to reappoint someone to the station was a true indication of how badly he feared his nemesis.

With a shrug of dismissal, Darrow forced his soaring ambitions back into place. It was time for him to get moving. He had an appointment with Prince Vargoss in thirty minutes. He dared not be late.

Vargoss had undergone an amazing personality change in the past week. Gone was his relaxed, open manner of dealing with his brood. Instead, the prince had become a harsh, sadistic tyrant, capable of turning on a loyal subject for the most minor of infractions. Darrow felt like he was walking on a tightrope. With a fiery pit burning beneath his feet.

The prince no longer relied on advisors. Darrow had quickly been relegated to the position of occasional bodyguard and lackey. Vargoss preferred his independence. He trusted no one. The prince appeared at the club at odd hours, and conducted city business when the mood struck him — or not at all. None dared argue with him. Those few who had ventured to raise a voice in mild dissent had disappeared, never to be seen again. The memory of Uglyface's execution was too fresh in everyone's mind for questions.

Darrow had his suspicions, but he kept them strictly to himself. He knew that it was impossible to match Vargoss' power. But what Darrow lacked in strength he made up in deceit.

He arrived at the club at ten minutes to the hour. Though it was a weeknight, the place was packed. There was no parking anywhere in the area. Thankfully, Darrow steered his car into the delivery zone at the rear of the building. He suspected that Vargoss would be extremely displeased if he was late for this particular appointment.

Time crept by. Every few seconds, Darrow checked the clock on his dashboard. There was no sign of the prince, though the minute hand crept closer and closer to the midnight hour. The bodyguard waited nervously. Vargoss' instructions had been very specific. Darrow was to be at the back door of the club at exactly midnight. He was not to mention his meeting with anyone. And he was to bring several gallon cans filled with gasoline.

"You are early," said a voice from the back seat of the automobile. "It's a trait I like about you, Darrow. You don't take unnecessary chances by being late."

The bodyguard stiffened in shock. None of the doors had opened. Yet, somehow Prince Vargoss was now sitting behind him. Darrow was positive that the prince had not been there a second ago. He had appeared from nowhere. This was a power Vargoss had never demonstrated before.

"I do what I'm told, Prince," said Darrow, keeping his voice as steady as possible. "You know that. I follow instructions to the letter, no matter what they are. I'm your loyal servant."

"You are a vampire of no morals and no firm convictions, Darrow," said Vargoss, chuckling. "But, don't worry. I like that in my assistants. You have ambitions and you are willing to do anything necessary to further them. That's true, isn't it?"

"You hit the friggin' nail on the head, Prince," said Darrow. "I'm bloody damned already. I figures whatever I do now ain't going to make a friggin' difference in what happens to me afterward. There's no forgiveness waiting for any of us on the other side."

"A pragmatic view of the world," said Vargoss. "How refreshing compared to the sickening code of honor held by the Assamites and others like them. Of course, talk is easy. Words mean nothing without action. Tonight, Darrow, I think it will be time for you to demonstrate that you mean what you say."

"I'm not sure I follow your meaning, Prince," said Darrow.

"Next week, a major conclave will be held in Europe," said Vargoss. "The elders of the Camarilla are going to discuss the matter of the Red Death. As the target of the fiend's first strike, I will naturally be called to present my tale at this august gathering."

The prince chuckled again. It was a grisly sound. "It will take more than my story to convince the lords of the Camarilla that harsh measures will be necessary to deal with this menace. The deaths of a few minor Kindred is of no concern to such esteemed Cainites."

"There were the other attacks," said Darrow. "And the Sabbat assault on Washington."

"Agreed," said Vargoss. "But you assume they believe that the Red Death was somehow involved in the blood war. Too many argue that the attack was driven merely by the ambitions of the archbishop of New York. And that it was thwarted by the reappearance of Melinda Galbraith.

"The Camarilla elders are set in their ways. It requires a great deal to change their opinions. Despite all that has taken place, I fear that they'll decide to let things remain unchanged. The only action they will take against the Red Death will be no action."

"It doesn't appear that there's much we can bloody do to change that, Prince," said Darrow.

"On the contrary," said Vargoss. "There is something that we can do, quite easily. You brought the containers of gasoline as I instructed?"

"That I did," said Darrow, his eyes narrowing in disbelief. "What's your plan?"

"The Red Death used hellfire to destroy his victims," said Vargoss. "However, most of his attacks attracted little attention. They focused on Kindred, not kine. Thus the stories were suppressed."

The prince's features were serene as he outlined his devilish scheme. "The Camarilla strives to maintain the Masquerade at all costs. It will do anything to protect the secrets of the Kindred. One deadly blaze with numerous mortal casualties, generating national publicity, would force the elders to act."

Darrow was no fool. "You're proposing to torch the club?" he asked. "And blame the fire on the Red Death?"

Vargoss didn't say a word. He merely smiled.

"The building won't burn," said Darrow. "It's protected by all sorts of spells to ensure that nothing like that ever happens."

"Minor incantations," said Vargoss. He opened the back door of the car. "They are easily neutralized."

The prince's gaze burned into Darrow's back. "Are you with me, or not?"

Darrow knew that refusal was tantamount to signing his death warrant. The Club Diabolique was going to be destroyed, with or without his cooperation. Though he had avoided senseless bloodshed whenever possible, his existence meant more to him than his scruples. "You want the friggin' joint burnt to crisp, Prince," he answered, "then it's toast as far as I'm concerned."

"A wise choice," said Vargoss. "I expected no less. Take the gasoline and spread it by the doors and windows. If possible, barricade the entrance and the emergency exits from the outside." The prince smiled, a death-head's grin. "I want as few survivors as possible. The higher the toll, the bigger the headlines."

Darrow did as he was instructed. Inside the club,

the music blared with ear-shattering intensity. The band playing was a popular goth group known as Descent into the Maelstrom. Darrow estimated that there were at least three hundred humans crowded into the building. A dozen vampires were upstairs, at the club's special bar. If the flames spread quickly, there was little chance that many kine or Kindred would survive.

"It's done," he reported to the prince fifteen minutes later. "The place is set to explode. All you need is a match."

"Start the car," said Vargoss. "I will join you in a moment. It would be best if we are nowhere near the club when the fire starts."

Nodding, Darrow climbed into the automobile and turned the key in the ignition. Out the front window, he could see Prince Vargoss stretch his arms to the gasoline trail. The Cainite had pulled off his white silk gloves, revealing long, slender hands. In the moonlight, the tips of his fingers glowed blood red.

Chapter 11

Sicily — March 29, 1994:

Don Caravelli, Capo de Capo of the Mafia, sat alone in his study. A sheaf of dispatches, reports of organization activity from a hundred different cities, sat on his desk unread. He was not in the mood to work.

The wall behind him was covered with edged weapons. There were dozens of swords — long swords, short swords, broadswords and rapiers, swords made of copper, of iron, of the finest Toledo steel. Mixed in with them were daggers. The collection included Stone Age knives crudely made of flint and wood, ornate curved daggers used by the warriors of Islam and incredibly sharp blades from the Italian Renaissance with secret poison compartments in the hilts.

Axes, single- and double-bladed, had their place. As did lances and pikes. And there was even a section of scythes and sickles. No edged weapon of war was missing from this veritable wall of death.

During his life, Don Caravelli had been renowned throughout Italy as the greatest duelist of his time. Like many Kindred, in undeath his skills had increased a hundredfold. Along with Salaq Quadim, weapon master of the Assamite assassins,

Don Caravelli was considered the finest swordsman in the world. The Capo de Capo had not inherited his position as lord of the Mafia; he had carved his way to the top with the black blood of his superiors. A student of Machievelli, he believed in one truth: As a leader, it was better to be feared than loved.

For more than a hundred years, he had been the undisputed ruler of the Mafia. Under his guidance, the crime organization had risen from a disparate group of Sicilian bandits and vampires to the most powerful force of illegal operations in the world. Both the Camarilla and the Sabbat treated him with respect. His whispered commands were obeyed by princes and archbishops alike. Only one person defied him: Madeleine Giovanni. She was his nemesis. She was, he feared, his doom.

The Giovanni assassin had murdered Don Lazzari, then dared send word of her actions to him by messenger. Don Caravelli snarled at the thought of the news. In his blind anger, he had given Tony Blanchard to his guards for amusement. The Syndicate boss had died a terrible death. In retrospect, the Mafia chief realized that he had probably acted exactly as Madeleine Giovanni wished. Don Caravelli shrugged. The death of a kine was of little importance, even if the mortal had been one of his allies. Men lived and died. But the Mafia endured.

The handle of the door at the far end of the chamber turned. Don Caravelli's eyes narrowed in surprise. No one entered his inner sanctum without permission. To do so would mean being staked out in the sunlight to meet the Final Death. Leaning back in his chair, he casually reached for the double-bladed Norse battle-ax. The massive weapon, capped with a steel spike, was meant to be used with both hands. Lifting it from the display, Don Caravelli rested the ax on his desk. He liked to be prepared for unexpected guests.

The door swung open. A stranger stood there, unmoving, as if waiting for an invitation. Though steeled for treachery, Don Caravelli was surprised to see that his guest was a woman. She wore a long hooded cloak that shrouded her features in shadows, and gripped in her left hand an elaborately carved wooden staff. The presence of the mystic talisman identified her as a mage. But there was no mistaking her for mortal. She was a member of the Kindred. And somehow she had walked undetected into the heart of his fortress.

The Capo rose from his chair, though he kept one hand on the handle of his battle-ax. "Please enter," he said smoothly. "I am Don Caravelli. You are looking for me?"

"Of course," said the stranger, stepping into the room. The door closed soundlessly behind her. With a shake of her head, she threw back her hood, revealing the attractive face of a young woman. Don Caravelli, however, was not interested in her pure white skin and thick golden hair, done in long braids that extended nearly to her waist. Instead, her potent blood called to him, as did the inner fire that burned in her bright blue eyes.

"I am Elaine de Calinot," she announced. "I

assume you have heard of me."

"Who among the Kindred has not?" said Don Caravelli, graciously. He gestured with his free hand to the chair in front of his desk. He did not, however, release his grip on the handle of the ax. "Your fame, like the tales of your beauty, precedes you. I am honored by this visit from a member of the Tremere Inner Council."

"My appearance here is a secret shared by just us two," said Elaine. "Etrius and the rest of the council have no idea that I have come to see you. Nor will they be told. No others in the citadel are aware of my entrance, and neither will they see me depart. I think it for the best."

Don Caravelli nodded. "Whatever you wish."

Elaine smiled. "Thank you. I'm sure then that you don't mind that the hidden video cameras monitoring this room are no longer functioning. Nor are the microphones built into the walls."

The Mafia Capo grimaced. "They are, I must admit, a waste of time and money. Any visitor possessing powers such as yours immediately senses their presence and disables them." He chuckled. "My most interesting tapes are all blanks."

"We are a secretive race," said Elaine. "It is a trait perhaps inherited from Caine, the master of secrets."

"Perhaps," said Don Caravelli. "I suspect it's more the result of hundreds of years of backstabbings, doublecrosses and betrayals."

"True enough," said Elaine. "No doubt you wonder why I have come to you in such a manner."

Don Caravelli shook his head. "I no longer wonder at such things. My guests always reveal their purposes to me without my having to guess. You are not the first clan elder to visit my citadel. You will surely not be the last."

"I am interested in forming an alliance," said Elaine. "My control of Clan Tremere is nearly complete. Once that is secured, you are the logical choice to help me to attain my final goal — the total domination of all the Kindred. As allies, the Tremere and the Mafia could be the most powerful force in the world. Together, we could master the Camarilla. And wipe out the tiresome rebels of the Sabbat."

"There are always the Giovanni," said Don Caravelli. "They are aligned with neither sect. And their ambition is as boundless as yours."

"Taking care of those abominations would be child's play," said Elaine, "once the Camarilla and Sabbat are brought to heel. Even the Inconnu would fall into line, or be destroyed."

"You are ambitious," said Don Caravelli. "Most elder Kindred are. I have my ambitions as well. What makes you think that you will succeed where many others have failed? Just recently one of your own kind attempted to exterminate the entire Kindred race and return magic to the world. It was an insane scheme, and with the help of the nether powers, it nearly succeeded. Yet, in the end he was defeated and destroyed."

"I have extremely powerful allies," said Elaine. "Unholy allies. They are stronger than even the forces of hell. Their might added to my own makes me nearly invincible."

"*Nearly* invincible," repeated Don Caravelli, emphasizing the first word.

"Just as I have powerful allies," said Elaine, "I have powerful foes. Lameth, the Dark Messiah, stands against me. As does Anis, Queen of Night."

"Lameth and Anis?" said Don Caravelli. "I thought they were legends. It is depressing to discover that they truly exist."

"They are very real," said Elaine, "and they command great powers. However, they rely on human avatars to advance their intrigues. Destroying the Methuselahs may be impossible. But, killing their puppets is not."

"Interesting if true," said Don Caravelli. "I admit to being tempted. However, I have not remained Capo de Capo of the Mafia for over a century by taking chances."

"The mortal agent for Lameth is a man called Dire McCann," said Elaine.

"I have heard that name," said Don Caravelli, his grip tightening on the battle-ax.

"McCann is a mortal detective with two Kindred bodyguards," said Elaine. "One is the Assamite known as Flavia, the Dark Angel. The other is Madeleine Giovanni."

"What a tangled web fate has woven," said Don Giovanni. He released his grip on the battle-ax. "I believe we have a deal. Assuming that if I arrange McCann's demise, your allies dispose of his protectors."

"Of course," said Elaine. "I thought the notion would appeal to you."

"Unholy allies," said the Capo de Capo of the Mafia. "I like that phrase. It fits the two of us quite well." He paused for an instant. "These entities who are providing you with aid, you said they are more powerful than demons. I know of no such creatures. What are they named?"

"They are beings that consist entirely of sentient flame," said Elaine de Calinot. "They are called the *Sheddim*."

UNHOLY ALLIES

Chapter 12

Somewhere in the Atlantic — March 29, 1994:

Dire McCann stood by the upper-deck railing of the cruise ship *Demeter*. The night was peaceful and the sea quiet. The powerfully built man stared out at the ocean. The moonlight played strange tricks with his shadow, twisting it into odd shapes across the deck. The detective's eyes, moody and dark, stared across the water, his thoughts on events long past.

Moving soundlessly, a dark shape floated out of the door leading to the deck from the ship's lounge. As it approached McCann, the shadowy figure took on form and substance. It was Madeleine Giovanni, wearing as always a short black dress, black stockings and heels, and a silver necklace about her neck.

"You commune with the sea, Mr. McCann?" she asked, curious. "I never would have thought of you as a sailor."

"The ocean is eternal," said Dire McCann, without turning. "It is written in the Bible: *Man comes and goes. But Earth abides.* So it is with the waters. In the beginning, God created the heavens and the waters. Land followed. Man and thus the Kindred came days later. Our presence is quite unimportant."

"You sound like my grandfather," said Madeleine. "When business is difficult, Pietro takes to looking out across the city and expresses similar thoughts."

McCann smiled. "Many years ago, your sire and I spent several days debating the meaning of the universe. We ended up deciding that even the Damned in their cosmic arrogance were not privy to the secrets of the Creator." He laughed. "It was not an answer either of us accepted with good grace."

"You have known my grandfather for a long time?" asked Madeleine.

The detective turned to her. His expression was unreadable, though he sounded amused. "A very long time."

Madeleine frowned. "You have a terrible habit of avoiding direct answers, Mr. McCann. I find it quite annoying."

"I suspect," said McCann, with a laugh, "that our friend Elisha would say exactly the same thing about you. Where is he, by the way?"

"Inside, on the main promenade," said Madeleine. "He is fascinated by the Demeter and its passengers. I believe he and Flavia are having their fortunes told in cards by a crazy Malkavian child named Molly."

Madeleine shook her head in dismay. "Elisha never realized that there are entire ships that cater to the undead and their ghouls. For all of his knowledge of the inner workings of the universe, he is incredibly naive."

"He's a fast learner," said McCann. "Don't

underestimate his ability to put facts together and reach the correct conclusions. Anyone who studies with Moses Maimonides is special."

Madeleine nodded. "I realized that immediately when I met him. Elisha burns with raw energy. As he grows older and wiser, other mages will tremble at the mention of his name."

"He won't be very popular with certain groups," said McCann. "The Technocracy destroys what it cannot control. Magic unless disguised as science is unacceptable. Someday, Elisha will come to their attention and the Men in Black will be set on his trail."

Madeleine's eyes narrowed to thin slits. "The Nephandi, the maniacal rogues who serve the monsters of the Deep Umbra, will fear him as well. They hate anyone who opposes absolute chaos."

"It sounds like he could use a bodyguard," said McCann. "A trusted companion to protect his back."

"I am the Dagger of the Giovanni," said Madeleine, her voice unemotional and distant. "I exist to serve my sire and my clan."

"He could make you mortal again," said McCann, casually.

"What?" said Madeleine, startled.

"Rambam knows the transformation spell," said McCann. "He has used it at least once in the past. I am sure he would teach Elisha if he asked."

"Enough talk of such nonsense," said Madeleine, angrily. "I don't want to hear any more."

"Whatever you say," declared McCann. "I just

thought you might find the news interesting."

"And completely distract me from what I originally came out here to ask you," said Madeleine, exasperated. "I do believe, Mr. McCann, that you enjoy playing these mind games with everyone you encounter."

McCann turned back to the ocean. "Let me raise a point," he said, after a moment's silence. "Give it some attention, but don't answer. Agreed?"

"Agreed," answered Madeleine instantly.

"Do you suppose," asked Dire McCann, a strange distant sound to his voice, "*do you really suppose* that any thinking being could survive for seven thousand years without going insane unless it possessed a sense of humor?"

"I—I never thought of that," said Madeleine, momentarily caught off guard.

"Very few ever do," said McCann. "Spend some time contemplating the idea. Now, consider the subject closed. You said you came out here to ask me something. What was it?"

"Elisha told me why he came to find you in America," said Madeleine. "He saw no reason to keep it secret. I wondered if you had any clue as to what Rambam considers so desperately important that he needs to speak to you in person?"

"He wants to tell me the truth about the Children of Dreadful Night," said McCann. "I suspect the news is not going to be particularly cheering. But it can't be avoided."

"Who are the Children of Dreadful Night?" asked Madeleine. "I don't remember hearing that name before. Am I correct in assuming they are associated in some manner with the Red Death?"

"When I first encountered the monster," said McCann, "I discovered he used an unknown Discipline, *Body of Fire*, to transform his entire being into a living mass of flame. The process involved several Kindred working together to complete the necessary rituals. At first, I believed that the magic affected only one vampire. It wasn't until the fight at the Navy Yard that I realized that the rite affected all of those involved. They are the Children of Dreadful Night, the progeny of the Red Death."

"An entire bloodline of vampires capable of turning into hellfire and destroying others with a single touch," said Madeleine. "It is a frightening thought."

"The Kindred have existed for a hundred centuries," said McCann. "I know more than most do of their history. Yet, in all of my studies, I have never encountered a Discipline known as Body of Fire. That's what bothers me."

"The Red Death has directed a great deal of its attention to destroying you and Alicia Varney," said Madeleine. "What makes two mortals so dangerous to a monster as powerful as the Red Death?"

McCann shook his head. "I don't know. Somehow, Alicia, I, and the Red Death are linked together. The creature considers us the only possible threat to its schemes. There has to be a reason. When I learn what unknown element connects the three of us, then I will finally understand the deepest secrets of the Red Death."

"And what happens then?"

"Then," said Dire McCann, in a voice that sounded only faintly human, "the Red Death will learn that the fury of Lameth, the Dark Messiah, is inescapable."

Chapter 13

Seven of them gathered around the dining room table in Moses Maimonides' home as the clock struck eleven. Introductions having been concluded, it was time to speak of serious matters. The group, they had determined quickly, was too large for the library and none of them worried about secrecy.

Rambam took the chair at the head of the table. Sitting on his left was the short, gray-haired man called Ezra. To Rambam's right sat the female mage known as Judith. Simon, they had been told earlier, was unable to make the meeting because of continued unrest in Germany.

Directly across from Maimonides was Dire McCann. He was flanked on his right by Flavia, and on his left by Madeleine Giovanni. Elisha sat next to Madeleine, between her and Judith. The chair opposite him was empty.

"Thank you for accepting my invitation," said Rambam. "I appreciate you making the trip on such short notice. You are welcome in my home. As are your two companions."

Rambam smiled. "When I told Elisha to find you," he declared, "I didn't realize he would return with a crowd."

"The perils of being popular, I guess," said McCann. "These two serve as my bodyguards. They refuse to let me travel unprotected. Whatever you need tell me can be revealed to them as well. I trust their discretion."

"As you wish," said Rambam. "You are familiar with my associates, Ezra and Judith."

McCann nodded. "I know them by reputation, if not perhaps by those names. It is an honor to be among such distinguished mages."

Ezra growled something indistinguishable into his thick beard. Judith sighed. "I speak for my brother and myself," she declared, "in welcoming you to this gathering."

Elisha's jaw nearly dropped to the floor. Hurriedly, he closed his mouth. He had never realized that the two mages were related.

"Enough of the pleasant stuff," said Ezra gruffly. "We came here to discuss the Red Death. Let's get on with it."

Dire McCann folded his arms across his chest. "I agree. Elisha made it clear that you somehow feel the Red Death is a threat to both kine and Kindred. I am concerned with the survival of both races. It's time for straight talk."

"To understand fully the menace presented by the Red Death," said Rambam, "we must delve into the darkest secrets of the mystical tome known as *The Kabbalah*. There, hidden in a language so obscure that only the most dedicated scholar can unravel it, are many of the basic truths about our world and its creation."

"Seth," interrupted Ezra, "the third child of Adam and Eve, was the first mage. He learned these secrets from his father, who was in turn told them by the Archangel, Gabriel. Over the millennia, the sacred dialogues of Seth, the *hokmah nistarah*, were passed down from mage to mage, until they were finally transcribed by the occult scholar Moses de Leon in *The Zohar*, the basis for that which became *The Kaballah*."

An odd look passed across Dire McCann's features. His eyes widened, as if seeing something not visible to anyone else in the room. "Seth was the first magician. But, equally important to the Kindred, he was the first ghoul. He was Caine's ghoul. He disappeared when the First City, Enoch, was destroyed."

The detective gazed at Maimonides. Elisha, sensitive to his teacher's habits, saw Rambam tilt his head as if answering an unspoken question.

"No wonder she looked so familiar," McCann murmured. Then, he shook his head as if to clear his thoughts. "According to Cainite tradition, the dialogues of Seth formed part of *The Book of Nod*. But those sections have been lost for thousands of years."

"Unfortunately," said Rambam, "they were recovered. By the being who calls himself the Red Death. But, I am getting ahead of my story. Please let me continue. Otherwise, it makes no sense."

"No more asides, Ezra," said Judith. "Otherwise we will be here all night."

ROBERT WEINBERG

"My apologies," Ezra grumbled, the tone of his voice indicating that he was anything but sorry. "Put three philosophers in a room and you get three different versions of the same story."

"In the beginning, the Lord God said 'Let there be light' and there was light," said Rambam. "Afterward, he created the heavens and the earth. However, if there was a need for light, originally there must have been darkness. Why darkness? The answer is simple. Before our world there were other worlds.

"Our universe was not the first created by God. There have been other spheres. How many, I have no idea. That was not something revealed by Gabriel to Seth. Others existed, but they were destroyed, either by God or by their inhabitants."

"Inhabitants?" asked Elisha. "People existed before our world?"

"Inhabitants, yes," said Rambam. "People, no. God in his infinite wisdom created the denizens of each sphere in his image. However, as the Lord is all-encompassing, the forms of those beings were not the same as ours. Not even the substance."

"The substance?" repeated Madeleine Giovanni. "They were wraiths?"

"Those beings who inhabit this plane of existence, this material dimension, have form and shape," said Rambam. "Humans, Kindred, Garou are creatures of flesh and blood. Demons and faeries when they manifest themselves take on physical form as well. Even the inhabitants of the Umbra, creations of psychic energies, and wraiths, spirits of the dead, have tangible presences on our world. This fact was not always true for those spheres of reality that existed before our own."

"The broken spheres," said McCann softly.

"That is the name given to those earlier universes," said Rambam. "For though they were destroyed, nothing created by the Lord God and thus touched by his presence can be totally annihilated. Fragments of those other realities still exist outside our universe. And, dwelling on them are creatures totally alien to our dimension."

"I am beginning to have a very bad feeling about this story," said Dire McCann.

"The news," said Judith, her features drawn, "is worse than you can imagine."

"Our reality and those of the broken spheres do not intersect," said Rambam. "The universes have no points in common. Travel between this world and those that existed is impossible. But, using the proper ritual, an inhabitant from one plane can be *transported* to another."

"Why?" asked Madeleine. "Why would anyone dare? The risks associated with such a spell must be enormous."

"There are those for whom no gamble is too great," said Rambam. "Who are willing to do anything if it means power."

"The Red Death," said McCann.

"The fourth-generation Kindred who calls himself the Red Death was such a schemer," said Rambam. "In his quest for total domination of the Cainite race, he discovered the spell that enabled him to contact the inhabitants of the broken spheres. Beings of living fire, they offered him a bargain. The flame creatures wanted access to our world. They cannot exist in this plane of reality, as they have no physical form. The Red Death and his brood, the Children of Dreadful Night, desired a Discipline that would enable them to wipe out all those who opposed their takeover of the Kindred. The two forces made their deal. They became partners in destruction."

"Unholy allies," said Dire McCann, "in body and mind."

"Each member of the Children of Dreadful Night shares his body with one of the fire creatures. Drawing on the monster's natural powers enables the vampires for a short period to transform into beings of living flame. In that shape, they are nearly indestructible. And capable of terrible acts of destruction."

"I can see why the Red Death agreed to the bargain," said Flavia, speaking for the first time. "But I wonder what the fire creatures gain from this alliance."

"That is why we summoned you here," said Judith. "The Red Death is a menace to the Kindred. We do not interfere with the Children of Caine. But, his diabolical partners threaten both vampires and mankind."

"Each time the Red Death or his brood use their Body of Fire Discipline," declared Rambam, "it further strengthens the monsters sharing the vampires' forms. The Red Death thinks the fire beings are content to be mere observers in our plane of existence. They are not. The creatures are slowly but surely taking control of the bodies of their hosts. A few more transformations and the Red Death and his followers will *become* these monsters."

"And once that happens," said Ezra, grimly, "once these horrors have established a foothold in our universe, we are convinced that they will be able to transport the rest of their kind from the broken spheres into our reality."

"Creatures of living fire, they will turn the world into a blazing inferno," said Rambam. "It truly will be hell on Earth."

"Can they be stopped?" asked McCann.

"There is still hope," said Rambam. "The monsters cannot exist, at least for now, without a physical presence as their host. They share their forms with the Children of Dreadful Night. If you can destroy the Red Death and his entire brood before they employ Body of Fire the proper number of times, the creatures will be exterminated as well."

"The proper number of times," repeated Flavia. "How many is the proper number?"

"That, I am sorry to say," declared Maimonides, his eyes bleak, "I do not know."

"The fate of the world depends upon us stopping the Red Death and his demonic partners," said Dire McCann. "But you are not sure how much time we have left? If the facts weren't so grim, I think I'd find them amusing."

"These fire monsters," said Madeleine Giovanni. "Do they have a name?"

"They are the dwellers in the outermost dark," said Rambam. "They are called the *Sheddim*."

Resting his massive arms on the table, McCann leaned forward, his gaze sweeping across those present. "I don't see that we have much choice," he declared. "The Red Death and the Children of Dreadful Night must be destroyed. And we're the only ones who have any chance of success."

"The odds," said Flavia, dryly, "appear heavily weighed in their favor."

"Our position does seem quite desperate," added Madeleine Giovanni.

"I agree," said McCann. "Still, we either sit back and wait for the apocalypse, or try our best to prevent it. I'm not the waiting type, never have been, never will be. I plan to stop the Red Death or perish trying."

"I always considered terrible odds a challenge," said Flavia.

"I feel the exact same way about desperate situations," said Madeleine.

"I'll help," said Elisha. "Any way I can."

"As will we all," said Rambam, gesturing to his companions.

McCann smiled. "The Red Death and the *Sheddim* are unholy allies. But then again perhaps so are we."

UNHOLY ALLIES

Epilogue

In the desert, a few miles outside of Tel Aviv, a huge shape stirred in the moonlight. A gigantic monster, standing nine feet tall, with blazing red eyes and two curved horns, it was hunting. Thousands of years before, it had been imprisoned beneath the sands by a powerful mage known as Solomon the Wise. Freed after millennia, the creature thirsted for revenge. Raising its head, it mentally searched for a mind with the power of its tormentor. A few seconds passed, and then Azazel grunted with satisfaction. Its enemy was close at hand. Now was the time for revenge. Purposefully, it set off for the city and the home of Moses Maimonides.

Demon eyes, of a wild and ghastly vivacity, glared upon me in a thousand directions, where none had been visible before, and gleamed with the lurid lustre of a fire that I could not force my imagination to regard as unreal.
>   from "The Pit and the Pendulum"
>   by Edgar Allan Poe

ROBERT WEINBERG

Robert Weinberg is perhaps the only World Fantasy Award-winning writer ever to serve as the grand marshal of a rodeo parade. He is the author of nine novels, five nonfiction books and numerous short stories. His work has been translated into French, German, Spanish, Italian, Japanese, Russian and Bulgarian. A noted collector of horror and fantasy fiction, he has edited nearly a hundred anthologies and short story collections of such material. At present, he is serving as Vice-President of the Horror Writers of America, teaching creative writing at Columbia College in Chicago, and finishing work on *The Unbeholden*, the third novel in his Masquerade of the Red Death Trilogy.

"When you bite into Bob Weinberg's books, they just melt in your mind."
    Brian Lumley
    best-selling author of the *Necroscope* series

"Robert Weinberg knows horror from the inside out."
        Doug Clegg
        best-selling author of *Goat Dance*

UNHOLY ALLIES

EXPLORE
THE WORLD OF
DARKNESS

with these introductory anthology volumes.

☐ The Beast Within

A **Vampire: The Masquerade** anthology. Immerse yourself in the politics, history and psychology of the undead.

ISBN 1-56504-086-4

Retail price: $4.99 USA/$6.99 CAN

☐ When Will You Rage?

A **Werewolf: The Apocalypse** anthology. Follow the Garou (werewolves) as they fight to defeat the Wyrm, the evil force that seeks to destroy the earth.

ISBN 1-56504-087-2

Retail price: $4.99 USA/$6.99 CAN

☐ Truth Until Paradox

A **Mage: The Ascension** anthology. Discover the struggles of mystical as well as technologically advanced magicians as they battle for reality itself.

ISBN 1-56504-088-0

Retail price: $4.99 USA/$6.99 CAN

☐ The Splendour Falls

A **Changeling: The Dreaming** anthology. Join the struggles and journeys of changelings — half human, half fae — as they fight Banality and search for a way home.

ISBN 1-56504-863-6

Retail price: $5.99 USA/$7.99 CAN

Buy these titles at a bookstore nearest you, or use this convenient order form for mail order service.

White Wolf Publishing
780 Park North Boulevard
Suite 100
Clarkston, Georgia 30021

Please send me the books I have checked above. I am enclosing $_____ (please add $4.00 to cover postage and handling). Send check or money order (no cash or C.O.D.s) or charge by Mastercard, VISA, and Discover (with a minimum purchase of $15.00). Prices and numbers are subject to change without notice.

Car# _____
Exp. Date _____
Signature

_____
Name

_____
Address

_____
City   _____
State _____ Zip Code _____
For faster service when ordering by credit card, call 1800-454-WOLF.
Allow a minimum of 3-4 weeks for delivery. This offer is subject to change without notice.